I0524658

SYLVANS

The Apocalypse Series
Book Three

Patrick Astre

Without limiting the rights under copyright(s) reserved below, no part of this publication may be reproduced, stored in or introduced into a retrieval system, or transmitted, in any form, or by any means (electronic, mechanical, photocopying, recording, or otherwise) without the prior permission of the publisher and the copyright owner.

This is a work of fiction. Names, characters, places, and incidents either are the product of the author's imagination or are used fictitiously, and any resemblance to actual persons, living or dead, business establishments, events or locales is entirely coincidental.

The scanning, uploading, and distributing of this book via the internet or via any other means without the permission of the publisher and copyright owner is illegal and punishable by law. Please purchase only authorized copies, and do not participate in or encourage piracy of copyrighted materials. Your support of the author's rights is appreciated.

Copyright © 2016 by Patrick Astre. All rights reserved.

Cover and Book design by eBook Prep
www.ebookprep.com

February, 2016
ISBN: 978-1-61417-830-9

ePublishing Works!
www.epublishingworks.com

PROLOGUE

—◆—

Three hundred kilometers west of Jerusalem, 612AD.

The centurion stooped in the passageway descending to the bowels of the Earth. The flame of the torch held by the slave just before him reflected in the sweat bathing the corded muscles of his arms and the white scars crossing his face. As they descended, the centurion held the thick Object clenched between his left arm and ribcage. The knotted muscles of his biceps and forearms betrayed the strength of his grip.

As they moved downward, the surrounding blackness swallowed the light dancing from the slave's torch like demons lapping blood. The centurion's lips moved as he recited a single prayer, over and over, for he was of the new religion that was beginning to spread and take hold across the land. Beneath the armored breastplate, he felt the comforting weight of the cross.

Bloodlust danced before his eyes, filled with evil that fought to take control of his body and his soul. Oh he was no stranger to blood. He had led the phalanx that broke the back of the barbaric Germanic tribes on the northern borders of the Empire. He killed showing no quarter or pity, and when his men faltered he carried out the decimation, his sword running red with the blood of his *own. But this, this impossible and evil lust that came to grip the heart of men and even women, to kill their very young, slaying their children and babies, was beyond anyone's experience.*

He'd followed the rumors and the accounts of the hollow eyed and haunted faces of those who had succumbed to the unholy power. He traced the demonic evil to the newly arrived priest from the mountains east of Damascus. The torn rags of the wretched priest belied the power of his glittering eyes and the fanatic voice that rose in praise of the unspeakable Object.

The centurion had pulled his sword and with a savage cry beheaded the priest, releasing the Object, blood soaking it into the dirt of the street. It was barely the length of a man's arm and weighted no more than a few stones. He hacked at it with his sword but it was like striking the hardest granite imaginable and when he stopped, the thing bore not a mark of his fury.

He'd sought the council of the Sightless Sage who had also felt the evil loose upon the land, and had told the Roman how to defeat it. The centurion had followed the Sage's directions and found the cave funneling down into the earth to a narrow passageway. For ten days his legionnaires piled the vast mountain of rocks and when the preparations were completed, the centurion had said his prayers and entered the mouth of the cave. A lone slave preceded him as he gripped the evil Object and descended into the cave.

Orange licks of torchlight melted into dancing black shadows as they came to the end of the worn steps. The air smelled of ancient dust, and beneath his leather boots he thought he felt the crushed bones of the forgotten dead. The flames of the torch shook with the trembling of the slave's body and the centurion's eyes watered. His throat felt dry and his stomach knotted. He dropped to his knees, struggling to release the Object from his left arm that refused to obey.

In less than a breath, the slave whirled, swinging the torch, striking the centurion in the face. The pain and shock of the sudden blow broke the blood spell. With a savage cry, he released the Object, rose and drew his sword. The slave struck him again, blinding him. But the attacker was no match for the battle-tested reflexes of the Roman warrior. The sword whistled through the air disemboweling the slave.

The centurion knew what he had to do, had known since he'd found the cave. He took the small crucifix hanging from his neck and placed it in his mouth, continuously mumbling his prayer. In the satiny darkness of the cave, laced with the foul smell of the slave's entrails, he laid the hilt of the sword against the rock floor with the sharp blade pointing upward. He balanced himself against the sword, the tip of the blade just below his ribcage and fell with all his weight, transfixing himself on the blade.

As he swam away from the ocean of pain to the bright light of the shore, the centurion's last thought was that he had won after all.

The dying rays of the setting sun glinted off the top of the mountain when the centurion's aide gave the order that sent the huge pile of rocks hurtling down into the cave, sealing it. His commander had not reappeared and the Roman officer had been compelled by the iron discipline of the Legions to carry out their centurion's last order.

Brookhaven National Laboratory, Physics Building, Upton, Long Island, New York, September 2008

Doctor Pravin Prabinwah thought Duncan Wesley was like an overheated pressure cooker with undercurrents of violence leaking out the edges like wisps of steam. The doctor's colleague sat next to him with bulging eyes peering out under thick glasses like a frightened owl. Although the two scientists sitting across from Wesley represented the best minds in the world of physics, they seemed nothing more than timid mice before a lurking hungry tomcat.

Duncan Wesley rose from his seat. He placed his hands on the table and leaned forward from the waist until his face was less than two feet from the scientists. They both craned their heads back as Wesley swung his gaze from one to the other.

"I don't give a damn about your protocols and procedures or any other academic bullshit," Wesley said. "You may be on the Government tit, but right now I control the flow of milk. In other words gentlemen your ass is mine. I want that test run in forty-eight hours. Do you understand that? Am I clear enough?"

Dr. Prabinwah glanced at his colleague who blinked furiously as he licked his lips with little cat-like furtive movements of his tongue. Prabinwah realized he would have to be the one to make this volatile man understand, if that was at all possible.

"Uh, Mr. Wesley," he said, "these are not military exercises we can run on demand. Our protocols and procedures are not the problem. Even eliminating all safety concerns, we must still deal with laws of physics. Five days would be the absolute minimum."

"Why?"

Dr Prabinwah sighed. This was not the first time he had explained this. He felt as if he was being interrogated, as if the man was trying to trip him up somehow. He also knew he had no choice but to play along and comply. In the last two weeks the Physics Science Department had been hostage to Duncan Wesley and his National Security Agency mandate. Since the arrival of the Artifact from Israel, all operating time of the Ion Collider and the new Phased Pulse Array Nuclear Aligner were locked in by the Agency. All other projects had been placed on hold.

"Well, uh," replied Prabinwah, "without Dr Wu…"

Both scientists jumped as Wesley slammed his hand on the table, the noise violent and alien against the muted whisperings of the computers lining the opposing wall of the room.

"Screw Dr Wu. He's already facing Federal charges for

his disappearing stunt. You can bet his ass is in a major sling when we catch him, and that won't be very long."

"Yes, I understand," replied Prabinwah. "But that leaves only Dr Hashimo and myself to interpret the data and set the Frequency Arrays. The Artifact's ionic pulses must be correctly interpreted and the alignment frequencies properly set before the Collider and the Phased Pulse Array Nuclear Aligner can be effective. Any error would not only negate the experiment but possibly ruin the Artifact for further tests."

"How about I get you a couple dozen NSA computer geeks or a couple more physicists?" Wesley asked.

Dr Prabinwah smiled for the first time as he replied.

"That would be like getting a clerk-typist to do a dissertation on surgery because she knows how to use a keyboard. Dr Hashimo, Dr Wu and myself, *invented* the theory and the machinery that is the Phased Pulse Array Nuclear Aligner. This is a brand new science, even to us. Bringing in outsiders would mean at least a year of training."

Wesley leaned back, his eyes never leaving the scientists. He sat for what seemed endless moments before he replied.

"Five days, five fucking days maximum."

Dr Prabinwah nodded. The undercurrent of threats and possible violence, the intensity of the man, even the profanity had shaken the academic's gentle soul. He wanted out, away from this man.

After the two scientists left, Duncan Wesley raised his face toward the ceiling and rotated his head like someone trying to get rid of a crick in his neck. It always began this way, that unpleasant buzzing in his head like a bee loose in his cranium. The noise settled to a sort of background hum as he felt the presence of the Sylvan.

It was late evening when Duncan stepped outside the main Physics lab. He could recall how he got there, where his feet went for each step, the feel of the handrail as he descended the stairs. But he was not in control. He felt as if he was tied on the front seat of a car while someone else drove. They might take your directions, or they might not. He felt the force, the push and pull of the alien presence. He didn't sense any threats, but still wondered what would happen if he tried to push it out.

Five days from now it wouldn't matter, he thought as he took another step toward the dark patch of woods at the edge of the Lab.

Where the Sylvan waited.

CHAPTER 1

———◆———

The Rocky Point Pine Barrens Preserve, Ridge Road, Rocky Point, Long Island, New York, September 2008

Even if Joe had not been drinking, he probably still would have hit the child. It was almost as if the kid fell out of the darkness above Joe's headlights directly onto the road. Before his alcohol-laden reflex could even begin to apply the brakes, the small body hit the hood of the Camry with a plunking sound. He bounced over the windshield with flailing arms, hit the roof with a dull thud and disappeared. Sick with horror Joe stood on the brake, stopping the car fifty feet away.

Because another DUI would land him in jail, he had deliberately chosen the long way home, thirteen miles of deserted road winding through the desolate Pine Barrens forest of eastern Long Island.

Joe wrenched open the glove box, half tearing off his fingernail, the pain drowned by the vast amount of adrenaline crowding out the alcohol in his blood. *Flashlight, gotta have a flashlight*, he thought. *I own a hardware store godammit*. He found a pencil light and pushed the switch. A feeble beam illuminated the open door of the car as he jumped out.

Oh please God, don't let this child be dead, please,

please. He knew to the core of his being that he had to take care of this kid, no matter what the consequences, to somehow make this right. He ran toward the small huddled form dimly lit by the glow of his taillights. He stumbled and fell, his hands painfully scraped by the rough blacktopped road. The little flashlight rolled away. He rose with a curse, picked up the light and ran the last few feet to the child.

It happened so quickly that for a split-second, he almost believed it was a booze fantasy. This child suddenly stood, impossibly fast after suffering such a hit. It was no more than four feet tall with strangely elongated limbs. *What was he wearing?* Joe thought, *some sort of black bathrobe?* Its dark facial skin was riddled with folds and wrinkles, the eyes, yellow and luminescent. They were large eyes like those cartoon kids you see in toy stores, only not cute, not cute at all. With impossible speed, the child-creature darted from Joe's weak flashlight beam into the viscous blackness of the woods.

Once Joe had been sitting in a gin mill, minding his own business when a drunk sucker-punched him, knocking him off the stool. He had sat there, dazed and uncomprehending, blood from his nose gushing on his shirt and pants. He felt the same way now, only much worse. He had caused this, he was responsible, what could he tell the parents of this strange child creature?

He pointed the flashlight, barely illuminating a pitiful few square feet. He swung it back and forth. Nothing. He stood still and listened. There was no rustling, not even a breeze to stir a few leaves. The internal humming in his ear punctuated the silence, mocking him. He felt the grit of the road under his feet and the sweet pine scent of the forest sat like ashes in his nostrils. He wanted to vomit. The flashlight died out and he threw it to the ground with a curse.

He ran back to the car. A sob escaped from his throat as he jumped into the idling Camry. He slammed it in reverse and jammed on the accelerator, the car weaving, barely in control as he reached the approximate spot where he had been standing. He whipped the wheel sharply to the right and stopped the car sideways in the middle of the road, blocking both lanes, headlights pointing into the woods.

The underbrush was so thick the lights barely penetrated a few feet. He switched to high beams. The halogen headlamps lit the big oaks and pines rising above the low vegetation, washing out the colors rendering everything in black and white.

For a long time, Joe stared at the empty woods and thought about the child-creature? Grief and self-loathing rose in his throat like a noxious cloud. He pounded the dashboard, feeling the pain of each blow through his shoulder. He sat there until the lightest tinge of the eastern sky announced the coming dawn, before he finally drove away.

CHAPTER 2

It was daylight when Joe pulled into the garage of his empty house. He found the note from his wife telling him she would be gone a few days and ending with a terse "We need to talk." He knew what the talk would be about. He vowed to turn things around when she came back, but first he had to settle last night's event somehow.

He spent the morning sitting with the remote, switching the TV to all the various news channels while listening to local radio stations at the same time. Nothing about any missing kids or hit and run. For hours he agonized over the next step until finally he picked up the phone.

His words stumbled as the desk sergeant answered.

"Sixth Precinct, Middle Island, Sergeant Malone."

"I was wondering, ah, would you have any, ah…reports of kids missing?"

"I have a whole wall of them. Are you making a report sir?"

"Uhm, I'm not sure, I ah…maybe. Were there any hit and run?"

There was silence on the other end. Joe's hand started to shake and he felt himself sweating. *Don't feel so guilty*, he tried to reassure himself. *You're only trying to do the right thing now.*

"Are you Mr. Joseph Gray?" the officer suddenly asked, startling Joe.

He sat in stunned silence. Of course they would have caller ID.

"Sir?" said the voice on the other end.

"Oh, uh, I'm sorry, yes, I'm Joe Gray."

"Would you like to talk to a detective sir? Would you like to make a report?"

Joe felt the drumming of his heart. Although he'd just showered, he thought he could smell his own acrid sweat. He had a sudden need to unload his burden. He desperately wanted help no matter the consequences.

"Yes, please, I can be there in a few minutes."

CHAPTER 3

The Sixth Precinct is located a short drive from Joe's house so he got there pretty quickly. Even though the building is a fairly new concrete structure, the inside smelled of old wood, paper and ink. Police officers came and went as Joe sat waiting and twitching on the rough wooden bench.

After about ten minutes, a dark haired, pleasant looking middle-aged man wearing an ill-fitting sport jacket, introduced himself as Detective Figueroa. He led Joe into a windowless room containing a table and four chairs. The glare of the bright fluorescent lights hurt his eyes, adding to his discomfort.

"I understand you have information regarding a missing child," Figueroa said.

"Uhm, not exactly, I think, maybe, I might have hit someone."

Joe stopped and put his face in his hands, pressing his eyes as if that single action could just make the whole thing go away.

Figueroa looked at him, not unkindly.

"Maybe you would like to have a lawyer present?"

Joe placed his hands on the table, opened his eyes and shook his head no. Then he began to talk. He told this detective as much as he could remember, answered his frequent questions and only left out the amount he drank that night. When he finished, he looked at Figueroa expectantly. The detective's notes filled two pages.

"Mr. Gray, you said you know exactly where this happened. Could you take me there now?" Figueroa asked, putting down his pen.

The detective led him out of the precinct house toward his unmarked sedan.

"How many cars do you have?" he asked, like an afterthought.

"Two," replied Joe. "Well, more like one. The second one is my wife's. She's been gone a while."

"Do you mind if I look at your car?" Figueroa asked.

Joe led the detective to the Camry. Figueroa spent the next 15 minutes going over every inch of the vehicle. Apparently satisfied, he took Joe back to his sedan and followed his directions to the desolate spot on Ridge road.

"Are you sure this is where it happened?" Figueroa asked.

"Very sure," said Joe, picking up a small steel tube in the weeds at the edge of the blacktop. "Here's my flashlight."

Figueroa spent what seemed to Joe an interminable amount of time examining the road surface and surrounding shoulders. He asked about the spot where he thought the child had run into the woods. He looked into the weeds and scrub oak bushes until the daylight began to dim. Finally, they rode back to the precinct in silence.

Joe found himself back in the brightly lit room.

"Let's summarize what we have," said the detective, "There are no local missing persons at this time, kids or otherwise. You said you hit what appeared to be a child, or perhaps a strange little old man with glowing yellow eyes. Whoever or whatever it was, you claim it fell out of a tree and you hit it with your car. But there are no marks or dents on your car. All of this happened in the middle of the night on one of the most deserted roads in the area. You found the exact spot, found what you said was your flashlight, but there's no blood or any kind of evidence of any thing being hit anywhere on the road or the surrounding woods."

Joe's stomach ached as he realized how stupid the whole thing sounded. He pulled his lower lip between his teeth, making a sucking noise. Figueroa looked at him and continued:

"Now let me give you my version Mr. Gray. Before you came here I looked at your record. You have two DUI's. Am I correct?"

Joe nodded, feeling worse by the minute.

"You said you own a hardware store. Hardware stores close early, usually between six to eight PM, nine the latest. You said you worked late on inventory, then had one beer and found yourself in this incident at about two in the morning," Figueroa emphasized the "one beer" as he continued.

"Here is what I believe happened, Mr. Gray. You were tired, feeling the effect of that *one* beer–or however many there were. You decided to take the long way home through the Pine Barrens, probably because of the scenic value, or maybe because we seldom patrol it. But it is heavily wooded and has a large deer population. The thing here is that deer don't run flat out, they hop. A small one hopped on the road in front of your car, you probably just brushed it, then you saw it run away."

"That was no deer," Joe said, trying to speak with conviction and hearing his voice coming out in a muffled tone. God he was tired. Now he suddenly craved sleep, relief from this nightmare.

"Late at night, tired, one beer, sometimes our eyes play tricks on us," said Figueroa. "Here's what we're going to do," he continued, "I'm going to write this up as a possible animal collision. I'll send a patrol down Ridge Road twice a day for the next couple of days. We'll keep our eyes open for missing persons. If nothing comes up in the next few days, we'll put the matter to rest."

CHAPTER 4

It was past nine PM when Joe got home. He had not slept in two days. His shoulder was sore and his finger throbbed where the nail had been torn off. He changed the bandage, and lay down on the couch.

It was still dark outside and the early October dawn was at least a half hour away when Joe opened his eyes. He saw that the entire east end wall facing the backyard and woods had vanished. He sat up, feeling his pulse racing as bile clawed at his throat. He rose from the couch. It seemed as if he was a stranger watching himself, detached yet not remote. He walked to the edge of the second floor on legs he couldn't feel as a part of his mind shrieked in alarm. Below he could see several furtive small hooded figures. One of them looked up with a flash of yellow eyes in a face filled with dark venom. He backed away from the edge as a sense of palpable menace enveloped him. He heard muted hissing and creaking noises outside as if the figures were climbing.

He backed away until his heels touched the opposing wall. His hands trembled as fear washed over him. He knew he should run and cry for help but his feet would not obey. He backed into the wall, feeling his body shaking, and his breath like ragged bellows in his chest. Two of the figures appeared at the edge of the floor, dark, barely visible against the night sky. A corner of Joe's mind noticed the symbol painted on his floor. A twelve-point Star of David with the inside missing.

More figures appeared and as they began to move forward, Joe knew he was in the greatest danger of his life.

He bolted upright with a stifled scream, almost falling off the couch. His heart raced and his hands shook from the nightmare. A vague sense of fear lingered. Daylight poured through the window and the digital readout on the microwave said 8 AM as he walked into the kitchen. He needed coffee more than any morning he could remember. As he opened the cabinet, he glanced at the window and froze.

Beneath the slightly opened window, resting on the counter just below, was an exquisite shape made from twigs lashed together. A twelve point Star of David with the inside missing. As Joe picked it up, he noticed the perfect craftsmanship. No more than a foot in diameter, each delicate twig tied with some kind of dried plant matter in perfect symmetry. Joe closed and latched the window and put down the object. He told himself that he must have seen it when he got home, that he must have missed the open window, that it was just one of the many curio things that Becky always bought, that last night's events had so unsettled him, it all came together in that horrendous nightmare.

But a tiny part of him whispered it wasn't so.

CHAPTER 5

Joe called the hardware store and told his manager that he wouldn't be in. The visit with the police had not resolved anything. Tortured by thoughts that he had injured or even killed someone, he knew he had to find the answer to this puzzle if his life was ever going to be right again. He felt a need to revisit the scene.

It was mid afternoon when he drove to Ridge Road and found the spot at the end of a sharp curve. He parked on the shoulder of the road and started walking the area and searching. He didn't quite know what he was looking for. Did he expect to find a child or some kind of midget huddling wounded in this primeval untouched section of the Pine Barrens?

He continued walking until he reached a narrow footpath and came almost nose-to-nose with a homeless man.

At least he seemed like a homeless man as they looked at each other in silence. The stranger was tall with a salt and pepper beard and long ragged overcoat. Joe spoke first.

"What are you doing here?"

"I live here," the man said. "I know what you're looking for and you won't find it here."

Whatever remained of Joe's confidence left him like smoke out an open window. He backed away, mumbling some unintelligible noise. He also felt like he was being watched. The feeling grew as he turned back to the road, walking quickly to his car.

Joe drove back home and spent the rest of the day and evening doing small household chores. All the radios and TV in the house were tuned to local news station but still no reports on any pedestrian accidents or missing people. No calls from the police either.

I know what you're looking for and you won't find it here.

The words of the homeless man kept coming back to him. At first he tried to dismiss the encounter. Joe volunteered monthly in the church soup kitchen and had firsthand experience with homeless people. He knew some of them were mentally ill and irrational. This was probably just the case with this man, but still, Joe thought, the words seemed to have meaning directed at him and the man had a certain presence.

That evening Joe decided on a course of action. He noticed with satisfaction that he had not had a single drink since that night and did not feel any desire for one now. The first order of business was to keep it that way. Tomorrow he would go to the store and arrange for his absence for a few days. He had to get away and clear his head. He would find Becky. She had to be with one of her two sisters, maybe Jeanne in Connecticut.

Tomorrow evening he would take the ferry from Port Jefferson and stay at a hotel in Bridgeport. Starting fresh the following morning he'd do whatever he had to do to get Becky back.

When he went to bed late that night, he fell asleep soon as his head hit the pillow.

He woke to a chilly breeze blowing through the house. The digital clock read four-thirty AM as he got out of bed to check the windows. The walls had vanished, and the house had turned into four corner pillars holding the two floors and a roof.

A sibilant hissing punctuated by scratching noises filled

the air. As he moved closer to the edge of his second floor bedroom, Joe saw the surrounding homes had also vanished as if he'd been transported into some otherworldly realm. A gibbous moon shed a dim light on the scene below. Dozens of hooded figures surrounded the house and to Joe's horror, they climbed the pillars to his floor. As he backed away from the edge, his feet seemed to walk in molasses, each step painfully slow as the small figures reached his floor and circled around him. He felt the wild pounding of his heart as he saw they each carried a gleaming white thin bone sharpened to a wicked point. Yellow eyes glowed bright in the dark hoods and small fangs gleamed with drool in the moonlight as the circle closed in on Joe.

This time he screamed as he bolted upright in his bed. He felt the sweat bathing his shaking body, his hands shook and he smelled his own fear. He looked around wildly at the four walls of his bedroom, and the clock on the night table: five AM. He might as well get up. No way he was going back to sleep after this nightmare. Warm oily nausea rose in his throat as he got up and turned the light switch. His heart jumped at what he saw: The top drawer of his dresser leaned out, open, and this time he knew for sure he had closed it. The middle stack of underwear had been removed and neatly piled on the top of the dresser. In their place, standing in the drawer and leaning on the edge, rested a duplicate of the twig symbol he had found in the kitchen yesterday morning. This one was larger, about a foot and a half in diameter. Joe approached it cautiously, as if it might come to life and attack him. It had the same intricate workmanship and symmetry, but instead of twigs, this one was made out of the bleached small bones of animals. He closed the open bedroom window that he knew for sure had been shut when he fell asleep last night.

CHAPTER 6

Joe ran a shaking hand through his thinning hair. Could these nightmares be some sort of elaborate prank or was he truly losing his mind? He knew he had to get out of there as he hurriedly packed his bag and threw it in the trunk of the car. He left the house as the sun came up, and drove to the diner next door to his hardware store. He ordered only coffee. He had no appetite as he sipped the hot liquid, waiting for Donald, his manager to open the store.

I know what you're looking for and you won't find it here.

The morning passed, failing to cut through the fog in Joe's head. He couldn't concentrate as Donald reviewed the inventory and new orders. A dim corner of his mind realized how strange he acted.

"Ordered another hundred bags of salt...ran out last year...fifteen extra packets of ice scrapers...stock-boy Billy not pulling his weight..." Donald's voice droned on.

Come!

The word boomed in Joe's head. He jumped, startled as his face suddenly turned pale. Donald stopped talking and looked at him.

"Did you hear that?" Joe asked.

"Hear what?"

"That sound, that voice."

"Joe, are you all right?"

"No," Joe replied, shaking his head, "I'm not all right."

"Why don't you go home, or see a doctor?" said Donald. "I have things under control here."

Joe nodded, picked up his jacket and left. He did not want to go home and he couldn't leave for Connecticut just yet. Something else had to be done, something that danced just out of his conscious reach yet pulled at him, beckoned him to return to the scene.

He drove back to the spot on Ridge road and parked his car close to a large fallen oak on the side of the deserted road. A breeze rustled some dead leaves as Joe stepped into the woods. The air was clear and brisk, laced with the tang of rotting vegetation and pine sap. The underbrush and scrub oaks formed a clearing surrounded by tall evergreens. He walked farther into the woods until he could no longer see the road or the roof of his car.

Joe was being watched, he knew it, and felt it. There was a presence here. The feeling grew stronger and it seemed as if the pit of his stomach fell away as he crossed a sandy fire-trail, and walked deeper into the Pine Barrens.

The vegetation changed to tall scraggly pines, their trunks black from the last brush fire. He felt the ground under his feet, a deep soft pile of brown needles and greenish moss. A part of his mind started to worry about getting lost. *Christ,* he thought, *I don't even know what the hell I'm looking for, much less where I'm going.*

A scrapping cough startled him and he whirled toward the sound. A man sat on a log about twenty feet away. *How did I miss him? I'm losing it,* he thought, *I'm really losing it.* A small, strangled noise escaped from his throat as he walked toward the man, stopping a few feet from him.

I know what you're looking for and you won't find it here.

"You," Joe said.

"Yes," the man replied. "Actually, I have a name. It's Duncan Wesley."

The name sounded vaguely familiar. The stranger had a

well-modulated voice, distinguished, with a hint of a British accent. He wore a clean overcoat and his beard was trimmed. Up close, he didn't seem like a ragged homeless person. But didn't he tell him he lived in the woods? What else could he be?

The two men stared at each other, Joe standing and Wesley sitting at ease on the log, an amused smile, curling a corner of his lip. The feeling of being watched like a bug under a microscope increased. Joe suddenly knew, was completely convinced, that there was something else out there. A pinecone fell from one of the trees, landing nearby with a muffled thump, breaking their silence.

"What did you mean yesterday, and who are you?"

"You mean how did I know what you hit?" Wesley replied, ignoring the second part of Joe's question.

"Dammit, answer me. No one was around that night, how did you know?"

"There might not be anyone around, but there's always something around, even if you don't quite understand it or know about it. Did you ever have a dog bark at a bunch of trees or bushes and you can't see anything? Does your cat jump from a quiet spot, run to a window and stare at the woods or just a tree or two? You see nothing, but your cat or dog clearly sees something disturbing."

Joe squatted until his eyes were level with Wesley's.

"Please tell me, Mister Duncan Wesley, please tell me, in one simple sentence or less, so even I can understand it, what did I hit with my car that night?"

Wesley's pale eyes locked on Joe's with perhaps a hint of pity.

"You hit a Sylvan," he replied, his voice soft as the falling pine needles.

The meaning completely escaped Joe. There was a Sylvan avenue near his house. Joe always thought it had been named after some obscure historical figure.

"What the hell is a Sylvan?" asked Joe, his voice rising.

"That's what I named them. I discovered them about a year ago," replied Wesley calmly, his British inflection increasing, "When I worked at the Lab."

Something rustled on a branch, the noise loud in the stillness of the tall pines. Joe looked up, and saw nothing.

"Don't worry," Wesley said. "You'll see them only when they want you to. You'll hear them in your head only."

"The Lab?" Joe asked, ignoring the implications of Wesley's last statement.

"Brookhaven National Laboratory, I was head of the Long Island Pine Barrens Biological Study Program."

Something clicked in Joe's head as he suddenly remembered where he had heard the name Duncan Wesley.

It had been in all the Long Island papers about a year ago and caused quite a stir in scientific circles. Duncan Wesley had come straight from Washington, the National Security Agency. He had been placed in charge of several projects at Brookhaven Lab. He expanded the projects to include the Long island Pine Barrens. Editorials had speculated that the NSA used the projects to cover up some hush-hush programs transferred from Los Alamos. Wesley never commented to the press and never submitted to interviews. A few weeks later the newspapers lost interest. Stories of the Brookhaven Lab projects were swept off the front pages by the sensational Play-For-Pay murders.

"What are you doing here?" Joe asked. "You're supposed to be a high-end government official with a big position at the Lab."

"What I am doing here and what happened to me is what is happening to you right now," replied Wesley. "I discovered the Sylvans—just like you will, soon enough."

CHAPTER 7

A small corner of Joe's mind noted his trembling hands and the way his breath came in shallow bursts. It felt as if he teetered on the edge of a black pit while something slithered in the darkness below. He lowered his head and cradled his forehead with his right hand.

"Please help me," Joe said, his voice reedy. "I don't understand what is happening to me, what are those things you call Sylvans?"

"They are a species mankind never discovered, or perhaps we discovered them thousands of years ago and lost the knowledge, they might even be an offshoot of humanity. As mankind evolved, we learned technology and neglected our mental powers. They developed mental powers, never adopting any technology."

"You mean like some kind of Elves?"

"No," replied Wesley. "Not like Elves at all. These are rather nasty little buggers."

"How can they be around all these years and no one discovered them?"

"They are creatures of the woods and forests. They live in trees, and their bodies conform to tree limb shapes, their skin changes color instantly. Their camouflage is so perfect, you could take pictures of a tree with dozens of them and the photos would not reveal a thing. But here's the real trick they have: They can reach into your mind and cloud the image your brain is getting from your eyes. You could look right at one and see only a branch or a bush."

"So how could you ever have found them?"

"In a way, I found them like you did, by being in the wrong place at the wrong time with technology. Your technology was the car. Mine was my invention, a spectrographic camera that films the imperceptible magnetic field of every living creature. I was using that device when I started seeing their fields as auras. When I became aware of them, they became aware of me." Wesley gazed away and his eyes glittered as he continued. "My life as I knew it, was over from that day. I am their servant. I have no choice. " Duncan looked at Joe again. "Like some kind of dammed pack mule," he added, his words clipped and bitter.

"But surely there's something you could have done," said Joe standing up, unable to control his shaking hands. "Even if half this crap is true, you could just have run to the cops or people at the Lab."

Duncan looked up at the gray sky, his head shaking slowly from side to side. He stood up and returned his gaze to Joe. Suddenly, without warning, he rushed at Joe, his large body covering the distance in a split second. Duncan grabbed the lapel of Joe's jacket with one hand and used his forearm to pin his shoulders against a large oak tree.

Wesley's face was inches from Joe's. Surprised by the sudden move, pinned against the tree by the bigger man, Joe smelled his sour breath as he hissed at him with frightening urgency.

"Run," said Wesley in a fierce whisper, "just run as fast as you can. Get away from here, get to the city, go live in somebody's basement or the subway. They can't follow you underground. " His whisper rose with ferocious intensity as he continued, "Don't go anywhere where there are woods, don't go to Central Park, they have a colony there."

Joe had the feeling of falling, of being caught up in a

living nightmare at Wesley's next words: "I know what you're going through, the nightmares, finding the symbols, hearing the voices, it's just the beginning. Run, maybe you can save yourself. It's too late for me and I know that my time is playing out anyway."

Engulfed by a primitive terror, a consuming fear, Joe pushed Wesley away. The feeling of being stalked by something powerful and evil overwhelmed him. He turned and ran, crashing through brushes. He ran the way he believed he had come. Nothing looked familiar until he crossed the sandy fire trail. Something grabbed his arm, he screamed and turned, pulling away the branch that had snagged his sleeve. He came stumbling out of the woods, almost falling on the roadway just a few feet from his car.

Strangled crying noises echoed in the woods as he fumbled for his keys, and realized they came from his own throat. He yanked open the door.

His peripheral vision barely perceived the impossibly fast movement of the tree limb in the split second before Joe's world exploded in a flashing consuming whiteness, changing to total darkness as he slid down the side of the open car door.

CHAPTER 8

————◆————

The place held power, trapped by mysteries steeped into the ancient weathered stones of its walls. The boy felt the spirit of his ancestors reaching out across the centuries, caressing his soul. Inside the stone structure in the midst of the old burial ground, he experienced a sense of timeless belonging.

The old man had brought him here before sunset. As the waters of the bay absorbed the last dregs of daylight, the boy watched evening shadows race across the inside of the moss-covered walls. They sat cross-legged, the old man and the boy, facing each other. The man removed a long-stem, decorated pipe from his leather bag. He chanted softly as he filled and lit the pipe. He took deep puffs and closed his eyes. A small fire burned between them, the smoke curling upward and escaping over the roofless walls. The pungent aroma of the old man's pipe penetrated the boy's nostrils, setting his head spinning. The beads and feathers in the Shaman's vest glittered and hung loose on the old man's sparse frame. Deep canyons ran through his features, marking his years like age-rings on a tree, and his skin was dark as dried blood. Contrasting his rough features, the voice was surprisingly gentle as he spoke to the boy.

*"At the beginning of time, the people had the third eye.
They shared dreams with the animals and the spirits of the
earth. It was as Elohino, the Great Creation, our Mother
Earth, had made them, to be one among all living things.
But as time passed, the people began to lose the third eye,
the vision, and the consciousness with life. As the people
spread throughout the world, they lost some of their spirits,
their memories and abilities. But they developed new
abilities. New things came into the world, things that
carried them over the seas, and the land, and even into the
skies.*

*A few of the people remained as they were. Their bodies
and their spirits changed. Their third eye and their visions
grew as they became a separate tribe of men. They learned
how to hide themselves from the rest, to live among them
unseen. They became the spirits of the woods and the land."*

*The Long Island Pine Barrens preserve, Rocky Point, Long
Island, New York*

Joe struggled in an ocean of darkness and pain. Something
tugged at him. Unseen tentacles rooted in his mind, in the
very essence that was Joe. He tried to fight back, to push
away the tendrils of energy that seemed to hold him, driving
out his control. His body refused to respond and he could not
feel his limbs. He fought as he imagined a giant axe
swinging wildly, striking the ligatures with a noise like
splitting logs. The presence slowly retreated, loosening, as he
began to float upward from the darkness.

A smell of burning wood filled his nostrils. He opened one
eye then closed it again. Waves of dull pain crashed over his
head and nausea gripped his senses. He retched violently and
opened both eyes, looked around, dazed, uncomprehending.
He was lying out in the open on a woven grass mattress. The
sky was the color of faded roses and brightening with each
passing minute. He could just make out the outline of trees in
the budding dawn. A few feet away a small fire was down to
embers, the smoky trails spiraling upward.

A large black woman sat cross-legged, watching him. Occasionally she threw a few twigs that flamed for a moment before turning to glowing red charcoal. Joe raised his head, tried to sit up. Another wave of pain stabbed through his head. He moaned softly and put his head down again. The mattress smelled of decaying vegetation, the surrounding air gently rustled the pines, whispering to him in a language he couldn't understand.

"It's tough the first time," the woman said.

Joe slowly moved his head again. This time the pain subsided a bit. He raised himself on one elbow, becoming more aware of his surroundings.

"You probably feel like two pounds of shit in a one pound bag," the woman said. "Like the world's biggest hangover."

Joe was no stranger to hangovers, that's for sure. But this was much worse, in a class by itself, like a migraine, a virus and a hangover ganging up on him.

He sat up slowly, shivering under the thin blanket. He ran his hands over his face and looked at the woman. His voice hurt, like the chords in his throat were burnt raw.

"What happened? I remember falling by my car, on the road." He winced and coughed, each little spasm bringing fresh needles of pain in his head. "Where are we?"

The woman smiled. Joe noticed a pot bubbling on the hot coals. She poured some of the liquid and passed him a fragrant cup. Wisps of steam rose from the container, the aroma both rich and strange.

"Better drink some of this first," she said. "That's one benefit we got here. They know all the herbs and natural medicine. We don't ever get sick."

Joe drank with tiny sips, blowing on the scalding liquid. The aches and stabbing pains lessened as he finished the cup. It was light now and he saw that he was in a clearing. Several wood shelters leaned against surrounding oaks and pines. Across the meadow, three people huddled around a raised stone pit. Smells of grilled meat and bacon fat made his stomach churn. The pain had receded to a muted dull drumming. He stood up, shook his head and stretched to clear the dizziness. The woman looked at him, her broad mouth upturned in a crooked grin.

"You don't know what's going on, do you?" she said.

Joe sat down, holding his head in both hands. No, he didn't know what was going on. Things had seemed to spin out of control. From that horrible moment when he'd felt his car hit—who—what?—to his panicked flight through the woods, events had taken control, jerking him back and forth like a marionette under a crazed puppeteer.

The sun rose and Joe felt its morning warmth on his face, driving out the remaining pain as he answered the woman. "No, I don't know what happened to me. I don't know where I am, how I got here, or why all this happened."

He paused as a breeze ran through the surrounding forest. Across the clearing three people sat, eating from plates in their laps. One of them gestured in Joe's direction with his fork, the others laughed, their voices soft.

Joe turned his attention back to the woman, searching her face.

"I'm Miriam," she said. "You just went through the Mapping, that's why you were hurting so bad this morning. Duncan asked me to look out for you until he got back."

"The Mapping?"

"Yeah, that's what Duncan calls it," the woman replied. "He says they map your brain patterns, like fingerprinting, but painful. Didja' ever get fingerprinted? Cops used to do that every time they busted me. Don't do that no more nowadays, got no choice. Gotta do just what them Things want so's I don't get the fire in the head."

Joe looked at Miriam, seeing her clearly for the first time since he woke up. Her rough black face reflected the difficulties of her life like a dirty mirror. She placed her hand on his bare arm. Her fingers felt heavy, like stones wrapped in leather.

"Come on," she said. "Let's get you something to eat. Duncan will be along pretty soon, you can ask him all them questions, don't quite understand everything myself."

CHAPTER 9

Joe sat with the small group, helping himself to some rich smelling stew in a dirty and chipped ceramic pot. They ate with slurping noises from a variety of tarnished spoons. Red stew juices dripped onto tattered shirts and sweaters, piling on top of dried spilling from previous meals like elevation rings on a map. Joe thought they seemed strange and fragile, like lost children. The sunlight grew hot, its rich brightness contrasting the lush natural vegetation of the pine barren forest with the shabby little camp.

By now it was well past midday and Joe felt much better. He was deciding which direction to head in, when Duncan Wesley arrived. The rest of the group had disappeared.

Wesley spoke a few words to Miriam and sat next to Joe. He didn't wear the overcoat, and he looked cleaner than the others with his beard neatly trimmed.

"How are you feeling?" Duncan asked.

"Better than before. Apparently I got through the Mapping okay."

"I'm sure Miriam explained some things, but there's a lot she doesn't understand," Wesley said, the British inflections making his words sound clipped.

"I understand well enough what you told me. There're some kind of creatures with mental powers that have caused me to lose control of my life in just two days. Only I don't quite buy it. Maybe there's something wrong with me, maybe I'm having a giant hallucination, maybe it's anything but Gremlins, Elves, Sylvans or any other fucking thing you want to call it."

Wesley looked away. His gray eyes remained calm and his demeanor was not agitated like the previous day.

"Take a walk with me, I want to show you something," Duncan said, heading out toward a clump of large oaks.

Joe thought how absurd this was, going on a stroll like a couple of old friends in a park. *Could Wesley be dangerous,* he thought, had he been involved in some strange drug experiments at the lab or was there really something to this weird story? Joe's mind kept wandering back to the last few days. The events had been as inexplicable as they were real. Even the nightmares had a terrible clarity.

They walked in silence, taking a narrow footpath between the shrubs into the deeper vegetation until they came to an unusual formation of trees. Two giant oaks, their trunks twisted at an angle, crossed thirty feet in the air by a pair of tall spruce growing at an opposing angle. The effect was of two leaning crosses, naturally formed by the trees. Joe had never seen anything like it before.

"They caused them to grow like this. It's one of their places," Duncan said, his voice a whisper. "Now just listen. Just open your ears and your mind."

Joe again had that feeling of being watched, of a presence in the still and hushed air of the afternoon. An unpleasant sensation washed over him. He felt as if he was naked inside a giant glass cage.

Then he saw it.

The creature was small, no more than four feet. One spindly leg hung down, the clawed foot digging into the trunk of the tree. The other leg folded under as it sat on the first branch six feet off the ground. It wore a loose fitting garment that ended at its knee. The arms were too long and spindly Joe thought, but the thing that held him was the creature's face.

It could have been a double of the one he hit. He had only glimpsed the face a moment, a terror stricken second before the creature disappeared into the woods. But this one held his gaze unflinching. The eyes, large and luminous even in the bright sunlight, a snub of a nose rested above a tiny mouth. There were no ears and the flesh was a dark wrinkled leathery cover.

Joe heard his heartbeat pounding in the stillness. A feeling of empty vertigo flooded his chest as the creature held his eyes and disappeared. It wasn't suddenly gone. It sort of faded, to be replaced by a foliage-laden branch. Joe blinked and searched the branches when he felt the probe.

It was a distinctly unpleasant feeling as if a tiny snake had entered his ear and wiggled in his brain. He shook his head so hard his neck hurt, trying to drive out the probing sensation as a flood of sensory images poured into his mind. Visions of forests, cities, and people all flashed before him in blinding succession. It ended abruptly and he saw himself standing in the clearing. A wave of fear washed over him, the probe felt cold and alien as the mind of a Praying Mantis. Joe knew the fearful emotions had been injected into him, the message unmistaken:

Don't leave.

Joe tried to swallow, his dry throat refusing to work as the alien presence withdrew and his heart slowly returned to normal. He felt Wesley's grip on his arm, strong and steadying as he led Joe back to the clearing.

They sat on a crude bench made of two by fours nailed between logs. Wesley brewed some tea over a Coleman stove and passed a cup to Joe.

"That chap you met is Multiplex," said Duncan.

"Multiplex?"

"They don't communicate like we do," Duncan said. "They send a stream of pictures and emotions. They don't have names like we think of. The nearest identity had sounded like a bunch of M's, P's and X's. Multiplex is as good a name as any. He seems to be the big cheese around here."

"He wanted me to stay, ordered me to stay," Joe said. "I could feel it, clear and unmistakable."

"We all stay, the five of us here and now you. We get things for them, do things that they want, as long as we return when they want, usually by nightfall, they leave us pretty much alone."

"And what happens if you don't come back, if you just leave?" Joe asked as he remembered Miriam's words; fire-in-the-head.

"The worst pain you can imagine," Duncan whispered. "That's what I believe the Mapping is about. They knock you out, physically, like they did with you. Then they probe and explore your brain's neural pathways, memorizing the patterns. They can reach over distances and activate your pain centers."

"Did you experience that?"

"Once. It's something you never want to feel. Trust me on that," Duncan paused, his eyes narrowing.

"I've seen them kill a bloke that way. Poor bastard had gone nuts, kept running at night. I found him in the morning. They led me to him. I had to drag his body four miles and leave him by a road for people to find. He died by some sort of cranial pressure. His eyes bulged and he had hemorrhaged. The autopsy probably showed natural causes, massive stroke or some such thing. But the truth was, he fought too hard. They killed him."

"What exactly do you and the others do for them?"

"Mostly get them things from our stores," replied Wesley. "Sometimes it's various food items, other times it's gadgets. They're fascinated by our technologies and they love our junk foods. Sort of strange you know. I mean here we are completely under the control of damned near invisible creatures who can't even buy potato chips at Walmart."

Joe knew the layout of the Long Island Pine Barrens. He had spent his childhood on the Poospatuq Indian

Reservation in Eastern Long Island. The reservation consisted of two hundred and twenty five square miles of the same Pine Barrens with sprawling Brookhaven National Lab to the North. He knew that he could be no more than a few miles from any of the major surrounding roads.

A plane flew overhead, a jetliner, probably on its way to Islip McArthur airport or JFK. The engine noise was unnatural in the wild forest. It seemed to mock his predicament. A wave of anger swept over him. He was done getting pushed around.

Joe selected a straight branch with a heavy knotted end. *Good walking-stick/head-basher combination*, he thought. He hefted it, testing the feel of it in his hand. Wesley looked at him, his head slightly cocked, a bit of amusement in his eyes.

"Let me see," Duncan said. "It's too early for baseball practice, so I would say you're planning to light out of here and if anything gets in your way, you're going to smash its head in. Is that about right?"

Joe felt his blood racing. He gripped the branch hard, the rough bark digging into the flesh of his palms, "You can stay here if you want," he said. "I'm not buying anymore of this crap. I'm getting the hell out of here."

CHAPTER 10

Joe turned and headed out of the camp. He followed the foot-trail in the opposite direction of the spot where Duncan had showed him the creature. As he walked farther from the camp, his anger dissipated, replaced by a malaise tinged with fear. The emotions grew stronger as twilight set in. He experienced a kind of emotional white noise—alien and disruptive. His breathing grew ragged and his steps faster but less assured.

The end of the walking stick kept getting snared in the thickening vegetation. He knew he had to walk in a straight line. The direction didn't matter as much as avoiding going around in circles and getting lost in the gathering darkness.

After what seemed hours, he finally found the road. The glow of a solitary set of passing headlights appeared in the thick darkness. A moment later he felt the first needle stab of pain behind both eyelids. He cried out, dropping the stick, stumbling.

Hundreds of white-hot shards entered his skull, pulsing with explosions of pain. He dropped to his knees, felt the horrible fire in his skin as if he had been forced face down into a brazier. He fell to the ground in a fetal position. Waves of unbearable raw agony slithered over every pore of his skin. At that moment, he would gladly have willed his heart to stop if it would end the screaming pain riding each heartbeat.

He crawled on the ground, making gurgling noises and retching unintelligible pleas, muffled in the dirt, decaying leaves and pine needles. He drowned in an ocean of unbearable torment. The flesh of his face felt charcoaled by the white heat howling through to his bones.

Suddenly as it had begun, the pain stopped. Joe remained curled on the forest floor, sobbing into the dirt, tasting the bitter grit mixed with his saliva. Gradually, the after-effect subsided. As he rose to his knees, he felt the wormy coppery tendrils of the Sylvan in his mind. Distant, alien but soothing, like someone who had kicked his dog and didn't want to do it again.

He lay down on the forest floor, the total darkness superimposed by the dancing, fiery images in his head. His eyes closed as his consciousness evaporated.

CHAPTER 11

Joe came awake to Duncan Wesley gently shaking him. He sat up, groggy and stiff, but otherwise fine. The vicious memory of the previous night was burnt on his consciousness and he was mildly surprised that he felt good. He rubbed his hand gently over his face, amazed that he didn't find incinerated flesh. The pain had been that intense.

He looked at Duncan who sat facing him. A grin softened the man's angular features. Joe thought he looked like a tall and slightly demented David Niven.

"They say experience is the best teacher," Duncan said. "But it's the most expensive. I would wager that perhaps next time you will take my warnings a little more seriously."

Duncan took a small thermos from the pocket of his overcoat, poured steaming liquid into the cup and handed it to Joe.

"I never," Joe said, taking small sip of the tea, "never experienced anything like that before. I hope to God I never do again."

Duncan's eyes were flat and his grin vanished as he spoke. "A few doses of that and you would kill your mother if they wanted you to. You'd do anything to avoid it. This is the world's worst drug addiction—in reverse."

The walk back to the camp took a short while. Joe followed Duncan. He felt numb but the desperate edge wore off as they walked in silence. At the camp Miriam gave him a plate of ham and eggs with a hard roll. She watched as he ate, suddenly ravenous, the egg yolk dripping from the roll back to the plate. He looked up, caught her watching him. She reached over, gave his arm a quick squeeze.

"It ain't so bad," she said. "Ain't so bad once you get used to it."

CHAPTER 12

Joe found new things about the camp since his painfully aborted attempt to escape. New details unnoticed the previous day. He washed and shaved at a basin by a nearby pond. A water purification unit, powered by a small solar panel, constantly filled a five-gallon jug. Another solar panel ran a large electric cooler. The huts that seemed crude at first glance were actually sturdy and tight. The roofs had vinyl sheets secured with nylon twine and covered with branches. The floors were soft and cushioned by a thick layer of pine needles.

The following afternoon Joe experienced a demonstration of the powers that held them all. A group of hikers entered the clearing, two men and a woman trailing a dog, a young black Labrador. Joe was in front of them, not more than twenty yards. The rest of the group a few feet away, ignored the hikers.

As the hikers approached, the dog ran toward Joe, tail wagging, barking. The woman jogged toward him, chasing the dog. She stopped a few feet away from Joe, patting the dog, speaking softly. As she looked directly at Joe, he realized she didn't see him. He felt an undercurrent, a charge in the air that seemed to float on the fringes of his mind and tugged at his consciousness.

The dog broke away again, and stopped a few feet away from the sole tree in the center of the clearing, a twisted pine three times the height of a man.

The dog's demeanor changed. Tail down, hackles up, it growled, a primitive feral noise, the long canine fangs bared like a wolf about to defend its young.

The three hikers stood in the center of the clearing as the woman hooked a leash to the dog's collar. They had walked right past Joe and ignored him. He spoke to them as they passed. He might as well have been on the other side of the world. He didn't exist for them. Nothing in the camp did. They stood in the center of the clearing, the dog straining and growling and they must have felt it. They must have sensed something as their eyes darted around the darkening woods. Perhaps it was something like Joe had felt that first day he had entered the forest after hitting the Sylvan.

"There's something about that tree he doesn't like," said one of the hikers. "I've never seen him act like this."

"I'm not too crazy about this place either," the woman replied. "Let's get going before we get caught in these woods after dark."

Miriam and the others ignored the hikers. They were used to this kind of thing.

"Now you know why none of us were ever found," Duncan told him.

In that moment, the reality of this absurd situation hit Joe with all the subtlety of a nail-studded two by four between the legs. In less than one nightmare of a week, he had gone from seemingly normal citizen to prisoner-slave, and all within the largest suburb of the greatest city in America.

He stepped closer to the hikers, cupping his hands around his mouth. He shouted. The loud noise echoed off the surrounding trees. Incredibly, the hikers did not react. Something blocked the noise signal in the nerve from ear to brain. He felt a humming in his mind, like a scout to the coming pain. The air thickened about him.

Duncan put a hand on his shoulder, the fingers like steel claws. Joe whirled, rage screaming in his blood, he shoved the man in the center of his chest, a two-handed violent shove that sent him staggering back.

"Fuck you," Joe said, the force of the scream rasping his throat. He turned to the nearby trees, "And fuck you, all of you little bastards," he screamed at the empty branches as he blocked the hikers.

Duncan's muscled forearm slid across his throat, the hand grasped the other arm, forcing his neck and head down. The chokehold was immediately effective and Joe's shout changed to a muted gurgle. Large spots, impossibly bright and black at the same time, bounced in his eyes. He felt his strength drain as he gasped for air from his pinched windpipe.

Joe fell to his knees then Duncan pushed his face down into the sandy soil. The pressure on his neck eased and he sucked a jagged breath. The arms remained around his neck, the chokehold ready to squeeze again. Duncan's head touched his, the lips close to his ear in a ghastly intimate parody as he whispered, "You bloody fool. Shut your mouth. I don't need another corpse."

An eternity seemed to pass before Joe breathed normally again. He could still feel those iron arms around his bruised neck. Duncan came off Joe's back and both men sat up slowly, facing each other. The hikers had gone, still oblivious and only Miriam was left in the clearing. She leaned against a tree, ignoring them as if nothing had passed.

"Look, you just can't fight them headlong like that," Duncan said. "There's a way, don't think about it, just go along with everything. Tomorrow you'll understand, but for God's sake calm down or I'll kill you myself."

Joe nodded. Fine, tomorrow is another day, he thought, and there was no way he was accepting the situation. Sudden thoughts of his childhood on the reservation resonated in his mind. *The warrior spirit of his people,* his grandfather has said, *you can deny it,* but you can never deny your own soul. He would fight, he would never give up.

CHAPTER 13

The next day Joe woke with the sun on his face. The morning was radiant and heavy with dewy pine scents. Duncan had shed his overcoat for a worn leather bomber jacket. If he had a pith helmet he would have looked like Dr. Livingston exploring Africa for queen and country. Joe followed him out of the camp. One of the other men, a lanky silent individual with wild eyes, came along while Miriam and the others remained behind.

"Mind what I told you yesterday," Duncan said. "Just watch and learn, you'll have your explanation before the day is out."

The oak leaves were changing to their fall colors in riotous explosions of red and gold amid the tall evergreens. Joe began to enjoy the hour walk and the autumn woods, deliberately putting aside his situation. *At least for now*, he thought, as he felt the aura of the Sylvans resonating in his mind, cold and watchful.

They emerged from the fire trail into Middle Country Road, the main thoroughfare bordering the Rocky Point Pine Barrens to the South. Walking along the shoulder, they soon reached a large strip mall containing a Wal-Mart and King Kullen supermarket.

In the Wal-Mart they loaded two baskets with a hodge-podge of things. Recorders, Lava-Lamps and battery powered computer toys from the electronics department, CDs and tapes from records, tools from hardware, clothing and toiletries, all piled together.

The register scanned $283.47. Now the resonant buzzing in Joe's head increased as Duncan laid out three singles. The cashier gave him change for three hundred.

Here's a mystery cleared up, Joe thought. No money needed, just another benefit of life under the Sylvans. The same performance was repeated in the supermarket, and they were back in the woods with loaded packs.

This time they took a different way back through a wide fire trail, the soil sandy but firm, easy on the feet. A few miles in the woods they came upon a steel tower. Lying on its side, the heavily rusted struts worn through in spots, Joe could see the top of the concrete base it had once stood upon.

"Let's take a rest here for awhile," Duncan said. "Bloody packs weight a ton."

As their companion sat on the ground, silently lighting a cigarette, Duncan motioned to Joe to follow him. They walked around the concrete base until they reached the other side. It rose about six feet above ground and Joe could see steps leading down. The base of the tower was a concrete bunker set into the earth.

"Let's go in there," Duncan said. "I want to show you something."

They went down a narrow short flight of steps. Most of the room remained in darkness since the only light came from the above ground entrance. Duncan produced a flashlight and swung the beam slowly across the room.

Against a far wall lay a steel bench. A panel of ancient instruments was bolted to the bench and wall. They were the old kind with large faces and dials and vestiges of heavy wires that had been cut out long ago. On the opposing wall, arrays of large switches with ceramic handles were held in place by decayed fasteners. Except for the tarnished copper contacts the switches were rusted solid. Throughout the metal framework, specks of olive drab pain clung here and there, witness to meticulous care now long gone. The chamber smelled of damp concrete and mold.

"This section of the Pine Barrens used to belong to RCA Corporation," Duncan explained. "During World War II, the Government hired RCA to build a huge communication center for the American armed forces throughout the world. This tower was one of eleven that carried forty-two miles of wires acting as a giant antenna. We're standing in the room that controlled the operations of the antenna. The system continued in use until the early sixties when satellites and microwave transmissions made it obsolete."

Joe turned to Duncan, his face a mass of domino shadows in the dancing light of the electric torch.

"You brought me here for a history lesson?" Joe said, spitting out each word like a bitter olive pit. "I'm beginning to think you're just plain scared shitless, or maybe you enjoy being a dancing monkey for these, these…"

"Sylvans," Duncan completed. "No, I don't enjoy it, but I'm not a bloody suicidal jackass either. If you ever want a chance at escaping, clear your addled brain and listen carefully."

As Joe stood in bouncing shadows, he remembered the agony he had endured just two days ago, a lifetime of pain that probably had not lasted more than a few seconds. He thought of the man who had kept trying to escape until he died. It must have been like falling into Hell's deepest pit.

"Look Duncan, I'm sorry, okay? I apologize. I'm having trouble dealing with this rationally."

"That's because it's not a rational situation," Duncan replied. "No hard feelings old chap."

Duncan walked to the entrance and stood at the foot of the steps leading up. "Look around you, notice the level you're at," he said.

"Level?"

"The level of your head in relation to the ground."

"We're below the ground."

Patrick Astre

"Bingo old boy," Duncan said. "I'll make a scientist out of you yet. We are below ground. That is our main ace, our protection. You see, Sylvans have no power below ground. Their minds cannot penetrate one centimeter of dirt. I'm not sure how they get around but I think that normally, their feet never touch the ground. In here we're safe, shielded from them, and we can speak and think freely."

"Are you saying they can read our minds, our thoughts?"

"No, not in a traditional sense," Duncan replied. "But they do read emotions, feelings. They can also pick up pictures we have in our heads. That's how we think, you see. If I give you a method of escaping and you think about it, your brain will create mental images of your running out of the woods, escaping. They will pick that up along with your feelings of elation. Immediately after, Soldier comes along and sets your head on fire. That's what happened to you the other night."

"Soldier?"

"Yeah, that's what we call him. He's the only one who ever metes out punishment. After a while you can even tell them apart by their mental auras, like you can recognize people by their voices."

"I don't have all the answers, Joe," continued Duncan. "But there's one thing for sure. You can't just run out yelling like a maniac. You'll be dead long before that, just another body found in the woods. There is one chance. I believe it's coming up soon. What you have to do, what you must do, is commit everything I tell you to memory, burn it in your brain then don't think about it anymore. Every time it comes up in your mind, think of something else. Think about the first time you got laid, think about anything, just get your head off the subject before you start sending out pictures for them."

Duncan's voice took on a professorial tone, like he was back in Sandhurst Military Academy lecturing to sophomore students.

"Most important point to remember is they are not geniuses. They are smart, but no smarter than we are. They have control through mental powers, and they have limitations. We are taking advantage of one of those limitations now. None of their powers penetrate underground. It's like a human eye in pitch darkness. It just doesn't work. Their second limitation is daylight. Their power wanes at sunrise and surges at sunset. I believe they may have contributed to the vampire legends."

"If that's the case," replied Joe. "Why can't we just walk out of here in daylight? Why were they able to block us out from the hikers, and what about the Wal-Mart cashiers that saw hundred dollar bills instead of the singles you gave them? That all happened in daylight."

"I said wanes, not vanishes. It simply decreases in intensity and range. They can still control or kill you in daylight if you're in range. Which brings another point, their range is not unlimited, best guess is about ten to fifteen miles, at least for this group."

"For this group? How many groups are there and how far are they spread?"

"World wide, they're all over the globe. But unlike humans, their ranks are rather thin. Each group consists of four to twelve individuals. This group has six. It's the only group on Long Island. There's one group in Manhattan's Central Park and two more over the Hudson, all together about thirty five individuals in New York State."

"How the hell do you know all this?"

"Those people," replied Duncan, waving toward the camp, "had something wrong in their lives. Miriam was a drug-addicted prostitute. The other two were borderline schizophrenics. I was a scientist, a normal well educated individual. It's like taking an aborigine who never left the deepest recesses of a hidden wilderness and plunking him down in a big modern city with six individuals in charge of him. If he's normal, he'll learn the basics of that civilization. It's been done and documented many times. " Duncan paused, his next words soft as a silk ribbon passed over a table. "I have been here a little past a year."

Duncan paused as a draft rustled some dead leaves in the

dark stairwell. "Until you came along," he continued, "I couldn't figure out a way to escape them. Now I believe we have a chance."

He looked at the dimming light from the opening. The sky had grown cloudy as the afternoon passed. He turned back to Joe, his voice now urgent.

"We don't have a lot of time left. You're going to have to listen carefully to what I tell you, memorize it and stick it in a corner of your brain until your time comes."

"My time? What about you?"

"Only one will be sent," Duncan replied. "They will not release me. Do you remember the nightmares before they assimilated you? They were induced, that's why you remember them and you also remember that figure, that twelve-pointed hollow star. It has tremendous significance to them, like a cross to a Christian. It's the closest thing to a religion they have. It exists in the form of an amulet that is passed from group to group. Each group holds the amulet for a certain period then it must be passed on to the next group. That's the difficult time for them. They are forbidden to touch the amulet. It must be carried by a lower life form."

"Like us."

"Yeah, like us. But they have a problem here. They don't want to let me go. I became too valuable to them. The others are no longer capable of rational actions without their controls. Within the next three or four weeks the amulet has to be carried to Central Park in New York, you will be the carrier."

"Don't they realize that the first thing anyone would do is run?" Joe said.

"Of course, and it's happened before, but never successfully. They will hunt you down. In time they would get you. No one has ever escaped them. But as they say, the times they are a-changing. You have three advantages, three unique circumstances. If you're smart and resourceful, you'll break free, you'll find a way to deal with them and come back for old Duncan Wesley"

Joe listened, silently, intently, cramming the information in his brain like a miser's money in a safe.

"First you'll be in Manhattan," Duncan continued. "You'll take the train and get off at Penn Station. You should be safe during the day if you stay away from Central Park. Oh you'll feel them all right, but you should be able to handle it. Night is when their power increases and blankets the city. You must spend each night underground. Basements, the subways, even the sewers, you must spend each night below the earth. Second: I wasn't alone in discovering the Sylvans. I had a partner, another scientist at Brookhaven National Lab. His name is Doctor Wu. He knew much more than I did, and when he realized the danger, he fled. I was too late. He left me a one-word message: Chinatown. He's out there, somewhere in Chinatown, hiding, and he knows enough to help you."

"How on Earth am I supposed to find a Chinese man hiding in one of the biggest Chinese communities in America, with a name that's the English equivalent of Jones?"

"Unless you have a better idea," replied Duncan, "any idea besides suicide that is, what choice do you have? Here's the third item; on 27th street, between Seventh and Eight Avenues, there's a bookstore called Teller's Rare Books. This store specializes in old and out of print books. You'll find an eighteen-century text called *Silva Nocturna*, Night Forests. According to Wu, it was written by a German who was captured and escaped from Sylvans. The book was reprinted in 1949 and has some useful information."

They walked to the stairwell until their feet touched the bottom step. "Are you ready?" Duncan asked. Joe nodded and they climbed the moss-covered steps into the fading light.

CHAPTER 14

Keeping his mind closed was easier than he thought it would be. The information Duncan had shared with him, and the idea of escape, simmered below the surface of his thoughts, the emotions well hidden.

When he felt the probe of a Sylvan enter his mind, he tried to examine it, attempted to form some rudimentary communication. Occasionally he would feel a swap of mental images. He'd send emotions of curiosity, softly murmuring questions, trying to send them in a sort of mental package. Most times, he would receive a feeling of a conscious entity, listening, watching. Occasionally, a stream of images, some familiar, others unimaginably alien, like the works of an incurably insane artist.

As time passed in the camp, he began to differentiate between individual Sylvans. He recognized the one Duncan called Multiplex, remote, detached. There was another individual he called Bird, its probes hovering, barely alighting on his consciousness before fluttering off.

Then there was Soldier.

The touch of its probe conveyed raw power leashed by a disciplined entity. It felt colder than dry ice and more alien than all the others, leaving a feeling in his mind like the taste of a mouthful of blood.

Outside of the daily excursions demanded by the Sylvans, very little work was needed in the camp. During the many idle hours, he turned toward his inner self, his life on the reservation suppressed for so many years. He recalled that he'd just passed his seventeenth year when he turned his back on the Shinnecock tribe and his grandfather.

Joe had tried to deny who he was, and embraced the Anglo culture. He never returned, even changing his name along the way. As he searched inward, he remembered the nightmare of what had come for him, so many years ago, resting on the surface of his memories like a sleeping demonic Cobra. He had asked his grandfather many times. The reply, if it came at all, was elusive as a parable.

Only once the old man had said, "There is something waiting for us, it is not of our world, it waits across the river of time. When you are ready you will face it as a Shinnecock warrior." He liked to think he left because of the poverty. Perhaps it began when he entered the Anglo high school outside the reservation. He envied the white kids, their money, fine clothes and cars. He'd desperately craved the affluence they had been born into. *That's why I left*, he told himself, as whispers of doubt blew across his thoughts like the rustle of leathery wings.

Time passed, and the foliage changed to the red and gold hues of autumn. The air grew chill and the group spent much time hauling kerosene to warm the little huts. Duncan repeatedly disappeared for days, rarely sleeping at the camp. When Joe asked him about it, he would just reply that he had to "do things" for them.

On a cloudy day, among the falling leaves and chilled portents of coming winter, Duncan pressed a small packet into his hands.

"You'll be leaving tomorrow, and you'll be needing this," Duncan told him, his breath little plumes in the air. "Much later, when you're well on your way, remember our conversation."

Duncan removed something from the pocket of his

overcoat and held it out to Joe. It was a pendant of the twelve point Star of David. The material felt cool and smooth, sort of like ivory, but different somehow, thicker and finely crafted. A flexible material seemed to grow out of the top forming a necklace, thin and deceptively strong. Duncan slipped it over Joe's head, tucking it into his shirt.

At daybreak the next morning, Joe left the camp. He walked to the edge of Whiskey Road, seeing the images flashing in his mind, understanding he must simply wait there. Moments later an old Ford drove by slowly and stopped in front of Joe. The young woman driving held an aura of confusion as she opened the door. In total silence she drove him to the Ronkonkoma station of the Long Island Railroad and dropped him off like a suburban housewife sending her husband to work. Joe thought the young woman would always wonder what had possessed her to take a long detour on deserted Whiskey Road, pick up a complete stranger and deliver him twenty-two miles out of her way in total silence, no questions asked.

It had only been a few weeks since Joe had started his episode with the Sylvans, yet there was a strange sensation to being in the bustling commuter crowd. He felt as if he didn't belong, *but had he ever truly belonged to their world?* He wondered. It seemed as if he was outside of himself, watching his actions through the eyes of a stranger, like an out of body experience. He bought tickets to Penn Station, took his seat among the commuters, and watched the Long Island towns roll by, Huntington, Bethpage, Mineola, all the New York City bedroom communities. Finally, the train passed through Queens and plunged into the tunnel to Manhattan.

CHAPTER 15

Joe felt as if giant scissors had suddenly severed a connection plugged directly to his brain, a connection that had grown as familiar as the feel of his own hands. He blinked and turned to the next passenger, a young man with pierced nose and eyebrows. The teen's shaved head nodded in rhythm to the booming base from an MP3 player. The noise leaked from the earphones like a faucet without a washer.

Joe wanted to shout that it was gone. The watchful controlling presence of the Sylvans had disappeared. He looked out the window as the train rocketed through the tunnel.

Spurts of yellow and white lights illuminated grimy walls like demented flashbulbs.

The train reached Penn station and Joe exited. He let himself be swept by the crowd until he reached the upper level. Standing there like a dog cautiously sniffing the air before venturing out, he sensed the familiar undercurrent returning, that buzzing in his head—familiar, yet not familiar, a little different, and much distant and weaker. *They must be the ones who are supposed to get the Amulet,* he thought.

Stay away from Central Park, Duncan had said. *Oh don't*

worry about that. I will stay far away until I figure out how to beat them.

He found Teller's Rare Books on 27th Street just like Duncan had described. It wasn't at all what Joe had expected. Instead of a dusty old place stacked with ancient tomes, he found a large and bright store complete with snack bar and coffee shop. This was more like a Borders or Barnes & Noble, except that half the store was devoted to rare and out of print books. Many were ancient, and locked behind glass cabinets.

It didn't take him long to find *Silva Nocturna*. As he removed it from the shelf, he noticed the woman. She looked at him, and for a moment their eyes met. She was pretty in a tough Jamie Lee Curtis sort of way. Somewhat scraggly, brown hair that didn't quite reach her shoulders, not a trace of makeup and a baggy sweatshirt gave her a take-it-or-leave-it look.

Joe turned away and sat down at a small table near the snack bar. He had just started turning the page when she took a seat opposite him. He looked up into startling eyes so blue they could almost be turquoise. She sat back in the chair, one hand casually draped over the thick armrest.

"You like that book?" she said.

For a moment he was completely bewildered. It had been weeks since he had spoken to any person away from the relentless control of the Sylvans. He felt a tremor begin in his hand. *Damn it*, he thought, *I'm like a kid on his first day of school meeting the Prom Queen.*

"Take your time sport. Is the question, like, too tough?" she said, her words softened with an easy grin.

"Ah, no, it's that I just started…" Joe replied. He felt lame, and the feeling grew with each passing minute.

"You started what? Looking for it? Reading it? You just went for that one book, you didn't look or pick up anything else."

Her stare burnt into him as he held her eyes. Unspoken questions passed between them.

"Hey you want some coffee?" she said.

"Uh, yeah, wait, I'll buy. You want something to eat?"

"Sure, I'll have whatever you're having."

Joe selected two cheese and tomato sandwiches on croissants. As he made his way back to the table he noticed the sunlight outside. It poured in horizontal streaks between the buildings, bright orange and shadowy with the late afternoon. The going-home traffic of commuters sounded heavy and noisy. Not much time left before he had to somehow get underground.

They opened the sandwiches, the clingy Saran wrap stuck to their fingers. Joe hadn't realized how hungry he was until he opened his food. She ate in silence with quick dainty movements and small bites. Afterward, as they finished their coffee, she started her questions again.

"So what do they call you?"

"Joe."

"That's original. I'm Charly, Short for Charlene."

He began to relax a little, enjoying the company of this curious woman and her friendly aggressive way.

"Actually it is original. It's Joe Gray, shortened from Joseph Gray-Wolf."

"It sounds so, like, Indian."

"It is, Shinnecock tribe."

She stared at him, her eyes steady and unblinking, hands flat on the table. She leaned forward slightly as she spoke, her voice a steel wire drawn across soft cotton.

"Is that why you have that book Joe Gray? You just want to know more about night forests, or is it something greater than that? Something that chases you, something you think you can't even talk about." She leaned back and looked outside at the vanishing sunlight. "Because if that's the case," she continued, "you're not alone you see. There's a group of us, trying, like, to warn people. It's difficult. All we've managed so far is to survive. We need more like us. That's why I'm here, in this bookstore, to find people like you. There's only one reason you would go for that one book and that one book only. It's the only book with answers."

Joe heard the pounding of his heart in his ears, loud with hope and anticipation. *Others like him?* He felt as if doors suddenly opened before him, what lay beyond them filled with possibilities. He'd encountered his first real hope since that night on Whiskey Road so many weeks ago, or was it another lifetime?

"Look," she said, "Why don't you come with me? You know you have to get underground for the night."

She knows, he thought, *she knows. What choice does he have anyway?*

CHAPTER 16

Charly led the way out, her gait fast and steady, holding his arm, pulling him along. They reached 31st Street, and she continued tugging at his arm with growing urgency.

"The sun has already set," she said. "We need to move."

A little more alarmed, Joe followed her down the grimy steps of the subway. She reached in the pocket of her jacket, and pulled out two tokens. Now she led him through the turnstile to the end of the platform where she pushed open a service door.

He heard a distant rumbling, building in volume as she climbed down the short flight of steps and came nose to nose with a policeman. Joe stopped suddenly behind her. The cop had his gun drawn, a few feet to his left, two more officers, also with weapons out, stood over two men in windbreakers lying face down on the soot covered cracked cement.

"What the hell are you doing here?" The officer shouted, startled, nervous, his gun pointing at Charly's stomach.

"Uh, I don't know officer…"

The cop took in their shabby clothing and Joe's unshaven face and tousled hair. He lowered his gun and said in a softer voice, "You don't belong here. Get out. This is police business."

Charly turned and went up the steps, emerging back on the subway platform with Joe close behind her.

"Shit," she said. "We're going to have to take the long way in."

A loud rumble accompanied by excruciating metallic screeching announced a train pulling into the station. Charly grabbed Joe's arm and led him through the sliding doors into the train. They stood by the exit, holding a pole, even though almost all the seats were empty. Three stops later they got out of the train. The newly whitewashed sign read "Lexington."

"Stay close to me," Charly told him, leading the way across the platform to the end wall. "Jump exactly where I go, and watch out for the rail in the center, don't get near it. Some are electrified."

He puzzled over that for an instant. Then Charly jumped down the platform, landing just outside the tracks. He paused, all his civilized instincts rebelling against leaping down a subway platform, with a dark, dangerously forbidding, tracked tunnel their only obvious destination.

"Come on, you can't just stay there and look," she said impatiently.

He jumped.

"Stay close to me and you'll be all right. I've done this a thousand times," Charly said. She grabbed his arm and led him into the tunnel, their bodies brushing against the stones of the wall.

He heard some shouting back on the platform as they ran, but he didn't dare look back. Soon, dim caged service bulbs, spaced every thirty yards, replaced the bright station lights. The center spaces between the bulbs were filled with pools of thick blackness as if the meager light didn't have the courage to penetrate. A thick, foul, dark film coated the rough cement walls, the accumulation of a century's worth of grime.

Charly ran now, holding Joe's outstretched arm. He felt a pulsing vibration coming through the slimy stone floor. A light shone on the bend ahead, steadily growing brighter as the rumbling din in the tunnel grew alarmingly loud. The train suddenly rounded the bend, flooding the tunnel with its stark white headlamps.

Charly pulled him into a six-foot wide depression indented three feet into the wall. Joe tried to make himself a part of that wall, every nerve screaming as a blast of foul metallic smelling air, pushed ahead by the train, washed over them. The subway passed in front of them, the incredibly loud noise a pulsing living energy, riveting them even farther against the wall. Joe saw the faces of the passengers in the brightly-lit coaches, flashing by in split second frozen segments. It seemed to go on endlessly. Then, as suddenly as it had appeared, the train vanished down the tunnel, the noise dying to a muted rumble.

His body shook as Charly led him back on the track.

"You get used to it after a while. It's really quite safe."

"Yeah, a real treat," Joe replied. He saw the corners of her mouth slightly curling in a grin, her only concession to his terror.

They went on for another twenty yards then turned into a smaller tunnel that ran at a ninety-degree angle to the track tunnel. A few more yards and they emerged into a high ceiling, large room, barely brighter than the tunnel.

"Stay real close," Charly said. "Don't slow down. Don't make eye contact."

He wondered about that last statement until he noticed the people. The air in the room had the substance of a place that has been damp for a long time. It was overlaid with a foul mixture of smells, a miasma of unwashed bodies, rotting materials and urine. He tried to breathe through his mouth, tasting the decay. There were about two-dozen people in various postures and positions, mostly leaning or lying against the walls.

Each individual or small group had its own space and bits of junk and piles of trash that probably consisted of their total belongings. Joe noticed with horror that there were children and what appeared to be several families. One man lay on his side, naked to the waist, dried blood caked below his nostrils. A rat the size of a small housecat sniffed at the man's toes poking through filth encrusted socks.

They made their way rapidly through the long expanse of the chamber until they approached a support pillar. A stocky man emerged from behind the pillar, blocking Charly's way.

"Gimme your coat, bitch," the man said in a voice burnt raw by cheap whiskey. His red eyes glared unfocused, and he swayed slightly on his feet. The stink of the man amplified the sense of menace.

Charly didn't slow down, didn't miss a beat. She whipped something long and white from her coat, hitting the man on the side of the head with a hollow thud. He staggered back, stopping against the pillar.

"Fuckinbitchilkillyou," he mumbled. But he stayed against the pillar as Charly and Joe passed through.

"There are more lost and dammed people in these tunnels than you can imagine," she said. "Most of them are mentally ill or have sunk so low they'll probably never recover. The shame of it is that it's easier to ignore them under the rug than raise taxes to take care of them."

As they left the chamber, Joe's last impression was an incredibly filthy child, perhaps seven or eight, squatting half-naked, defecating on a pile of garbage.

CHAPTER 17

They continued through the service tunnels, but now even the few working lights ended. Charly pulled a long flashlight from the hidden recesses of her coat. The beam lit up a trio of rats that scampered away at their approach. Joe shuddered as he heard them squealing on the outskirts of the bouncing pool of light.

"Not too far now," she said. "We're approaching the PCC tunnels."

"What's a PCC tunnel?"

"Stands for Pneumatic Communications Corporation. The company was formed in the early 1900's. They dug miles of tunnels beneath Manhattan. They were supposed to hold pneumatic tubes that could send messages packed in containers, within minutes, across town. The idea was good but the telephone systems made the whole thing obsolete. The company went bankrupt and the tunnels remained. We mapped them and use them."

Charly turned into a tunnel that was shorter but somewhat narrower than the previous. The air held a dusty pungent quality, but to Joe's relief, the rotting stenches had vanished. The walls seemed rougher and coarse, as if crudely hewn from the bedrock. Beams from Charly's lantern threw strange and constantly moving shadows from the crevices and raised stone faces of the walls. Their footsteps echoed in the darkness even though surface noises had been reduced to the muffled rumble of trains passing overhead.

The tunnel slanted downward. Joe found this manageable but somewhat worrisome as they advanced farther into the depths of the vast rock base of Manhattan Island. After a while, he detected a glow a good distance away.

Charly slowed down and pointed her light on the left side of the wall until she came to a plastic conduit fastened to the limestone by U bolts. Several different colored wires protruded from the plastic housing, their ends stripped of insulation. She chose a yellow wire with red stripes, and a blue wire. She touched the ends of the wires together causing a small spark. As if in answer, a strobe blinked four times at the far end of the tunnel.

"Come on, we have three minutes," she said, trotting down the tunnel with Joe close behind.

As they reached the end of the shaft, it curved and expanded into a large, well-lit chamber. Joe blinked while his eyes adjusted to the sudden brightness of the room. Ancient large oak beams buttressed the ceiling. Secondary trunks protruded into the tunnel from the chamber. The strobe light was mounted on the end of one of the beams. Charly reached over and pushed a button next to the light.

"What was that about?" Joe asked.

"Booby trap. If you miss the wires, there's a pressure pad and a motion detector that will set off a shaped charge. The tunnel blows up and gets sealed. Touch the wrong combination of wires and you set off the charges. It's our protection system against hostile intruders."

"How could you know how to set this up?"

"We have an electrical engineer and a demolition expert down here," she replied.

Joe clenched his fists, trying to stop the shaking of his hands. The realization of the dangers he'd just faced, hit him hard. First they'd run this gauntlet under the streets of Manhattan and now the perils of the last few feet left him shaken.

"What if you screwed up and touched the wrong wires?"

Her eyes danced and the corner of her mouth turned up in that little crooked grin.

"Then, like, you wouldn't be here to ask me now, would you?"

Before Joe replied, a voice interrupted. The tones boomed in the cavernous stone room.

"Well Charly, what did you bring back this time?"

CHAPTER 18

The voice caught Joe by surprise. He hadn't seen the man sitting on a makeshift stool along the wall of the cave-like room.

"Hey Bill," Charly said. "This is Joe Gray. I found him in the bookstore. Joe has the same problem we have."

"Bill Darien," the man said as he rose from the stool. He was bearded and bald on top with side hairs tied in a ponytail. He had a nose like a squashed tomato and a big belly. He reminded Joe of those aging bikers who dress and groom themselves like they're still twenty years old.

Bill's face broke into a wide grin as he extended his hand. Friendly eyes and a slight grin softened his face. His grip was firm as the men shook hands.

"Well maybe we can use some help here," Bill said. "Don't look like we're getting any closer to settling anything."

"How long have you been here?"

This time it was Charly who answered. "Bill's been here the longest. He discovered the PCC tunnels. Life would have been real shit without those tunnels."

Joe remembered the oppressive grime of the subways and the undercurrent of danger that ran through them like a dark tide. How could anyone live in there? At least the PCC tunnels seemed cleaner and maybe even safer, *unless you count explosive charges that will shred you to pieces if you forget what color wire goes with what.*

"It's been a little over two years," Bill said.

"Two years. You've been living here two years?"

"What would you suggest? They've been in my brains. I've been imprinted. I can barely go two to three blocks before I feel them, and that's in daylight. I wouldn't survive an hour at night."

"Can't you contact the authorities? Can't you do something?"

"Like I said, what do you suggest? Let me tell you a little story. Charly's only been here a few months, but a year ago we had this guy named Sam. No last name, just Sam. Now Sam had been here only a few weeks when he decided that if he just yelled loud enough, they would believe him. Well he did yell loudly and he convinced the NYPD he was delusional. They held him in Bellevue, kept him overnight. According to the papers he had a seizure early in the evening and died. I followed the story in the Daily News. There'd been allegations that the staff at Bellevue had been at fault. The autopsy showed multiple cerebral aneurysms. Now do you have any ideas how that happened? Because if you have any doubts, I can tell you exactly: They killed him."

Joe didn't answer as he remembered Duncan Wesley's story about the man who tried to get away and died in the Pine Barrens near the lab. He felt Charly's hand on his arm, a gentle touch, just a bit shy for her forceful demeanor.

"Maybe now with more of us, with someone like you," she said almost in a whisper, "we can come up with some ideas."

"Who else is in here?" Joe asked.

"Two more," Bill answered, "Jesse and Manuel. They'll be along soon as they finish rigging some wires for lights in the lower reaches. We're trying to see if these tunnels connect to the ones under the river. If they do, maybe we can get far enough out of Manhattan to get beyond their range."

Joe circled around the room, searching, not quite knowing what he was looking for. He wondered how these people could spend two years living in this room carved out of the Manhattan bedrock. Time had a strange ephemeral quality here. No reference points existed, no window or door to look out and see the progress of day or night. Time itself became subjugated to the surroundings, as if the rock lived and ate the moments like some kind of food.

Joe's watch told him it had been only an hour since he had arrived, when the warning lights on the edge of the tunnel blinked and the strobe light went off.

As he thought about it, two men walked in.

They strutted into the cave-room with the easy manners of people familiar with their surroundings. "That's Manuel and Jesse," Charly told him.

Jesse was a surly, wild looking man with hair like dried plastic spaghetti, long, scraggly and white. He ignored Joe and seemed in his own world, responding only to the other man accompanying him: Manuel.

Joe liked Manuel immediately. The short Mexican had a wide smile that made his bushy mustache dance as his eyes twinkled. His laugh came easily and quickly, along with his rapid-fire speech peppered with Spanish words.

"Hey *amigo*, good to meet you. Glad to have another *Pandejo* down here. Could use the help. Bet you ain't so happy to deal with those *maricones* either."

As the evening passed, Joe learned their stories: Bill Darien had been discovered by Sylvans during the design and upgrade of electrical lighting systems in Central Park. He was the only one from Manhattan.

Manuel's parents had been illegal immigrants who made sure their son would be born in the US. He grew up in Texas, and visited Mexico often. It was during one of those visits that he met his great aunt, the white witch.

"It was like spooky, man," Manuel told Joe. "I mean I never met this woman before. I was seeing this real fine *guapa*, when suddenly this old woman, about a hundred years old, starts to spout all kinds of shit from my life that nobody could have known. It was so weird. Then she starts with the spirit world and shit, tells me I have a destiny.

Now I was a little rattled. It ain't everyday somebody comes to you and knows all this stuff about you and you ain't never seen them before. I knew from everything she told me that she really was my father's sister. He told me he had a sister once but it was like he didn't want to talk about her, you know?"

Manuel had spent a few days with his great aunt in her small cabin at the foot of the Sierra Madres. He discovered a world he never knew existed, a world of nature, wilderness and mystical spirituality.

He also found Sylvans, or as his great aunt said: "*Los Onos.*" The Ones. The old woman, his great aunt, lived with the creatures as far back as her prodigious memory recalled. Manuel was something else. As he felt the slow and steadily increasing control of the Sylvans, he fled.

Manuel made his way to Mexico City and took a flight to New York. Pursued, always pursued, he didn't find the safe harbor he sought at his cousin's apartment in Spanish Harlem. The nightly presence and psychic assaults intensified until he found refuge in the subway tunnels.

In turn, Joe related his story. It seemed easier with Charly next to him. When he told them what Duncan Wesley said about finding Doctor Wu, Manuel broke into cackling laughter.

"Sure, just like that, you gonna find this *pandejo* Chinese with a name like Wu."

"I'll damn sure try," Joe said. "Why don't you and Charly help me, we could start tomorrow."

Every time Manuel laughed, the deep creases at the corner of his mouth made his mustache tremble. It shook as he laughed even harder.

"Man," Manuel said, "I can picture that, the three of us in Chinatown. Just imagine it. You said you're Indian, Shine Cook or some shit."

"Shinnecock."

"Whatever. You still look like white bread. Then we have Miss America here and me, a spic, in Chinatown. *Madre De Dios*, are you nuts? This is gonna be worse than the

Three Stooges."

Charly gave Manuel a light slap on his arm and a tiny smile.

"Well I think he can help us out of here," she said, "Your only plan so far has been to bring cases of Corona down here."

"Hey, that's got value too you know," Manuel said, holding up a half empty bottle as they ate thawed packages of pizza and drank tepid bottled water.

CHAPTER 19

Joe, Charly and Manuel set out early the next morning. They emerged from an underground passage into a service storage room at Lexington Station, and carefully re-bolted the door behind them. As they came out of the station into the street, Joe felt the presence in his mind again, like a light switch just turned on. Now it had a different quality, a buzzing undercurrent of anger like a disturbed beehive.

They walked to Chinatown. The sidewalk and streets glistened from the light drizzle and the entire city seemed as gray as the clouds peeking between the Manhattan skyscrapers.

None of them really had any idea where to begin. Joe and Charly just asked in stores loaded with knockoff merchandise and cheap souvenirs. No one knew anything. There were hundreds of Wu's in the Manhattan directory and a dozen were labeled as Doctors.

They spent the day chasing and calling. They were met everywhere with blank looks and negative headshakes. The clouds grew fat as a sheep in a pasture and the air turned serious-cold. After the umpteenth negative muttering in Chinese or broken English, they decided to pack it in.

They made their way back to the subway well before dark.

"Hey Geronimo, you got any money so this spic don't have to panhandle," Manuel asked Joe.

Try as he would Joe couldn't get mad at the laughing Mexican. He gave him a twenty to bring some food down for them, but he was a bit disturbed. He had a pretty good idea how they obtained money to buy necessities. They probably took turns panhandling. When he asked Charly about it, she said only Manuel and Jesse did that. She had some other source. She also gave them some cash but wouldn't tell him where she got it.

Later that night, he found that both Manuel and Bill had guns. Manuel owned a thirty-eight Police Special and Bill a Glock nine. They carried them all the time in the underground. When they came to the surface they had special hiding places where they stashed them.

"Can't take a chance getting caught with guns up top," Bill told him. "That's a night in jail for sure, and for us, an automatic death sentence."

"Down here we need the guns," Manuel said. "This place is crawling with *hijos de putas* and *locos*. They haven't made their way down here yet but we don't know how long that's gonna last. That's why we got the booby traps and all."

Joe thought back on how Charly handled the homeless man who had wanted her coat. She didn't seem to need a gun for that, but there certainly were harder cases prowling the tunnels.

The next morning Manuel refused to go with them.

"*Madre de mentiras*," he said. "It's useless. None of them Chinese are gonna talk to you. I'm better off looking for my cousin Paco. He got a basement apartment I could share. I just ain't got his address, but I keep looking I'll find it."

"Manny," Charly told him. "You been looking for that cousin of yours since you got here. I don't even think he exists."

"*No es verdad*, it's not true. I got a cousin, I'll find him eventually then we gonna look to mess with these *Los Onos*, those Sylvan things."

CHAPTER 20

Joe and Charly left without Manuel the next morning. They stopped at a small breakfast nook on 28th Street. Joe ate and barely said anything. He looked up as he felt her stare and their eyes locked. She reached over and took his hand in both of hers. Her grip felt warm, reassuring somehow. He squeezed her hand.

"Penny for your thoughts," she said. "Or the cat got your tongue, or probably a rat," she grinned.

"What a lovely thought."

He noticed a dimple on the side of her cheek when she smiled, and he thought it gave her face a little girl quality, a feminine impish look that he found delightful.

"Look, Charly, it's just that I'm not staying here months or years. These three guys," he waved back toward Lexington Station, "they seem to have taken roots here. I can't live like this. I don't give a damn how long these things have been around. We've got to fight it until we convince others to help us or we break free somehow. I think Duncan Wesley and Doctor Wu may be the key."

She leaned forward and he felt he could happily drown in those dark blue eyes. He realized with some surprise that he was thrilled she was here with him.

"When I first saw you and met you in that bookstore,"

Charly said, "I thought you were someone who would be able to really handle this. Maybe not right away because you were a little lost, still are." She grinned and gave his hand another squeeze. "But I knew," she continued, "I sensed you would find the way out of this. I just want to be there with you when you do."

"Yeah, but we have to change tactics. Manuel is right about one thing. We can't blunder around Chinatown expecting to get results. It's about time we got some help."

"Get help? What do you think we're trying to do Joe? Join the society debutante ball?"

"I know someone in Manhattan."

"Christ Joe, we all know someone in Manhattan. What good does that do? They won't believe you. They'll try to get you put away for your own good. I went through that shit all ready."

"Maybe," Joe replied. "But this one is a Manhattan Police Captain."

"He better be a real good friend or he won't believe you either."

"He's better than that. He's my brother."

It took only one phone call for Joe to reach his brother. He was the sole family member Joe had kept in touch with. They made arrangements to meet a little later that day.

CHAPTER 21

Captain T.R. Jackson, Joe's brother, met them in the early afternoon at a quiet diner on 31st Street. He was in plainclothes and Charly immediately recognized the family resemblance.

T.R. hugged Joe with such pleasure, and their smiles were so wide that Charly thought they'd be able to eat a banana sideways. She grinned at the idea and let out a little chuckle.

"What's so funny?" Joe asked.

Charly pursed her lips, and said, "Nothing. You going to introduce me to your brother, or what?"

"Sorry. Charly, my brother T.R."

They shook hands and Charly liked him immediately, He looked like someone happy with himself, at peace and confident. She liked him as much as she had liked Joe. Well, maybe not as much as Joe. There was something special there. She turned to Joe, smiled, then back to his brother.

"So what's T.R. stand for?"

"Nothing particular."

"I'll bet no one at the precinct knows. You've never told anyone, have you? Mind if I tell her?"

T.R. looked up as if seeking help from some indifferent

deity. He shrugged and said, "Go ahead."

"T.R. stands for Tall Rider."

"Tall Rider?"

"Yeah, our father always admired the native tribes of the great plains. TR was the first-born son. Our father said he would learn to ride like a Comanche. He would be a Tall Rider."

"If word of what TR stands for gets around in the Department, I'll personally place you both in Rikers Island's deepest dungeon. By the way, did this character who calls himself my brother give you his real name?"

"Yeah," grinned Charly, "Gray Dog."

TR laughed uproariously. They all started laughing, and as they talked, Joe realized he longed for nothing more than just forgetting his troubles for a while.

The waitress brought their coffee, and TR fixed his eyes on Joe. He waited until she left before talking.

"Joe," TR said. "I know this is not a social call. You said you were in real trouble and needed help. I guess that's about the time you call an older brother or a cop. You're in luck. You got both in one package, so tell me, who's after you?"

"I wish it was that easy. But first, I want you to remember certain things. I want you to remember Grandfather and the burial ground, the shrine by the bay and the Shaman's Vision Stone rites. Do you remember? I want you to think like a Shinnecock warrior, like our father and grandfather and our ancestors. Can you still do that TR?"

TR blinked, the wide forehead wrinkled above bushy eyebrows and the laugh lines settled. He was older than Joe and it showed.

"That's kind of a strange thing for you to say, Joe. You were still a minor when you left the reservation. It's been what, twenty years, maybe more? Sure I remember. Certain things you carry always and eventually take them to the grave. It's what you are, like your eyes, your toes, it's you."

"I know that," Joe replied. "I want you to remember because I think that somehow, and I can't explain why, it might help you understand and believe the kind of trouble we are in right now."

"Hell, Joe, I'm going on my twenty second year as a cop in Manhattan. I've seen things most people can't even begin to imagine. You don't really think I need to dwell on native Shaman rituals to handle your problem?"

"You might in this case," Charly cut in.

Once again Joe told his story. He left nothing out, from the drinking to hitting the strange creature to his flight into Manhattan. Charly sensed that telling all this to his older brother was a catharsis, like being a child again and unburdening guilt, cutting loose a problem to a responsible adult who would make it all well again. But of course it wasn't that way at all. By the time Joe finished and answered TR's questions, two hours had passed, punctuated by several rounds of coffee.

"Joe, if it was anyone else than you," TR said. "I would either pass them off as harmless nuts or send them for a psychiatric evaluation."

But he listened to both their stories. He took notes in a little spiral pad, and when they were finished, most of the notebook was filled. He sighed and there was something in his eyes like someone who's had a disturbing diagnosis confirmed.

"You know," TR said, "until a couple of weeks ago, it would have been difficult for me to swallow this story, even coming from you. But things have happened lately."

He held a fork in his hand, twirling it between his fingers like a tiny cheerleader's baton. His other hand tapped on the table as if he needed the rhythm to center his thoughts. His eyes alternated between Joe and Charly as he spoke.

"I've been through the Beame and Dinkins administrations, times of high crime and low budgets. Then Giuliani with the tough-on-crime attitude and the World Trade Center horror. I've been through all that, but something's happening now. I can't quite explain it. It's a *feeling*. In the last two weeks we've had more murders and assaults than any six-month period I can recall. Most of these violent episodes come from people you would never expect. It's like there's something in the air or the water. You can sense it, everybody feels it on some level, but no one wants to talk about it."

A flash of worry passed across TR's face like distant summer lightening. For a second Joe thought he read fear in his brother's eyes.

"Well, I agree with you on one thing," TR continued. "We have to find this Doctor Wu. If I can get independent corroboration, we could get some serious wheels turning on this."

Joe looked out the window and frowned. When he turned back, he saw TR watching him. The afternoon grew late. Much later, Joe would remember this day. He would wonder with agony if he could have avoided the coming horror by simply struggling without seeking his brother's help. This moment however, he remained blissfully unaware, simply concerned about getting underground before dark.

"You and Charly don't have to go back to the subways," TR said. "I know this retired cop. He's one of my former partners when I was on patrol. He owns a grocery store with a deep basement storage room. He's got it furnished and he'll let you stay there if I ask him, no questions asked. You should be okay at his place."

"No, I don't think so," Joe replied, shaking his head, "I don't really know the power of whatever's out there. Those tunnels are the deepest thing in Manhattan and safe from them."

"And besides," Charly added, "there're these other people that helped us. We should get them out of there. Its better if we go back, at least for a while."

"All right," TR said, "but here's how I can help you. You don't have a chance of finding this Doctor Wu, if he even exists, but I have the people who can find him. I'll put Cheng and Li on it now, tonight. They're Detective Sergeants, Asian Crime Task Force. They know Chinatown like their own face in a mirror. If this Doctor Wu is in there, they'll find him, and they'll find him fast."

TR paid the bill and they left the restaurant into the gloom of the coming Manhattan fall evening. A light drizzle brushed their faces like wet fog. They had agreed on a time for Joe to call the next morning. Charly looked back and saw TR just standing there, watching, as they disappeared down the stairs of the 32d Street subway entrance.

CHAPTER 22

Joe called TR the next morning. His brother had already assigned the Asian Task Force detectives to help them. He'd told them it was urgent they find Wu since he was a key witness in an important missing person case and he was hiding in their own backyard: Chinatown.

For Joe, the rest of the day passed so slowly, time seemed frozen. He roamed the area around Lexington Station and the surrounding streets, restless as a dog with fleas. The day ended soon enough and he was driven into the subterranean station by the approaching night. It was just about ten PM when he called TR from a station pay phone and got the news he waited for.

"They found him," TR told him.

"Christ that was fast."

"I told you they knew the place. They were born and raised there. If somebody farts in Chinatown, Li and Cheng will know what they had for dinner."

"Nice, when can we talk to him?"

"They arranged a meeting for tomorrow," TR said. "It's set up in a back alley restaurant called Dragon Scale."

"Why can't you just bring him in?"

"That's not the way it works, you've been watching too many NYPD reruns. First this guy hasn't done anything wrong. I can't just tell two detectives to bring him in without some good reason. Second, in Chinatown, everything's contacts, favors and assurances, without all that, my guys don't have any links in there. Wu will meet with you because they guaranteed his safety and his daughter's safety."

"He has a daughter with him?"

"That's what they tell me, twelve or thirteen years old. I understand she never leaves his side and from what Li says, the guy is scared shitless. But there's more, there's something strange going on with this whole thing."

"Tell me about it. What kind of weirdness did you find, TR?"

"Well, there's this guy I know, a real good guy, an old friend. His name is Donohue. He's with the FBI, a Special Agent. We worked together on a number of cases that involved NYPD and Federal jurisdictions. He's tough and smart and I trust him. I asked him to look into this on the FBI side. Here's some stuff he came up with: Wu's background: entry from China in the fifties, college at Harvard, physics career, the whole nine yards check out, now get this, until he vanishes from Brookhaven National Lab. This Duncan Wesley is a different story. Donohue says it's like he popped out of nowhere at the same Lab. Inquiries have been shut down. His records are black– classified. They don't exist. Plus this Wu is taking too many precautions for somebody hiding from creatures like you described. It's like he's also hiding from any authorities, like some kind of deep cover. Donohue's intrigued. He'll keep working it. Meanwhile you and Charly meet Li and Cheng at the old Nedicks on 18th street at nine-thirty AM tomorrow."

"Got it, we'll be there"

CHAPTER 23

Joe met with Charly that evening at ten thirty PM at the nearly empty IRT platform at Lexington station. She led him through a service tunnel and they linked up with the old PCC tunnels to the underground room. He found it difficult to fall asleep in the damp air filled with echoing noises and squealing shuffles from a variety of rodents that shared the underground passages.

Joe rose early the next morning, washed and shaved best as he could. He longed for the luxurious steaming showers of his abandoned home in Long Island. As he shared a couple of stale bagels with Charly, he wondered if he ever would see that home again.

When they emerged from the station early in the morning, Joe felt like he had become a mutated creature, a quasi-rodent, human underground dweller.

Last night's drizzle and clouds had lifted and the early morning sunlight glinted off the top of the Manhattan towers like steady orange flames. The air held a hint of decay as they walked toward their meeting with the detectives on 18th street. Arriving early, they waited nearly a half hour, sipping coffee out of cardboard containers from the Nedicks on the corner.

The two Asian Crimes task force detectives picked them

up in a battered, blue, grime covered, pock marked Ford. Punctuated here and there with rust spots like bleeding wounds, the vehicle looked like a refugee from a car-crushing machine. That was one automobile that didn't scream "undercover police." The men driving it fit right with the image. Detective Li was a tall jovial young man wearing a knitted wool cap on his head and a two-day beard on his chin. Li's partner, Detective Cheng, sat on the front passenger side, and his bulk took most of the front seat.

Cheng turned his head to face Joe and Charly as they sat in the back. The interior of the car smelled of stale smoke and mold. Crumpled fast food wrappers littered the rear floor of the Ford. Li caught sight of them in the rear view mirror and grinned.

"Sorry, we didn't have time to clean up for you," the detective said. "We usually only do that for ranks of Inspector and higher."

"Okay, here's the deal," Cheng said, lighting a cigarette. "We tracked this Doctor Wu thru one of our contacts named Long Wo. We've got an understanding with Long Wo, he's one of our most important informants. TR said you needed to talk to Wu. We guaranteed his safety. This Wu is badly scared of somebody, has to be with all these precautions. You're going to have an hour to talk with this guy, beyond that, we can't guarantee anything."

"What kind of shit are you people involved with anyway?" asked Li.

"We've got some problems," Joe replied, "but we're not involved in anything illegal if that's what you want to know."

"Hey I'm a detective," replied Li. "Curious is my middle name. I know whatever problems you got, you're not the bad guys. If you were, TR never would have asked us to help you."

They left the Ford double parked on Mott Street with a Police card on the windshield. Joe and Charly followed the detectives through an alley littered with empty boxes and torn trash bags. Cheng led the way, ducking under an overhanging fire escape rail. In spite of his bulk, he moved with the smooth grace of a basketball player. Joe thought his goatee and shaved head made him look like a cross between Dr. Fu Manchu and a nasty-looking Buddha.

They emerged into a tiny courtyard. Clotheslines loaded with various garments blocked out most of what little sunlight managed to filter down. Steam rose in clouds out of a grate in one corner and a pungent smell of curry and onions stung their nostrils. Li walked to a corner of the yard and squatted in front of an old man sitting cross-legged on the pavement. The old man's voice came in a high-pitched singsong as he pointed to a partly opened, ancient wood door. They went inside, and followed an unlit corridor of mostly broken tiles. Sounds of rushing water, banging pots, crockery and loud voices arguing in Mandarin, poured through the greasy brick walls. They continued through a second door leading to a cramped space between two buildings, emptying into yet another courtyard.

Two Chinese men waited there. One looked distinguished, and old. He wore a traditional Chinese gown, red with gold trim and high black collar contrasting with his short white beard. The other man was young and slender, with features like knife blades. A tight black sweater stretched over steel-roped muscles. Thin scars ran from the bridge of his nose through the length of his cheek. The white scar lines set off the olive skin before they ended below the ear. Li and the old man spoke briefly in rapid Mandarin.

Joe had a feeling of disconnect, as if he stood in an alien land far away. Waves of strange sensations filled the atmosphere and echoed with the buzzing continuous tendrils of the Sylvans. He felt Charly's hand holding his arm. She leaned closer and whispered.

"It's like we're on another planet. I don't even think we could find our way out of this place without these guys."

"I know. We never had a chance of finding Wu by ourselves."

They followed the old man through another corridor until they came to a heavy steel door. He produced a large key from the folds of his robe and unlocked the door.

Nothing could have prepared them for what they saw.

They stepped into paradise. At least it seemed like it to Joe and Charly. Through this labyrinth of doorways, seedy alleys and filthy courtyards, they had reached a hidden treasure of beauty and tranquility.

The space was a courtyard about a hundred by sixty feet, enclosed by the back of four buildings each five stories high. Climbing vines and unidentifiable heavy vegetation completely covered the walls giving the appearance of being surrounded by a thick jungle. The ground was a meadow grass that Joe had never seen before. It felt soft and pliant and intersected with two footpaths covered with brightly colored pebbles. A weeping willow grew in the center against one of the walls. Its branches spread overhead so the sunlight came down in diffused beams. Vines hung from the branches, swaying back and forth in a soft breeze that seemed to come out of the green vegetation of the walls. Colorful birds flitted in the branches, their chirping blending with the soft tinkling of hidden wind chimes. Flowers and lush plants grew in a controlled profusion of riotous colors and shades, and the scent of roses and lilacs filled the air. Joe felt suddenly at ease. A sense of peacefulness emanated from every corner of the courtyard.

"God it's so beautiful," Charly said, "I could just take my shoes off and lay down right here."

"Man, I lived and worked here my whole life and I never heard of this place," said Cheng, turning to Joe and Charly, "It's incredible."

A voice came from behind them.

"My brother built it as a tribute to our mother."

He might have materialized from the very walls. Neither the detectives or Joe and Charly had heard him coming. The newcomer was short with close-cropped hair and fine features, almost feminine in their delicateness. An adolescent girl stood at his side, beautiful with dark hair, a hint of an Asian fold to the almond shaped eyes. Blue pupils crowded out the white, and she carried an air of otherworldly exoticness that hung about her like a shimmering veil.

"I am pleased you like my little garden," continued the man, "I am Doctor Wu."

CHAPTER 24

They stood facing Doctor Wu, and didn't quite know what to say until Joe spoke first, "I am Joe Gray and this is Charly. We've been looking for you for days."

"I want to tell you we're dammed glad to see you," Charly said, as she reached out and gently shook hands with Wu, "Who's the young lady?"

"My daughter, Mai Lin."

Both Cheng and Li bowed to Wu in the Chinese custom.

They sat around a small table decorated with delicate Chinese ceramics. As Cheng and Li stood a few feet away, Wu prepared green tea, his movements sparse and ceremonial. He filled small round cups and gave one to each with a small bow of his head. They drank in silence, savoring the pungent aromatic brew. Joe felt Wu's eyes examining him, gauging him. Their glances locked, and for a brief moment he sensed a wave of kindness from the Doctor, as if something long-asleep stirred within him like the hint of an approaching dawn. He glanced at Mai-Lin as a smile unfolded like a flower across her face. He thought she looked like the obedient child putting up with her elder's tiresome customs, yet the almost non-existent pupils of her eyes lent an unearthly quality to the girl's features. He felt Charly's hand around his arm and for the briefest moment he sensed the aura of the girl's presence.

"You have gone to a lot of trouble to find me," said Wu.

"I am amazed we did find you," replied Joe. "I thought it would not be possible."

Wu gave a small pleasant laugh as he spoke. "Normally it would not be possible. Your friends helped certain people whom I am fond of. I learned long ago that one of the secrets of life is returning one's obligations."

Joe licked his lips and made a small noise deep in his throat. He felt a complete loss of words. How could he possible explain all that had happened? It still didn't make sense to him. He couldn't even remember how he had told all this to his own brother.

"I don't quite know how to begin," said Joe, "I don't even see how anyone could believe it, but so help me it's the truth."

Dr. Wu smiled again. There was something about him that felt reassuring as he replied.

"We have a saying from my birthplace in Gansu Province. It is from a man you know as Confucius."

Joe felt Charly's hand tighten on his arm as Wu continued.

"It is man that makes truth great…Not truth that makes man great."

Wu leaned forward, the heavy lidded eyes held Joe's.

"Just talk to me," said Wu. "Tell the story as if you were telling it for yourself."

For the second time in as many days, Joe told his story. It was a release for him, this outpouring of words. As he spoke, he tried to glimpse some answer, some reason, but it hovered on the edge of his consciousness, elusive as a Mayfly. He wasn't aware of the time that had passed as he spoke. When he finished, the air was noticeably chillier and the light had begun to fade.

Wu sighed and looked away. His eyes locked on Mai-Lin's and they exchanged a brief smile. He looked down on the table and spoke softly.

"So it has begun. I was a fool to think that if I left, if I took my knowledge with me, they could not progress on this terrible path. I am at fault. The signs were all around me and I ignored them."

CHAPTER 25

Joe felt the heavy pummeling of his heart and it wasn't just because of what Dr. Wu had said. Something hummed in the air like a galvanized charge, a precursor to a violent storm, something you feel in your pores, in the depth of that still and primitive part of the brain.

He heard the commotion first. A series of muffled thuds and shrieking, the noise burst in the quiet garden, muted from just beyond the wall. He saw the detectives, Li and Cheng, get up from their seats as the vegetation-covered door flung open from the outside. The young Chinese man who had waved them inside walked in. For a moment it seemed as if he was drunk, staggering, his eyes opened wide in surprise as he stared down the front of his white shirt at the spreading satiny red stain. He tried to grasp a pigmy palm but the sapling was too weak to hold him, and he pitched forward, eyes still open. He struck the rock border face first with a noise like crushing a cantaloupe. Bright red arterial blood pumped inside his shirt and seeped on the thick grass.

It took Joe a few frozen minutes to even begin understanding what happened. Everything seemed to slow down into little segments of time, Cheng running toward the fallen man and the door as he reached inside his sweatshirt, pulling out a black sleek pistol.

He never had a chance. They came thru the door like deadly black shadows, heads bandaged leaving only slits for the eyes. They raised the Mac-10 automatic pistols, the twin salvos pouring out bullets at an appalling rate, catching Cheng in the crossfire, the rounds walking across his chest. Joe saw the exiting bullets as they exploded out of the detective's back in gouts of blood. Cheng seemed to leap backward, spinning and falling across the path, his pistol sliding across the slate flagstones. Li dove behind a carved stone dragon and pulled an automatic from a shoulder holster under his jacket.

Both arms resting across the top of the dragon-head, holding the gun in a two handed stance, he fired six rounds. The first assailant's head snapped backward as the bullet blew out his left eye. The second man dove back through the door. Joe knocked over the heavy table and pushed Charly, Wu and Mai-Lin behind it. Li rushed to his fallen partner as blood soaked the grass beneath. He crouched by Cheng, one hand on his partner's chest trying to staunch the red torrent, the other hand holding a portable police radio, shouting officer down and giving his location.

It flew in through the partially open doorway. The size of a large orange, the grenade bounced on the grass and landed with a clatter on the slate pathway six feet from Li.

Time seemed to stretch again for Joe as he stood, yelling at Li to get away. Li's eyes went from his partner to the grenade. He rose from his crouch like a sprinter, reached the grenade and kicked, sending the black sphere rolling across the slate and grass toward the door.

It might have worked if it wasn't for Buddha.

The grenade struck the terracotta statue of the god and bounced back, stopping a few feet away. Li dove to the ground as it exploded. The blast hit his body mid-air, flinging him a dozen feet. When it stopped, blood poured from dozens of wounds as the detective's eyes stared wide and lifeless.

Joe dashed from behind the table with Charly close

behind. He picked up the gun that Cheng had dropped. His mind numbed as he looked at the body of the two detectives, two men who had been living breathing humans, now reduced to battered meat. He felt Charly hold his arm, felt her limbs shake as she moaned at the sight of the detective's bodies. He forced her into a crouch and picked up Li's radio. A piece of shrapnel had blown away the faceplate and smashed electronic fragments rattled inside. He flung it away. He heard Chinese voices arguing urgently behind the partially opened door. Someone's head emerged, peeking from the doorway. Joe raised the pistol and pulled the trigger.

Nothing happened.

More chattering came from behind the door. This time Joe pulled the safety and fired two shots into the doorway. He grabbed Charly's arm and ran back to the overturned table where Wu crouched holding Mai-Lin. Her eyes widened like bright jewels on a satin cushion. The pupils had disappeared.

"Is there any other way out?" asked Joe.

Wu seemed dazed and Joe saw the shaking of his hand over the girl's head. He suddenly thought that it was Mai-Lin he should be talking to. The girl said something incomprehensible in Chinese, her voice like musical notes, high and sweet. Wu shook his head and looked up at Joe.

"There," Wu said, pointing to the opposing corner, "there is a service door, it latches from both inside and outside."

Charly helped Wu and Mai-Lin to their feet, herding them toward the hidden door. Wu found the latch buried in the mass of foliage and yanked it open into a dim hallway. Joe pushed them through just as another man ran crouching in the garden, firing while running, the bullets hitting the wall by Joe's ear with a vicious plunking noise. Joe dove through the doorway, pulling the heavy steel door shut.

It bounced open again.

"The latch, where the hell's the latch?" Joe screamed as he shut the door again.

Wu stepped to the door. He grasped a long deadbolt from

a recessed notch and slammed it home. He turned and held the girl's hand and pointed where the hallway appeared to turn into yet another door.

"This way, we must go through there."

Joe grabbed Charly's hand and pushed her forward with his other hand between her shoulder blades. From behind the latched door came the sound of rapid firing and hollow pinging as the bullets passed through the door. Joe pushed Charly against the wall as they ran forward. He turned in time to see Wu shove the girl ahead. His eyes opened wide as he stopped. He took two slow tentative steps, like someone just learning to walk again. Joe turned back, hustling both of them forward.

Another volley of gunfire hit the door, bursting through, the bullets whistling over Joe's head. He looked up at Charly, saw her eyes pleading, fearful.

"Move, godammit, move," he screamed.

Instead of going toward the doorway, Charly ran back to Joe and crouched on the floor. She put both her hands on the girl's trembling shoulders. Mai-Lin's scream turned to deep sobs as Wu held her, and Charly's eyes met Joe's.

"My God Joe, those poor detectives, we've got to get them help."

"They're dead. There's nothing more we can do. If we don't get out of here now we're all going to join them."

As if to emphasize his point, the door was battered from inside, chunks of metal and wood, already weakened by bullet holes, broke from the door. Streams of daylight from the garden inside penetrated the gloom, lighting pathways of floating dust.

Joe hustled them through the open doorway at the end of the corridor. He had no idea where he was going. He just ran, ushering them through corridors, and alleys between buildings as the noises of pursuit faded.

They emerged into a dingy litter-strewn side street, the shadows of the coming evening stretching to the top of the grimy brick buildings. They continued running until they ducked into a subway entrance just off the Bowery. Two chains stretched across the entrance. A "closed for repairs" sign hung from the chains. They ducked under the chains and went down the steps as the last rays of the sun vanished from the top of the buildings.

Part of the platform had crumbled. Cement mixers, construction supplies and machinery lay about like abandoned children's building blocks. A single caged fluorescent light cast a shadowy glow that didn't make it to all corners of the empty station.

They stepped gingerly around the gaping holes in the concrete under repair. They reached a bench just past the construction equipment. As he led Charly and the girl toward the bench, Joe felt his heart beat wildly and his hands tremble.

At least four men have died tonight. Why? The two Asian crimes task force detectives, TR's friends, and two assailants. Joe's mind reeled. Above all, he wanted to talk to his brother, explain what had happened, maybe he could get some answers. The idea of not contacting the police, alerting them to the violence that had taken place, was abhorrent to him. Yet, as his eyes took in the single destroyed pay phone propped up on a rusty pole, he knew there would be nothing he could do in this place until morning.

They sat on the deserted platform bench, hugging the girl between them. Her sobbing subsided leaving her with eyes the color of burgundy in a blank expressionless face. It was as if she had gone elsewhere, some place only she could go.

"Can we get back to the PCC tunnels from here?" Joe asked Charly.

"No, at least not any way I know off. It's across town. We'd probably get lost. It's just too dangerous wandering around in unknown tunnels. Trains still go thru this line and some spots are so narrow you'd be unable to avoid getting hit. Best thing for us is to just spend the night here."

Joe turned to Wu as he spoke. "What about you, Doctor Wu? What do you think we should do? Do you have any idea what the hell is going on? Do you have a place we could hide until morning?"

"No," the older Chinese replied. "Even my refuge is no longer safe. We must stay here tonight. To be above ground this night would be too dangerous."

Something was building, some kind of energy. Joe felt it like an invisible undertow lying in wait just below the surface of consciousness. He turned to Charly and saw in her eyes that she felt it also.

She shook her head gently.

"Don't say it. I sense it too," she said, "Never felt anything like this. It's new or something."

Whatever it is, Joe thought, *it doesn't seem to get worse.* After the ambush and deaths they had witnessed, this didn't seem that important, at least not for now.

They held the silent girl between them as the shaking of their bodies slowed. It was hours later that they fell asleep, huddled in a dark corner of the silent station.

CHAPTER 26

The Sylvan squatted on the ancient oak, way up in the limbs stretching to the skies. He remembered a time when such trees were the highest things on the island. All those many time-cycles came back to him like silent ghosts haunting the night, the eras when his kind populated the island in hundreds.

There were no men those many time-cycles ago, at least not enough to make a difference. A few tribes of men, scattered throughout the island, a few more in the lands they now called Brooklyn or across the other side they called New Jersey where the cliffs towered like guardians to the river and the headways of the ocean.

In those old times they had rarely bothered with the humans. They would enter the minds of the men who made war and hunted. Their brains would receive the signals like messages from their gods. Indeed he thought, they were their gods.

They were not demanding gods, didn't require sacrifices. Food, hand-made articles of clothing and other artifacts were sufficient. In return, the Sylvans would give them peace and timeless feelings of serenity.

The changes had been slow. Not as slow as the age-old retreat of the glaciers that had formed this land, but slower than many time cycles. What humans called centuries, passed.

They had come hesitantly, even timid, as if the race of humans could ever be timid. They came from vast distances crossing the expanses of the great ocean. Distances so great that he could feel no thoughts, no emotions from those far away lands. The psychic waves were absorbed by the great span of water.

The men had come, just a few at first. A few in fragile wood ships driven with cloth sails like white cotton clouds. Then they came in waves of hundreds, many ships with masts from the tallest, straightest trees. As they grew in numbers they changed the shape of the island. Buildings sprouted everywhere like toadstools. In the beginning days, they were simple dwellings built from the surrounding woods. Later, many time-cycles later, the humans learned the wondrous technology. Buildings upon buildings in vast towers that reached to the skies like mountains, marvelous bridges that spanned huge expanses of water and crafts that carried humans in untold numbers across the land, the sea and even in the very skies.

The humans expanded until they crowded out the entire island, the island they called Manhattan, until this enclave of greenery, Central Park, was the only spot of woodland that remained.

But enough woodland remained. That was where the humans had come from and where there are humans there are Sylvans. At least it used to be so. That's what all the racial memories he carried told him. The racial memories Sylvans held from the times of the Coming. Those times were so long ago that it defied comprehension, even for him. Times when life on Earth with all it's myriad of animals had no resemblance to the present days.

Days before humans existed.

Now after all those eons, he could see the future. It would be a future he would craft, a future where the Soul Singers and the Memory Tellers would sing his praises. Where it would be told how he had resurrected the waning race of Sylvans to a glory beyond their best times so long ago.

It was time to raise the Maarzuk...

The Maarzuk awakened slowly as sensations flooded into its receptors. Perhaps awakened was not the right term. For something to awaken, it must first sleep. The Maarzuk had never been asleep nor had it really awakened.

It had stopped being, ceased to exist and now it simply was again.

It writhed in the rocky cavern far below the city. It's receptors sent out the waves of energy that had not been felt on this planet for millions of years. Far above, on the surface it dreaded, the Maarzuk sensed the weak psychic life forces of millions of beings. Small entities, weak, it regarded them as no more than a man would regard ants.

But men kill ants without a thought.

The flow of energy coursing through its body composed the essence of its mind, or the closest thing to a mind that it could possess. Its body was made from the basic blocks of the universe, silicon and carbon atoms in a fluid state like molten lead. Nothing like it had walked the earth since the Sylvans had managed to drive it deep underground and lock it in fields of timeless psychic energy. If it had memories of the old times, it would have sensed the difference. It would have sensed that now, in this time and place, the power of its Sylvan master was greatly reduced, its control weak. The links of psychic energy from the Sylvans were like gossamer strands of a fragile invisible web.

Unlike a fly in a web it had no constrains. The Sylvans guided it like a living bolt of energy sent to find, to destroy.

Its body shifted, the molecular structure constantly changing, moving through the fissures in the rock, flowing upward like mercury imbedded with hundreds of sharp pins and razors. It formed and re-formed, flowed and ebbed, moving from semi-liquid to steel-solid and back again. It moved upward, guided by the Sylvans. It moved toward its target of just a few individuals among the teeming entities of the surface. It reached a tunnel and took form.

John "Digger" Martin and Abraham "Chappie" Chapeau, would have been a lot less happy if they had known what was coming for them. Well perhaps not specifically for them, but it really didn't matter. They were in the way.

Right now though, they were happy. Digger had scored some free methadone at the clinic and Chappie had two "B" rocks. *Yesiree,* thought Chappie, *two mighty fine grade number one rocks of primo crack cocaine.* Along with the B rock, they had two cans of Dinty-Moore beef stew and a quart bottle of Muscatel.

Funny how things work out, thought Chappie. He had given up the faggot dealer to that big undercover cop in exchange for a tip, a favor really. The cop had come through. When Chappie approached Dicey, the faggot dealer's rival, Dicey had given him two B rocks for getting rid of the competition. Payday was mighty fine.

Digger and Chappie were in the service tunnels, the ones that ran beneath the branch of the IRT on 38th street. The grimy support columns held one light bulb each. At the moment only two bulbs worked, rendering the wider bend in the tunnel where they stayed most nights, into a stark black and white world of dancing shadows.

A breeze blew through the tunnel from God-knows-where. It carried a stench of decay, warm as summer rain and filthy as a leper. Of course Digger and Chappie weren't very particular, but they did have standards. Perhaps not the same as most good folks, but standards nevertheless, and those standards made for a rather short list. High up on that list was inaccessibility, away from cops and the varied predators and victims that roamed the subterranean world beneath the streets of Manhattan.

Digger had a good buzz from the methadone and half the bottle of Muscatel he had already poured in his ulcerated stomach. *Time to catch up*, thought Chappie as he stuffed one of the crack rocks in the half burnt-out corncob pipe he had found in the gutter by 42nd street. He lit the rock with his flame-thrower lighter, always had to have a good lighter, and inhaled the metallic dead white smoke.

The rush came instantly. *Goddamn that feels good*, thought Chappie. He was on top of the world at the bottom of the world. He laughed at his little joke as Digger looked at him, eyes heavy with coal-dusty lids.

Digger got up, his breath came in polluted wheezing noises as he walked off to the edge of the tunnel.

"Gotta piss," he said, not looking back, "Howzzabout you gimme a hit of that rock when I come back."

"Fuck you man. I'm the one taking the heat if the faggot finds out I ratted him. S'ides, you got the meth."

Digger looked around the wide tunnel. The shadows and carved rocks and bricks, cast in extremes of black and white, reminded him of a painting he had seen in school long ago. It had been some artist's idea of what hell was like. He raised his head and sniffed the air like a prairie dog coming out of its burrow.

"Hey man, you smell that?"

"What? What smell?"

"Chappie man, you better slow down with that B rock crack shit. Your nose is getting fucked up. Don't you smell it? It's like…I don't know, sulfur and almonds. That's it, sulfur and almond. Ain't never smelled shit like that before."

"Chill man," he replied, "Probably some new kind of chemical shit they're spraying somewhere."

Chappie closed his eyes and took another hit of the rock. He was on top of the world again, the dope always made him feel like that. Maybe it was time to go back up, do some panhandling. His line of shit was always better when he was high. Maybe he looked meaner and the citizens were just scared of him. He liked that idea.

"Hey Digger, what say we go up top, maybe score some cash and more dope?"

Digger stood about twenty feet away, pissing into the

dark. Things were fuzzy as he swayed. The methadone edge was starting to wear off and he saw shapes shifting and moving in the gloom of the sloping tunnel. He zipped up, closed his eyes and shook his head. Things hummed and buzzed in his brain like electric bug zappers. He rubbed his forehead and closed his eyes. Maybe he had taken some bad shit. Happened before, he thought as he opened his eyes.

He saw it coming out of the gloom of the tunnel toward him. All blackness like the interior of a dead mine, full of moving shadows and punctuated with glittering sharp things, medleys of huge needles, razors, fangs and knives.

A strangled choking sound came out of Digger's throat as he tried to turn, to flee anywhere from the dark monstrosity that erupted out of the bowels of the earth.

It moved like quicksilver. Fluid, constantly changing and impossibly fast, it was on Digger in a New York second. It sprouted tentacles ending in onyx sword-like claws tipped with shiny edges.

Digger saw a black and silver blur passing like a demonic whirlwind, he felt a sting around his throat and hot wetness suddenly spurting down his chest. Before he could even think about reacting, he felt an immense pressure from his heart and stomach as a smoky black tentacle tore him from chest to groin. Eyes and mouth opened wide, without a sound, Digger fell face forward on the stone tunnel floor as the smell of blood and intestine rose in undulating noxious waves.

The crack he had just smoked almost saved Chappie. It would have killed him for sure in another four or five years, but this night, in the Maarzuk's path, it almost saved him.

Almost.

The crack coursing through his blood fired up his nerves and heightened a paranoid fear. Something ancient and primitive reacted in Chappie at the sight of Digger's corpse hitting the floor twenty yards away. A rope of intestine splattered away from the corpse as blood splashed in dark shadows. The smell of sulfur, almond and bloody carved body parts filled the dusty air.

A choked and strangled scream came out of Chappie's throat as he ran. He ran without looking back, ran as if all the minions of hell were on his heels. Maybe they were, or something close to it.

He hit the narrow stone stairwell to the upper level track tunnel. He took the stairs four at a time in adrenaline-cocaine fired up bounds. He reached the last few steps, almost to the top, when it hit him.

A bolt of wild energy, as powerful as it was alien, entered his mind like a psychic flamethrower. He felt unbearably excruciating pain as the energy flickered and burned through the synapses and neural pathways of his brain. His face hit the stone steps hard with a cracking noise as facial bones fractured. But Chappie didn't feel it. He died before he hit the ground, eyes bulging and thin whispers of blood trickling from his eyes and ears.

The Maarzuk felt Digger's blood splatter on its shifting body. It savored the spilt essence of life like a carnivore inhaling the scent of bloody torn prey. At the same time it felt the aura of the second entity escaping, filled with panicked fear. It sent the awakened power of its silicon and carbon mind hurtling in a bolt of focused energy.

The aura of the fleeing entity ceased to exist.

Now it turned its attention toward the upper levels, the stratas of hollow tunnels and rocks, concrete and sandstone that composed the earth between him and the surface. He felt the hundreds of entities all about those levels. It was like the odor of grilled meat and spices to a starving man. Dimly he felt the presence of the Sylvans, the urging presence that guided him toward just a very few of those sentient auras, those human entities that didn't exist during his previous stalking of the planet.

Later it would obey the Sylvans, but now, its hunger was an ogre of a monstrous desire, too powerful to be controlled by anything.

CHAPTER 27

   Mai-Lin opened her eyes and moaned, a pitiful mewling sound of terror and fear, awakening the others immediately. Now the girl screamed. The high-pitched ululating howl reverberated around the empty station as Wu and Charly hugged her.

   The girl's screams turned to a continuous howling cry of two words.

   "It's coming, it's coming, it's coming, it's coming, it's coming, it's coming, it's coming, it's coming, it's coming, it's coming, it's coming, it's coming, it's coming."

   Wu held the girl, rocking her and crooning in soft Chinese. She quieted, her eyes round saucers filled with terror.

   Joe felt Charly's arms holding his, the girl like a needy throbbing heart between them and Wu. As he stroked her hair, her head, Joe felt an extra sense awaken. The essence of the girl's thoughts, her unconscious psychic power, her very being projected itself into his mind. He realized part of it came from a source deep within his own self. Maybe the contacts with the Sylvans in the Pine Barrens had created this ability. Perhaps it had always been there, latent beneath the surface.

   Mai-Lin's eyes locked on his. She felt it also, their contact through her fear. A psychic empathy, piercing and alien, not unpleasant, and completely unlike his previous experiences with the Sylvans.

It formed like a warm apparition in his thoughts, images, within images, within images. First Mai-Lin, warm and sweet and innocent as a new flower, and he sensed her in his mind, surprised that he could, that he had the ability and also aware that Charly did not seem to have that ability.

Within the frame of Mai-Lin's thoughts, there lay the core of her fear. Joe sensed it and recoiled as if it was a rattlesnake. It hovered on the edge of her consciousness. A dark alien presence, full of strangeness, vicious and predatory, a psychic echo of something alive out there, something deadly that finally tasted blood.

And wanted more, much more.

The cop didn't really mind riding the late night train, after all, that's his job as a Transit Police Officer. At first, he had been miffed at the waiting list for NYPD. He was a second-generation New York Irish cop, but the waiting list had been so dammed long that when the Transit Police slot opened for him, he took it.

He grew to like the night patrols, their solitary aspect on the late night trains at this shift. He enjoyed the peace and the feeling of security beneath the earth. He never would admit it to his fellow transit cops, but he thought he knew how submariners felt on good tours of duty: deep and steady.

The student felt his weariness to the marrow of his bones. He sat on the seat, swaying like a reedy black corn stalk in a Kansas field. Classes for most of the day, two hours of messenger work, and four more hours at his night job, pushing broom, just plumb wore him out.

Hell, he thought, *I ain't got too long to go. Another couple of years maybe, and this black ass is graduating, going on to a law firm, or maybe private practice, anywhere but in this ghetto.* His old man had lived and died young in Harlem, his mother old before her time, but he remained determined to break this cycle through sheer tenacity.

As he dozed, he thought he smelled sulfur and almonds while the train hurtled toward 38th street with a handful of late-night riders.

Once aroused the beast could not be easily reined in. Its nature was a state of enraged blood lust that the Sylvan found impossible to control, at least for the moment.

High on its perch atop the giant oak, surrounded by the lights of the city, the Sylvan's mind struggled with the sole survivor of their race's ancient enemy. The lust for destruction and death was too well ingrained within the Maarzuk. It would have to run its course before the Sylvan could guide it, force it, to accomplish what it had been awakened to do.

The beast moved up the stairwell, all blackness and glittering edges and death. It moved and flowed past Chappie's corpse and stopped at the top of the steps. The alien mind sent out probing beams of energy, felt the presence of the human minds in the tunnels like a bloodhound on the trail.

Now it sensed many of them, the energy of their auras like so many twinkling specks, most of them unreachable on the surface, but not all. He sensed many in his world, his environment within the earth. He sensed a number of them now, hurtling through this tunnel inside a metal cocoon.

It went through the stonewalls of the stairwell, passing over Chappie's corpse, flowing through the cracks and crevices, through the very atoms and molecules of the structure. It flowed, arranged and re-arranged itself within the stones and bricks. It sensed the structure, the strength and weak points of the materials like a snake feels the air with its tongue. It positioned itself, became solid and pushed. Flickers of energy flew within the stone and fissures appeared with cracking sounds like a demented earthquake.

The conductor wore his Walkman even though it was against New York Transit Regulations. Motormen are supposed to be alert at all times while conducting the trains. He was very alert in spite of the Walkman and kept the volume low so he wouldn't miss any radio calls.

Eleven years on the job and he knew every twist and turn on the line. He knew if a stone was out of place, a light bulb burnt or some new trash dropped on the tracks. It was a routine late night shift, one cop coming off shift, about a half a dozen passengers and the conductor. Routine that is, until the train approached the bend before the 38th street station.

The left side of the tunnel bulged out and boulder size rocks broke from the wall and flew onto the track. The conductor reacted immediately, hitting the screeching brakes as the wall collapsed, all black and white shadows in the train's headlamp. A boulder the size of a Volkswagen struck the front of the train, crushing it, and sending it careening off the track. The collision knocked the conductor from his seat, and flung him to the side. The metal caved in like a stomped empty beer can, crushing and pinning his legs. The conductor's scream rose, lost in the violent howling of the train hurtling off the track into the sides of the tunnel.

The train hit the wall still propelled by the forward momentum. The sides peeled off like skin from rotting fruit, spilling seats, jagged metal, poles and people throughout the length of the track. The noise of the wreck reverberated in the confined spaces of the subway, reaching upward through the ventilation grates and outward to the stations. Showers of sparks and flames erupted through both sides as the four cars telescoped one into the other.

The student came awake to the biggest jolt of his life. The seat flew up from the floor as the car disintegrated in a hellish nightmare of twisted metal. The student held on to the seat, both hands pale from the force of his terror-driven grip. The car bounced from the stone tunnel wall and the side windows, doors and frame fell away. The seat flew out and landed upright with the student still hanging on.

The transit cop walked by one of the structural center poles when the car crashed. He stood close enough that he wasn't slammed into the pole with enough force to seriously hurt him. He held on for his life as the storm of crashing metal raged about him. Others were not so lucky.

The noise died down to a medley of creaking settling metal as the cop rose to a stooping crouch. The car rested on its side with the top exposed, ripped away from scraping against the wall. He stood up, tasting blood and smelling smoke and burnt metal and something else; Sulfur and almonds.

The student gripped the metal top bar of the seat and leaned against it. Gingerly, feeling every joint aching, he rose to his feet. He had kept a death grip on the seat as it ejected from the train. He could have been inside a great tin can while a giant shook it mindlessly. The train settled a few feet away, wheels horizontal with great holes in its side bounded by jagged metal where the insides had spilled out.

The crash set off alarms at the Transit Control Center. The main board looked like a pincushion dotted in red. People rushed about frantically, phoning for help, shouting orders. It was a scene of controlled chaos, of disaster management.

All trains stopped and diverted from the 38th street line. Emergency Medical Services, Transit Police and Rescue units all rushed to the scene. The Mayor, Police, Fire Commissioners and ranking Police officials, including NYPD Captain TR Gray, all awakened. Sirens sounded throughout the city as Police and emergency vehicles converged on the disaster scene. The entire 38th Street branch and its stations shut down to the public as rescue personnel and equipment crowded the platforms.

CHAPTER 28

If it had such emotions, the Maarzuk would have marveled how easy it had been to stop the strange things hurtling through the tunnels. Even though they moved at great speed, the things were lifeless hulks. It didn't stop to wonder how such inanimate objects moved so quickly and purposefully. Such thoughts were beyond its abilities. It focused on the glowing life force of the beings inside. Some had winked out, destroyed in the crash. The others enticed him, beckoned to its hunger, accelerated by the emotions, the fear and pain that coursed through the beings as their conveyance crashed inside the tunnel.

Now it would feast.

It moved from the rock, flowing around and over the train in long black and silver tipped tentacles, like a giant snake with mobile slicing razor fangs and psychic bolts of lashing energy. It absorbed the victim's life force as it died, its pain like a delicate spice flavoring the gruesome psychic meal.

It killed as it moved. First one survivor trapped in twisted metal, then the next two, dazed and uncomprehending. It slit them open from gullet to groin, beheading, tearing huge chunks of flesh from the living bodies. The putrid stink of blood, death, and released excrement mingled with the smoke and metallic stench of the crash.

Screams of terror and desperation filled the tunnel, each ending abruptly with the moist thudding sound of savaged flesh. It reached the end of the train. Every life had been extinguished, fed into a feral hunger that had not stalked the earth for tens of thousands of years. Up ahead, retreating, two more lives were in the tunnel. It felt their panic and terror like a gourmet sniffing fine cuisine. It moved toward them, tentacles forming, reshaping and reforming into steel-like clawed razors.

The transit cop pulled the dazed student from the tangled seat that had been hurled through the side of the derailed train. They were at the front of the car in a haze of dust and smoke and dimmed emergency lights when they both felt it.

It hummed in their minds like high-tension wires buzzing on a damp day. Strange and alien emotions echoed from incomprehensible images flashing and disappearing inside their brains like scenes out of a surrealistic movie. But there were physical sensations also. They heard screaming from the rear cars followed by squishy thudding sounds. The student took a few steps back as he felt sweat breaking on his forehead and hands.

Something happened in the dark center and rear of the train, people died. The cop smelled the bloody odor of death and terror sweeping along the tunnel. He pulled his service automatic and the long flashlight hooked to his belt. He fumbled with the catch as a corner of his mind noted his shaking hands. *Like a leaf,* he thought, *I'm shaking like a leaf.*

Something was coming. Primitive waves of psychic energy washed over them, and the air filled with raw terror and pain and hatred. It felt like the psychic equivalent of being forced facedown in a boiling cauldron. Permeating throughout, the strangeness boiled, an otherworld aura, alien, vicious and implacable.

Something formed in the dark tunnel ahead of them, indigo blacker than the surrounding gloom. It moved and flowed like a bloodied midnight steam with silver edges. A primitive feral terror swept the two men, an ancient racial fear from the earliest dawn of earth.

They both ran, stumbling over track debris. The policeman looked back once, feeling the rolling darkness closing. He raised the automatic and fired nine shots until the hammer clicked on the empty chamber. He pulled the flashlight and turned it on and the shaft of light danced outward on his shaking hands.

The powerful beam reached into the boiling black and silver cloud. Where it touched, the cloud shrank away, creating a moving shifting tunnel for the light. Moving streaks of silver and black flecked the edges of the tunnel as if attempting to cauterize a wound against the infection of light.

The cloud stopped and withdrew back toward the wreck of the train. The student tripped as a wave of screaming raw emotions entered their minds. It was like someone screaming into their ears but without sound. Rage and frustration howled inside their brain, the emotions clenched with *strangeness* as their human minds tried to interpret the alien psychic waves in some understandable term.

The policeman grabbed the student by the upper arm, helping him to his feet. They stumbled back as the shifting forms melted against the walls and floor of the tunnel until it was absorbed by the stone and concrete—like a swimmer entering water.

They ran toward the station, its light an expanding glow as they passed a curve. The emergency lights exploded on as they approached the station. The first of the arriving rescue workers helped them onto the platform.

CHAPTER 29

Something happened to Joe, or rather something went on *within* him. A change, maybe perceptions of something that had been there all along like an unnoticed shadow on a wall. But Joe *had* been there before, felt and *tasted* the strangeness and fear so many years ago.

He sat on the bench against the wall of the closed down station, leaning back with his head touching the cool stone. Mai-Lin calmed down, and now slept curled between Joe and Wu. Charly dozed on Joe's other side, her body rolled in a tight ball. But Joe couldn't sleep as the memories returned.

The change happening within Joe re-started as if the years hadn't passed at all. He remembered as if he were thirteen again, the age for the Vision Stone Ceremony. The Second Son of a Second Son of a Second Son, he would become the tribal Shaman on the passing of his grandfather. He was the product of a line of Shaman stretching back to the days before the white men had come to the waters of Long Island and the Hudson River.

In a way, he had known that he was different, that somewhere within him was the mystical power of the Seer passed along his ancestral lines. Now it was time to awaken the abilities locked in his mind and body.

It happened on his thirteenth birthday. Following a two-day fast, he donned the deerskin robe with the great Osprey plumes and swatches of bright stones, smooth and glistening from the oceans, their beaded holes patiently carved centuries ago by long dead tribal women.

He sat with his grandfather in the high-walled stone circle as the sky darkened and the moon rose, casting its glow like a pale shell on the roofless top of the inner walls. He remembered his grandfather's voice and the chants rising to the black skies like a timeless dirge. He recalled the cool breezes of the nearby ocean and bays, carrying salty-sweet water smells and the pungent, pleasant scent of the smoke as he inhaled the mixtures of herbs made from a particular dried moss and mushrooms that grew only in certain places at certain times.

Gradually, his mind lifted and moved above his body, as if he could see his form, small and still against the circle of stonewall while his dream-spirit soared high above.

The circle began to spin, faster and faster until it became a vortex that pulled him in, flying effortlessly without sensations. He became aware of other forms flashing by him on either sides, moving whispering strands of dizzying colors and he sensed their individuality and their life force.

It is the spirits of life, of Elohina, Mother Earth.

It had been his grandfather who talked to him in the language that had no words, no sound, the language that came into his head. Now, clear and strong, and even though there was no tone or voice, he knew his grandfather guided him on the journey.

The whirling vortex stopped and faded as he floated gently down and landed on sand soft as cotton wisps. He stood on the bank of a vast river, the waters moved swiftly under a coppery black and white light diffusing everything into the dream state. He felt the sand under his feet and the wetness of the small waves that splashed by his toes as he inhaled the smoke scented air. He realized the dream-like trance had brought him to the spirit realm. As he looked across the river, he saw dim shapes, shifting fluid shadows, familiar yet uncertain.

It is the river that separates us from the other side, the world of the Ancestors. Now you must take your first journey of the Vision Stone. There is one who needs you, one I cannot help.

He marveled at this. What could he do that his grandfather could not? The old man who had been the all-powerful Shaman of the Shinnecock tribe since time knew when. What could Joe do? He was just thirteen.

The path, walk the path.

Something rustled at his side as a foot-wide stretch of grass bent, the blades seeming to crush themselves in the reddish smoky light, forming a clear footpath along the river. He walked, his feet feeling the scratching coarseness of the ground. Soon he came on a boy, laying on the dream-grass, still as a stone. He could not see the boy's chest rise in breathing. But did anything breathe in this place? He thought. He could not even be sure if he himself breathed, yet he felt awake and sensations continued to flood through his mind. He squatted and looked at the boy's face, suddenly recoiling when he realized what he saw. The eyes, oh the eyes, black with the dancing light of the maroon day highlighting the utter depth of the interior of the skull. There were no eyes, only that terrible emptiness. He stood back, blinked eyes that did not blink and whispered without sound.

Red Hawk. But how is he here? It is said he will die soon. His eyes, where are his eyes?

His grandfather's reply came like a dream memory.

An Abaasy has stolen his soul. Even I cannot help him. Only a boy who is no longer a boy but not yet a man can cross the river to the spirit world and bring his soul back from the Abaasy.

He felt a tendril of fear like a scaly serpent invading his body. The Abaasy had been part of the Shinnecock legends even though they originated with the Yakut tribes. Fearsome netherworld inhabitants with teeth of iron who roamed in packs of seven, they were the nightmare spirits who crossed the river stealing the souls of warriors and children. Grey-Wolf felt the unseen presence of his grandfather like the invisible wind that blew from the ocean. Confusion and questions arose as scattering of seeds while he heard his grandfather speak to him in the voice that had no voice.

Follow the stone path and lead with your heart.

As he tried to understand his grandfather's thoughts, he turned toward the riverbank. Ghostly swirls and eddies appeared in a straight line of disturbed black water. Rocks poked through the stream, their flat surfaces glistening with a dark-red patina, an almost purple sheen. Roiling clouds, dark as squid-ink, chased themselves across the brownish red skies and the odor of decay soaked the air. It seemed as if a coming storm blew gales of unfelt wind that passed through his very body. Murky swift flowing black waves passed around the rocks, occasionally lapping their shiny surface. He walked to the edge of the river where the first rock touched the shore. He felt the fear rooted in his gut, as he thought of Red Hawk, a happy, gangling boy who had run and played with Grey Wolf at the reservation school on the Bay.

Lead with your heart.

He put a foot out, gingerly feeling the surface of the stone. It felt steady and sure, not slippery as he had expected. He stepped from one stone to the next and the next. Soon his side of the riverbank retreated, much faster than his steps would seem to indicate and the other side approached, too rapidly as if it had moved on its own accord, meeting the boy who had the temerity to brave the river-barrier to the spirit world.

Grey Wolf stepped on the opposite bank. He heard the beating of his heart throughout his body, a great pounding that should not exist on the spirit side of this otherworldly river. It felt like the pounding of a great drum in a still forest, a beckoning of fanged shadows.

Shapes moved back and forth and shady fog enveloped him as he moved forward. He felt a warm presence, a lightening of shadows as a moon glow light appeared flicking along the rocky bank. Almar waited, his grandfather's father, whom he had known only by the tribal stories and the words of his grandfather. He heard his whisper and the air came suddenly alive with sussurrant buzzings that were somehow familiar. He sensed the warmth of the Vision Stone and its smooth surfaces bonding to the ethereal flesh of his hand. He felt his ancestors moving, flicking about, shadowy streaks just behind his vision, sensing their message without words.

We cannot interfere with the Abaasy. Trust your spirit and the Vision Stone.

Had that been the Ancestors or his own thoughts? The Vision Stone throbbed in his hand and a weak light escaped from it, passing through his fingers like starlight through an opaque window. He stepped farther away from the riverbank.

It erupted from the gritty mud like an ancient Golem, formed of primeval ooze and decaying souls. In a flash it materialized with oversize head and great yellow eyes above a wide mouth where rows of thin needle-like iron teeth gleamed the color of red arterial blood.

Grey Wolf seemed to move in a tub of sucking fluid mud. He ran his left arm forward as if he could push the nightmare creature away. The Abaasy grasped his arm and its head struck in a serpent-like move, the iron teeth embedding themselves in the flesh of Grey-Wolf's shoulder and neck.

The most intense pain he had ever felt in his thirteen years seared his flesh like a living thing, pulling and biting with horrible ferocity. He screamed, his right hand reaching and lashing at the creature, the Vision Stone growing larger and smooth in his grip and its magic was a living power. Where he struck the Abaasy, wide gashes appeared that ran with a sickly putrid fluid. A scream echoed in his mind, a shrill wail of rage and demonic hatred as the creature dissolved in front of him, its wounded body evaporating in blasts of dark steam flying off into the nightmare sky. Another creature appeared, lower still to the ground and fastened its iron-needle fangs on his leg. He screamed at the white-hot agony and struck out again and again until the creature dissolved. Waves of hell spawned rage filled the spaces of his head.

Seven, there are always seven.

He backed away toward the water. The horrible pain of the bites had gone and there were no marks on his body. As he looked down at the translucent flesh of his leg, he could see through it to the dark shore he stood on. In spite of the living nightmarish quality, Grey-Wolf knew with certainty that if he lost this fight he would never awaken. His body would die as his soul would be unable to return from this place. The fearful legends were all true. Sobs arose from his throat and his pounding heart filled the universe, bitter saliva leaked from the corners of his mouth as he spun frantically like a fearful rabid creature, trying to find his tormentors. Seven, there had only been two. How could he possibly survive the rest? Yet, he had to or Red-Hawk would die, his soul captured forever.

They came together, gathering in a semicircle, five creatures of primordial terror. The river flowed at his back and wherever he moved, the path of rocks leading back to the other side always appeared there, beckoning. Every shred of whatever being he had become in this place, wanted to turn, to run to the safety of the other side and back to his world.

He hesitated, trembling as he saw what the two middle Abaasys held between them. It looked like smoke caught in a transparent bag, shifting and evanescent, formless, yet held between the two creatures. Deep in its center were two glowing eyes, alight with fear and desperation: Red-Hawk.

Grey-Wolf lashed out at the nearest Abaasy. The Vision Stone leaped in his hand, stretching and piercing the creature's body. Where the Vision Stone touched, a white hot circle appeared, dissolving the creature in a spasm of fierce malignant energy.

They pounced on him with incredible speed. Not the kind of speed that happens in a very short span where there is a certain period of time, no matter how little. One moment they stood in that semi-circle, the next they were on him. No pause, no movement.

A pounding ocean of pain and terror suddenly engulfed him, a shrieking-hot agony that filled every corner of all the universes he had ever known. It felt as if a pack of giant rats clawed him apart, eating him alive, tearing chunks of his living flesh. He had never imagined there could be this much pain in the world. He couldn't retain a speck of rational thought. He turned into a blob of primitive fear and hurt as he fell back into the black water. Everything ceased to exist except his tormentors.

He fell under the water, breathing, or perhaps not breathing. Maybe he had never drawn a breath in this netherworld. The Vision Stone glowed and pulled him along as he broke the surface. He hung on grimly. To let go was to die in hideous torment. He found himself running, flying across the stones until he threw himself into the red grit of the other shore. He lay face down for long moments before he dared sitting up and looking across the river. Even though it seemed distant, he could see Red-Hawk's eyes as if they were directly in front of him. The despair, pain and futility of all worlds had focused in those eyes. The emotions poured out from them in waves that battered Grey-Wolf like an ocean of acid. He cried out in agony as the vortex sucked him up in its black whirling heart.

He had awakened hugging the cold stone of the circular wall, his face speckled with grit and moss and dirty tear-runs on his cheeks. A sour taste filled his mouth and mixed with the smell of sulfur in his nostrils. His body trembled and his palm crusted with dried blood where the Vision Stone had cut into his flesh. He had run, the fear a living sobbing entity. Oh it had been much more than nightmares, much, much, more.

The next day he heard White-Hawk had died during the

early morning.

That terrible night had marked the beginning of his estrangement from the people, his departure from the ways of the Shinnecock. He would never be the Shaman and there was no replacement after his grandfather died.

He had been changed that night. Something had awakened deep within him. No matter how he tried to suppress it, to deny it, he had felt it all these years, a great dormant part of himself waiting to be awakened, called to its rightful place.

Maybe now was the time.

CHAPTER 30

Joe felt Wu's hand on his shoulder and shook his head, returning from the terrible memory of so many years ago. Mai-Lin and Charly still slept. The stairwell leading upward to the street grew a tinge lighter, the shadows of the stone steps retreated the merest shade from black. Silent construction machines lay about the station and resembled sleeping dark gargoyles outside of the dim pool of the caged emergency bulbs. He turned his head and his eyes locked with Wu.

"Your eyes were open but you were having a nightmare," Wu said.

"I wish it were that simple. It's more like reliving an old nightmare, one that may be connected to this somehow. I can't explain it. It's a feeling, an intuition."

"It's been said," replied Wu, "that if your prayers are you talking to God, then perhaps your intuition is God talking to you."

"Something's talking to me. I just wish I knew who or what it is, and just what the hell it's trying to tell me."

Something moved within the distant blackness of the interior of the subway tunnel. Or maybe it had been his imagination. He felt a resonance inside his head, a feeling of strangeness as if something wild and primitive stalked him, but somehow stalked him within the confine of his own brain, his psyche. It wasn't a Sylvan. He knew the *feel* of them.

Distant muted noises wafted from the tunnel, their volume too low to figure out what they were. A slight but constant breeze, washed over them carrying smells of decay, sewage, smoke, and a hint of sulfur and almonds. Charly stirred and mumbled in her sleep. Mai-Lin opened her eyes and sat up, looking directly at Joe.

Joe felt his heart hammering in his chest, felt the pounding pressure of the very blood in his veins. A feeling of dread, of approaching danger seized his senses.

He felt as if something forced him to stand on a railroad track, bound, blindfolded and ears plugged. He roused Charly and left the bench they had slept on. He walked over to the edge of the platform and peered into the tunnel.

He felt a probing, a telepathic outreach filled with malevolence and unknown darkness. He turned away from the platform and went back to the bench where Wu, Mai-Lin and Charly waited.

"Come on," Joe said, "let's get out of here. Let's go up top."

"Wait a while," Charly replied, "It's not daylight yet."

"Don't you feel it? Don't you sense there's something out there that's not too friendly for us? It's not a Sylvan. It's different, more, well…evil."

They walked slowly to the base of the station stairs, Mai-Lin holding Wu's hand while Joe ushered them along. They stopped at the first step as they felt the draft from the tunnel wafting around them and passing up the stairway to the street above.

The odors of sulfur and almond grew stronger with each moment.

Wu gently disengaged Mai-Lin's hand and placed it in Charly's. The old man turned around and took a few steps back, peering into the darkness of the distant tunnel.

Mai-Lin's eyes opened wide and she looked at Joe. Fear and pleading mingled in voiceless emotions.

No…Don't go there…No…

Joe felt his hands begin to tremble. Something in the hidden corner of his mind screamed hysterically. He tried to suppress the urge to run, to just leave everything behind and run from this amorphous menace pressing on them like a greasy anvil.

Wu took a few more steps until he stood at the edge of the platform.

"Hey Doc," said Joe, "come on. Let's just get the hell out of here, okay?"

Wu ignored them, turned toward the tunnel entrance and walked a few more feet along the platform.

No…No…No…

Wu raised his hand in a slight, indistinct wave. The odor of sulfur and almonds filled the station and stung their nostrils. Two more steps and he stood just outside the circle of light from the emergency bulb, his form murky and blending in the shadow.

Charly held Mai-Lin's shoulder with her right arm, her left hand gripped Joe's arm. He felt the pressure of her fingers, the digging tips of her nails, through his jacket.

"Joe, what the hell is Wu doing? Get him back here."

Right now Joe felt as if he stood on the edge of a pier over a stormy ocean, seeing someone drowning and knowing if he jumped in, he would drown also. A menacing buzz, a continuous rumbling echoed through his mind, closer with each second.

It was Mai-Lin who saw it first.

No… No… No… No…

Now Joe and Charly saw it also. A finger of swirling darkness reaching from the blackness beneath the platform, a snaking arm of indigo tinged with flashes of swirling silver, reaching like a tentacle from a demonic octopus. It looped around Wu's left leg as curling smoke and tightened like a bullwhip.

Wu's face registered surprise, then pain. It knocked him from his feet. His glasses flew off as it pulled him toward the black void below the station and outside of the reach of the dim light. He grasped a stanchion and held on as the pull of the tentacle increased with ferocious intensity like a predator reeling in prey.

Joe could never rationally explain what he did next. Maybe he reached the culmination of the last few days, like some sort of last stand. Or perhaps he had just reached a point where it was time to gain a little control by action. He knew for certain that if Wu got pulled below the platform, he would surely die by whatever horror had come out of this subterranean hell.

He just let himself go, reacting like someone stepping on something alive in a dark forest. He sprinted to the other side of the station where Wu held on to the stanchion, his face grimacing in surprised pain. He tackled the Chinese, the full impact driving him away from the edge of the platform, just a few feet, but enough to bring him into the pool of light. The smoky tentacle vanished in wisps of disappearing black and silver steams. He dimly heard screaming noises from the entrance to the stairwell, of Charly yelling something incomprehensible at him. He grasped Wu beneath one arm and around his chest and turned toward the stairwell. He had time for one solitary footstep when he was hammered to his knees.

It felt like a physical blow. He dropped Wu and heard a groaning noise of pain originating deep within his own throat. A force like living electricity entered his mind, numbing in its pain and intensity. A small part of him observed with detachment as Wu's eyes rolled inside his head, the whites showing in his pain contorted face.

Joe retched and held up his head as if to ward off a blow from above. He felt his mind, his essence, curling into a defensive ball under the hammering telepathic assault. But even as he felt shards of agonizing pain trying to reach his very core, something else welled up from deep within. A rage boiled up in him, a deadly bubbling brew, it rose from the hidden recess of his mind driving a psychic wave of energy. He felt that suppressed reclusive corner of his mind, the part that held denied latent psychic abilities, he sensed it coming alive like a deadly fanged bear emerging from hibernation.

He lashed out against the psychic assault of the creature and he felt something wrapping itself around the waves of energy whipping out from his mind, something strange but yet oddly familiar, it combined with his energy adding strength and power.

The air roiled with the smell of sulfur and almonds and filled with a buzzing roar. Waves of rage and frustration pounded the dusty atmosphere of the closed down station. But something else grew, a yielding, a touch of fear as if their attacker encountered resistance for the first time.

It only amounted to a scant yielding, but it was all Joe needed. Holding Wu around the waist, he dragged the old man back into the circle of light and pushed him toward the bench where Charly held Mai-Lin back. As he reached them, his eyes locked with that of the girl and he suddenly understood: That surge of friendly telepathic power had come from her. The burgeoning strength of her mind combined with his own power, broke the creature's psychic hold.

Joe staggered back toward the stairwell, holding Mai-Lin in a fierce grip with his right arm, driving Wu and Charly ahead of him. Wu tripped and sat heavily on the bottom step, his injured leg giving way. Faded gray morning light streamed down the stairwell in dusty shrouded beams. Joe saw a patch of grizzled sky between the dark building walls. He hustled them up the stairs, his breathing rough and fraying. Wu leaned on him, each step sending a lance of pain from his injured leg.

They emerged from the steps onto the pavement, ducking under the chain festooned with the closed for repairs sign. Barely five thirty AM and the sidewalk began to fill with the early shift workers. Sirens wailed, the strident warbling notes seeming to come from mixed directions, their echoes bouncing around the concrete and brick canyons. A hundred feet ahead, a barricade blocked the intersection with two NYPD cruisers, and manned by several uniformed officers in yellow and blue slicks. A misty drizzle came down, overlaying everything with a greasy sheen. The absence of cars on the street gave it the artificial feeling of a movie set.

Joe tightened his grip on Mai-Lin. His hand enfolded her hand and part of her wrist and he had been squeezing it so tight. Mai-Lin turned toward the dark subway entrance, peering into the darkness pooling at the bottom of the stairs.

Bad...afraid...very bad...

Mai-Lin looked up and her eyes closed on Joe. Something passed between them, that the lurking menace below had awakened in both of them.

CHAPTER 31

The Sylvan cradled itself in the upper branches of the tallest tree in Central Park, its elongated limbs grasping, holding. Its mind blocked the senses of any humans that happened to look in its direction so it was truly invisible. It did this in the same way an experienced person would ride a bicycle or drive a car, by rote, by subconscious.

It sensed the savage aura of the Maarzuk, the awakened ancient enemy from the time of the Coming. A tremor, a sort of human shudder ran through the Sylvan's body as his mind made contact with that of the Maarzuk. It felt like stepping into a whirlpool of acid, a vicious energy that was the very antithesis of life. The Memory Tellers spoke of the Maarzuks, how they had once been the soldiers and guardians of the Sylvans, even hinted they had been created by Sylvans until they turned against their masters, and had to be obliterated in a conflict that spanned the planet, eons before Mankind crawled out of the woods and stood upright.

The Maarzuk absorbed the life energy of its victims and while it could never be sated, the edge of its deadly primordial hunger had been worn sufficiently so it could be somewhat malleable. It took the directions from the Sylvan, the imprints of specific living entities, specific humans, their mind-maps as unique as facial features, retina prints or fingerprints.

The Maarzuk oozed into the granite and concrete, its shape constantly shifting as its atoms traveled between the molecules of the stone. Alien senses and rudimentary thought system sought those particular humans directed by the Sylvan. Its kind had been spawned on a dense planet thousands of times the size of Earth. The enormous gravity kept all matter that would have been solid on a smaller planet, in a flowing liquid state. Under those conditions, a bizarre alien life and intelligence evolved.

Captain TR Jackson sat up and ran both hands over the sun burnt coppery features of his face. He looked at his watch: six AM.

The time had been closing in around three AM when he crashed on the beat up sofa in an empty squad room at One Police Plaza. Hours had been spent locating the bodies of the two detectives inside Chinatown's maze of alleys and interconnected buildings, with dozens of detectives and uniformed officers assigned to the murders. They were still putting together a task force, when the subway disaster happened. TR struggled with the report he would have to file and his brother's involvement in all this. How do you put together Chinese gangsters, invisible telepathic forest creatures, (in Manhattan?) groups of refugees hiding from them in subways and missing Chinese scientists?

Most of all he worried about his brother. He hadn't heard anything from Joe since the call came in from the detectives before they died. He knew Joe would have called if he could, if he wasn't lying dead in some remote alley or captured by God knows what. That girl he had with him, Charly, she seemed swift. What happened to her? *Goddamnit, why doesn't somebody call with something?*

TR listened to his cell phone messages as he walked to the lobby downstairs; Nothing from Joe or Charly, two messages from Donohue at the FBI regarding his brother. The last message said he would be at the subway disaster on 38th street investigating possible terrorism. TR grabbed a cup of coffee and headed toward his car. At least that's one bad tradition the NYPD had managed to ditch: putrid coffee. Now it was Starbucks all the way.

TR drove toward the 38th street station, flashed his badge at the barricades and parked his car among the assortment of emergency, rescue and official cars crowding the streets like a herd of abandoned metal animals. He walked past uniformed cops and firemen and paramedics, and down the stairs of the subway station. Two EMS technicians carried a stretcher with something covered under a sheet dotted with ragged red patches, stark against the brilliant white. A coroner tag hung on the stretcher, and the form beneath was lumpy and irregular as if pieces had been hastily assembled in a futile attempt to give human appearance to whatever lay beneath.

TR paused at the bottom of the station steps. Bright arc lights had been setup and the scene was lit like a sun-baked desert at noon. No shadows existed anywhere, and even the inside of the tunnels were bright as far as TR could see. Deep inside, flashing lights and sparks resonated against the stone of the shaft, the actual work hidden by the curving wall. A beefy sergeant leaned over a crate, using it like a desk to sort reams of official paper work. Sweat ran down his face and a drop fell from his nose onto the papers below as he saw TR.

"Hey Cap," the sergeant said, "Glad you're here. We need all the help we can get."

"I'm not sure the feeling's mutual. So what have we got?"

"A cluster fuck is what we got. Looks like something blew out the tunnel wall and derailed the train as it came around that bend. Then some unknown perps decided to play slice-and-dice with the survivors. Got sixteen dead, cut up like Chop-Suey, two survivors who said they were chased by a cloud or a ghost or some other thing. I'd say they were set for Bellevue or Creedmore except one of them is a Transit cop. Glad I'm not a detective and have to sort this shit out. No offense Cap."

TR shrugged and headed toward the end of the platform as the sergeant called back, "Oh by the way, your buddy is here. He asked about you."

Joe, it had to be Joe, thought TR. He suddenly turned back toward the sergeant.

"Who's my buddy and where is he, Goddammit?"

"Take it easy, Cap. The fun just started. It's that guy that looks like a vampire, the one from the FBI with the Irish name, Donnoly or something. He's in the tunnel. Probably wants you to join the party."

TR turned and jumped down the platform. He walked between the rails, following a compact pay loader toward the scene. The oversized tires on the big machine covered the tracks. Clouds of diesel fumes blowing from its exhaust were immediately sucked up the vent tunnels by the giant emergency fans. Somebody yelled at him something incomprehensible, then pointed to his head and tossed him an orange hard hat. TR put it on and walked until he rounded the tunnel bend.

The train was lying on its side like an obscene crushed metal caterpillar. Torn pieces of seats, parts of huge metal objects ripped like paper, tons of rocks from boulder to pebble size, even articles of clothing and glass and paper strewn about as if a giant demented child had decided to destroy all his toys. Everywhere emergency crew people pulled at debris, ran back and forth with tools and equipment. Workers dressed in black protective suits and helmets with dark faceplates operated arc welders, cutting away great swaths of metal in eruptions of orange sparks reaching the ceiling. Dust filled the air, dancing and floating under portable sodium lights that swallowed all shadows. Acrid smells of ozone, burnt metal and smoke stung his nostrils and the grit of the place filtered into the pores of his skin. Detectives wearing yellow NYPD jackets worked alongside several men in FBI sweatshirts. Evidence gathering, dusting, bagging, the grunt work of police investigation that would go on until, hopefully, answers were found.

About a third of the way down the length of the wrecked train, a pile of various size boulders, smaller rocks and bricks lay in a scattered arc as if a giant boot had kicked in the rock tunnel from the inside. Four men in FBI jackets worked around the rocks with an assortment of electronic devices and lights. TR walked toward them.

One of the men bent over a group of mid-sized rocks, scanning with a hand held plastic box filled with flashing diodes and digital readouts. Donohue was embroidered on the front of his FBI windbreaker.

He stood up, tall and bony with a face full of angles and a thin sharp nose, wide eyes, brimming with intelligence and punctuated with dark bags and circles. He noticed TR and smiled revealing a slightly protruding canine tooth. He managed to do that without losing the cigarette dangling out of his mouth. TR couldn't help but chuckle as he recalled the sergeant's description. *I'll be a monkey's uncle if he doesn't look like a vampire*, thought TR.

"Welcome to the party TR," Donohue said.

"Yeah, thanks. Did they assign places yet?"

"Sure, NYPD called us in just about right away, terrorism of some sort. You're the liaison man, coordinating our joint efforts, bringing about effective communication and cooperation to bring the full weight of combined law enforcement to bear and all the rest of the bull shit."

"So, bull shit aside, what have we got here Bill?"

Donohue frowned, pulled a cigarette out of his pocket and lit it with the first one. He took a deep pull, his features threatening to cave in around his mouth.

"Well, right now, it's like the man said. We got a mystery wrapped in an enigma. See this shit," Donohue said, waving around the pile of blown out rocks and boulders and the gaping hole in the tunnel wall, "Obvious explosion right? I mean you don't need an investigative genius to figure it out. So what kind of explosive did they use? What was the detonator? We can detect any trace of any explosive ever made, from Semtex and Plastique to good old Dynamite and Nitro. In addition, we can determine how it was detonated.

We usually figure it out within an hour or so. This one, zip, first time I ever ran across an explosion that left no residue."

Donohue took another deep pull on the cigarette, his face scrunching up as he grabbed TR's arm and walked him out of earshot of the working technicians.

"Look TR," Donohue said, "between your brother's screwy story and this case tonight, I got a whole career's worth of strangeness."

"You telling me you don't believe it?"

"I wish I could tell you that you're full of shit and to go piss up a rope, but there's two things stopping me: First I've known you too long, personally and professionally. Now somebody might say because it's your brother it affected your normally good judgment. Maybe, but second, I got some awfully weird stuff from Washington that, if anything, corroborates your brother's story."

"What kind of stuff?"

Donohue pulled a pack of cigarette from his jacket, took one out of the pack and lit it with the short butt in his mouth. He spat out the butt, replaced the pack and pulled a handful of folded sheets of paper out of the same pocket.

"Here's the printouts, the squiggles on the ends indicate blocked and classified. No access whatsoever, not even for the Bureau. But there's enough in there to tell me something's going on and it ain't strictly Kosher. Way I see it, your brother might be a few brews short of a six pack but there's still something to his story."

TR took the papers and started to unfold them. Donohue placed his hand over TR's in a stopping motion.

"Don't open it now," Donohue said, "take it with you and when you can get away from this situation, contact your brother. Get him to one of our safe houses in Brooklyn. The address and contacts are in there. I've already made arrangements. Get him and his friends over there soon as possible. The place is shielded and secured. They'll be safe until we sort this out."

TR took the papers, placed them in his jacket pocket and closed the zipper.

CHAPTER 32

———◆———

They walked away from the closed station, Wu limping and leaning on Joe. They crossed the empty street and Mai-Lin stopped, staring at the cast iron sewer cap set in the blacktop and leaking clouds of steam like an old boiler.

Below, bad, afraid, below, bad, below bad

He sensed Mai-Lin's presence in his mind, in his consciousness. It felt as if someone walked into a room and you didn't see the person but you knew who it was because of the sound of their movements, their scent, or maybe the way they breathed. He looked at her and realized that she felt his gaze in her mind and she knew it, understood it. He felt her fear, her terror of whatever lurked below. Yet back at the station when Wu had been in danger, something flared in her, something surged in both of them, a new sense, filled with strange power. Or maybe it had been hidden, suppressed. He understood that in his case, perhaps it had been suppressed since his encounter with the Abaasy in the spirit world of the Vision Stone quest.

He squeezed her hand and she looked up at him. A thin smile crossed her face, quick and beautiful as a shadowed moonbeam. Joe gave a gentle pull on her hand and she followed across the street.

"Okay, we're still alive, that's something," Charly said,

"but what about Manuel and the others? We've got to warn them, help them get out. "

"If they are not out, they are already dead," Wu said.

"What are you talking about?" Charly replied, "The PCC tunnels start more than twelve blocks away and run a quarter of a mile deeper. That thing was nowhere near there."

Wu turned to Charly. His face carried a withered look, suddenly aged and bone-deep tired. His hand grasped the girl's shoulder and his voice had a reedy thin quality as he answered Charly.

"Would that distance and depth mean anything to a shark? This creature passes through stone and the ground like a fish through water. It's telepathic and guided. If it was set on your friends like it was set on us, they are already dead if they were anywhere below ground."

"Let's at least go to a meeting place we set up in case of emergency. It's off Mott Street just past Little Italy. God I hope they'll be there. That's where they would run to, where we agreed to meet in case we were run out of the tunnels."

She looked at Joe and he nodded. Right now, he couldn't think of anything better except getting to a phone and calling his brother. They started walking toward Mott Street when Joe stopped Wu, turning him around so they faced each other.

"How do you know all this about that…that thing below ground," Joe said, "We sought you out because you were supposed to know how we could get away from these Sylvans. You haven't told us anything or helped in any way, yet you know what this thing is. It's time to tell us, what is it? Where does it come from?"

The old man stood a little straighter as he looked away from Joe. At the end of the street a group of ragged people emerged from a subway station as four transit cops closed off the entrance with hastily made up signs and yellow tape. A woman and two men in torn filthy army surplus jackets carried plastic bags and yelled at the cops, their voices high with fear. Sirens wailed like background music in a macabre movie. The misty drizzle and low-ceiling gray clouds washed the color out of the city leaving only shades of tan and black and dirty white.

Wu looked up at the sky for a moment then faced Joe. Mai-Lin wrapped her hand around his arm while leaving her other hand in Joe's. A shadow passed across Wu's face as he seemed to come to term with something deep within. His voice was firm and he spoke as if lecturing physics students.

"What is that thing and where does it come from? Those are questions we have not yet been able to answer, but we have some idea. It originated in a place of unimaginable pressures and temperatures where human survival would be measured in nanoseconds. Until today, I wasn't sure that these creatures still existed. We just haven't deciphered the language that well."

"We?"

"Yes, I was at Brookhaven Lab, remember?"

"So where in hell did this thing come from, how can we fight it?"

"Not hell," replied Wu, "not hell at all, although the physical description comes close. Near as we can tell, they originated from a planetary system near Rigel, a star in the Orion constellation, a huge dense planet with gravity so powerful that most elements would remain in liquid or gaseous states. Under those conditions any life that evolved would have to be built to handle molecular density hundreds of thousands of time greater than that of Earth. It would travel through our rock strata's and soil like a crab burrowing in mud. Its intelligence, its mind would be on a sub-atomic level where electrical currents and synapses carrying thought could still exist. At least that's what we theorized when we studied the codes and records in the Artifact at Brookhaven."

"You were some kind of wheel at the Lab weren't you?"

The corner of Wu's mouth turned up in a slight crooked smile.

"You could call it that. I held the position of Director of

the Sylvan project and head physicist. My team found the link with the Sylvans, the Artifact and SETI."

Joe struggled to understand, he felt like he swam against a powerful tide without direction or knowing where the shore was. He had heard of SETI, Search for Extraterrestrial Intelligence, but he couldn't tie it together with the Sylvans, the horror underground or whatever this Artifact thing was.

"But if you were finding all this out, if you were studying this, why did you suddenly leave, disappeared like a thief?" Joe asked.

"Because it was the only way I could stop an experiment that would have meant the end of life as we know it."

CHAPTER 33

They walked for a dozen blocks as the drizzling rain reduced to a sort of wet fog. Joe found several public phones but still couldn't reach TR. Always that recorded voice, "cell phone user is unavailable." He debated calling the station but decided to wait and keep trying until he got through.

They stopped in front of an appliance store with half a dozen TV's tuned to CNN. The situation in the city worsened with appalling speed. The subway system had been completely shut down. Pictures of yellow rain-coated cops with blue NYPD letters closing down the stations and hustling hordes of confused straphangers dominated the news. TV anchors speculated endlessly about terrorist attacks on the subway system and multiple murders across the city. Grand Central Station turned into a scene of barely controlled madness. Thousands of stranded angry commuters milled about yelling and shouting at cops. Taxis were rare, having been mostly taken by travelers anxious to leave the city. Gridlock took a firm hold, and countless numbers of automobiles lined the streets. The entrances to the Midtown and Lincoln tunnels remained impossibly jammed, and the sound of futile angry horns mixed with the wailing sirens of emergency vehicles as they rode whatever sidewalks and alleyways happened to be clear. Homeless people of all descriptions emerged on the streets in force having come out from their underground refuge. A CBS news crew interviewed a small group emerging from the Lexington Street station. A tall, lanky middle-aged man wearing a hodge-podge of tattered clothing shouted into the anchorwoman's microphone. Greasy yellowish strands of hair fell over his forehead, bushy eyebrows danced over agitated bloodshot eyes and his voice had the tone of a slightly hysterical old time gospel preacher.

"Its the devil coming at us, the Lord done let him loose at all the sinners, I seen him myself, I seen the devil coming up from hell, he's running in the tunnels and he's killing and taking the sinners, that's what this is about."

Her professional mask firmly in place under flawless make up, the anchorwoman prodded the man with questions.

"So you have actually seen what is causing these attacks in the subway system?"

The anchorwoman held the microphone with the bold CBS sign toward the man. A black woman grabbed the mike. The skin of her face resembled pressed leather, tears had left streaks of caked dust from her eyes, crossing her cheeks and disappearing down her necks under folds of filthy ragged fabric.

"I seen it, I seen it too. It killed my man, it was a cloud of black with a devil inside. It sliced my man, just cut him in two. Pigs don't wanna listen, don't wanna do nothing cause we ain't upstanding-like citizens. They gonna let us die like dogs. But it ain't over, no way is it over. It gonna come for them too. Ain't nothing can stop it. Yo'all gonna get the surprise of your life when it comes slinking for you and ain't nothing can stop it."

Another man tried to grab the mike. The woman pushed him back, someone in the crowd shoved him forward and he collided with the anchorwoman, knocking her down. Screams and shouts came on the sound track and the video careened wildly as the camera bounced, caught in the sudden altercation. The picture flashed off and returned to another confused anchorman sitting behind a wide empty desk.

While the Mayor pondered asking his political rival, the Governor, for National Guard assistance and a possible declaration of martial law, trouble continued spreading in various forms.

Random acts of senseless and inexplicable violence occurred throughout the five boroughs and Long Island. On Pelham Parkway in the Bronx, a man in a NYCFD firefighter's uniform calmly got out of his car at a light when a motorist behind him sounded his horn. The man carried a fireman's ax, the kind designed to batter down doors. He blasted out the windshield of the car behind him and killed both occupants as they tried to escape. Then, he went on to batter two more passersby until he was killed by shotgun blasts from a patrol car as he lunged after the officers. On swank Park Avenue, a nurse brought both her wheel chair-bound employers to the spacious patio-balcony of the 30th floor apartment. She picked up each one from the wheel chair and flung them over the railing. In Queens and Brooklyn sniping incidents occurred in numbers unprecedented even during the race riots of the sixties.

Although Manhattan was affected more because of its population density, Long Island had the most number of incidents for the amount of people living there. It seemed the farther East on the Island you went, the greater the violence. From road rage incidents on the Long Island Expressway, to neighbors settling disputes with knives and guns, to random senseless attacks, a wave of violence radiated outward with Brookhaven National Lab as the epicenter.

Wu stared at the TV sets. Joe put his hand on his shoulder and spoke, "Come on Doc, its time to go. There's enough bad news on TV."

"Yes. Its time to go," said Wu, his eyes never leaving the TVs. It seemed as if he spoke to himself, arranging his thoughts out loud, "I never believed it would go this far.

They must have unshielded the Artifact in spite of all the warnings I gave them. I should…I must go back. What if they somehow figure out how to conduct the experiment? They must be stopped."

Joe looked steadily at Wu as the elderly Chinese seemed to come out of a trance, turned his head slowly toward Joe and spoke, "Whatever happens, you must swear you will care for Mai-Lin, you and your friend Charly. You are good people caught in something beyond your understanding. Mai-Lin is an innocent with immeasurable undeveloped abilities that cannot help her at this early time. You must protect her. There is no one else."

A pall of anticipation hung over Long Island and the Metro area. An undercurrent of energy ran through the area, and everyone felt it, like an electric spring slowly winding, building up. It intruded into every person's sensibility, from the milling crowds around Grand Central and Time Square to the senior citizens in the lonely upper towers or nursing facilities and the suburban families in the lawn studded homes of Long Island. It lay like a shadowy psychic cloak over everyone. The news services did not discuss it in their continuous coverage. How could they? How could they talk about something they felt like a sentient shadow or an orchestra off by a single note.

They walked until they passed Mott Street and entered the area bordering between Chinatown and Little Italy. It was one of those quintessential New York neighborhoods, a mix of a little Chinese, a little Italian, with smatterings of Indian, Far East and European cultures. The twin stone towers of the Brooklyn Bridge stood out in the distance, ghostly in the thin misty drizzle. Odors of warm and wet tar rose from the street and sidewalks mingling with the floating smells of frying meat and curry from the local restaurants.

"There," Charly said, "that's where we agreed to meet if there ever was a problem." She pointed to a crescent shaped small lot about thirty by sixty feet.

Someone, perhaps the city, had tried to make it into a

little park. A couple of dilapidated wood benches stood on opposite corners and a semblance of weed choked lawn had been recently cut. An overturned trashcan spilled a pile of greasy wrapping papers toward the sidewalk, punctuating the opposing building wall, filled with bright graffiti like an explosion in a Pittsburgh Paint store. The wall bore the signature of its urban artist: Morca69.

Charly looked around. Noon just passed, and the crowds thinned. Those on the street bustled toward some purposeful destination with the New Yorker's accomplished trait of avoiding eye contact. Small groups of teenagers sporting tattoos and pierced faces, loitered with mixed groups of people in varied clothing ranging from shabby sweatshirts to ethnic robes and expensive suits. Police cars with flashing lights blocked two streets emptying into the avenue. The officers walked back and forth or leaned on the hoods, not going too far from the squad cars. Tension hung in the air, a feeling of pressure and pent up violence and fear. It gleamed in the eyes of the people hurrying past, hoping to get away before something unseen started. It echoed in the eyes of the police officers, in their tense movements and uneasy looks.

No signs of Manuel or anyone else they knew. Charly bit her fingernails, spitting out a tiny cuticle, "Joe," she said, "we've got to find them, help them. If they try to return to the PCC tunnels, they'll be killed. We should warn them."

"How would we ever find them? If they're still down there, they've got to have figured out something bad is going on and they would have come up."

"And what happens at night? How are they going to survive that?"

Joe ran a hand over his face. He felt a layer of grit over his pores and inhaled the thick air with its miasma of smells. God what he would give for a long hot shower.

"I don't even know what *we're* going to do in another six or seven hours when the sun goes down. I do know that gallivanting back and forth doing Mission Impossible, trying to find them, just raises the odds of all of us getting killed a whole lot quicker."

Charly bit her fingernails again but didn't answer. She looked off toward the bridge and hissed "shit" through clenched teeth. She looked down at Mai-Lin. The girl pulled on Charly's jacket and pointed toward the edge of the avenue.

A man walked toward the little park. He wore a Yankees jacket with strips of materials hanging almost to his knees where the cloth had been slashed and holed. The upper part of his head was wrapped in strips of blood spotted white towels covered with a layer of black dust. He walked with a limp, his eyes pocked with red streaks and looking off toward something no one else could see. A long scratch carved a straight line from his forehead and vanished under the jacket. Even in New York, he would have drawn attention on a normal day.

This was very far from a normal day.

"Manuel," yelped Charly as she grabbed Joe's arm and shook it, "look it's him, it's Manuel, over here, Manuel, over here."

Manuel looked toward the sound of their voices, his eyes focusing just a little more. A slight smile played across his lips mingled with relief. Charly and Joe hustled him to the bench and sat him down. Wu bought two hot dogs and a Coke and Manuel ate while he told his story.

"I don't know man, it was like, the middle of the night you know, I kind of felt it first," said Manuel. He shook his head, swallowed and started again, "It reminded me of those Sylvan things, you feel it in your head, but its different, its like… like… something bad, you just know its bad and it wants to kill your ass. It killed John and Willie and the others, it… it came through the wall, through the fucking wall man, that *Pandejo* blew in through the wall."

Charly covered her mouth and bit her finger. Her lips quivered and the gray light of early afternoon reflected wetly in her eyes. A drop rolled slowly down her cheek as she spoke.

"All of them Manuel? They're all dead?"

Manuel nodded, his eyes dull and flat as he continued.

"Its horrible man. This… thing, this *Maricon Diablo*, it came out of the wall, it was a black cloud then it changed to things, sharp solid things like knives or giant razors. It was so fast, they didn't have a chance. It was like they got dropped alive in a giant blender with razor blades."

Manuel raised his head and his eyes met Joe's. It was like a physical shock Joe thought, staring into those eyes, haunted to a few short steps from insanity.

Manuel took a long swallow on the Coke, put down the empty can and buried his face in his hands. Charly placed her arm around his shoulder as a muffled sob escaped from under his clenched fingers. He wiped his face with his sleeve, leaving brownish wet dust streaks across his cheeks.

"You know what the worst thing was? The very worst thing? This *Diablo* liked it. It… it, like… projected it, it projected it into your head, it loved the pain, the fear and death. You ever feed a cat? You know how they let you know they love it, they purr and rub against you, man, you know they love it. This thing *purred* when it killed. It loved it, it *purred*."

Manuel stopped, his eyes on the ground. Wu offered him the second hot dog. Manuel shook his head no.

"Thirsty man, just so thirsty."

Joe bought a six-pack of cans of club soda and gave one to Manuel. He drank it down, speaking between greedy gulps.

"I'm still not sure how I made it out *Amigo*. You know how we sleep in that room, just those two little twenty-five watt bulbs in the corners like night-lights. This thing came between the bulbs, in the dark middle. I was sleeping on the outside, just near the doorway where the bright tunnel light is. I think that's why it didn't get me right away like the others. It doesn't like the light. It's a true *Diablo*, a devil of darkness. I could feel it in my head, like it's talking to you all the while its killing, it's saying, okay *Pandejo*, I'm coming for you now. I ran out the tunnel to the next bulb.

You know there's only three and then you got this long stretch without light. It was going to get me there, it knew it, and I knew it. It followed me from one bulb to the next, it was inside the wall, you understand, *it was inside the fucking wall tracking me.*"

Across the avenue from the tiny park, loud voices suddenly resonated, a shout, a popping noise like a firecracker and someone ran holding his side, blood dripping on the sidewalk, more noises and shouts and running as two police officers with guns drawn waded into the dispersing group. Screeching sirens approached, the noise increased and a helicopter passed overhead, the whomp-whomp sound reverberating in the concrete canyons. The drizzle stopped and the wind picked up, pushing low dark clouds across the ambergris sky.

Manuel returned his gaze to Joe, Charly, Wu and Mai-Lin as he continued.

"I was running for the third light, didn't know what I was going to do after that. I mean not a clue. I had just reached it when it kicked out the light."

"Kicked it out?"

"I don't know how else to describe it little *Amiga*, a chunk of rock blew off the wall like somebody kicked it from inside. The light was fixed to that spot and it went flying and everything got real dark. I felt it yelling in my head, it had won. Now I know how a mouse feels when a big tomcat pounces on it. I was a dead man. *Muerte.*"

"So how'd you make it out?"

"Suicide, I guess that's what I thought I was doing, anything's better than getting swallowed up by *El Diablo* of the underground. I yanked out the wires, even in the dark I knew exactly where they were, I helped lay out the booby trap. Soon as I pulled the wires, the whole thing blew up. I got flung down the tunnel with rocks and shit and I passed out. When I came to, I was covered with debris and bleeding, that's how I got so messed up. That thing was gone. It probably thought I died. The *Hijo De Puta* must have been mighty disappointed. Then I made my way back up. You had all kinds of people there. The word's getting around fast that there's some kind of unnatural *Hombre*, or something, killing people. Junkies, homeless, they're all coming out. They got *mucho* Cops, even SWAT teams down there. They think its some kind of terrorists. There's so much light that thing ain't gone go near them. They ain't gonna find shit and they sure won't listen to people like me who could tell them what it's all about."

Joe felt Mai-Lin's presence in his mind. Her telepathy had increased in power throughout the day. He sensed her thoughts, her communications clearly. He also felt an intensity emanating from the girl, a growing strength like a Toledo blade being forged.

Bad, near, it knows where we are. It waits. Bad. Near.

Joe walked out to the avenue. Only a few people loitered, just hanging out. He got the feeling they were waiting for something to happen. A stretched feeling danced in the air, an anticipation of some violent event like the charged atmosphere before the strikes of a powerful electrical storm.

He walked to the corner and called his brother once more from the payphone at the luncheon counter.

CHAPTER 34

TR climbed the subway station steps and paused outside. The early afternoon lay damp and chilly for a Manhattan October. The wind picked up and debris from knocked over trashcans flew about in the breezes like giant oily butterflies. The dead had been taken away from the subway and there were no wounded. It had been determined no risk of fire or hazardous materials existed, so most of the emergency vehicles were gone. With mutilated bodies turning up throughout the underground system, thirty-three so far, the mayor had ordered the New York City subways shut down for the first time in history.

But there was more going on.

Throughout the city, violent crime skyrocketed. For the most part it wasn't premeditated nor was there any sort of understandable motive. People just seemed to be attacking other people without definable cause. Most disturbing was the rise in attacks against children. When the guilty persons were apprehended, they seemed dazed, as if they had been drunk or drugged. Of course some of them were, but most had little or no history of aggressive behavior. The largest part of the violence remained confined to the poorer sections below 118th street and Harlem. The West side with its blue-collar Irish and Italian populations, had also been heavily affected. Other sections of Manhattan, such as the financial district, suffered fewer incidents but were not immune to various horrific cases. All police shifts had been called and still there weren't enough. The most disturbing incident had been the young patrolman on 44th street who calmly shot a mother and daughter as they hurried to their apartment building. Commanders with rank of Lieutenant and above received confidential memos from the police commissioner to be aware of "aberrant" behavior among the ranks.

What constituted "aberrant" behavior, wondered TR, aside from shooting passersby. *Hell, the entire city is in a state of "aberrant" behavior.* Most people, civilians that is, were off the streets. Cars lay scattered where they had been abandoned, their owners unable to make headway in the impossible gridlock. Pathways were made for emergency vehicles that wandered up onto sidewalks in spots where street congestion remained un-passable. Smoke rose from varied locations and TR felt the pall of apprehension and tension settling across the city. Riots broke out in Harlem and on the docks of the waterfront. TR had been told that the Governor called out the National Guard, and Martial Law was the next step. Things were only slightly better across the river in Brooklyn and Queens.

The tinny musical theme of racetracks sounded from TR's cell phone hooked to his waist. He picked it up and punched the answer button.

"Captain TR Jackson."

"TR," Joe said, "I've been trying to call you all day. Your cell has been out of reach."

TR squatted, concentrating on the tiny cell phone almost lost in his hand.

"Man, am I glad to hear from you little brother. I know what you mean about the cell phone. I've been in the subway since six AM doesn't work down there. We got an incredible situation. I think I have an idea what happened to you yesterday and why my two detectives are dead. I need to get to you and your friends fast. Right now you're in danger. You've got to get out of the city where I can get you somewhere safe. We can figure it out and track down the bad guys from there."

TR could almost feel his brother wincing on the phone.

"And where the hell would I be safe TR? The last two guys who tried to help us are dead, two good detectives who weren't slouches either. I guess you know that, but still, I haven't any idea who killed them or why."

"Joe, listen to me. You've got to stay calm and think. There's a safe house in Brooklyn run by a friend of mine, an FBI agent. It's used mostly for the temporary protection of mob witnesses. It's about as safe as it can get."

"Christ TR, these are not half-assed gangsters we're worried about. Haven't you been listening to me?"

"I know about that Joe, the telepathic and psychic attacks. I never doubted you, no matter how strange the story, but now I have evidence, enough that I have FBI backing. We're even beginning to believe it's tied to all this stuff going down throughout the city."

"Okay, so how do I get out there? Everything's shut down, cabs, buses, everything. Maybe you want us to take the subway?"

TR couldn't help but grin. *Attaboy Joe, keep your sense of humor and stay strong.* "Not a good idea sport, besides, the fares just went up. Here's how you do it. You'll owe me a couple of beers when you get done."

"Hell," said Joe, "I'll buy you a whole goddamned brewery."

"All right, can you make your way to the Brooklyn Bridge?"

"Yeah, we're not that far. I can see it from here."

"Okay, listen carefully," said TR, "how many of you are there?"

"Charly, me, two other men and a kid."

"What are you doing, starting your own commune? Here's what you do. Pay attention and repeat it back to me. Get to the Bridge. There's a pedestrian walk there. Take it across to Brooklyn. Stay on that road, you'll pass Henry street on the right, keep going, you'll pass St Francis College and you'll go through the Polytechnic University and pass the Civic Center on your left. Keep going, don't stop and don't wander around. You'll run into a large avenue about a couple miles down, that's Atlantic Avenue. Can't miss it. Go left on Atlantic Avenue until you get to a very large intersection. That's Flatbush Avenue. I'll pick you and your friends up at that corner. Atlantic Avenue and Flatbush Avenue."

"How TR? How you gonna get there?"

"Hell Joe, I don't paint houses for a living. I'm a cop, a Captain no less, remember? I've got an official car complete with sirens and radio."

They agreed on a time, between five and six that evening. TR listened as he repeated the directions back before hanging up.

CHAPTER 35

Joe told everyone what TR had said they should do. Manuel listened, lethargic and beaten by the events of the previous night. Charly and Wu hammered him with questions. Evidence? Safe house? how? why? Joe told them everything TR said, which really wasn't that much. He felt Mai-Lin's gently probing thoughts. The girl ceased making any noises at all as if she had discovered a totally new sense, a means of communications much superior to the speech she lacked.

They walked across the extension of Park Avenue and crossed East Broadway, continuing until they were under the elevated road, the FDR Drive. It was there, within sight of the huge stone bases of the giant towers of the Brooklyn Bridge, that they ran into their first mob.

About a dozen people stood around a blazing bonfire of old tires, wooden crates and cardboard boxes. Great clouds of noxious black smoke carried a stink of rubber and burning offal to the dark ribbon of overhanging highway. The smoke cloud accumulated on the underside of the elevated road where gusts of wind pushed it toward New Jersey. A body lay face down on the sidewalk a few feet away, his head hanging down to the street where it lay in a pool of congealed blood like a wick in a gory candle. Two men and a woman turned from the fire and looked at them, their eyes feral and wild. The woman bared her teeth, black gaps like a carved pumpkin in a face full of madness.

Joe hustled the group across the street, walking rapidly as the people stood watching them. He heard shouting, the voices slurred, and some of the people started toward them.

"Run," Joe said, "go, go, go," as he pushed Charly and the rest forward. Four people started running after them, while the rest seemed content to just watch.

It took only a few yards for the four wild-eyed people to catch up to them. Joe knew the girl could run like the wind, and Manuel, Charly and him, could hold their own.

Wu was another matter. The old Chinese doctor wheezed like a battered teakettle, practically carried between Mai-Lin and Charly. Joe and Manuel brought up the rear. Their pursuers came so near, Joe could almost feel their breath as they closed in. He reached down and picked up a half broken broomstick and turned facing their assailants. A part of his mind noticed faces peering out from inside cardboard boxes and rotted panels of plywood leaning against the walls of the underside of the elevated FDR highway. There's no one else around, not a remote chance of help, he thought. They were truly on their own in a place turned into a savage battleground overnight.

Joe faced the four people, his heart pounding, his vision turned into a narrow tunnel focused on his attackers. The first one held a long butcher knife, a wicked foot long blade that gleamed wherever it wasn't spotted with dried brown material. The second one had the thick half of a baseball bat in which penny nails had been driven to make a sort of medieval mace. His eyes were red and dried spittle crusted the corners of his mouth. There was no mercy anywhere, no hint of the possibility of any kind of civilized behavior. Joe knew he would die, right there in the street, in the filth of the road under the FDR amid a city brimming with insanity. Underneath it, burned a solitary beam of hope. He felt the soothing presence of Mai-Lin filled with radiance and energy.

Stay strong. Must be strong.

He held the ridiculous thin piece of broomstick as he faced the man with the knife. The one with the mace/bat sidled over to his left. A woman, her face twisted with mad hatred, the whites of her eyes yellow and streaked with leaking broken red capillaries, moved to his right. She reached under her dress and a straight razor appeared in her hand. The fourth man, a brute with a deranged grin and mumbling lips, remained behind the man with the knife. Somewhere, maybe from one of the cars abandoned in the debris strewn roadway, came the strain of an old disco song.

Oh yes its lady's night, oh what a night.

Oh yes its lady's night, and the feelin's right.

The woman held up the razor, the blade chipped in places and her eyes soaked in wild savage bloodlust. She began to chant, a horrible reedy parody, "Oh yeah, its lady's night, oh what a night, its lady's night mother fucker…"

That's when they closed in on Joe.

CHAPTER 36

Brookhaven National Laboratory, Physics Building

Doctor Prabinwah always thought the room had started out as gymnasium. On the only wall not obscured by the Collider housing or the giant magnetic coils of the Aligner, there was a narrow series of windows opened outward. All that could be seen were patches of sky because the windows began sixty feet from the floor, their upper edges inches from the light studded ceiling.

At this moment the doctor wished he could be a bird, soaring high above the Lab where he could choose to fly as far away as possible from this place.

To say Dr. Prabinwah was upset would be like saying the Himalayas were a hill. Everything about this series of experiments felt wrong. It was more than the enormous time pressures exerted on him and his tiny staff, more than the bypassing of numerous protocols or the safety shortcuts. But the most disturbing aspect was the reckless headlong plunge into a scientific unexplored darkness. His entire life and career had been devoted to the meticulous step-by-step gathering of data, interpretation of information and postulation of theories to be proved by experimentation. Now they forced him to barge ahead like a grade school student with a new chemistry set. To make matters worse, the experiment involved the greatest scientific unknown on the planet today: The Artifact.

Since that meeting with Duncan Wesley three weeks ago, he had been effectively boxed in. Born in the teeming hovels of Bombay, Dr Prabinwah clawed his way through life until he arrived in the United States under a Federal science grant some fifteen years ago.

When Wesley gave him that mandate with its preposterous shortcuts, the Doctor refused, so Wesley lowered the boom.

Until a few weeks ago, the doctor never dealt with Duncan Wesley. Wu had been in charge of the project and Dr. Prabinwah always thought Wesley was just a project manager sent from Washington. By the time he discovered Wesley's true role, it had been way too late. Immersed in his science, Dr Prabinwah never paid much attention to the running of the lab and the physics department. It was all peripheral stuff secondary to his research. He was happy to ignore all of it and let Wu and others deal with it.

Three weeks ago a merciless reality in the form of Duncan Wesley had hit him between the eyes, or as Wesley would put it, kicked him square in the balls.

This type of thing wasn't supposed to happen in America. Wesley laid out the internet transmissions that Prabinwah sent to colleagues in India and China. The transmissions had been encrypted and coded. Classified sensitive information filled most of the transmissions. The scientist knew he never sent this material, yet records of access with his signatures were produced, bank account statements with large amounts of deposits from foreign sources were also placed in front of him, all with his signature.

He felt bewildered, dazed with fear. The internet transmissions were his, but they never included any classified materials nor had they been encrypted and coded. He didn't have any knowledge of any bank accounts but the signatures were his, no questions about that at all. His explanations sounded lame and weak in his ears as he voiced them to a grinning Wesley. He tried to explain that his only real interests were his family and science. He just signed everything his secretaries and assistants placed in front of him with scarcely a glance.

He felt acid saliva in his mouth and a tremor in his hand as he recalled the insulting arrogance of Duncan Wesley.

"So you see Gunga Din," Wesley said, "if you don't dance at my little party, it's off on Federal charges you go. Your family will be totally screwed. I might even be able to arrange a deportation. Your kids can write you about their adventures pulling rickshaws twenty hours a day for scraps in Calcutta or Bombay. It should help pass the time. Your only experiments will be with cockroaches. We got plenty of them in the Federal incarceration system."

Dr Prabinwah sweated in the bulky radiation suit, and not because of the temperature. The state of the art suit kept a steady seventy two degrees with optimum atmosphere. The Artifact had now been out of its special shielded case for over two hours. It lay on the stainless steel table in the center of the leaded-glass walled room, incased within still another shielded room. The precautions were nowhere near the shielding afforded by the special case where they normally kept the Artifact. That case had been designed and created at Los Alamos Laboratory in New Mexico.

Dr Prabinwah detected the radiation six miles from the site. He suspected he could probably detect it sixty miles, or maybe six hundred. There just wasn't any way of knowing. Wesley allotted no time to such crucial data gathering. Prabinwah immediately spoke to Wesley, pleaded with him to lengthen the time scale because of the radiation emissions.

"What kind of radiation?" asked Wesley.

"Kinoshita level four, first discovered at Los Alamos during initial studies of the Artifact. We identified it and classified it by intensity levels here at Brookhaven. We invented a new science that is barely beginning to scratch the surface of the Artifact."

"Okay sport. I must have slept through the initial briefing. What the hell is Kinoshita level four and why should I care?"

Dr. Prabinwah felt a hollow lightness in the pit of his stomach. He tried to push out of his thoughts the effect the

Kinoshita level four could have. Now his worst fears came bubbling up to the surface of his psyche. He sensed how tenuous all this was, even to a physicist. Now he must convince Wesley, whose agenda didn't include a whole lot of science or concerns of human safety.

"Kinoshita radiation," began Prabinwah, "is named after the work of Doctor Toichiro Kinoshita, a particle physicist from Cornell University. Doctor Kinoshita spent over thirty years using Quantum Electrodynamics to calculate certain detailed properties of electrons. Kinoshita's calculations filled thousands of pages and ultimately required the most powerful Cray computers available to complete. We used Doctor Kinoshita's work as a basis for…"

"Cut the crap doctor. Just get to the bottom line quick before I send your ass back to India. I'm asking you one more time: What is Kinoshita level four radiation and why should I give a damn?"

"Kinoshita radiation is the result of the combined studies of Quantum Mechanics and Unified String Theory, Einstein's missing link in relativity, something that only existed as mathematical models until the Artifact. Our work showed that it existed through the Artifact. We were unable to create or find this radiation anywhere in the universe. Anywhere that is, until the Artifact. It emits this radiation with Kinoshita four being the highest level we are able to detect. It's the result of aligned vibrations of sub-atomic particles. Our studies just grazed the surface of sub-atomic particles aligned vibrations when…"

Duncan Wesley shook his head with impatience and snarled at Prabinwah.

"Let me ask you one more time. If you don't give me an answer in one or two sentences, so help me I'll stick your head through this Benson burner. Why should I give a shit about this new radiation?"

Dr Prabinwah sighed and looked down at his feet. He raised his head and faced Duncan Wesley's eyes as he answered him.

"Because it drives people mad."

* * *

Central Park, New York City.

In the narrow branches atop the highest oak in the park, the Sylvan held its link with the raging Maarzuk. Tendrils of gossamer telepathic energy bound the raw elemental power of the creature with the guiding consciousness of the Sylvan's mind. Some of the targeted humans had been eliminated but with more loss of human life than it had anticipated. Reining in the stark savagery of the Maarzuk had been much more difficult than the Sylvan had believed it would be. There had only been legends, the stories of the Memory Singers, to guide its effort. The casualties, what the human Accomplice termed "collateral damage" alarmed and horrified the Sylvan.

All around him he sensed the upheaval in the vast city. Great tides of fear, anger, pain and rage washed all around him in battering psychic waves like storming ocean breakers. Overlying it all was the pulsing energy of the Channeler, what the Accomplice called the Artifact. For the first time the Sylvan felt the soothing pulses, the dancing vital force that previously had existed only in the stories of the Memory Singers. Sadly, the Sylvan knew the harmful effect of this newly-released power on the teeming humans. Still, the energy beckoned him with its potential and its promise.

A promise the Accomplice, the one who called himself Duncan Wesley, would soon help him realize, a potential that would revitalize the Sylvans while placing the Accomplice at the pinnacle of human power.

The Sylvan felt the tracking Maarzuk as it followed the small group of escaped humans, the ones who knew, the ones the Accomplice said were a threat that could destroy their plans.

It was time to move, time to put the final stage of the plan in action. Soon the gray afternoon light would yield to the darkness of night. He climbed down, each step guided by tens of thousands of years of evolutionary experience. It could no more fall than a bird could suddenly forget how to fly and fall out of the sky.

He walked to the great roadway, the one the humans called Park Avenue. It's mind touched and altered the perceptions of every human in sight. The spindly alien shape of the Sylvan instantly changed into visions of familiar objects. A trash can for one, a stray dog for another, anything a human would disregard because of its normality. The Sylvan did this like a human would ride a bicycle or roller skate.

Its mind now focused on a human couple in their steel conveyance. The man's thoughts were filled with fear at the events around them. The Sylvan felt their anxiety, their urge to escape the troubled city and reach a refuge in a place they called "the Hamptons." The Sylvan reached in their thoughts, manipulating emotions until it overrode logical actions.

The man could never explain why he decided to stop his car, right there on the inner lane of Park Avenue. He pressed the remote button that opened the rear window of the Lexus SUV. His wife looked at him and smiled. It was all perfectly normal and they suddenly felt better. Their apprehension at getting out of the city to their tranquil summer place just vanished like morning fog. The rear of the SUV dipped ever slightly, as if a weight, certainly not a great weight, had been tossed, or in this case jumped, in the back of the vehicle. The man raised the window and pulled the SUV out, heading toward the Queensboro Bridge. He had originally thought about trying the Mid-Town tunnel but had a sudden aversion to traveling underground. Normally the SUV would not have gone more than a block or two before becoming hopelessly mired in the gridlock, but this time, the SUV carried a different cargo in its rear passenger compartment. Police officers obeyed a sudden urge to get this vehicle through, ordinary people helped push vehicles out of the way and paths suddenly cleared on sidewalks where the streets were hopelessly blocked. The

SUV made its way toward the entrance to the Queensboro Bridge where other traffic yielded their places. Helmeted police waived them ahead to the bridge roadway exiting the city.

The man and his wife thought it was all so normal.

CHAPTER 37

New York City, Under the FDR

The woman lunged first, her face contorted in a hideous grimace of hate. The razor slashed down in a vicious arc toward Joe's face. He stepped back, tripped and fell backward, the broomstick knocked out of his hand by the woman's razor. It was the only thing that saved his life for the moment. He fell, one arm raised, deflecting the razor. He felt a dull stinging pain and a thin welt of blood from his forearm and chest painted a spreading red line across his shirt. Things seemed to slow down, time stretched like an old black and white movie in slow motion. He knew he was going to die, there was no way out for him and somehow it had a calming effect. The woman raised her arm high above her head, and the straight razor clenched in her hand began its descent toward Joe's throat.

From Joe's right side, above him as he half sat-half lay on the ground, an arm appeared, an arm holding something metallic and dull blue. A flash came from it with a cracking noise, the woman stopped, an astonished look on her face as she lunged again. The second shot took her high in the chest, just below the throat and she fell backward as gouts of blood flew from her back and mouth.

Joe got up, blood now dripping from his forearm and

down his hand as Manuel fired again, this time at the man with the knife.

The round hit him in the shoulder, spun him completely around, sending the knife flying and clattering to the pavement. He fell and got up holding his shoulder, then backed away stumbling. The other two men just ran, leaving the woman's body laying face up, eyes open as a satiny stream pooled and congealed in the gutter near her head.

Joe barely stood, dazed as vertigo ran through him and his legs wobbled. The blood pulsed from his forearm and splashed on the filthy concrete. He felt hands holding him up, felt Charly's arm around his waist, her other hand cutting the sleeve of his shirt.

"Oh God baby," she whispered, "your arm. They almost killed you, oh God Joe."

He leaned on Wu and Mai-Lin as Charly tied a strip of cloth around his forearm near the elbow. She found a small metal rod and applied the cloth around it and twisted then tied another knot anchoring the rod in a makeshift tourniquet. Manuel looked steadily at Joe while inserting bullets in the empty chambers of the revolver. He nodded and let out a low whistle.

"Nice work, *Amigo*. You put your ass on the line. You got *Cojones*."

"You're the one who saved our ass with that gun."

"No, *Amigo*, I knew I had the gun. You just stood them down. You were ready to die to buy us a little time." Manuel cackled as he added, "You're all right, but you sure ain't no Bruce Lee."

Yeah, Joe thought, he had been ready to die, he had accepted it but he would have fought like a tiger, fought to his last drop of blood. He remembered the trance-induced foray into the mystic spirit world so many years ago, the nightmare fight against the seven Abaasy demons for Red Hawk's soul. Was that a precursor of things to come, some part of Shamanistic training? He had a sudden longing for his grandfather. He yearned for the old Shaman-warrior's wisdom, the voice like deep gravel and soft thunder.

Charly opened his shirt and ran a cloth soaked with club soda across the long wound on his chest. The razor had cut a shallow line. It stung like hell but wasn't serious. His left forearm was a different story. The cut ran deep, the blood flow had stopped and it felt numb from his elbow down. Somewhere above it all he sensed the telepathic probing of Mai-Lin, saw the images the girl sent him. He saw himself, impossibly tall, light radiated around his features as he protected them. He caressed her head, running his fingers gently down her cheek. She reached up and held his hand.

Still below…Bad…Danger…Below…Bad…

"Come on," Joe said, "we've got to cross the bridge and get to that corner in Brooklyn before dark."

They walked down the middle of the road, looping here and there around abandoned cars and a couple of overturned vehicles. Signs of rioting abounded all around. Glass from storefronts and automobile windows littered the sidewalk and streets, the shards like hard shining gems in the dull light under the FDR. Wafts of acrid smoke from burning tires fired their nostrils and stung their eyes. Groups of people stood around blazes in big trashcans, others threw all sorts of materials into open bonfires. There were no police in sight. Here and there bodies lay strewn about, some alive, some obviously, and violently dead. They passed an overturned car with the crushed corpse of a man half under its side. Two black men with long dreadlocks and machetes stared as they passed. Manuel walked close behind the group, the gun in his hand, out in the open and visible as a skull and crossbones warning sign. They continued unmolested and reached the foot of the bridge. They followed the century old walkway onto the bridge toward Brooklyn.

CHAPTER 38

Numerous killings fed the Maarzuk's painful gnawing hunger, and now, somewhat sated, it followed the Sylvan's imperative. It killed the humans in the deep tunnel that the Sylvan had wanted killed. Now it stalked the last five that still roamed above ground. It felt them with its psychic/telepathic abilities, sensing them in the dreaded light above ground. Biding its time, it waited for the chance that would surely come.

It sensed them getting onto an elevated roadway and as the height increased, the Maarzuk lost the prey. But the creature knew where they had been headed: across the water.

It flowed through the crevices and molecules of the bedrock below the FDR. As it passed, the people above felt a kind of foreboding, a disquiet that mingled like an evil brew with the strange and deadly events of one of the most terrible days in the history of the city.

Deep under the river at the base of the Brooklyn Bridge, a tentacle black as the surrounding water rife with pollution, slowly extended out from within the rock and concrete and muck. The Maarzuk felt the new medium, the water. It was no more difficult to negotiate than any other particle of matter. It flowed out of the rock, anchoring itself

in the silt-covered rock bottom of the riverbed. The
Maarzuk moved like a jet of ink from an octopus, swaying
in undulating black wavy clouds, its alien intelligence and
psychic senses continually probing the life energies that
abounded on the surface, seeking the prey.

They came to the first police barricade at the entrance of
the Brooklyn Bridge. Two squad cars blocked the incoming
lane as a steady stream of people crossed toward Brooklyn.
Many commuters coming from the suburbs had been
stranded when the subways shut down. A line of cars
headed outward but no vehicles were allowed inside the
city. Boom boxes blared the emergency channel at full
volume. All outbound lanes of all bridges remained open,
inbound lanes closed. The tunnels and the entire subway
system had been shut down. Police sources quoted over
two hundred recorded killings with unknown numbers yet
to be discovered. The deadly pace seemed to slow down as
the city returned to a semblance of calm like a great
behemoth coming to a stop after an exhausting gallop.

Joe led the group, his left arm in the improvised sling
made from the sleeve of Charly's jacket. The wind picked
up, coming straight in from the ocean. Unfettered from any
obstacles in its path, it blew across the bridge driving them
in crooked steps toward the railings, pelting them with
occasional stinging raindrop. A military convoy passed
them, heading toward the city. Dozens of Vietnam-era two
and a half ton trucks, deuce and a halfs, emblazoned with
the New York National Guard insignias from some upstate
armory. Each truck filled with somber soldiers carrying M-
16's with fixed bayonets.

They reached the center of the bridge, the highest point,
and Joe stopped to savor the moment, the feeling. He
looked at Charly as the wind blew her damp hair in a
straight line from her skull. She had to feel it, the others
must too.

"Charly, can you sense it?" Joe asked.

She frowned and sniffed the air. Her head shook slowly

as she replied.

"No, I don't feel anything."

"That's it man," Manuel said, "that's what he's talking about. You don't feel anything here, no Sylvan, no Diablo. The *Maricons* are gone, they're out of our head. Maybe we can live on the bridge."

"I doubt we could do that," Wu said.

"Relax Doc, just making a joke."

Joe felt Mai-Lin's thoughts. Images flashed across his mind, blending with the reality around him, images of something dark with long slimy fangs circling in the depths beneath the bridge, circling like a school of piranhas waiting to devour any prey that fell in the water.

Bad...Still...Bad...Still waiting...

Another image entered his mind, a form indistinct, hazy and blurred. It changed into many shapes huddled within groups of trees. Some glowed with inner white light shedding a feeling of benevolence, most were just a grouping of ambiguous neutral and harmless shadows. A few, just a few, glowed a pulsing malevolent red and orange.

Sylvans, good, and bad. Sylvans.

The girl's mental projections grew in strength and clarity. Joe felt an aura from Mai-Lin that communicated itself to him. He seemed to be the only one that received her thoughts with such clarity. It was a developmental stage, like a child just crossing the speech threshold and rapidly expanding his skill.

By the time they crossed the bridge into Brooklyn, Wu had weakened considerably. This long hard day had taken its toll on the older man. Leaning on Manuel on one side and Mai-Lin on the other, he barely kept up, his face worn and haggard.

They got off the bridge and rested underneath the Brooklyn-Queens Expressway. The BQE is notorious for its potholes and generally poor condition. It's an elevated road like its cousin the FDR across the river, but its rutted surface is miserable and sometimes has been compared to roads found in third-world countries. The traffic jams are also legendary.

Traffic certainly wasn't the problem on this rapidly closing afternoon. With the violent insanity going on across the river in Manhattan and to a lesser extent, the surrounding boroughs, most people either hunkered down in their apartments and houses, or, if they were able, had left the city for the refuges of Long Island, Westchester and New Jersey. Still, some traffic remained, cars whizzed unseen over their head producing clanking and banging noises as they hit potholes and ruts.

The grimy littered roadway was just about deserted. Two old men, or maybe middle aged, scruffy beards hanging from their faces like filthy Spanish moss from a tree, pushed two supermarket carts filled with assorted debris. Plastic bags, loaded with God-knows what tied to the sides of the cart like mangy clouds as they passed Charly and Joe sitting on the ground, leaning against the massive concrete base that held the steel posts supporting the roadway above their heads.

Joe rested against the concrete, his eyes closed. Charly's arm rested around his shoulder, her hand lightly against his neck. A few feet away Wu sat on a plastic milk crate, his back resting on the concrete. Mai-Lin squatted on the ground next to him. Manuel had taken out his gun and wiped it with a rag as he sat cross-legged on the sidewalk.

"We don't look much better than they do," Charly said softly.

Joe opened his eyes, looked briefly at the two homeless men pushing their carts and grinned at her.

"Yeah, I'm ready for a GQ photo shoot."

"Maybe you better get a hold of a razor and a bathtub first," she replied.

A full twenty-four hours passed since the shootings in Chinatown. They had been on the run ever since. Joe felt like his skin was covered by a sooty layer of crud. A bath sounded like a wonderfully absurd luxury right now. He longed for his house in Ridge, out on Long Island with its great amenities.

Charly took his left arm and gently loosened the tourniquet.

"What are you doing?" he asked.

She looked up at him, her eyes just inches from his face. She leaned forward and kissed him, her lips soft, warm and pliant. Joe thought she looked good in spite of all the events. He slid his right hand over her shoulder, and up her neck, his fingers entwining with her tossed damp hair. He pulled her face to his and kissed her, his tongue probing and caressing.

The moment passed, sweet and delicious and Joe leaned back again, their eyes still locked.

"Let me see that arm," she said, reaching for the tourniquet on his left forearm.

"Its fine," Joe said, but he let her take the arm and place it in her lap as she moved to his left side.

She looked up at him, holding his arm in her lap, "Joe, I've never met anyone quite like you before. I don't know where exactly this is going to lead to, but I'll be dammed if I'm going to lose you to an infection or blood poisoning."

She removed the tourniquet and the bandage. A trickle of blood oozed from the scab-crusted razor slash. She pulled her shirttails from inside her pants and tore out long strips. She cleaned the cut with the last can of club sodas they had bought on East Broadway. She bandaged his forearm and tied it off with loops of strings from her pocket.

"You're going to need stitches on that," she said.

"That'll wait till we get to the safe house. Let's get going."

They got up, stiff and slow with creaking and snapping joints. They left the overhang of the BQE and walked on through the wide street.

The wind still gusted strong and the sky changed from dull gray to a patchwork of dark racing clouds interspersed at rare intervals with spots of welcomed sunlight. As the afternoon closed they walked past the college and the civic center until the street widened and became Flatbush Avenue.

A dozen miles away, the Sylvan sat in the rear of the SUV, tendrils of telepathic energy projected around him like ripples in a still pond. The ripples were a live extension of its mind, constantly seeking, searching out the elusive prey. As the vehicle moved halfway through Queens County on Route 25, Queens Boulevard, he felt the sun behind the patchy wet clouds beginning its descent below the horizon.

CHAPTER 39

At this point they could not be too far. They had walked all the way past Fulton Street and now Lafayette would be next, on their left. Beyond that it was no more than about a quarter mile where Flatbush Avenue met Atlantic Avenue and TR would be waiting to take them to safety.

The wind slowed down, or maybe it was just because they were away from the exposure of the empty spaces of the Brooklyn Bridge. Joe vaguely remembered that October was hurricane season and something was expected soon. He tried to recall the last weather forecast, before all this happened. All he remembered were some trite sentences about the calm before the storm.

Flatbush Avenue was just about deserted. A police van passed with loudspeakers barking about a curfew, everyone must be off the street by nightfall. A few cars hurried past on the wide avenue, the faces of the drivers stretched and fearful. Two military vehicles drove slowly by, the armed National Guardsmen tense, clenched hands grasping weapons. No one seemed to understand exactly what went on.

The sky grew gloomier with each passing moment. They would make it, but just barely, before darkness truly settled in. As if the events of the last few hours weren't enough,

there was something else going on. The tension had
returned. They had had a respite on the bridge from the
buzzing alien sensations that had followed them the last
few hours. Now it returned, strong as ever, like it wanted to
make up for lost time, punish them for their temerity in
daring to escape the fate that had been set out for them in
the city.

They kept going, kept walking and the feeling of
disquiet, of being hunted, grew. The air around them
thickened as if infused with steam.

At one point Joe stopped. A psychic wave of energy
suddenly hit him, a telepathic hammer blow. He leaned
against a pole and cradled his forehead in both hands. The
others felt it too but it didn't seem to affect them as much. It
was like a hand reached into his very core, into his heart
and his brain, activating all the nerve centers, lighting them
up in flaming beams of pain.

He felt Mai-Lin's probing touch in his mind.

Shield...Protect...Shield...

A wave of hurt racked through his head, a violent ache
like sharp blows. Dimly, he barely heard Charly speaking
to him as if from a great distance.

"Joe, what's wrong? You okay?"

His knees buckled and she held him up. He tried to
speak, tried to tell her, but the words wouldn't form.
Through the daze of pain, he suddenly saw an image of his
grandfather. The old man was weaving leather ropes
through tough hide in a wood frame, building a warrior's
shield, strong enough to deflect a war club. His eyes looked
directly at Joe as he worked, his face brown and crinkled
like pine bark.

Joe understood.

Then he started building the shield.

*The Sylvan felt their aura, their very being, some twelve
or fifteen miles away near the place called the Brooklyn
Bridge. With ferocious exultation he lashed out, the
telepathic waves filled with focused energy toward the one*

human, the one who had the awareness, the one who eluded him. In the gathering gloom, the Sylvan's power surged like a thunderbolt and he felt the human target weaken and begin to crumble under the psychic assault. A telepathic swell of triumph rode the next wave of energy as the Sylvan lashed out again. But something changed very quickly. Somehow, they diverted his power.

Near, so very near to the group of now shielded humans, the Sylvan felt the Maarzuk's hungry power below the concrete sidewalks and blacktop road. Best to let the creature take care of these humans. After all, that's why he had awakened it.

It was a warrior's shield. A magnificent protective shield built in the recesses of his mind. Joe visualized the tanned and cured deerskin hides, tough and impenetrable as steel shutters, woven in and around hickory and cherry wood laced with hundreds of feet of leather string like metal cables. He extended the shield until it formed a half oblong like a giant split eggshell that surrounded him and his companions. Over and around the shield, a glowing white light enfolded it in a protective cocoon. Mai-Lin projected her own aura, strengthening Joe's mental shield. He felt the hostile presence, now distant and frustrated, unable to penetrate their combined defenses. He recognized the telepathic probe of the Sylvan from Central Park, its distinctive aggressive signature. But for the first time, he felt a puzzled unease from the alien presence. Moments passed as Joe and Mai-Lin held the shield and the Sylvan presence withdrew.

Joe felt the girl's steadily burgeoning powers bloom and expand. It reminded him of the rumble of distant thunder carrying a vision of crashing unimaginable violence. He felt its promise like the electricity that makes the hair on the back of your neck stand up like wires. His own awakening psychic ability had detected the Sylvans and the stalking creature under the ground, through the ground, but he did not feel any human minds, no thoughts or emotions from any persons, except Mai-Lin.

Strong...Stronger than the bad...Not afraid...Strong...

He saw the images she sent out. Feelings, emotions that translated into flashing photos from the depths of his subconscious, an unwitting deciphering, blooming into communication.

He felt her difference, her strangeness, and she was like no other person. Something eluded him, an answer, flitting around in the twilight of the outer edges of his mind. What was it about her? How did it all fit in the great mysterious puzzle of the last seven—had it only been seven days?

He swam back, upward from the nightmare landscape of the Sylvan's psychic assault. The glowing shield slowly dissolved in his mind like a fading movie scene as he opened his eyes. A taste of burnt bitter ashes lingered in his mouth and the grimy residue of their smell clung to his nostrils.

Joe half sprawled like a sack of twigs on the edge of the sidewalk among blades of brown grass poking up through cracks and the curbed edge of the concrete meeting the blacktop of the roadway. Manuel held Joe's back as Charly stroked his forehead, making gentle dove-like cooing noises. Dr Wu rested a few feet away, his back curved against a beat up garbage can at the foot of the stoop of a building.

"*Amigo*, you alright? You gave us a scare man," Manuel said, the sharp corners of his voice changed to concerned whisperings.

"Joe," Charly's fingers gently traced the outline of his cheek, "You were zombied out while you walked. Your had your eyes open but you weren't there, then you crumpled, you stopped and just sort of *melted*."

Joe stared, a hint of bewilderment in his eyes, like someone coming out of anesthesia. He felt his mouth move a bit but no words came out. He looked at Mai-Lin. The girl's pupils were wide and not quite in focus as she saw through him like he was a smoky pane of glass concealing some vast truth.

"You don't know the half of it," he whispered.

CHAPTER 40

Joe thought he must have walked a while without seeing as he held back the Sylvan's attack, and meanwhile, the neighborhood had changed. The taller, maintained buildings of the Civic Center on the right and Long Island University on the left had been replaced by shorter, seedier structures.

He knew this part of Flatbush Avenue was quintessential Brooklyn, filled with the kind of buildings Neil Diamond sang about in *Brooklyn Row*. Two story railroad flats, long and narrow in front with straight roofs bristling with TV antennas and covered with tar that dripped black sticky ooze on hot days. Here and there, a brownstone would break the low roofline like a dark fang in a mouthful of decayed teeth. Most of the buildings had stoops that jutted to within three feet of the curb, and Joe saw that most contained storefronts with signs proclaiming Beepers-Illamadas, Bodegas, Afro-Salons and Soul Food. One storefront sported hand painted letters that advertised the First Haitian Church of God in Brooklyn.

Signs of leftover rioting abounded, storefronts with boarded over windows and glinting sidewalks of crushed safety glass as if a giant had sprinkled diamonds over a hapless urban landscape. Paper, plastic and assorted trash lay scattered everywhere and residues of oily rain that would not evaporate on such a damp, cool day, covered everything. Throughout the street and sidewalk, demolished articles of looted consumer goods, televisions, stereos and smashed pieces of furniture, stood forlorn as cactus in a surreal desert of concrete and asphalt.

Joe stood, helped to his feet by Charly and Manuel. He felt okay. He could have managed on his own, but their touch was reassuring. He wasn't alone. Never mind that without him and Mai-Lin, their brains would probably have been as fried as one of Manuel's tortillas. Even though he hadn't yet figured out the depth of it, the four people added a dimension that had not existed twenty-four hours ago. They were the answer and the salvation to the muddy enigma that had been his life until now. More than ever he understood that deliverance would ride the road of his heritage.

Four teenagers walked past them on the roadway. Ball caps turned around, rolling aggressive gaits and hard ghetto eyes turned on them. Manuel's pistol butt stuck out of the belt in the front of his pants over the torn and bloodstained shirt. One of the teenagers said something to the others and they laughed as they kept going. This was the edge of the Bedford-Stuyvesant ghetto enclave of Brooklyn. The area competed constantly for the most violent murders with the South Bronx, Harlem and East New York. Years ago the neighborhood had been a working class fortress of people embracing what came later as a political cry called "family values." All that changed in the early sixties when drugs devastated block after block of humanity.

The power remained on and streetlights were lit even though early evening had not yet turned to night. They passed by a group of people, their eyes shifting back and forth with the look of the hunter who could turn into the hunted at any moment. A radio blared the voice of a newscaster whose tone slowly grinded out as if his vocal chords were worn from overuse.

"…all private vehicles except for food and emergency

deliveries have been ordered off the streets. All vehicles with registrations outside the city may use the streets for exits only. Private vehicles are banned from entering the city. All tunnels are closed."

The announcer paused, cleared his throat, and Joe pictured him frowning. The merest hint of an I-don't-believe-this tone flashed for a fraction of a second before the professional voice resumed control.

"An emergency taskforce consisting of NYPD, FBI, National Guard and ATF officials issued the following statement: The Governor declared a state of emergency to exist in the boroughs of New York City and Long Island. National Guard units have been deployed and airports are closed to civilian traffic. We do not yet have answers to the great tragedy that has suddenly struck the Metropolitan area and its suburbs, and while we do not have an exact casualty count, it is now known to exceed six hundred killed with thousands injured…"

Here the announcer's voice trailed off. He coughed, excused himself and resumed a moment later.

"Investigators are working around the clock and have determined the following sequence of events: Shortly after midnight a group of yet unknown terrorists attacked a train approximately a quarter mile from the 38th street subway station in Manhattan causing heavy casualties. Simultaneously throughout the city, terrorist bands attacked people in the subway system. It is also believed there has been a release of hallucinogenic agents into the air which has been the cause of violence and rioting. Testing shows the air is clear and we believe we have weathered the worst of the attack.

Although a terrorist attack of such treachery and cunning has caught us by surprise, as it can any democratic government, our citizens should rest assured that we will not rest until those responsible are brought to a swift and merciless justice."

The announcer continued with details of martial law procedures and block-by-block accounts. The voice trailed off as Joe, Charly, Manuel, Wu and Mai-Lin continued up Flatbush Avenue.

They passed Fulton and now they crossed Lafayette. For an instant Joe wondered what the French general would think about his name on this avenue filled with decay and human hope ground into the acid mud of poverty that soaked Bedford-Stuyvesant.

Joe remembered from TR's directions that they had to be close to where Atlantic Avenue intersected Flatbush. The sky darkened moment-by-moment, and the air felt like burning excrement. Only a few people prowled the streets and they passed with predatory looks at Joe and his four companions. They were being viewed and judged as possible victims, opportunistic glances that found them wanting, capable of too much resistance. Those were the only kind of people that remaining on the streets this evening. All the good citizens huddled behind their doors, eyes glued to their TV sets.

The deserted avenue reminded Joe of one of those Science Fiction movies out of the fifties where alien invasions emptied the cities.

Fifty yards ahead a National Guard Humvee turned slowly out of the upcoming intersection. The vehicle headed away from them, the helmeted soldiers inside, bare shadows, their weapons held ready. Beneath it all, Joe felt the hulking presence of the Maarzuk. He sensed the menacing edge of the creature pouring itself under and through the ground, seeking what the Sylvan had unleashed it to destroy.

"Joe," Charly said, "I'm scared."

He looked at her. Her short hair scattered in wet ringlets that clung to her forehead, her eyes wet blue spaces between puffy lids. Fear gave her mouth a pouty full look as her lower lip trembled slightly. He felt a wave of affection for her. *Affection or love?* Was he capable of love? Isn't that what had happened to Becky? She had deciphered his desperate attempts at creating a facade of normality. No love existed, just a different form of running away, of running from what he should have embraced.

Joe put his arm around her as they walked. He felt like a protecting oak branch as she reached his hand over her shoulder and squeezed his arm.

"Don't worry," he told her, "we'll get through this. I'll get you through it."

She squeezed his hand harder as she replied. For the first time he sensed the hesitation and fear in her voice.

"I don't know Joe, this is different, stranger," she frowned, pausing, "more dangerous is what it is. Like, I know we were living in the subway and we had those things, those Sylvans after us above ground at night, but nobody died."

"How about the guy I heard died in Bellevue?"

"Yeah, he did die in Bellevue, but it wasn't like this. He died in a *hospital.* Lots of people die in hospitals. Maybe it was like they said, maybe the Sylvans killed him, but now, look around you. Hundreds are dead, and what about that thing, that smoke creature that follows us under the ground?"

Joe felt her shudder, and he held her back, slowing a little as Wu and Mai-Lin walked ahead with Manuel leading. They had only about twenty yards or so to go before reaching the big intersection ahead. Darkness enfolded the avenue except for the sidewalk and parts of the street washed in pools of glowing white light from the big sodium bulbs arcing on their tall aluminum poles. Up ahead, two traffic lights glowed a changing red yellow and green as the two large avenues intersected. On both sides of the corners small groups of people loitered, their arms gesticulating, walking back and forth, arguing and laughing. The pulsing base of a boom box tuned to some rap station pounded, the molecules of disturbed sound waves washing through them, felt in the marrow of their bones rather than their ears.

"What about them? What do you think?" Joe asked her, waiving toward Wu and Mai-Lin ahead of them.

"I'm not sure," replied Charly as her left arm curled

around Joe's waist, her fingers moving up his back under the jacket, "but there's something strange there. He says she's his daughter but look at her; no Asian fold to her eyes, she looks nothing like him. That's no proof of anything, I know, but still, it's strange, it's like they really don't belong. And her, there's something there, like, she acts like a child sometimes, but other times you feel its an act and she's really this older person, pretending. I'm not sure if I'm making sense, but it all seems strange, like everything is a show."

Joe nodded slowly and didn't reply. He had felt sort of the same thing. The very power of Mai-Lin's mental projection had startled him. It was like watching a small child suddenly overturn an automobile.

"I tell you one thing," continued Charly, "I'll sure be glad when your brother picks us up and we're at this safe house. I'm tired of this running, tired of being afraid all the time."

They reached the intersection and stood back a few feet from the curb. Dark shapes poked up all about the crossing avenues, round and a foot or so high. Joe stepped a little closer to one leaning upright against a light pole. White letters proclaiming Firestone stood in bas-relief against the dark rubber. *Tires*, thought Joe as he looked across the wide street. The front of a vee shaped store had its window shattered. An overturned tire stand hung half out like a piece of spilt intestine among shards of glass reflecting dead white light from overhead. Every three seconds the giant red neon Firestone sign blinked sending out a wash of blood-red light to the wreckage below.

As they stood on the corner, Joe saw that Manuel had taken out the gun from his belt. He held it at his side, loose and casual, like a painter with his brush. The two groups of people across the avenue, about a dozen young men in all, ignored them, except for wary glances here and there. Joe knew that in Bed-Stuy you don't lock eyes and you don't show fear unless you want to rock and roll. On the other hand, you keep an eye on the man with the gun while you keep yours loose, if you got one, under the baggy gangsta-rap sweats.

"Hey, *Amigo*, your brother," Manuel said, his head swiveling, looking down both avenues, "he going to show up? We're a little late you know."

"He'll be here. Either that or he'll be looking for us the way we were supposed to come."

"And what if something happened to him?" asked Wu.

"He's not alone in this," Charly said, "he's bringing us to an FBI safe house. I'm sure he told them where and how he's meeting us."

There was an edge of tension in her voice as if she was answering her own doubts instead of Wu's question.

Joe was pretty edgy himself. There were probably hundreds of things that could have happened on a day of calamities like the city had just been through. He thought how good it would feel to just let go, let his brother and the FBI with their resources, their *authority*, take over. Let them track these things down while he tied his life together. He thought that he had some answers now. No, not all, definitely not all, not even very many. But just enough, just barely enough to get on track, to get where he should be, to do what counts. He rubbed Charly's shoulder through the jacket, felt the knot of tight muscles at the base of her neck.

"It'll be alright," he told her.

"I know baby, I know."

CHAPTER 41

Brookhaven National Laboratory, Upton, Long Island, New York, Physics Building

While Joe and his three companions crouched, hidden in the darkness surrounding a decrepit brownstone on the corner of Atlantic and Flatbush in Brooklyn, awaiting NYPD Captain TR Jackson, Dr. Prabinwah sat at his desk in the physics building.

The Indian physicist put his head down until it touched the rumpled computer printouts covering the desk like litter topping an unattended lawn. He felt tired, so tired that his very skin ached. The settings had been mostly completed, and only about twenty-four hours or so remained before the test began--the test that would bring what? Prabinwah held deep anxieties as to the results. There was so much they didn't know. Duncan Wesley had been gone most of the day and had not yet returned. *That's the only good thing about today,* thought Dr. Prabinwah. The vast amount of work he and his team accomplished this day focused his mind, his energies. The drudgery and the weariness it created also served another purpose. It helped to stifle the screaming voice of that corner of his mind that peeked into the world of horrendous possibilities this test could bring about. *And all for what?* That was a question he didn't have to ask. He knew full well the answer was Duncan Wesley's ambitions. The man was like a ruthless shark, devouring anything that stood in his way, driving all before him like schools of frightened minnows, a true human predator, uncaring, unforgiving and deadly as a basket of black mamba snakes.

Brooklyn, Corner of Atlantic & Flatbush Avenue

They huddled beneath the stoop of the brownstone, the darkness about them like a black quilt cover. Joe heard the steady rustle of Wu's breathing, a sound resembling dry leaves stirred in a breeze. The old man wasn't holding up very well. They practically carried him the last quarter mile. His face looked pale and mottled at the same time and an odor of illness enveloped his body. Mai-Lin stood by him but Joe had begun noticing certain things, details he had missed before. Although Dr. Wu said the right words regarding his daughter, the gestures were missing from both of them. The little touches, the infinite varieties and nuances of every moment that defined father and child relationships. It was like two decanters bereft of the wine they were designed to carry.

A set of headlights appeared in the depths of Flatbush Avenue, rolling toward their corner, the beams bouncing as the car ran over the potholes. The automobile slowed when it turned into Atlantic and entered the bright pools from the overhead arc lights. Joe stood, awakening Charly as he recognized TR in the dark sedan. He let out a whistle and called out his brother's name. The brake lights glinted, red spots bouncing from the glass shards in the roadway as the sedan stopped. TR reached under the seat, placed a "bubble gum machine" portable flasher on the roof and activated it. The pulsing red beam bounced up and down the avenue, reflecting from two story flats and storefronts and moldy brick walls. The sedan backed up, stopped in front of the brownstone where Joe hustled the others from the overhang of the stoop.

TR got out of the sedan, the interior light threw out white beams from the windows mingling with the red flashes like a strange Christmas scene. He wore civilian clothes with a badge latched to the front of his belt and a nine millimeter Glock NYPD regulation automatic on a shoulder holster. He met Joe and the others as they came out of the darkness.

"Come on," TR said, "get in. We're twenty minutes away."

As TR turned and stepped toward the sedan, Joe heard a loud plink like someone hitting a pan with a ball peen hammer. A small chunk of roof suddenly glinted bright metal in the dark paint. TR stopped and turned back to Joe. He started to say something, his mouth had barely begun to open, the bronze leathery face crinkled with surprise.

It created a moment that would live with Joe forever. A scene of life burnt in the neuron pathway of his memory, indelible and drenched in ageless sorrow.

A spot on the front of TR's shirt erupted in a red star as if a firecracker had exploded from his chest. When the bullet exited, it ricochet against the brick stoop with a whiny thumping noise. TR staggered forward as another steel-jacketed round hit high and to the left on his back.

A scream filled the air, an unbelieving bellow of mixed pain, rage and despair. Joe wasn't even aware the yell had come from his own throat as he grabbed his falling brother and dragged him in the darkness of the brownstone's stoop. Two more bullets hit the car. The window of the still-open driver's door blew out in thousands of exploding tiny pieces of safety glass. Another round hit the bricks at the base of the metal railing above the building's steps, blasting out bits of shattered hardened clay.

TR coughed, a gurgling choking noise rising through a throat filled with blood. His breath came in ragged, gasping wheezes. Charly kneeled on the other side of TR, her arms cradling his head. For a dark panicky moment, Joe felt he had entered the world of the Abaasy again, but this time, no bridge of stone provided and escape, and his own brother the victim.

"Hold him, just hold him," Joe told Charly, even as he realized the complete futility of his words, "Don't let him die."

Joe dashed from the covering darkness, ran the few feet to the idling sedan and rolled to the curb under the open door. Two spidery holes appeared in the windshield as the sniper targeted him, and the bullets passed through, one slamming into the open door, the other hitting the upholstered center post with a muffled thud.

He raised his head to the floor level of the sedan. *The mike, the radio, where was the mike? These unmarked cars had to have radios,* Joe thought as he tasted the fried-dust smell of the car and the street, and the spattering of his brother's blood turned to black congealed splashes on his face and clothing. He heard a yell, a Spanish curse behind him as Manuel ran to the car, firing shots from his pistol into the darkness of the empty street. A round plinked through the upper part of the roof with a metallic whining noise while another hit the red flashing bubble gum machine sending out showers of plastic casings. Manuel threw himself on the pavement beside Joe, under the protective bulk of the sedan.

"There, under the dash," Manuel said. He spoke in a loud stage whisper, as if the low volume could keep away the bullets, "See it, right there man."

Joe reached under the dash, part of his torso lying on the floor of the car. He heard the rushing noise and crackling static from the dash speaker as he keyed the button on the mike.

"Hey, emergency, police dispatcher, officer shot, Captain TR Jackson, send ambulance and officers to…to…"

Joe's mind went blank, he couldn't think of the name of the streets to save his life.

"Atlantic, Atlantic and Flatbush in Brooklyn," Manuel said.

"Atlantic and Flatbush in Brooklyn."

The police dispatcher's voice answered, all business, cool and professional.

"Emergency vehicle and response unit on its way. Corner of Flatbush and Atlantic. Are there perpetrators still shooting?"

"Yeah, somebody's firing, maybe a rifle, across the street. I think it's the west side of Atlantic, across from a Firestone building."

"Roger that. It's relayed to the response unit. Who is speaking? Identify yourself."

"Leave it man," Manuel said, grabbing Joe's hand over the mike, "We can't do your brother any good by letting them grab us. With your brother out of it, they'll just throw us in a holding tank. If it's a basement, we're really screwed. That thing underground will have us for a snack. Come on man, let's make a dash for the building."

Joe looked around wildly and nodded. It made sense. He ignored the squawking radio, dropped the mike and dashed for the building in a crouch. Manuel followed close behind, firing wildly behind him over the roof of the car while Joe dove out of the circle of light. He heard Manuel cry out and fall, heard the clatter of the gun as it flew out of the Mexican's hand. He ran back covering the five or six feet in one leap, grabbed Manuel under the arm and pulled him to safety as another bullet passed his ear in a whine of displaced air.

Joe couldn't see Manuel's face in the dark, but his breathing turned a series of painful gasps.

"Fucker shot my leg off man," Manuel screamed, the inflections of pain washing off the echoing buildings.

In the darkness, Joe couldn't see the Mexican's face but his eyes shone like silvery nickels as he moaned with the pain. He ran his hands down the wounded man's legs, slowly, one at a time. No bone fragments but the hands came away steeped in gluey blood, glinting black in the dim reflected light.

Down the avenue, an armored car bristling with antennas turned the corner on six big round wheels. A flak-jacketed soldier manned an M-60 machine gun on a short pivot behind armor plating. On the front of the vehicle, a remote spotlight sent an incandescent round beam sweeping the buildings continuously from basement to roof. It looked like a huge combination of a firefly and beetle on wheels. Ten feet behind the armored car an EMS ambulance followed with flashing red lights and close behind, an NYPD squad car with two riot-equipped police officers in the front seat.

The little convoy stopped in front of the sedan. The unmarked car's door was still open, the interior lights on and the engine idling as if passengers and drivers were just waiting to get in the bullet pocked car like taxi riders in a rainstorm.

"Help me, *Amigo*," Manuel gasped between spasms of pain, "Just help me walk, we can't let them catch us and put us where that thing's gonna get us." The pain from the gunshot wounds in his legs had not overridden the fear of the Maarzuk pulsing beneath them in the atoms of the Earth.

"No, you need medical help and I'm not leaving my brother."

TR lay on the pavement by the brownstone stoop, his head cradled in Charly's lap. She removed his jacket and placed it over him like a blanket. Satiny black crimson seeped from his chest through the jacket. His breath turned to barely perceptible little wheezes sounding like cracked ancient bellows. His face was a mottled pasty gray, hardly visible in the murk. Joe felt a choking helplessness, and a deep rage welled up from some pit within his very soul as he turned to Dr. Wu.

"Can't you help him? You're a goddamned Doctor aren't you?"

"I'm a Doctor of physics. I study atoms, not human bodies."

"Joe, Manuel's right. We can't help TR, but they will." Charly said, waving toward the armored car and ambulance stopping in front of the idling automobile. She took off her jacket and placed it under TR's head. His eyes closed and each breath seemed to take an eternity as if his body decided which one would be the last. The pavement seemed awash with his blood. Joe thought he could die before the ambulance attendants arrived.

In the street, the rear gate of the armored car came down with a whining noise. Five soldiers wearing flak jackets and holding M-16's at ready fanned out in a wide circle encompassing the car and the ambulance. The beam of the powerful spotlight turned and moved ceaselessly, a glowing oval playing across the faces of the buildings as the machine gunner searched for the sniper. Behind the ambulance, both policemen left the squad car. They wore riot helmets and flak jackets and held shotguns aimed level at the deserted streets. The prowling young men had disappeared at the first crackling of bullets hitting the sedan. They didn't need to hear the shots, couldn't hear them because the rifle had probably been equipped with sound suppressors. In the Bedford-Stuyvesant ghetto of Brooklyn, if you didn't recognize just the sound of whining bullets, and failed to make yourself scarce, you would never live to see twenty candles on your birthday cake.

"Joe, come *on*," Charly whispered, her tones urgent, "they'll be here any minute to find him. We can't take care of him, they can."

One soldier approached the sedan. He played the beam of a strong flashlight over and around the car while another soldier covered him with his M-16. Thirty feet away a policeman covered his other side with the riot gun.

Slowly, like his feet were stuck in a sea of sucking mud, Joe turned and walked down the alley between the buildings, away from the street and his fallen brother. Manuel leaned heavily on him while Joe supported the Mexican around the waist. The wounded man's feet dragged on the ground, his legs barely responding, unable to carry any weight. This time it was Charly who hustled them forward with Wu in the lead.

Unnoticed, silent as a desert breeze, no one saw Mai-Lin as she turned back and stopped at TR's feet. She took another two steps and fell to her knees next to the dying man's head. A gurgling noise like a stopped-up sink came from his chest and a thin red bubble formed out of his mouth following the pencil line of blood trickling down his cheek. An abattoir odor clung to the man and the girl felt the aura of death about him.

She placed a hand on the clammy white skin of his forehead and the other hand on his chest amidst the gore.

She closed her eyes and stood very still.

Her breathing stopped.

Out on the street, just a few feet away from Mai-Lin and TR's body, the soldiers yelled "clear" over and over as they searched out the surroundings. The one with the flashlight moved the beam toward the stoop, catching TR's feet and legs. He yelled at the armored vehicle and the spotlight came down to the brownstone's stoop, bathing the area in noontime light.

Charly stopped and turned around soon as she realized Mai-Lin was not ahead, nor was she following them. When she finally saw the girl by TR's body, it was a moment she would think about often in years to come, a moment of suspended frozen time, of unearthly ethereal *strangeness*. Perhaps, she often thought, it had been magic, deep and primitive, the kind of magic that had been responsible for all the creations of all the ages.

As Charly watched, the spotlight beam descended on Mai-Lin kneeling at TR's body. The little group escaping could not be seen from the area they had reached deep in the alley. They were like members of an audience in the recesses of a hidden balcony, invisible to the players so brightly lit on their stage. As Wu shuffled forward followed by Joe carrying Manuel, Charly had been the only one to turn, the only one to see what happened next.

The soldiers stood like figures in a tableau, frozen, silent. Time seemed to halt, and the air thickened as Mai-Lin opened her eyes and raised her head. She slowly removed her hands from TR's head and chest. Tenebrous wispy tentacles of foggy smoke curled from her fingertips, thinning and disappearing as the distance between her hands and TR's body increased. She stood still as a church statue in front of the soldiers. She took three small steps backwards, still facing the men. The soldier with the flashlight was closest, "Over here," he shouted,"There's somebody alive here."

The two soldiers ran to the stoop. TR raised his head and torso on one elbow and coughed, a clear breathing cough, hurting but filled with life. Two paramedics ran toward the stoop carrying a stretcher and medical equipment.

They don't see her, thought Charly, *she's right there in front of them, but they don't see her. She's blocking their minds.*

The girl turned and ran toward Charly. As she caught up, their eyes met briefly and a sensation of soothing washed over Charly for a brief moment. Then it was gone like a flashing scent of alluring perfume as they exited the passageway between the buildings and turned down a larger alleyway. It was so littered with debris, garbage, crushed syringes and other odious unidentifiable objects that even a city sewer rat would avoid them. They walked through the filthy deserted path, the only light coming from the occasional glow of a barred upper story window. The buildings rose on either side of them like troglodytes of stone and crud covered brick.

CHAPTER 42

———◆———

TR, oh God, TR, hang on big brother, hang on, thought Joe as a silent prayer reached his lips, summoned somehow from a tribal past he had suppressed but never forgotten. It came to him unbidden, arising on wings of despair and fear.

Protect O Great One
For the beauty of all things
For those who walk alongside us
For those who have come before
For those yet to come
Protect O Great One

The alleyway ended, spilling onto pavement. Joe helped Manuel sit against the building wall as they stepped out of the alley. They entered a narrow street, an apocalyptic vision of decayed urban hell, the kind of place where politicians seeking inner city votes will visit for sound bites and quick photo opportunities. Accompanied by hordes of police and plainclothes security, they make short speeches filled with grandiose wording and swollen with promises that are immediately forgotten soon as they leave the area with their security.

The little group that was about to enter the street, certainly had no such security. Joe stopped as they looked to the darkened ends of the roadway that vanished in a yawning black pit of busted streetlights. Broken down hulks of cars squatted, some fully on the sidewalks others half on the street. The metallic carcasses weren't just classics broken-down-on-blocks, but the totally destroyed, no-wheels kind. Some had been burned and Joe could see signs of occupation in the rust filled shambles.

On both sides of the streets the sidewalks were backed by buildings, some as high as ten stories, others, single-floor squat ugly square things that settled like noxious rooting toads. Most had suffered fire damage, and some were partially demolished. People also lived in them, squatters, for this was not a neighborhood of rent-paying tenants. The owners had abandoned the buildings long after collecting whatever insurance money they could get. Their real homes would be in another world of neat single brick houses with tended lawns that sprouted sparkling fountains from in-ground sprinklers at the same timer-controlled moment each evening.

Here and there glinted the occasional unbroken windowpane amongst openings that held only shattered pieces of glass like shards of pointed demonic teeth. Halfway down the scarred road, a fire burned in a barrel and several people gathered, occasionally throwing unidentifiable debris into the flames. Two men rested against the building across the street, their faces covered in shadows like dark scarves. The odor of decay mingled with the stench of poverty and hopelessness so deep it formed a decrepit cover that penetrated the pores of Joe's soul. The very air held a timorous quality, an edge of palpable fear and apprehension. Underneath it all, like a circling great shark, unseen in muddy waters, rode the buzzing psychic *feel* of the berserk creature. They all sensed the presence of the Maarzuk, dogging their very footsteps beneath the earth.

Charly came up quietly behind Joe and held his arm.

"What do we do now?" she asked.

That was one of two questions he asked himself continuously since the moment TR had been shot. The other question being, would his brother survive and be okay? He shook his head gently, the gesture more an expression of confused doubt than negativity.

"I'm not sure," he replied, his tone so soft it wouldn't reach the others, "The only thing I can think of is to return to the reservation. I can't explain why, but I think, I feel, some of the answer is out there."

"How do we do that Joe? I don't think any of us know exactly where we are."

"Maybe not exactly," he replied, "but I have an idea. We're somewhere in Bedford-Stuyvesant, one of the worst areas in any American city."

"No shit!" She replied, "I didn't think we were outside the Waldorf-Astoria. How the hell we get out of here is the real question."

"We head North. Eventually that will get us out of Bed-Stuy and connect with one of the main drags like Myrtle or Metropolitan Avenues. We follow them northward until we reach the Jamaica section, not a garden spot either, but better than this area. From there, we can catch the Jamaica station branch of the Long Island Railroad. That's still running, it's all above ground and will take us to Mastic in Eastern Long Island. The Poospatuq reservation is a few miles from there."

"So which way is North and how do you know all this stuff?"

He grinned a little and placed his hand on her neck.

"I'm Indian, remember? I got something in common with these people," he said, his hand sweeping across the backdrop of the street, "we both got screwed by the white man."

She had a momentary flash of hope at regaining that little smile of his, but it was washed over by a wave of quick anger. She pushed his hand away and replied.

"Spare me the oppressed people sycophantic bullshit and tell me how you're going to find North. You got a compass on you maybe?"

"No, but like I said, I'm Indian. It's part of my heritage. Remember that clearing of the clouds for about an hour this evening? Well, I noted where the sun went down. That's West, and I kept track of it as we walked. The opposite side is East, and North is right about that way," he said, pointing down the street, "and what's more, I went to Queens College so I know some of the area and I understand big words. See, no sycophantic oppressed people bullshit, just common Injun horse sense."

"Shit, you're still a whackadoo. That's probably why I love you," she said and reached his face with her lips, her tongue trailing across his open mouth. He let her linger a second or two then broke it off.

"Now who's the whackadoo?" He whispered, "This area is not very conducive for long romantic moments. Let's get the others and move on."

She held his arm in a gentle but firm restraining grip.

"Wait Joe, there's something more, two things more. When you were calling for help with Manuel, I was holding your brother. He came to for a moment, he tried to speak but he couldn't, he could just move one hand toward his pocket. There was something he wanted me to take, an envelope. Then he passed out."

She handed him an unsealed brown envelope with a NYPD imprinted return address. Joe glanced inside at several sheets of folded computer printouts. He closed the envelope and placed it in his own pocket. The mention of his brother and his unknown fate had returned a fog of gloom and pain to his face.

"We'll check it out when we're in a safer area. Let's get away from here."

"Wait, I'm not done," she said, "It's about TR…I mean…well I think, he's going to be okay."

He stopped and turned to her. A little part of his mind noted how beautiful she was with her hair wild in the reflected distant streetlight. Another part of him surged in anger as he spoke.

"How do you know? He was shot in the back, twice. I saw the bullets come out of his chest. You're just patronizing me. How can you know he's going to be okay?"

"I'm not sure, maybe it's a feeling, a surge of intuition because I saw something strange just after that, something as strange as anything we went through the last two days. None of you saw it, just me. It was Mai-Lin."

She continued describing what she had seen down to the last detail she could remember, the wisps of fog from Mai-Lin's fingertips, the inability of the soldiers to see her in front of them and TR sitting up, coughing, but a different cough, not the rasp of coming death.

Joe took it all in, wanting desperately to believe her, to believe *in* her, to be certain it was not some kind of stress induced vision. Charly's story added to his doubts about Mai-Lin. There was more to this young woman than they saw. Joe felt like someone finishing a complicated puzzle only to find the last few pieces didn't fit anywhere.

Before Joe could sort anything out, he had to get this little strange and beat up group to a safe area. Quiet, warmth and food would also be a much needed bonus.

He led them out of the alley and out in the street. Manuel's leg had stiffened and he could barely move. Supported between Charly and Joe, each hobbling skip brought a muffled groan of pain. Wu followed close behind, his face an ashen mask of weariness and resignation. Only Mai-Lin seemed lively, as if the silent girl received infusions of power from some hidden source, some wellspring of energy she had secretly tapped. *Maybe it's just her youth*, thought Joe.

They continued down the long street. Eyes brimming with hostility and wariness followed them as they passed several groups of people. An emaciated man with cruel slit eyes wearing a full-length mink coat and a cane with a sharply knobbed edge followed their progress. A trio of haggard and dangerous looking whores perched on stilt heels ignored them. Two young children with aged hard eyes passed them at a run and looked back, appraising and measuring. A group of three men hunkered in the cavernous shadow of an overturned van as they passed. Their black skin shining and damp in the gloom and their arms erupted with running sores and countless track marks. One held a small flame under a spoon while another poked a filthy syringe in the bubbling liquid. The third one lolled against the side of the van, eyes white and empty, long rubber tube stretched tight around his upper arm. Someone called out something vaguely challenging from the edge of a pool of dirty light pouring from a solitary streetlight with a sole functioning bulb. Stray humanity, disease and death ruled this place like a medieval fiefdom.

They reached an intersection and Joe turned North, leading them into an avenue, wider, but equally decrepit, just another stretch of unknown and dangerous territory. They continued walking for another twenty yards or so, when he realized they were being followed. He looked back briefly, a stolen glance, trying not to alarm his companions. Two figures lurked behind them, their features shaded in the darkness. Joe saw they each wore bandannas and baggy shining black nylon pants and sweatshirts. One walked on the sidewalk, the other on the edge of the street. They swaggered in a rolling aggressive gait, a ghetto signal that said: to fuck with me is to fuck with death. As Joe watched, another man came from behind a car on the other side and took a place in the center of the street as they followed.

"Don't look back," Joe whispered to Charly, and Manuel stumbling between them, "We've got company. Try to go a little faster."

"Shit, and I dropped my piece back there," replied Manuel between painful gasps.

They picked up the pace, just a little, a small insignificant increase. Joe knew they had no chance of outdistancing the dangerous looking trio following them. He just hoped to reach some kind of safe area, perhaps even one with security before they closed in. Joe appreciated what his ancestors must have felt centuries ago. What it must have been like to be lost in a night forest filled with predators, tracked by hungry wolves with long white fangs that dripped saliva, anticipating blood.

Joe and his companions passed the end of a tall building and a rubble filled short empty lot. At the end of the lot, another building reared up. It was a long structure, one story high. Joe saw that it was the remains of a burned out building, nothing more than four or five feet of bricked walls encircling piles of crumbled concrete and wood debris. Flickering tongues of red light from a campfire in the basement, glowed in the spaces between the rubble.

They barely walked half the length of the building, when two shadows came out of the dark crumbled entranceway of the structure. One man was tall, wearing a tee shirt in the chill air, a baseball bat slung over his shoulder like a roadman carrying a shovel to work. Something long and metallic gleamed in the other man's right hand. Joe and the others stopped as they approached. He heard Manuel mumbling muffled Spanish curses under his breath. Charly's face wore fear like make up over her features. Wu's limbs shook with a slight imperceptible trembling. Only Mai-Lin seemed undisturbed. Her face was placid, like a child who had to go to a movie she didn't want to see. Not much fun, but no big deal. Joe didn't have to turn to know the three following them had also closed in.

The tall man in front, the one with the baseball bat, spoke first, his voice a deep rolling rumble, the tones carrying not a shred of pity or mercy.

"What you muhfukrs doin here? Ain't nobody told you this be Cripps territory?"

They all stood silent for a moment that stretched with promises of bloody, pointless violence, "Look, we're lost," Joe finally replied. He tried to sound confident, unafraid yet unchallenging. He knew he was failing as he felt the tension in his vocal chords.

"We don't want any trouble. We just want to get back home."

"You a long way from home, mother fucker," a voice said from behind him, the hostility so thick you could slice it like roast-beef.

The thugs closed in so they were only four or five feet from them. Joe saw the one next to the tall man with the bat, held a long thin knife in his right hand. He spun it in his fingers like a twirler with a baton. Beams of reflected light bounced from the blade as it flipped and turned and twisted.

"Hey," said the man with the blade, "this here's our street. You need to pay us toll to pass."

"We've got some money," Joe said, as he realized it would never be enough. They were completely at the mercy of these five men. As they stepped even closer, he saw they weren't men at all, kids, teenagers, the tall one probably no more than eighteen, maybe nineteen. They wore bandannas of the same red and white with yellow slashes, like some uniform. Their childhood had been violence, grinding poverty and hopelessness. Yet, they were the survivors, carrying their hatred and violence like badges of honor, lashing back at the world, experienced in death like a perversion of trained soldiers.

"You *had* some money sucka," one of them said behind Joe.

"We got us a problem, a bad ass problem for you," said the tall man/teenager with the baseball bat, "Let's get you all down in our war room so we can figger out what to do with all of you."

"I all ready know what to do with the ho and the little bitch," growled the one on the street. He was older, squat and ugly like a charcoaled fireplug. Trunk-like arms crisscrossed with prison tattoos and knotted muscles stuck out from the sleeveless sweatshirt. A thick steel rod the length of a yardstick, one end taped for grip, held dangling by his left leg. The others laughed.

"Jamal gonna ride some fine bitches tonight," one of the other teenagers said.

The tall one held his arm, bat straight out toward the entrance of the building and the stairs heading down.

"Down, in our war room," he said.

The dim muted fire from below bounced red flickering beams that lit up the graffiti covered walls. It looked like the entrance to Hades, the very vision of a demented Dante and his Inferno.

CHAPTER 43

Time slowed for Joe. He was no longer Joseph Gray. He felt the change within him, within his very core and accepted it with the peace of a Jesuit monk.

He became Gray-Wolf, the Shinnecock warrior, and tranquility washed over him as he prepared to die. He saw Charly's face, her lip trembling and eyes shining, ruled by an all-consuming fear. Manuel mumbled some Catholic Spanish prayer over and over as if coming from an invisible rosary. Wu began taking slow steps toward the building's entrance. The old Chinese's entire body shook, the slender limbs like reeds jerking on invisible winds.

Gray-Wolf's mind ran with the words of his grandfather. The old warrior's voice rose out of the depths of his memory.

The true warrior will fight with the shield, the spear, the arrow, the knife and the tomahawk. He will fight with the courage of his heart and the will of all his ancestors. But that is not enough for a great warrior. From a thousand warriors, all with strength and bravery in their heart, only one will truly be great. Only one will the generations of the People yet to come, sing his praises in the campfires that warm the teepees when the waters of the bays harden to ice. That one great warrior will have the fighting quality

*none of the others will have. Beyond the strength of the
shield, skill of the lance or flight of the arrow, he will have
the intelligence of the Great Spirit and the cunning of the
fox.*

It came to Gray-Wolf in a flash. The only hope that
existed, it could free them or it could kill them all, but what
choice was there?

Joe pressed Charly's back, urging her forward. She
resisted, just a little, took the first step then another,
following Wu. Behind them Joe held up Manuel as they
entered the building and descended the stairs followed by
the five men. At the last step, one of the teenagers shoved
Manuel, a hard driving punch in the small of his back. The
Mexican slipped out of Joe's supporting arm and went
down with a noise like a wet cement bag hitting the floor.
He laid a few feet from the last step as Charly rushed to
him, holding him by the shoulder. Joe moved toward them,
but the squat man with the steel bar poked him in the chest.
He poked him again, only this time it was Gray-Wolf who
responded.

In fragments of a fractured second, Gray-Wolf absorbed
the scene, the battlefield. The squat teenager in front of him
raised the iron bar, this time for a hard, killing blow. A gold
tooth with an inscribed initial shone among the gleaming
white mouth in a face like black hardscrabble. The eyes
glowed with a primitive hard-edged light. Behind him,
congregated at the foot of the pocked cement steps, Manuel
laid on the ground with Charly next to him and Wu and
Mai-Lin standing on either side. On the last step, blocking
any exit, the tall man stood with the bat held over his
shoulder and both hands on the grip. The other three were
in a semi-circle, blades and sharpened bicycle chains in
their hands. In the corner near the stairs, flames jumped
inside a fifty-gallon drum, fueled by a dozen two by fours
protruding from the open mouth of the smoking barrel.

A whooping noise erupted from the depth of Gray-Wolf's
body, a great war-cry of the Eastern Tribes, as instinctive as

ancestral memory. At the same time he launched a football kick. The straight-legged high thrust rode with the war cry. The loud whoop bounced off the concrete walls and Gray-Wolf's foot connected solidly between the surprised hoodlum's legs. There was a noise like a suddenly punctured tire, a rush of expelled air and the man fell to the floor, bent in two, both hands holding his crotch.

The surprise didn't last long. Much as Joe's spirit had taken the mantle of Gray-Wolf, the warrior, his body had not followed that path. He had no fighting experience and no instructions beyond basic training in a three-year tour of a peacetime army. His four remaining foes however, had been battle tested continuously almost from birth. Darwin's laws applied in the hard slums of Brooklyn as much as on the south-seas archipelagos the famous scientist had studied. Gray-Wolf faced the product of evolution in the ghetto. Survival of the fittest had turned into survival of the deadliest misfits.

The tall teenager just about flew from the step, the baseball bat whistling in a vicious arc at Gray-Wolf's head. Joe ducked and partially deflected the weapon. The bat caught him part shoulder-part upper arm and glanced off the side of his head. Flashes erupted in Gray-Wolf's eyes, his arm went numb his legs gave out and he fell. He tried to get up, propping himself on the arm as he faced his standing opponent, but the arm gave out and he slid to the floor again. He became dimly aware of the other men moving and surrounding him like predatory jackals, the knives gleaming fangs in search of blood. He half raised himself again and saw the tall teenager three feet in front of him.

He raiseed the bat to deliver a skull crushing, killing hit. The knives and chains would finish whatever remained.

CHAPTER 44

The Maarzuk hunted all day. It had crossed the medium of water to the other bank of earth and concrete. Following the Sylvan's imperative, unable to do anything else until its hunger reached such voracious longing that it would be forced to hunt any sentient being unfortunate enough to somehow be in its underground path. The day's killing in the subways of Manhattan provided some immediate satisfaction and the building hunger had not yet reached its crescendo. So it kept on hunting the five humans. It sensed them on gossamer wisps of psychic feelers reaching above the ground where it could never venture. It followed their path, dogged their footsteps, waiting, sniffing them out like a dog seeking a buried luscious bone. Nuclear synapses on a level yet unknown to human science snapped and hummed as it sensed the humans it wanted, sensed them descending into a lower level, a reachable level beneath the earth. As the very fabric of its atoms surged upward, it projected out the human equivalent of a delighted hand clap. They had entered its realm and along with them they had brought five more humans. Nine life forces to destroy, absorb their psychic energies as their lives ended in eruptions of agony. It flowed and spread on the underside of the great concrete slab.

The building had been constructed in the twenties, in the years of New York City's Tammany Hall, one of the most corrupt government organizations the United States had ever spawned. This building had been the showcase. Bribes and kickbacks and favors had flowed like wine at an Italian wedding. The building was a model of construction made with huge amounts of the highest quality concrete, bricks, mortar and steel. Investors had inspected every square inch and their hired engineers had probed all the crevices and nooks and crannies. It was one of the best-constructed buildings in all of the Big Apple. Of course, after the millions from investors and buyers had started to flow into the coffers, everything changed. The buildings sprung all around like mushrooms in a field after the rain. Oh they looked like the first one all right, but the materials and constructions had been cheap and inferior. Now, eighty years later, they had all crumbled with the accelerated decay of things that are shoddy and inadequate. But the original had stood, strong in this wasted neighborhood. Its upper structures had been devoured by fire and human predators, but nothing could touch its foundation, its base of massive reinforced concrete. Nothing that is, until the Maarzukk came.

Under the ground a black smoky silver-tipped cloud of sentient atomic particles covered the underside of the concrete in unimaginable trillions. It flowed and probed until it found the weakness; a settling crack in the remote corner. It flowed into the fissure, re-arranged itself over and over, hundreds of time in split seconds until it suddenly expanded and pushed with irresistible pressure at the exact weak spot.

Gray-Wolf expected death in the next moment. His only hope had failed. Or had it?

His nostrils filled with the cloying scent of sulfur and almonds. Across the room at the foot of the stairs, the huddled group guarded by a teenager wielding a foot long hunting knife, had smelled it also.

"Oh God, oh please," Charly whispered.

The man standing over Gray-Wolf had reached the upward travel of the bat so it would come down with maximum killing power. Before the weapon started its life-ending stroke, the corner of the wide basement exploded.

Chunks of concrete flew out, hitting what was left of the upper floor, sending debris flying out into the night. A whirling cloud of madness, black and smoky, onyx living fog tipped with silver edges that shifted states of matter like insects flickering in headlights. It flowed and whirled and swirled across the room. The startled squat teenager with the knife swung in a helpless gesture. It was not a gesture of defense for nothing could defend against the Maarzuk. It was an instinctive shielding, like putting up your arms when someone throws something at you. Silver tentacles became solid as steel blades, slashing sideways, upward and downward, through the man's neck, through the left arm and down mid torso. A hint of a cry immediately choked off as a fountain of blood sprung and erupted and soaked in the surrounding concrete.

This time, the little group's reflexes served them well, perhaps because they knew the nature of what they faced. As the four remaining gang members bolted toward the steps, Joe stood and grabbed the end of a two by four from the burning barrel. He threw the flaming torch into the moving cloud.

Waves of violent rage and alien frustration reached their mind, dug into their very core, but it was all the time they needed as the creature retreated from the light emitting flames. Gray-Wolf pulled up Manuel and they bounded up the stairs behind the four fleeing hoodlums. The stench of sulfur and almonds laced with spilt blood and human intestines followed them as they reached the top of the stairs and collapsed on the sidewalk under the open night sky of the city.

CHAPTER 45

They picked themselves up, slowly, savoring their aches, for pain meant they were still alive and that was a marvel, considering everything that had happened.

They moved on as quickly as they could. Joe feared their assailants would return once they got over the shock. They moved slowly, hampered by Manuel who passed in and out of consciousness and had to be carried half the time. Joe doubted they could have gone much faster anyway because of Wu. The older Chinese swayed with fatigue and stumbled like a man trying to find his way home from an all-night drunk.

They hadn't gone more than a few hundred feet before Joe heard running steps behind him. He turned and saw four men, shadowy troll-like figures under the sporadic streetlights. They were closing in fast on two hundred dollars, drug profit-bought sneakers.

"Shit. In here, quick for heaven's sake," Joe said as he hustled them into one of the alleys that ran like noxious abysses between the buildings.

They only went a few feet before encountering a courtyard wall. They were in a dead-end and to make matters worse, one of the few surviving building nightlights worked. The bulb may have been a dim wattage but it was enough to make them very visible from the street.

The four men reached the alley, saw them and walked in, abreast, blocking any chance of escape. Joe recognized the tall teenager, the leader. He had lost the baseball bat. Instead, he held a homemade ice pick, a two foot long steel rod embedded in a knife handle and sharpened to a blood curdling point, a sort of ghetto Samurai sword.

"You muffuckers got Jamal wasted. I'm gonna stick you so many times yo mamma ain't ever be able to identify your ass," he said. Painful death sparkled and danced in their eyes as the men advanced on the group huddled against the alley wall.

An explosion roared directly behind the advancing men. A tongue of flame and sparks swept inches over their heads. Brick and concrete and even a piece of the steel fire escape ladder flew in all directions as thirty or forty double O pellets struck the building just a few miles per hour short of supersonic speed.

Joe and the rest of the group covered their heads. The men fell to the ground in a crouch. The leader stood up again, and slowly turned around.

"What the fuck man…Who you?…You know who we be?…You gonna be one dead brother soon…"

Joe stood. He saw the man who stepped in the mouth of the alley. Big, and at least five inches taller than the gang leader, he was the blackest man Joe had ever seen. His face shining like Kentucky coal, highlighting a pink/white scar running from the left eye beneath the shaved skull to the tip of his jaw. The scar indented midway at cheek level giving it a zigzag like a bolt of lightning across the broad features. Muscles surged and boiled under a tight black sweater topped by a Roman collar surrounding a massive neck. A stainless steel chain dangled loosely around his neck, weighted down by a cross big enough to hang on a church wall.

The newcomer took a few steps forward. He moved like

a sedate jungle tiger, power lurking beneath the surface, ready to explode when needed. His large hands held a shotgun sporting the biggest barrel Joe had ever seen. The stock of the weapon had been carved and whittled into a single grip that fit the big man's hand like a Mario Andretti racing glove. His other hand became a blur as he pumped the shotgun. The empty shell ejected, landing at the gang leader's feet. A clank of smoothly operating machinery told of another round chambered and ready.

"I am the mighty hand of the Lord God," the man said. His voice erupted in thundering rumbles, a gravelly tone releasing the clear sentence like an exploding rocket. Each word dripped with the inflections of the deep South, the hill countries of Georgia and Alabama.

The gang leader tried to maintain the ghetto's swagger, the mantle of bravado.

"Hey brother, we ain't got no beef with you. If you knew who we is, you wouldn't…"

The man swung the shotgun so it pointed just four very short feet from the leader's head as he spoke again.

"Ah know exactly who you are. Yo'all are spawns of the angel of the bottomless pit, whose name in the Hebrew tongue is Abadon, the Devil. Yo'all should be concerned about who *Ah* am, the mighty avenging arm of Jesus Our Savior, carrying his ten gauge flaming sword. You got about a second to git, fore that sword sends you four heathens to your judgment."

Looking down the dark tunnel of the bore of a weapon like a ten gauge shotgun, all cocked and loaded, can change someone's perspective pretty dramatically. Joe saw the tall man with the ice pick, retrograde from swaggering gang leader, to teenager to child to pleading baby. Only bowel liquefying fear and the instinct to run remained. Ice-pick, chains and knives clattered as the four teenagers ran like an evil wind. The man lowered the fearsome shotgun and walked until he stood a couple of feet in front of Joe and his huddled group.

"I'll be jumped up and down if yo'all ain't the sorriest beat up group ah seen in a dog's age," he said, "yo'all don't know how lucky ya be ah caught up with you when ah did."

"I got a pretty good idea," said Joe as he helped Charly and Wu to their feet. Mai-Lin stood, staring fixedly at the man. Manuel stayed down but his eyes were wide and staring.

"This is Charly," said Joe as he pointed at each one in turn, "Manuel, Doctor Wu, Mai-Lin and I'm…I'm…"

"S'okay, take your time," said the man as his face stretched in a smile, an explosion of big white teeth, dancing eyes and a long flashing scar set in deep ebony.

Joe nodded, grinned and replied.

"Joseph Gray-Wolf of the Shinnecock Nation. Maybe now you can answer the question that thug asked: who are you?"

"A servant of God, humbly trying to do the bidding of Jesus Christ our Savior. Ahm the Right Reverend, Jedediah Mosely-Wilson. Mah momma believed two last names meant royalty so she added Wilson later. She got it from a basketball in a schoolyard in Atlanta, may God rest her soul. Now ah don't rightly mean to hurry you good folks, but those were Cripps and they don't take kindly to even me barging on their turf. They's coming back with lots of re-enforcements, sure as rain. We needs to move now."

He picked up Manuel and slung him over his shoulder in a fireman's carry as if the two hundred pound Mexican was a throw pillow. Charly and Joe picked up Wu between them and followed the big man's long strides, struggling to keep up. Mai-Lin trotted silently between them. They walked like that through blocks of seemingly deserted streets while unseen eyes followed them in the gloomy patches of darkness between the few operating streetlights. When they crossed a wide avenue, the big man's pace slowed and his demeanor relaxed, while the shotgun still dangled loosely from his hand.

"You walk around with that cannon all the time?" Joe asked.

"Mostly when the Lord sends me to rescue his sheep."

"Don't the police bother you about that?"

Jedediah's laugh echoed off the buildings and parked cars as he replied.

"The po-lice don't never come here. Nine-one-one ain't in their vocabulary for this neighborhood. They's figure, the more we kill each other, the better off they be."

Joe tensed as they passed a parked car. A young man who could have been a twin of the four they escaped, except for different color bandannas, sat on the hood. Three more were inside the car. Sticky sweet odors of marijuana drifted from the open window and a silver pistol barrel gleamed from dark jeweled hands inside the car. Jedediah and the man on the hood exchanged terse greetings.

"Sup"

"Yo"

"Yo'all can relax, we safe now," explained Jedediah, "The Bloods and the Cripps, they control everything, drugs, whores, even took the numbers from the old wops after the FBI took most of the big Mafiosi's down. Trouble is, there's major problems between the two gangs. Mah church and me, we's got an arrangement with the Bloods. I done'em a few favors, patched up some of their wounded and such. Because of that, they leaves me alone, even extends some protection if it don't cost them much," he paused, stopping against a corner building, "not that ah need a whole lotta protection as you can see."

They stopped under a steel cover adorning the storefront of the corner building. A solitary bulb, high over the awning and protected in a glass cage like a small zoo animal, cast a wide circle of light around the three story building. Under the awning, the storefront was lit from within by a single neon tube. A white sheet held by thumbtacks prevented any view of the interior. Large hand-painted dark red letters surrounded a big cross made of black contact paper, occupied most of the glass. Bars of thick steel crisscrossed the window, rendering it into square foot sections. Joe read the message behind the bars.

FEED MY SHEEP MINISTRIES
FIRST AFRICAN CHURCH OF GOD OF THE DIVINE REDEMPTION

"Be it ever so humble," said Jedediah, "You lucky white folks are going to be guests in the holy house of the Lord tonight. Probly do yo souls a whole lotta good."

He knocked on the metal covered door, great pounding knocks. A moment later there was a fumbling behind the door and a steel bolt slid back from a tiny peephole. A few seconds of silence followed by muted clattering and rattling until the door opened revealing a large black woman in a small front room behind the sheet-covered window. Her face stretched in a wide smile as she opened the door and they all came in. The woman closed the door and threw a series of deadbolts, chains and locks behind them.

CHAPTER 46

"Hey Mabel, we got us some more guests for tonight," Reverend Jedediah Mosely-Wilson said to the smiling woman. He put down Manuel who tried to stand and immediately collapsed on his bloody leg with a groan of pain.

"Damnation, don't try to stand on that shot up leg," Jedediah said, "Mabel, go fetch up some help and take this man to my office. Git Doc Jefferson, he should be sleeping upstairs right about now."

The woman came back with two old men following her, and they carried Manuel up a set of creaking worn steps.

"He ain't a real doc," Jedediah said, "but he's real close. He's a former paramedic and right now he's on the wagon. Bout the best we gonna do this time of night around here."

The woman came back down a few minutes later and spoke to Jedediah.

"Doc's got him now," she said, "We should know how he is in a little while."

"Praise the Lord," replied Jedediah, "now we need to fix our guests up for the night."

"Yes," the woman replied, a touch of the Caribbean, or maybe the West Indies in her voice, "I see you found your rescuees. Still got some stew left, and coffee's on. Beds for tonight won't be a problem. Tomorrow might be a bit tight, getting farther away from payday."

"We feed and give shelter to the needy," explained Jedediah, "round here that includes most people. Iff'n you gotta job, it usually don't pay enough to cover a whole week's worth of rent. Most of the rooms are paid by the day and whatever paycheck there is don't last from one payday to the next. Our patrons are usually too weak to take their chances with the squatters, junkies and predators, like the ones you met tonight. And then there's our regulars. They's mostly women with kids, sick or old people. We're their only refuge so attendance goes up comes the end of the week. I reckon we's one of the thousand points of light George Bush, the first one, talked about."

Jedediah led them in the second room, a big hall stretching the remaining length of the building. As they followed him toward the rear, he kept a running commentary of explanations, pointing here and there like the curator of a vast estate entertaining important guests. But no curator in the world could have matched the quiet dignity and strength of the Right Reverend Jedediah Mosely-Wilson. His drawling, rolling baritone oozed with pride and quiet humility while fairly bubbling with enthusiasm. Joe realized the man had reached something reserved for a very select few. He found his true calling and embraced it with the strength of a great black bear. Joe envied him.

Tables, benches and chairs of all kinds filled most of the room. Whatever had been manufactured and eventually discarded, the Feed My Sheep Ministries dragged in and painstakingly repaired. Crates, two by fours, even several lashed-together bamboo's, gotten from God knows where, served as legs, sometimes for tables and benches at once. One corner of the large room was set up as a kitchen where rows of pots, pans and various utensils hung from hooks dangling out of the walls. Cardboard boxes filled with plastic forks and spoons and Styrofoam plates shared space with assortments of canned foods under a long serving table. A big single pot simmered on the stove and a tall coffee urn sat on the end of the table with a red eyed bulb winking on its bent front, indicating available coffee. Everything was dented, dinged and used, but it practically glowed with cleanliness a hair short of fanatic. About two dozen people sat around the tables, sipping coffee out of paper cups. They were mostly older, with a sprinkling of younger women, some of them pregnant. Here and there a haggard young man or woman bore the haunted face of someone fighting desperately one of the many virulent addictions that infested the ghetto like a medieval plague. A dozen, maybe more, children ran, busy at play or sitting engrossed in some overused game or coloring book. Except for the children, yet untouched, all bore the damage of grinding year after year of blinding suffocating poverty.

Jedediah moved among them like a fairytale benevolent despot. He greeted most by name with a "yo," "hey," or "wassup?" Occasionally he paused at a new face, extracting their names and origins, and perhaps a sense of their problems as well. He doled out high fives to the kids, two handed shakes to the older people, their hand between his great paws as if transferring a double dose of toughness to his temporary charges. He exuded hope and strength out of every pore.

Joe and Charly's respect for the self-styled preacher cranked up through the roof as they saw his accomplishments all around. *Especially* Joe thought, *with the kind of budget he must have*. The man was a veritable Brooklyn Mother Theresa, spreading goodwill from a huge heart and protecting it with guns and muscles.

He led them to an empty table toward the corner kitchen where they helped themselves to plastic bowls heaped with stew. Someone placed a loaf of donated day-old Wonder bread (helps build bodies nine ways) and half a stick of butter on the table.

Joe didn't realize how hungry they all were until they started eating. All they consumed this day was a late morning hot-dog and gallons of adrenaline.

As they ate, Charly pointed to the large cross hanging from Jedediah's neck.

"So Reverend," she asked him, "Catholic are you?"

He laughed, a great booming cheery sound like a ghetto Santa Claus. The zigzag scar danced white and pink on midnight black.

"Call me Jed, but let me ask you little gal, do ah look Italian, like a pope maybe? Ahm whatchu call non-denominational. This here cross ain't but a symbol. It stands for Jesus, the Father, Jehovah, Allah, whatever name you apply to the great power, the lord thy God. Whatever name you choose to call Him, that's who ah follow."

Jedediah paused as two little girls, maybe six or seven, came up to him holding a doll carriage donated from some toy drive, its axle and wheel bent. He said something to the girls, got up and pulled some pliers from the kitchen drawers and returned to the table. He started fixing the carriage while everyone watched him work like a surgeon in the operating theatre. His big hands straightened the little axle as he resumed speaking.

"Looka hear, when you look at me, you see a man with a burden, a burden ah will carry all mah days until the Lord calls me for His final reckoning. Ya see, ah was a bad man. A great rage and evil will burned inside me. Ah spent most of my teenage years in juvenile institutions. Back then in Georgia, probably still are, juvenile institutions weren't nothing but a breeding ground for abuse, violence and criminal training. Ah began my graduate course when they released me at nineteen. They got me a job as a dishwasher. Ah lasted for three days until the owner, a mean ole white cracker, put his hands on my young ass. Ah busted a luminen pot over his head and got me a new job. This new job paid enough to get me new clothes, a nice pad upstairs from a bar filled every night with fine young foxes and a shiny red Oldsmobile convertible 442."

Jedediah stopped to put down the carriage. The girls watched him with grave eyes that filled their faces like a full moon in a desert sky. They mumbled barely audible

"Thank you Reverend Jed" and wheeled the little carriage away as they inspected its renewed workings. At that age, doll carriages can be very serious business.

"Must have been a hell of a job," Charly said.

"That it was little gal," replied Jedediah, his eyes traveling around the table as they watched him, "A hell spawned job. Y'see, ah was big with steel muscles and very good with mah fists, even better with a knife. Part of my curriculum in the juvenile homes. Mah employer was the kingpin Skag, Heroin dealer between Atlanta, Rome and Augusta. Most of his customers were combination users and small dealers. Mah employer extended credit at five percent a week. Every so often, someone didn't pay or just skipped out with the dope. When that happened, the bone cracker went after you. That was me, ah was the bone cracker. They give me that name when ah busted the arms of five brothers in mah first week. Ah'd feint like this," Jedediah's forearm and fists flashed across the table like black clubs as he spoke, "when they'd put up their arm to block ah'd catch it with cross strikes. Break the forearm every time. They'd always pay the money before mah next visit. That week there was an epidemic of armed robberies from guys with bandaged forearms, anything to get that money. Payments went up across the board for mah employer. He was so happy with me, mah first weeks pay and bonus was three thousand dollars. Never saw so much money in mah whole life."

Jedediah paused, looked down at the table for a moment as they watched him. Joe noticed Mai-Lin's stare, her eyes steady, locked on Jedediah. Something very un-childlike peered out from the unblinking orbs, something that watched and judged as Jedediah continued.

"It went fine that way for a while. Word gets around real fast. Pay up, don't let the bone cracker come after you. Yeah, it went fine for a while, until ah killed a man. He was even bigger than me, twice as mean and filled with hate to the top of his head. He had the money, he just didn't pay so's the bone cracker would come after him. He wanted

Patrick Astre

mah reputation and mah employer's territory. That boy was fast. Couldn't break his arm, that's for sure. He come up with his prison shank, a straight edge razor latched into a wood handle. Carved mah face like a Halloween pumpkin in about two seconds. That's where ah got this."

He traced the lightening scar that zigzagged the length of his face as he spoke.

"It sure wasn't no birthmark. Ah was down on the ground and that boy was goin' for my throat, jumped right on me. Ah don't remember how ah did it, but ah managed to stab him afore he killed me. Stabbed him through the heart, oh Lord forgive me, took a life against almighty God's first law."

"But it was self defense."

"Yeah, that's what the court said, that's why ah only got a dime, ten years at hard labor. But ah don't sees it that way a-tall. Y'see, ah didn't have to go after that boy, didn't have to be doin what ah was doin. You could say he was self-defensing against me. His killing weighs on me. Ah carries his soul as my burden."

"Then you found religion?"

"There's an old saying, when the pupil is ready, the teacher will appear. At that point, ah was ready and the teacher appeared."

He paused as voices were raised at a table in the middle of the hall. He stared at the two men arguing. Joe thought he was like a great black Doberman ready to pounce on anything that invaded his territory. Mabel walked over and talked to the two men and things just quieted down as Jedediah continued.

"Mah teacher's name was Alizir Khan-23, a minister of the Nation of Islam, a Black Muslin doin life. He opened my eyes to the glory of God and his grand purpose. Ah came to understand that everything that had happened to me, happened for a reason so ah could do His great work. Under his teachings ah devoured all the books on religion in the library, ah studied the Bible and the Koran and their various interpretations. When ah was released on parole six years later, ah had the equivalent of a college education on theology as fine as could be found in any seminary. Ah also knew the path God wanted me to walk. He wanted me to help his children, them that cain't feed themselves, protect themselves against the wolves or shelter themselves from the storm. That's what ah'll be doin till the day ah die, right here in this place or a place like this. We ain't goin to run out of them that's for sure. So you see when the Catholics and their Christian offshoots get all fired up about things like the Vatican or what happened two thousand years ago, or no birth control, when the Jews carry on about bondage to the Pharaos and the fate of Israel, when the Muslims study the Koran to figure out what the prophets were saying and pilgrimage to Mecca, all that's not real for me. Mah reality is right here." He continued, his hand sweeping across the big room, "None of those ideas mean anything in a place where babies are born addicted to crack from their mothers, where children have to sleep on the floor away from windows because of stray bullets. Where the main hero is the local drug dealer flashing gold chains, silver pistols and new cars, where almost a third of the young males die by violence and the girls are putting out on the streets for nickel bags of dope afore their fourteenth birthday."

Jedediah leaned back in the creaking chair. He sighed heavily as he pulled a cigarette from a beat up pack, lit it and blew a great cloud of blue smoke toward the ceiling. He looked at Charly, Joe and Mai-Lin each in turn, his eyes wide open and serious like an appraiser of antiques contemplating a Louis WI piece. Dr Wu silently got up from the table and wandered away in the room.

"Now it's your turn," Jedediah said, "What's goin on that brought yo'all to this place?"

Neither of them said anything at first. Charly looked at Joe who gave a slight shrug of his shoulder. Finally she answered.

"Well, I guess you know there's been some trouble in the city, and uh, we were just trying to get away."

"Looka hear gal, ah been round long enough to know when someone's pissing in mah boots n'trying to tell me it's a rainstorm. Ah got a pretty gal, about as white as they come, an Indian who looks like a WASP accountant, a shot-up Latino, an old Chinese guy and a mysterious little Miss who don't talk. Yo'all just *happened* to get together and decide the safest way out is through New York's worst slum. You want to try that answer again gal?"

"There's not much point in that," Joe cut in, "You wouldn't believe it anyhow."

Jedediah stubbed out the cigarette in one of the plastic dishes. He stroked his face once, his hand following the long scar. He leaned forward, his eyes flicked back and forth between Charly and Joe. Now his voice became a whisper, a conveyance of things strange and secret.

"Try me. Y'see, one of the teachings ah never believed in was the Devil. Ah never thought ole' Satan existed. Always believed there was enough evil right here in front of us, didn't need any Beelzebub. But tonight, this very night, ah saw the horned one, the fallen angel."

He leaned back in his chair again and this time both Joe and Charly strained forward to catch each whispered word.

"Only he wasn't wearing no cape," continued Jedediah, "wasn't carrying no pitchfork and didn't have no horns. Oh no, none of that. Instead he came bursting out of the ground, up from the bowels of hell. He took the shape of a black cloud with silver edges and slashing swords that cut a man to pieces in seconds, a devil driven back by a burning torch from a brave man."

"But… how… how did you know? We were alone in that blasted building." Joe said.

"Yo'all *thought* you were alone. Ah was up at the top of them stairs, in the shadows where neither you nor them gangbangers could see. Ah was just getting ready to jump in and get you out, I'd been following behind them bad boys."

"But how did you know to find us and follow us?" Charly asked, "And please, don't say God told you."

Now Jedediah laughed, a great rolling belly laugh.

"Well, for starters, yo'all blend in like me and a couple of homeboys at Mrs. Rockefeller's debutante ball at the Four Seasons Country Club in Westchester. Ah mean you stand out around here. Word got to me pretty fast. In fact, ah got a grapevine system that would put to shame them Tom-Tom drums, white movies about Africa are always showing. And yeah, ah'm gone tell you, something said to me you'd need help. That part wasn't too hard to figure out, but that something also said ah was the only one round here who could do it. That wasn't hard to figger out either."

Charly suddenly reached across the narrow table and rested her hand on Jedediah's, like a soft white pebble on hard granite. She gave it a squeeze and whispered a gentle "thank you."

"We owe you our lives," Joe said, "All of us."

"Wasn't nothing," replied Jedediah with a shrug, "Now if you'll s'cuse, me ah got to check on mah guests and get'em settled for lights out."

The house held three floors, the second one being the main dormitory with the overflow of "guests" placed downstairs, or, on those really crowded days, in the cramped attic rooms that served as offices and storage to the Feed My Sheep Ministries. Tables were pushed back, mattresses laid out on cots or the floors as Jedediah and Mabel assigned spots, dispensed medication where needed, and tended to all the details required to safely host three or four dozen refugees for the night.

In the midst of the slowly winding-down confusion and clatter, a man came down the far steps. He was tall and skinny to the point of emaciation. He had the look of someone who had ridden the bottle all the way to the bottom and stayed there a while. Sharp bony corners filled his face, and hair, thin and almost orange, covered a patchy black and tan skull. He looked around, spotted Joe and Charly and walked to their table. When he spoke, it seemed as if he borrowed the voice, smooth and well modulated, the essence of the doctor explaining the condition of a beloved family member.

"I believe you must be Joe and Charly," the man said, "Manuel told me you'd be here."

"How's he doing?"

"He'll be fine. The bullet passed through mostly muscles. Very painful but not dangerous if treated properly. I cleaned and dressed the wound and applied sutures, pumped him with top shelf antibiotic and pain killers. Everything here seems on its last leg but don't let appearances fool you. The Reverend has medical supplies that rival any clinics in this neighborhood."

"Should we get him to a hospital?" Joe asked.

"It's not necessary, in fact, he's probably better off here, especially with everything that happened around this city today. I heard a dozen people died in Bellevue, in the hallways, awaiting triage. A week or so here and he'll be ready to fend for himself again."

"Will you be…I mean, are you going to stay that long?"

The man smiled, "Yes. I tend to drink a bit when I'm outside on my own. Here, I help the Reverend by running the equivalent of a mini-medical center. It's about all some of these people have. In return, the Reverend helps me with my own demons. It's a good arrangement. I'll be here longer than your friend needs."

CHAPTER 47

After the medic left, Joe opened the envelope TR had given Manuel as they were being shot at. Smudges of blood dried to black cloudy prints decorated the brown paper. He stared at the envelope for a while. The worst part, Joe thought, was the lack of information, not knowing if his brother survived or how badly he had been hurt. He worried every moment, the thought of his brother in an ICU ward, in a coma, dying or dead, haunted Joe, overshadowing his every thought.

He opened the two folded sheets of FAX paper and began reading. When he finished, he read it again. Charly came back to the table and sat next to him, her arm around his waist as he put the papers down. He felt the grinding of his teeth as each angry word squeezed out of his mouth.

"Son of a bitch, that son of a bitch, he set this up," Joe said, "He lied every step of the way. He used me."

"Joe, what are you talking about? What's in those papers?"

"Did you wonder about all the shit we went through, about how somebody or something dogged our every step. It wasn't enough for those Sylvans and that creature to stalk us, but how about the other killers? Those thugs with their machine guns who killed the detectives my brother sent to help us. How did they know we would be there? And how about that sniper who shot TR and Manuel? You think that's a coincidence? You remember that guy I told you about? His name is Duncan Wesley and he helped me escape, told me I was supposed to get this Amulet to Central Park, that it was supposed to be a holy object for them. He told me how to escape, told me about that bookstore where I met you and said the only way I could be free was to find Dr. Wu."

"Well here, read this."

He handed her the papers.

The top quarter of the first page served as a FAX cover. It proclaimed the information TOP SECRET under the National Defense Security Act, only to be sent over encrypted secured lines. It originated from the FBI central data office in Washington, eyes only for Special Agent Donohue, cleared for Top Secret, New York office:

Inquiry result, Individual: Wesley, Duncan.

Indicated individual currently third level Sub-Director National Security Agency. Assigned to project ARTIFACT as Director/Coordinator. Project originated Los Alamos Laboratory, New Mexico. Transferred two years ago to Brookhaven National Laboratory, Upton, Long Island, New York. Information on project ARTIFACT denied by NSA.

Individual Duncan Wesley born in UK, naturalized US citizen. Graduated West Point 1977. Served with Special Forces and 24th Infantry Division S-2, Intelligence. Left Army with rank of Major. Recruited by CIA in 1982. Sometime afterward transferred to NSA. Personnel file classified and denied. May only be opened with order from Justice Department.

Charly leaned toward Joe, her cheek resting on her hand, her head slightly cocked and frowning. She had found the women's shower. Her hair was still damp since the Feed My Sheep Ministries had no hair dryer. She had put on some light makeup and she smelled of soap and generic shampoo.

"But I thought you said he was being held by Sylvans in the Long Island Pine Barrens?"

"That's what he told me," Joe said, "Obviously the bastard lied when he gave me this amulet."

Joe reached in his shirt and pulled out the Amulet. He removed it from around his neck and they both examined it in silence. Charly stared at it as if her eyes could penetrate through the tightly woven plant materials, tiny carved bones and wood. She held it in her hand, hefting it gently up and down.

"You know," she said, "this thing is kind of heavy for something made out of dried weeds and stuff like that. There's got to be something heavier inside."

Joe took a small pen-knife from his jacket pocket. He held the amulet on the table and poked at it with the tiny steel blade. The tightly wound strands broke open with little snapping noises. Joe continued to dig and poke at the strange medallion as the crossed lengths fell off, each no more than two or three inches of intricately carved bone fragments and wood splinters. As the outer layer of the amulet came apart, a dull grey metallic surface was exposed. He continued worrying it until a disc the size of a quarter popped free among the litter of pieces of the dismantled amulet. Joe held the disc up and passed it to Charly.

"So much for the religious significance," she said, "but what the hell is that thing?"

"I think I know what it is. It would explain a lot," Joe said as he turned over the amulet, examining it like a jeweler about to repair an expensive Rolex watch. He brought it close to his left eye, squinting until he found what he was looking for. He inserted the tip of the blade in the tiny slit on the side of the disc. Small as the blade was, it was still too thick to fit in the slot. He twisted the tip back and forth as he held the disc.

"This is not going to be much harder than opening one of those Peconic Bay Little Neck clams," he told Charly.

Their heads touched as they both stared at the steel disc

and the tiny tip of blade twisting back and forth in Joe's hand.

"What kind of wine goes with that?" Charly said.

Joe stopped for a moment and turned his head so their faces were inches apart. He breathed in her clean fresh fragrance and noticed for the first time the small dimple at the corner of her mouth when she grinned.

"After what we went through, I'd even settle for Ripple."

He continued prying, forcing the blade through the small opening until the top cover of the disc suddenly popped off and landed on the table with a tiny metallic noise. Inside the disc was a packed labyrinth of miniature electronic components.

"What is that? How can Sylvans have something like that?" Charly said.

"They don't. Don't you see what happened? It's that bastard Wesley's doing. He's using me to get to Wu. As a bonus, he might get you and the others as well. He's tied in to them somehow. Dr. Wu and the rest of you are a threat to them. This is a tracking device. He's with the NSA, they have tons of sophisticated stuff like this."

"So all the time they knew where we were, that's how they tracked us in Chinatown and also ambushed us when we tried to meet TR."

"You got it," Joe said as he poked the knife in the innards of the device. He twisted and pushed the blade as tiny circuits came apart. A microchip and a battery, each about the size of a match head fell on the table. Little wires and tiny resistors broken and twisted stuck out of the ruined miniature gadget.

"Now find us, Wesley you bastard," Joe whispered.

As they both stared at the debris of the amulet, the main lights went out in the downstairs room. Mabel and two helpers had cleaned and put away the kitchen utensils. Smaller nightlights went on at each corner of the room. A half dozen or so people were already rolled up in sleeping bags and cots. Some slept upstairs where Jedediah settled down most of his charges for the night.

Joe and Charly went to a corner nightlight where she read the second part of the printout from TR.

Inquiry individual: Dr. Wu linked to Brookhaven National Lab. Reported missing eleven months ago. FBI and law enforcement agencies alerted nationwide due to classified and sensitive nature of research conducted. Physical characteristics and other details in search request NSA12991 from NSA to FBI. The following information is in addition to that bulletin and follow up bulletins.

Dr. Wu, full name Zhang Hai Wu. Graduated University of Kowloon, graduate studies University of Beijing. Doctorate Nuclear Physics in 1952. Married with only son born 1953. Member of Chinese Communist Party and Chairman Mao Council of Science for the People. Assigned to Khan Shu Pharmaceutical Development Laboratory (later identified by CIA as a major nuclear weapon development center.) Subject was instrumental in developing nuclear weapons and hydrogen fusion technology for the People's Republic of China. Went out of favor during the years of Cultural Revolution when his son was arrested in 1976 for plotting the return of the Gang of Four. Tried and found guilty of anti-revolutionary activities and treason. Wu's son was executed. Entire process lasted only forty-eight hour. Wu's wife was arrested and found to have nurtured her son's guilt by using the "Four Overdones." Over-indulgence, Over-caring, Over-protection and Over-interference. Wu's wife, nee Wang Xiao Jie, was sentenced to "Rehabilitation and Corrective Work Therapy" in the mines at the foot of Khafa Gumbaz, the Domes of Wrath Mountains on the edge of the great Taklaman Desert. Translation of *Taklamakan* is "go in, don't come out." Reported killed in mine car accident 52 days later. Dr. Wu was accused of practicing the "Four Olds." Old thoughts, Old habits, Old customs and Old ideas. Because of the importance of his research in nuclear weapons for the People's Army, sentence was never passed but from that day he was held as worker/prisoner at the Khan Shu research facility.

In 1979 he escaped by a complex (and still classified) CIA operation. Embittered and sworn enemy of the communist state, he became a naturalized US citizen and chief researcher in nuclear physics at Los Alamos Laboratory, New Mexico.

Dr. Wu is currently the world's leading authority on sub-atomic particles and radiation sciences. He pioneered and invented a new science of Nuclear Particle Alignment. Assigned Scientific Director of project Artifact thirty months ago.

Project transferred to Brookhaven National Laboratory twenty three months ago. Subject disappeared from BNL grounds without trace twelve months ago.

Subject never re-married and has no family in United States.

Joe and Charly looked at the far corner of the room. The small night-light cast a kind of electric moon-glow on a small figure lying on a canvas cot. Thin blanket over the lower half of her body, Mai-Lin resembled any young girl, sleeping peacefully after an exhausting day playing at a family picnic.

"Sooo..." said Charly, "if he has no family, who is that strange little lady?"

CHAPTER 48

The Right Reverend Jedediah Mosely-Wilson was a light sleeper. In fact, it could be said he didn't really sleep at night. While he gave all his resources, mental, physical and worldly, such as they were, to his mission, he kept a very little corner of time for himself. Seven days a week, he worked out with weights for one hour. Four days a week, he drove the ancient Ministries station wagon to a storefront Tae Kwon Do dojo where he practiced the martial art under the tutelage of a Korean master. Jedediah had followed this routine ever since he opened the Feed My Sheep Ministries in the worst slum New York offered. He embraced his workouts with fervor as strong as his religious belief, a routine that in itself had become its own holy grail for the self-styled and self-ordained minister. The physical exercises became more than just staying in shape. They were a focus point where evil energy, malignant temptations and doubts were banished through sweat, aching muscles and constant demanding repetitive movements. The workouts were Jedediah's personal therapies, more effective than any Park Avenue psychiatrist could ever be.

On days that carried particularly bad events, days where a previously rescued young addict had shown strength and promises of cures only to relapse and be found dead of overdoses of poison, the filthy syringe still imbedded in a collapsed vein on arms freckled with track marks, on days where he held a mother carrying the sorrow of the world, a mother racked with unspeakable grief whose baby had been killed in her crib by a stray bullet from the mean Brooklyn streets. On those days, Jedediah lifted the weights with muscle tearing efforts, lifted as if wrestling with the Devil. He attacked the heavy bags with kicks and punches thrown with such ferocity they threatened to tear the sawdust filled bags from their anchors in the ceiling, slammed the bags and padded punch board as if somehow the violent energy could be aimed and transferred, shattering and destroying the forces of misery that haunted and possessed Bedford-Stuyvesant.

After his morning workouts, Jedediah plunged back into the affairs of the Ministry. He instructed the volunteers that worked at the house and solved the numerous problems that descended like dirty summer rain. He drove throughout Brooklyn seeking donations, food, clothing, furniture, or anything that could be sold or bartered to finance the constant needs of his chosen flock. He caged donations from businesses, clubs and churches in the more affluent parts of Brooklyn.

There was a beat to the Ministry house, a rhythm of life that pulsed and rose and fell. Between the afternoon hours of three and six came a lull, a quiet space where nothing much happened. One or two volunteers rested, chatting, drinking coffee or playing cards with the "guests." Others cut vegetables and prepared other foodstuff for the evening's free meal for the hungry. Big soup pots simmered under gas flames and slabs of meat loaf or turkey, or on days when Jedediah had good fortune, roast beef, bubbled in slow cooking ovens. It was a quiet time where it seemed the forces of the great slum marshaled for the onslaught of mayhem that would ride the coming night.

During those brief hours, Jedediah rested. He would go upstairs to the cluttered office of the ministry, close the door and lay down on a wooden cot covered with a thin mattress donated from a used furniture store. He slept soundly for one, two or three hours, always waking up invigorated, and plunged back into the Ministry for its "rush hour."

When he finally turned in at night, after counseling, securing and settling his charges, he rarely slept more than a few hours. When he fell asleep his subconscious remained attuned to every creak, every shifting noise, every scratching or scuttling that went on, for the guests of the Ministry often brought the troubles of the harsh streets. It clung to them like burrs digging into sensitive flesh. Many an addict, unable to resist the lure of the crack B-rock in their pocket, many a thief, the desperate stealing from the needy, or maybe trying to settle a score from an obscure street dispute, those persons found themselves suddenly facing the Reverend, zigzag scar dancing and eyes holding a mixture of compassion and implacable strength. He was shepherd, comforter, savior, policeman and enforcer. Word went out on the street that you could always find refuge at the Feed My Sheep Ministries house, but you had best keep yourself straight and well behaved in there, for no one wanted to mess with Reverend Jed and his muscles and karate. Even the gang members respected the damage he could do with those kicks, ham-hock fists, flying club and as a last resort that customized alley-sweeper shotgun he carried at night.

And so later that evening, after the guests fell asleep, Jedediah's eyelids suddenly flew open. Something penetrated his wispy layer of sleep, something different from the snorting, snoring, shuffling noises of thirty or more people resting.

He barely moved as his head raised a few inches from the pillow, eyes darting throughout the great room, white iridescent orbs in the black shadowy face. Now he picked it up, a slight scuffing, soft as a night whisper. A hushed bent shadow passed among the sleepers, silent except for the occasional muted shuffling of bare foot or the tiny creak of a board.

Jedediah recognized the slight figure as it passed the nightlight and disappeared in the shadows of the stairwell. He heard the creak of the two middle steps that told him the figure climbed the steps. He got off the cot, the two-foot club that he slept with, attached to his belt. He moved to the stairwell on silent jungle-cat steps. Cautiously he peered up the stairs, his eyes adjusted to the gloomy shadows. The staircase ended into an oblique hallway. From the hallway came a white and greenish glow that illuminated the upstairs hallway where the figure had passed.

Slowly, his two hundred and twenty five pounds threading silently on the balls of his bare feet, avoiding the two creaking steps, Jedediah ascended the stairs and peered into the length of the upstairs hallway.

CHAPTER 49

<hr/>

Four thirty AM, Long Island Expressway, Exit 70

The Mercedes SUV slowed past the exit sign and stopped on the shoulders of the road. That part of the Long Island Expressway, the last twenty or so miles before it ends at the town of Riverhead, is a dark stretch of road. It is surrounded by Pine Barren forests, dotted here and there with patches of new home developments, a few strip malls and commercial centers sticking out of the woods like giant acne. Blending in with the forests, a few remaining farms sprawled out on flatlands, their potato, corn and strawberry fields, gentle throwbacks to earlier, less busy times.

But the driver of the SUV and his wife on the seat next to him didn't appreciate any of this. Sunrise was still two to three hours away and the expressway remained deserted. The headlamps threw out beams that were eaten by the darkness within fifty feet. Darker shadows of brush lands and trees rose around the roadway like thick hovering black spirits. The man and his wife felt as if they were half drugged. A smothering blanket covered their movements. They both experienced a sense of detachment with dulled senses as if they were outside of their bodies. The trip from Manhattan had been like watching a movie from the confine of their skulls. Roadblocks, checkpoints, State Police stops, all flashed by like scenes from a play. They participated, said the right words, did the right things and could never understand the tendrils of psychic energies that controlled those actions.

The rear compartment door of the SUV swung open. A night breeze passed through the vehicle carrying the rich scent of the pine forests and the acid tang of scrub oaks. A small shuddering movement passed through the vehicle as an unseen weight jumped from the rear compartment. The driver got out, walked to the rear and closed the back door. There was no conscious thought, no questioning, as if doors opening by themselves in the middle of the night along deserted highways was quite normal and simply had to be closed again. He got back in the front seat, rubbed his forehead and shut his eyes. His wife all ready slept. They would awaken a while later. The strange feelings and memories of the last few hours would overlay their brains like the sour covering on a tongue after a night of drinking.

After he left the SUV, the Sylvan crossed the Expressway and entered the woods on the north side of the road. He moved quickly, a scattered leaf or a few bent blades of grass the only testament to his passage. The large, luminous eyes took in available light like a cat's pupils. The night was his ally, his domain. The powerful brain emanated psychic waves that remained tied to him on gossamer strings of invisible energy. He sensed the gopher asleep underground, mice and rabbits in their burrows and the minds of humans in their dwellings among the woodlands and farms. A little farther west, near what the humans called Whiskey Road in Ridge, he sensed the emanations of others of his kind, the Sylvan tribe of the eastern Pine Barrens. He felt their dismay and the fear that ran through them like a swift underground current. His thoughts pulsed out to them, clear and powerful in the still night and he received their telepathic reply.

You have released the Maarzuk. It is an abomination that the Dreamsingers warned us about since the time of the Coming.

The Sylvan's answer came like an invisible night breeze:

It was necessary. Neither we nor the accomplice, were able to control the other humans. Our plan will fail if they are not contained. Our race will continue to dwindle until there are no Sylvans left.

They had all felt the great telepathic power, a malevolent energy that spread from its source under the ground of what the humans called Brooklyn. It widened, continuing like great waves in a lake where a boulder had been thrown, disturbing the still waters. It was a restless powerful energy, devouring and filled with ancient unspeakable hungers. The sensitive psychic response center of their brains felt the old awakened force across ninety miles as the Maarzuk waited for its human prey. The psychic reply from the pine barren Sylvan tribe was cast with concern.

How will the Maarzuk be put back to rest after it has accomplished what you set it to do? The old powers are gone. Not even the Dreamsingers have memories of the ancient time, the time of the coming when the Maarzuks were destroyed save for the one you have let loose.

The Sylvan's telepathic answer flashed across the dark miles:

There is the Maiglin. Her power is still nascent but will grow until it overshadows the strongest among us. There is the Accomplice. He will have to help us to retain his newly-found power. He will place the humans at our disposal. Their technology will surely vanquish the creature when the time comes. And most important, we will regain control of the planet as we were always meant to have.

But the pine barren Sylvan tribe did not share the same point of view as their brethren from Central Park. Their doubts filled and rode the waves of answering telepathy.

That is foolish. We have made a grave mistake. Ever since we saw the first humans using tools, we have hidden ourselves from them. Our mental powers have kept them unaware of our existence over the many centuries. Now, their machines have become so powerful, it is beyond our abilities to stop them. If they become aware of us, they will hunt us down. Our race will perish in an eye blink. You must stop immediately.

The answering thoughts brimmed with contempt.

You are weak as tadpoles in a pond. Your fears leave us all vulnerable. You fret and squeal like tiny birds abandoned in their nest. Our plan will not fail. Soon I will meet the Accomplice and the final step will be in place. We will push aside the humans and take our rightful place. They will truly be our servants as they were always meant to be, not just a few here and there so we can barely survive. Our power will be restored as in the great days of the Coming. The Maarzuk will be dealt with.

CHAPTER 50

Five thirty AM, Brookhaven national Laboratory

A few miles away at the Lab, Duncan Wesley awoke to the dusty smell of stored documents and office materials. The last few nights he had slept on a cot in the supply room of the Physics Building.

Fourteen to sixteen hours away, thought Wesley. That's the amount of time remaining before the realization of three years of planning. Since the start at Los Alamos to the transfer at Brookhaven National Lab, when he and Wu first realized the potential of the Artifact, a potential they had scrupulously kept to themselves. That is, until that gutless wonder Wu backed out and disappeared. Well, that was all right. Some things are meant to be. He didn't need Wu. He had contact with the Sylvan and he had that chicken shit Dr. Prabinwah to finish the work.

A perfect concept, Wesley thought as he remembered every word that Wu had spoken. He might be a bit fuzzy on the science of it, but that was okay. He understood enough to make it work.

They transferred the Artifact and the project to Brookhaven Lab to use the new science of Nuclear Alignment that would be blended with the sub-atomic particle experiments. That's when they discovered the

Sylvans, or maybe the Sylvans had discovered them. It really didn't matter.

According to Wu's theory, Sylvans were the descendants of an alien race that had somehow been marooned on Earth, or perhaps left behind deliberately, about ten thousand years ago. Experiments on the Artifact conducted at Los Alamos and later at Brookhaven National Lab, seemed to confirm this. Those same experiments led to the discovery of Sylvans by Wu and Duncan Wesley. Of course, this occurred before their disagreement. It had been a pretty fundamental disagreement and resulted in Wu fleeing to Chinatown with that creature from the lab, the one he called his daughter. Wesley remembered their last conversations when he complained to Wu about the snail-pace of progress on the Artifact project.

"Think of it this way," the elder Chinese scientist had said. "Suppose a modern F-16 somehow went back in time and crashed in Europe during the Middle Ages. Suppose some components survived intact, maybe the on-board computer, the Plexiglas pilot shield, wing sections, fuel tank, lights, how long do you think it would take them to figure out what it is, much less begin using it for their own purposes? A century? Maybe two or three? Well that's about where we are when you compare us to the technology of the Artifact. The Middle Ages, maybe even the Stone Age. The only thing we can say for sure at this point is that it's some form of intelligent communication device on a scale that we can't begin to fathom. Our research points toward direct brain-to-brain contact, unhampered by space or time. But there's something else we believe it could be."

"What?" Wesley had asked.

"A weapon."

But the work progressed nevertheless. When the Artifact radiation changed for the first time, when it had been charged with negative Ions and bombarded with sub-atomic particles, something happened. Something called out, emitting unknown radiation for nanoseconds.

Those nanoseconds had been enough time, sufficient to bring them in touch with the Sylvans. Wesley remembered that first contact. He had stepped outside and lit a cigarette when he felt it, a mental caress, tendrils of sentient *feelings,* somehow transformed into communication. They were drawn by the bursts of radiation, attracted like summer insects to a porch light. In moments Wesley understood better than anything he had ever realized before, like being on a higher plane of existence. Compared to his experiences with human communication, language and the written word, this was a whole new level. It was like trying to describe a picture to a group of people instead of passing around a photo.

He made a bargain with the Sylvan, the one he thought of as the most powerful one, who occupied Central Park in Manhattan. He recognized in that Sylvan a certain greed, a certain lust for power, for control. The recognitions of kindred spirit had been instantaneous on both sides even though they were different species. That was one thing with direct telepathy: There could never be deceit or subterfuge. And so what Wesley had called The Plan, was born. There had been no drawn out sessions, no reports or research, none was needed. Sylvan-Human telepathy bypassed all that. He brought Dr Wu into the plan, spoke to him and laid it all out.

Then the problems started. Wu balked at the collateral damage, called it inhuman and monstrous. But, in Wesley's eyes, it only revealed the fatal weakness of the scientist.

Wesley pictured the events to come in twelve to fourteen hours, the time it would take Dr. Prabinwah and his staff to complete the settings needed for the artifact to successfully undergo the nuclear alignment procedure. Moments afterward, the New Ion Accelerator would bombard the Artifact with a steady stream of sub-atomic particles.

Right now the Artifact was like an electronic device with a weak or dead battery. Its present capabilities were a shadow of its potential. The nuclear procedures Wesley directed would be like a jump start. They calculated an intense flash of radiation would be the first result. The initial burst would spread in concentric circles like radio waves. Unlike radio waves, the emanations from the ancient alien Artifact would not escape into space immediately. They would bounce off the Ionosphere then back to Earth and up and outward again. The radiation burst would circle the globe thousands of time at the speed of light, saturating everything on the surface of the planet before it dissipated. Following the initial burst, the artifact would settle into continuous pulsed radiation emissions. Those emissions would link the Sylvans, enhancing their mental powers, multiplying and channeling their psychic energy.

Wesley and the Sylvan, the one he had begun to think of as a kind of ruling partner, would control the mental process of the teeming billions of humans on the planet. He saw this as the ultimate power possible. Wesley, through the Sylvan's control, would command all human affairs. In return, he would cause human technology to be applied for the regeneration of the Sylvan race. Nations would rise and fall at his beckoning under his total domination. It would be absolute mind control with Wesley at the helm of the new human order. He would cut through the political infighting, the shallow and weak leadership of the ineffectual democracies that failed to realize his true worth. And that idiot Wu had shucked it away because of the collateral damage. *Just as well*, he thought, from now on, there's no room at the top for anyone else but Duncan Wesley and his Sylvan partner.

Somewhere in the hidden recess of his high IQ mind, Duncan Wesley must have perceived his actions as those of a sociopath. He refused to project thoughts and feelings toward other people. Compassion, kindness and regard for the welfare of others were hallmarks of weakness in his eyes. Only the strong and ruthless could ultimately rule. He shut himself away from suffering and wounded people because that's what the strong must do. A dead person to Wesley is either a problem to be disposed or an opportunity to gain an advantage. If they were not any of those things, then they were just so much dead meat.

Wesley understood the concept of collateral damage, it just didn't faze him a bit, in fact, he construed it as positive.

Wu had conducted numerous animal experiments at Los Alamos, exposing chimps to the unshielded radiations of the artifact with striking results. The presence of Serotonin, Dopamine, Adrenaline and other brain chemicals increased hundreds of time. Behavior changed dramatically with aggression and madness in the forefront.

Wu predicted the initial radiation burst would kill eight to ten percent of the global human population during the first twenty-four hour. Over the next few days, between forty to fifty percent more would die from violent, madness-induced conflict, before the magnified telepathic powers of the Sylvans could bring it under control.

That was fine with Duncan Wesley.

Scientist and politicians had debated for years about what to do with the world's overpopulation.

Tonight, he would solve that problem.

Duncan Wesley slipped the holster over his shoulder and placed a sleek automatic pistol inside. He donned a light jacket and stepped out of the storage room.

He walked into a large room with huge vaulted ceiling and metal sides large enough to be an airplane hangar. But the resemblance ended quickly. Within the room, like a surprise box within a box, the Artifact room was contained. Shielded steel doors flanked by thick leaded glass windows gave this area the appearance of a closed-mouth giant skeletal monster, an apparition suitable to populate nightmares. Wesley saw through one of the leaded-windows, a titanium table bolted to the concrete floor. On the table, a dark metal case held the Artifact and shielded its deadly emissions.

Another tube-like room stood at an angle to the Artifact room. A burnished metal tunnel connected the two chambers. Giant coils sprouted from the sides of the second room and disappeared into the floor. Thick power cables, broad as a man's thigh, looped around the room like massive Pythons crushing a victim. An array of junction boxes connected thousands of thin silver wires encompassing the room in giant metallic spider webs. At human eye level, banks of digital readout meters blinked out long sequences of numbers and letters. A half dozen computer terminals protruded from the lower end of the wall connecting all the vast gear in a snare of complex cyber-controls. In the remaining space, a dozen or so technicians worked at computer consoles, arranging and rearranging data in unfathomable sequences and structures. A low level hum permeated the room and seemed to come out of the very atmosphere. Smells of burnt ozone permeated the air like opening the inside of a fried television set. Bright white light from banks of fluorescent bulbs covered every square inch, permitting no shadows. Wesley felt the grit of the bare concrete floor reaching through the thin sole of his leather shoes as he crossed the room and poured himself a cup of coffee from a pot on a credenza. He walked toward the exit where two men dressed in black jumpsuits stood guard. The men radiated alertness and capability. Their jumpsuits had no insignias, and on their shoulders were affixed radio microphones. They each carried compact sub-machine guns with folding wire stocks. The men glanced at Wesley and nodded as he stepped outside.

The chilled October air caused vaporous clouds with every breath. The big building and grounds were bathed in light from powerful sodium arc lamps. Thick armored glass and wire cages protected the melon-size bulbs and their reflectors. As Wesley crossed the walkway to the street, two men passed at a slow walk. Their eyes shifted constantly to the surrounding shadowy buildings and woods. They carried assault rifles with curved magazines. On either end of the only road fronting the building, concrete barricades, each manned by three guards, blocked the entry. A black Jeep Cherokee, all its chrome stripped off, circled continuously around the building. The shadows of men and the barrels of more weapons showed through the open windows. In spite of their lack of insignias and markings, the guards had the look and movements of highly trained professional military.

Normal security at Brookhaven National Laboratory is usually lax. The armed Rent-a-Cops at the gate will waive almost anyone through who gives them some sort of credible purpose. Under Wesley's direction, the Nuclear Aligner project and the Ion Collider had been placed under special protective security. Wesley's assignment gave him enough latitude to handpick each guard from the CIA and NSA field operations division.

The strolling guards noted Wesley and ignored him as he crossed the street and stepped into the gloomy area between the blazing light of the building and the dark forest that bordered it. He leaned against the tree and looked to the East where the faintest lightening of the black sky hinted at the coming dawn. Moisture and the smell of autumn oaks and pine filled the air. The surrounding woodland was so still that he clearly heard every cricket chirping and the hum of the motor of the Jeep Cherokee patrolling a hundred feet away. He lit a cigarette, inhaled deeply and stared into the impenetrable blackness of the forest.

It came softly, perhaps so as not to startle him. Sure and steady, it carried the feel of alien strength and muted power. As the Sylvan's telepathic probe found and entered the receptor pathways of Wesley's mind, pictures and images flashed with incredible speed. Synapses and nerves in his cerebellum, received information bits at the velocity of light and translated them into terms his conscious mind understood.

Is all in readiness?

The Sylvan's probe carried a hint of anxiety, something Wesley had never experienced. He silently sub vocalized his reply. The Sylvan picked up the meaning from the confines of the human brain.

The event is one half day, or less, away. Before the end of

Patrick Astre

the next night, we will hold the power. I have lost track of our troublesome people. Have you been able to stop them?

The Sylvan's reply came instantly.

No. But it will be very soon. The Maarzuk cannot be held back. Sooner or later they will fall into its clutches.

A wave of repulsive alien feelings accompanied the blurred image of the Maarzuk like a cauldron of hate and voracious evil hunger. Wesley shuddered as a malaise ran through his body and he replied: *No matter. Once I activate the experiment, nothing can escape our control. There is no way they can stop this now.*

Wesley stubbed out his cigarette against the tree trunk as the Sylvan's reply flitted into his brain.

I will be here, waiting.

CHAPTER 51

---◆---

Feed My Sheep Ministry House, Bedford-Stuyvesant, Brooklyn, NY, 6:30 AM

Procedures ruled the mornings at the ministry house, things happened methodically at specific intervals. Subconsciously, the Reverend Jedediah Mosely-Wilson understood the comforting power of steady dependable routine against the despair of the mean streets.

The Reverend awakened before anyone else, always. Most times he'd been up hours earlier. He switched on the kitchen lights and made the first urn of coffee. If there was no coffee, then donated tea or some weak chocolate, but it was always something hot. Next he got out whatever they had available for his guest's first meal. Most mornings it would be porridge or generic donated cereal. On good days, there would be powdered eggs, maybe some fried potatoes or toast made from two days-old bread. On very good days, it might be real eggs with occasional pieces of ham or bacon or even fresh fruits.

Unfortunately there were not enough very good days.

Joe bolted up in the hard cot, throwing off the thin military surplus blanket marked with "gift of the Salvation Army." He had been having a nightmare where he was being chased by huge snakes that would pop up from under the ground like gophers. He slid from the cot and put on his shoes. He slept with everything else on. He looked around at his companions asleep on similar cots around him. Charly curled into a tight ball, one arm dangling to the floor. Wu lay on his back, mouth opened and gently snoring. He looked over at the next cot where Mai-Lin sat, legs under her in a sort of Lotus position. She turned toward Joe and their eyes met.

Joe felt a dancing swirl of gentle emotions enter his mind, like a warm smile from an old friend. For a brief second they shared a slice of time where words didn't matter, a tiny bit of advanced communication on a plane of the soul.

She looked away, breaking the moment and Joe experienced a sudden burst of longing for the fledgling contact. He shook his head, stood up and walked across the sleeping hall to the breakfast area.

Jedediah placed boxes of Cream of Wheat on the counter. He wore a cotton headband imprinted with crosses. The muscled arms gleamed as he put down the box and the zigzag scar danced white and pink on his cheek. He poured a mug of coffee and handed it to Joe.

"You gonna talk to me now?" he asked him, "Gonna tell me what yo'all's up to?"

"I still don't think you'd believe us."

Jedediah chuckled as his fingers intertwined around the hot mug. He drained the last of the coffee, put the mug down in the sink and silently waived to Joe to follow him up the stairs. His footsteps were surprisingly quiet for a big man. He opened one of the doors in the upstairs hallway and waived Joe inside an office room cluttered with assorted boxes. A couch lined one wall, the nearest end missing a leg and held up by two stacked bricks. A large and rusted old metal desk, overflowing with mounds of paper work, captured a corner of the room. Cracks went this way and that in the plaster wall where ancient bricks peeked through, and a vague scent of antiseptic floated in the air. Like every corner of the Feed My Sheep ministries, the room was dilapidated and cluttered, but scrupulously clean. Jedediah sat down behind the desk, found a remote under a pile of papers and turned on a small television perched on a metal filing cabinet.

Joe bolted upright from the couch and stepped closer to the screen. The volume came low and clear, but it took a few moments for the announcer's words to penetrate Joe's consciousness. He was riveted by the images on the corner of the television as the CNN announcer droned on.

Three photos appeared on the screen. Joe recognized an old publicity picture of himself taken five years ago when he first opened his hardware store. Below were two computer-enhanced pictures depicting what he might look like now and what he would look like with a beard. His photo disappeared from the screen, to be replaced by one of Charly. Her hair was long and she looked younger in the grainy driver's license ID photo. Below, were two more photos of what she may look like today with long and short hair. The shorthair one came close enough for easy recognition. Charly's picture disappeared and four photos of Dr. Wu flashed on the screen. His pictures were the most accurate since he had a security clearance and had been often videotaped and photographed. As the initial surprise wore off, the announcer's voice started to penetrate Joe's consciousness.

"...believed part of a blood cult that placed bombs in various locations in the New York City subway system. The death toll from the explosions is now up to two hundred and eighteen. It is also believed the group was responsible for the release of psycho-hallucinatory agents into the atmosphere at various locations in the city. The agents have caused massive outbreaks of psychotic violent episodes. The toll from these mass outbreaks has now reached over seven hundred and fifteen killed and nine hundred and twelve injured. Intelligence sources gave information to the FBI and NYPD revealing the group as a Satanic Cult offering sacrifice to Mythological Demons by violent killings."

Joe gripped the edge of the couch with such force that the

armrest gave out a snapping noise as the wood cracked. A picture of his brother flashed on screen as the announcer continued.

"It is believed the group is responsible for the ambush of NYPD Captain TR Jackson. Unnamed sources in the FBI have told CBS News that Captain Jackson scheduled a meeting with the group to affect their surrender when they ambushed him on Atlantic Avenue in Brooklyn. Captain Jackson is in Saint Vincent Hospital in serious but stable condition.

He is expected to survive..."

Joe closed his eyes and leaned back on the couch. *Thank God, TR is going to make it.* For the moment, the relief he experienced eclipsed the implications of the rest of the broadcast.

CHAPTER 52

Bedford-Stuyvesant doesn't normally come awake until late in the morning. Unemployment is rampant and only a very few leave for jobs most mornings. This particular morning was worse because of the events of the previous night and day. No one went to work and the gang-bangers, addicts, thieves and hustlers started their normal day as usual, after noon or later.

Dim gray light struggled to penetrate the dark clouds as they boiled and ran across the sky. The wind rose, filled with moisture and the smells of industries from the shores of New Jersey.

The Bell & Howell Jet Ranger helicopter raced across the Hudson, originating from the roof of a nondescript building in Staten Island. With authorities on high alert and the National Guard patrolling the boroughs of the city, it had taken Duncan Wesley and his NSA credentials hours to clear the flight to Brooklyn. Days later the inquiries from local authorities would begin. NSA would immediately realize the length to which their assistant director had overstepped his bounds. By then thought Wesley, it wouldn't matter at all. The world was just a little over a half a day away from having no NSA, no government, and no authority. None that is, except for the absolute power

Wesley would hold.

The helicopter flew in a direct line to the place where the last signal from the location device in the amulet had been detected. As the Jet Ranger reached the location directed by its electronic guidance system, the pilot banked the machine in an oval loop.

The team leader and his three men stared out the windows as the helicopter finished the tight circle above the Feed My Sheep Ministry Building.

"What a shit hole," one of the men said.

They were dressed in sleek black outfits, dulled to prevent any reflections. Kevlar body armor covered their chests and upper legs. Each man carried a custom designed short barrel submachine gun. Above each gun a mounted pencil thin laser-aiming device ensured accuracy. A thin curved magazine protruded from the belly of each weapon with two additional magazines held by quick-release clips and taped for silence. Twelve-round automatic pistols and commando knives completed their armaments. Dark nylon hoods covered their heads, stretched tight as a second skin under skullcap helmets with antiglare visors. They looked like demons from some subterranean hell. The team leader's helmet was adorned with a small silver hourglass shape for identification. His head resembled the round belly of a Black Widow spider.

The leader gave rapid instruction and the helicopter settled in a smooth hover fifty feet above the roof. Both side doors slid back and three ropes dangled from the helicopter ending a few feet above the ground. One man slid down each rope in a barely controlled descent while the fourth man remained at the open door and cranked down a swivel mount fixed to the inside roof of the helicopter. A black machine gun swung loose on the mounting with a long cartridge belt attached to the weapon like a scorpion's stinger. As the three men landed on the roof, the helicopter drifted back a few feet so the machine gunner could cover the fire escapes and the two exits of the building.

The three men ran to the narrow cement hut that held the

door and stairwell to the interior of the building. In well rehearsed moves one of them placed a small shaped charge on the heavy lock and latch mechanism that secured the steel door. He pressed the tiny electronic timer and the three men hid on either side of the structure. An LED red light, no larger than a pinhead, blinked steady for five seconds then started blinking rapidly. Another five seconds and the roof door latch blew off with a smoky flash and dull thumping noise. The leader kicked the door open and the three men burst into the stairwell.

They moved like professionals in quick coordinated bursts. Only one jumped at a time covered by the other two. Dancing pinpoints of intense light beams preceded them on the floors, steps and walls. Wherever the red dot of the laser sight landed, that's where the bullet would hit.

Joe savored the euphoric relief of knowing his brother survived when Jedediah suddenly stood from the desk. The big man shut off the television set and cocked his head. He stepped into the hallway and paused. Joe came up behind him but froze when the minister held up his hand in silent warning. A muffled whirring noise came from the roof, a rapid muted thumping like golf balls in a huge blender. The noise faded and returned as the helicopter circled and finally, it seemed to the two men in the hallway, settled directly above their heads. Soft padding sounds came from the roof with other muffled noises from the stairwell leading to the top floor. Jedediah reached in his pocket and thrust a set of keys in Joe's hand.

"Here." Jedediah said, "Take them keys. Mah station wagon's downstairs. Last door to the right is the garage. It's an ol'shitbox but it'll haul yo asses outta here fast as lightning."

Joe stood there, his face puzzled, his eyes directly on the Reverend.

"Don'be looking at me like that. I know a damn sight more than yo think ah do. That ole'Chinee an' I had us a long talk last night when ah caught him on the Internet with the computer in mah office."

An explosion sounded from the roof, soft and deep like a paper bag popped by a teenager. A whiff of something acrid and sharp drifted from the stairwell with the sound of someone kicking the door open. Jedediah turned and shoved Joe hard toward the downstairs at the opposite end of the hallway.

"Git. Now," he yelled, "Get yo're people and take off in the wagon. Talk to that old Chinese guy. Ah'll hold off whatever's coming."

"I can't just leave you here. Come with us."

A sudden grin and a flash of white teeth split Jedediah's face. The zigzag scar danced a dark pink in the dim hallway light.

"Ah got's me the Lord on mah side. That's a lot more protection than yo're sorry ass could ever provide, besides, who's gonna take care of my people? Now git, ah'm gonna be real busy in about ten seconds," replied Jedediah as he shoved Joe, harder this time, toward the end of the corridor.

Joe turned down the stairs. He didn't intend to leave at all. He wanted to alert Charly and Wu and Mai-Lin and face whatever happened alongside Jedediah. It seemed as if he was forever being forced to leave people behind. Just when he thought there might be a measure of control, of some distant possibility of returning sanity, something else came along. Joe felt like a driver gripping a steering wheel as the vehicle begins an uncontrolled spin.

CHAPTER 53

A red dot appeared on Joe's back for a split second and fastened on the wall just above his head as he dived down the stairs. Muffled popping noises came from the other end of the hallway and a burst of three bullets hit the external wall sending plaster and brick fragments in concentric circles.

As Joe ran downstairs, Jedediah dove back into his office and pulled the door behind him, leaving it open an inch or so. Son'sa bitches had shot in *His* ministry. *Evil bastards ain't getting away with this in God's own house,* Jedediah mumbled silently. He took the customized ten-gage and put the safety in the off position. In the hallway, footsteps came in spurts and the red dots danced everywhere like the eyes of malevolent Cyclopean devils.

Jedediah pointed the shotgun at the wall that separated his office from the hallway. He aimed the big barrel about two feet above the ground and pulled the trigger.

The magnum load buckshot tore through the interior cheap plaster wall as if it didn't exist.

Chunks of white pieces blew into the hallway with puffs of dirty gray dust. The explosive noise of the big bore shotgun rolled through the hallways and the rest of the house like packed thunder.

Soon as he pulled the trigger, Jedediah rolled into the hallway pumping the shotgun and firing twice.

The lead man in the hall took half the charge in his unprotected left ankle. If it had been a full hit, undeterred by the scattering effect of passing through the wall, it probably would have taken the leg off. As it was, the pellets tore out a ragged chunk of calf muscle and tendons, splattering a gory portrait on the opposite wall. The man went down with a scream, the involuntary tightening of the trigger sending a dozen rounds into the walls and ceiling. Yelling and screaming came from downstairs as the guests of the Feed My Sheep Ministry were jolted out of sleep by the gunfire.

Jedediah's next shot took the second man full in the chest. The body armor saved his life, preventing the buckshot from penetrating and shredding the man's heart, but it couldn't absorb the impact. It was like receiving a baseball bat strike from a major leaguer. The man flew off his feet as if shot out of a cannon. Breastbone and three ribs broken, the blast drove him backward into the third man behind him. Jed dashed for the stairwell leading downstairs.

He almost made it.

The third team member pushed aside the man who fell on him and fired a short burst at the fleeing minister. The rounds stitched from left to right, most hitting the wood banister and walls sending splinters and pieces of hardscrabble dirty white in all directions. Two rounds caught Jed in the lower back and upper thigh.

The minister felt as if a truck slammed into his lower body. The shotgun flew out of his hand and his legs seemed to disappear from his body. He saw the floor rush up at him and the walls tilt at crazy angles. For a moment he felt how strange it was, what he believed was his last moment on earth. As blackness closed in and his consciousness evaporated, his last thought was surprise at the lack of pain, and curiosity as to what the Maker he had so faithfully served, would really look like.

The third man passed by Jed's form sprawled with his

head and shoulder draped down the first step and the rest of his big body on the upper landing. He held the light machine gun on him for a second as he surveyed the downed minister. Satisfied there was no further threat he ran down the stairs, weapon at ready.

CHAPTER 54

Joe raced downstairs, hustling Charly, Wu and Mai-Lin toward the rear door leading to the garage. The fear returned to Charly's eyes, and the old Chinese scientist moved painfully slow. Mai-Lin preceded them as if she knew exactly where to go, like she had done this hundreds of times before. Joe intended to get them in Jedediah's car and have Charly drive away while he went back to help the minister and retrieve Manuel. He had no idea who or what came after them, but he felt prickly hairs on the back of his neck and a sensation in his stomach like falling in a deep well.

Three explosions blasted the large quiet room from above, followed by several more like strings of firecrackers. People still asleep suddenly jolted up screaming. The ones with a little more street wisdom rolled on the floor, hugging the bare concrete as if they could become a part of it. Others just screamed and ran toward the front door. One of the volunteers in the kitchen area knocked over a vat of oatmeal cooking on the gas stove. A large woman ran across the boiled grains spreading over the bare floor. Her feet gave out under the slimy liquid partly coagulated like gray blood. A thin old man in under shorts fell over her. His eyes glared wildly and his arms flailed like dark skinny windmills as short screams escaped his toothless mouth.

The smell of cordite and dust followed the third man from the raiding party. He came down the stairs, the smell like sulfur clinging to a devil. He paused on the last step, weapon shouldered, right eye on the sight. His head darted back and forth. The red dot followed his movements across the room, instant death hovering around the mass of screaming people trying to hide or find the exit. A stench of sweaty fear spread in the room like ghoulish perfume.

The man recognized Joe and Wu from the photos Wesley had them memorize. He brought the barrel of the assault weapon around toward them. The red aiming dot of the laser bounced around the heads, shoulders and arms of the people in the way. He raised the barrel and fired a long burst over their heads.

Two dozen rounds blasted over the room like whining screaming hornets. A small, barred window at the far end vomited shards of glass into the street. Bullets ricochet from cast iron radiator pipes and hit the steel cooking pots and utensils hanging in the kitchen area, adding to the din. One man in a ragged Nike warm-up suit went down with blood exploding in a satin gusher from his neck. Screams and sobs filled the air adding another dimension to the hideous stench of excrement, blood and acid-burnt gunpowder. The man from the raiding party had no thought about hitting innocent people. It didn't matter either way, it just seemed more efficient to get their heads down than to try and hit his two targets by sending bullets through a dozen or more bodies.

As the bullets tore the air above their heads, Joe pushed Charly, Wu and Mai-Lin into the garage and slammed the heavy steel door shut. He fumbled for a few seconds then found the light switch and rammed the safety bolt.

The man ran after them, slammed into a woman hugging a wide-eyed little girl and shoved them into a wall. People desperately tried to get out of his way as he screamed and pushed and clubbed at them. He paused a second to key a radio fastened to the Kevlar vest and spoke into the wire microphone running from his helmet.

"Nightbase, Nightbase. Two targets, possibly more, may be exiting from Northwest corner garage area. Possible vehicle exit, two assets down. Cover Team needed."

People continued to run from him like the Red Sea parting for Moses as he crossed the room. He reached the steel door, took a step back and kicked it. He was a big man, filled with rage and violence, but the powerful kick might as well have been a spitball. The door didn't move. Not one bit at all.

When the Reverend Jedediah Mosely-Wilson had first taken residence in the house, he had spotted the old dilapidated plywood door as a certain and easy point of entry for any junkie bent on an easy score. When the Safe-4-U security company on Avenue U went bankrupt, the Reverend persuaded the cleanup crew to leave the floor-model security door behind. Jedediah had "requisitioned" the hardwood door with the half-inch steel covering and security "dead bolts" for the garage area.

The man took three steps back, leveled the assault weapon at the lock area and fired a four round burst. The bullets imbedded themselves in steel and hardwood with a hammering noise.

The door didn't budge. It would take primacord explosive to get through and the man in the upstairs hallway with the shredded ankle was the only one who carried it.

CHAPTER 55

Manuel swam up from the clear blue and gold waters of his native Yucatan Peninsula. Rays of bright yellow sunlight streamed through the cool water and he noted without surprise, that he could breathe as he floated among a myriad of sea creatures. From out of the depth a dark shape floated upward, tentacles undulating and waving like seaweed as they wrapped themselves around one of Manuel's leg. Where they touched, a throbbing pain hammered his leg and a tentacle reached up and covered his mouth and nose.

Manuel pushed the sheet off his face as he sat up on the dingy cot. The wound in his leg throbbed, and he felt it hammering through the clean bandage. But that wasn't what awakened him. It was a feeling, a sixth sense experienced in his skin. When the first thundering explosions of shotgun fire came from the hallway, answered immediately by the sharp spitting noises of muffled automatic weapons, Manuel responded with the instincts of one raised in the Barrios of Mexico City and Los Angeles. He rolled off the mattress and slid under the bunk.

Noise erupted in the hallways and the downstairs great room like a series of volcanoes going off. Gunshot blasts, yelling and screaming, the sound of a body falling nearby, all rode on a wave of pungent sulfur and cordite. Someone kicked open the door and placed a foot in the entrance. Manuel could just see a black combat boot with tucked-in dark pant leg. He had no trouble imagining the gun barrel covering the interior of the small room, seeking a human target, a beating heart. He tried to blend in the wall under the cot, squeezed his eyes shut and silently prayed to the Madonna. The moment passed like hours, but it was less then one-second real time as the intruder scanned the room and moved on.

Manuel heard footsteps running down the stairs, more gunfire and now it seemed as if the yelling and screaming rose unbearably, reaching the tiny upstairs room like violent slices of dementia.

But no more noises came from the upstairs hallway connecting Manuel's room. He crawled from under the bunk and reached the door. His body hugging the floor, head barely inches away, he glanced up and down the hall. In the light of the blown out window and the emergency firelight, he made out two black shapes sprawled on the floor. One was silent while the other moaned softly as blood, thick and black in the dim light, spread from a shattered leg. But it was the third figure, close to Manuel, that held his attention. The Reverend Jedediah Mosely-Wilson had managed to raise his head and turn toward Manuel's room. His face twisted, mouth working and jumping as the zigzag scar danced with the pain. His eyes held a fierce shining, racing against the glaze that began to settle on them as he struggled against the coming shock of the wounds to his lower body.

Manuel raised himself to his hands and knees and crawled the few feet to Jed's side. The Reverend's lips mumbled, his face shiny with sweat and Manuel strained to catch each word.

"Roof.., the roof.., got to.., get em cover..," Jed's head fell the few inches to the floor and his forehead rested against the cement, patched with his sweat. His breathing came like a patchy bellows struggling against great pressures. Rhythmic staccato hammering of automatic gunfire came from downstairs followed by whining ricochets and clanking noise of steel jacketed rounds hitting walls and furniture and God knows what else.

Jedediah waved his hand toward the shotgun lying by the corner. Manuel disregarded the pulsing throbbing pain of his wounded leg as he followed Jed's eyes. He tried to stand but his leg gave out and he sat heavily with a whimpering mewling noise of pain.

Manuel was confused. His leg seemed to have gotten worse and he couldn't figure out what was going on, who had attacked them or where his companions had gone, but instinctively, on a level beyond words, he trusted the fallen Reverend.

"*Madre de Dios,*" he muttered softly as he grasped the heavy shotgun and used it as a crutch to get on his feet.

He hobbled down the hallway, his shoulder dragging against the wall, trying to keep any weight off his leg, and the shotgun barrel pointed toward the roof entrance at the end of the hall. He passed the two men; their black clothing and helmet made them look like giant sprawled cockroaches. One of the men curled in a fetal position, arms around an ankle slick with blood. A piece of white bone protruded from the torn pant leg soaked in gore. The other man remained sprawled out; arms and legs splayed back where the force of the shotgun blast had thrown him like so much meat.

Manuel tasted a bloody, sweet coppery smell as he passed the men and came to the roof stairwell. He stepped inside, all his weight on his good leg, leaned against the metal railing of the stairs and pumped a round in the chamber. He hopped one step at a time, little gasps of pain and mumbled Spanish curses erupting softly from clenched teeth. He saw dingy clouds racing across the sky and felt the wind coming down the stairs. The air smelled like dirty ashes and he tasted grimy dust on his tongue. The early light appeared grizzled, like a morning funeral. He stopped three steps from the roof and held the banister so tight with his free hand that one of his fingernails broke against the rusted metal. He heard the pounding of his heart, heavy and at the edge of panic. But now he became aware of another pounding. Heavy and thick, it resonated against the ancient brickwork of the building and washed over the black runny tar of the flat roof.

He took the last two steps and crouched so he could stick his head out, just a little, at ground level. No more than thirty or so yards away, a black helicopter with red and gold letters hovered, a few feet out from the edge of the roof. The blades cut the thick moisture laden air sending thumping waves of sound washing into the streets and roofs below.

Downstairs in the garage, Joe yelled at Charly and the others to get in the car. He went to the garage door, found the three retaining latches, threw them back, lifted the door open on its sliding track, and ran into the driver's side of the big station wagon.

It was an Oldsmobile Custom Cruiser, a big old car, over twenty-five years old, a leftover from the era of seven-miles-per-gallon vehicles. Powered by an Olds Rocket V-8-455 engine, the dilapidated vehicle was a precursor to the modern SUV's. Patches of rust dotted the body, brown and big as sidewalk puddles. The old wood grain decals peeled and oxidized, most of the chrome trim vanished long ago, and the cowl windows were fixed shut with wire. A rusted tailpipe protruded from the rear tied to the chassis with a twisted coat hanger. Black vinyl letters six inches high proclaimed the ownership of the vehicle as the Feed My Sheep Ministries, Brooklyn, New York. The two back windows sported foot long black crosses made from electrical tape. The headliner hung down inside and touched the top of Joe's head as he fumbled with the ignition key. The engine cranked over slowly on a wheezing battery inches away from it's final rest.

The engine didn't start, the starter cranked even slower and Joe released the ignition. He felt Charly's arm tighten on his as bullets thumped on the safety door from outside.

Suddenly it dawned on him. This was an old car with a carburetor. He was used to modern fuel injected motors. You had to pump these things to set the choke and prime their carburetors.

He pumped the gas twice, turned the key again and the engine caught immediately on the first anemic crank. He yanked the gearshift into drive and stepped hard on the gas. The big station wagon shot out into the narrow back street.

The pilot and the fourth team member left on the helicopter received the leader's radio message simultaneously. The pilot eased back gently on the control and the helicopter drifted from its hovering place above the roof so it floated over the back street. The other team member attached his safety strap and rotated the machine gun pivot so the weapon pointed to the street below. As the big station wagon pulled from the garage, the gunner drew his bead and prepared to release several bursts. Orders had been clear: no one should escape. If they could take them alive, all well and good, if they couldn't, killing them was acceptable.

Manuel saw the helicopter drift over the roof and the man pivoting the machine gun and pointing it down into the street below. Somehow, he understood he had to stop them. He stood on the last step, hidden from view by the roof entrance. He leaned out the top half of his body, braced his shoulder against the wall, held the shotgun steady as he could and aimed it at a point just ahead of the guy with the machine gun. He didn't want to take down the helicopter, just warn it off.

Manuel pulled the trigger.

Three things Manuel had not counted on: First, the raw power of the magnum ten-gauge shell, second, the scattering effect of the pellets with distance. It might not be possible to take down the helicopter with a shotgun, but he couldn't have aimed at a better spot if he had tried. The third item Manuel hadn't foreseen was the awesome recoil. He held the gun too loosely, and the kick slammed it into his shoulder and out of his hands.

Manuel fell back against his injured leg and rolled down four steps until he managed to stop, it felt like he'd been kicked by a mule on steroids. His shoulder and arm were numb. His leg hurt like someone twisted hot knives into it, and he tasted blood from where he had bitten his lip. He tried to get up but fell another step.

The gunner aimed the machine gun about where the driver would be, leading to compensate for the acceleration of the big station wagon. Once he wasted the driver it was a simple matter of emptying a full belt into the body of the car. The rounds would penetrate the thin metal of the auto killing all the occupants. Mission accomplished, its Miller time, he thought.

By the time the pellets from Manuel's shot covered the thirty or so yards to the helicopter, the pattern had spread to about a two-foot circle. The velocity was no longer sufficient to fully penetrate a human body, but could still cause havoc on soft tissue.

The pellets entered the interior compartment through the partially open back door and spread throughout the interior. Half a dozen lead shots struck the gunner on the arms and neck. Only the safety strap kept him from being thrown from the craft as the machine gun muzzle swung from the street to the sky.

The remaining pellets struck the pilot on the cheek and hands. He jerked the collective and cyclical controls. The machine tilted upward and began to swing clock-wise, the back fuselage clipped a TV antenna. The pilot frantically grasped the controls with bleeding hands and struggled with the machine. He applied power as the helicopter continued to rotate. It wobbled and shook, threatening any minute to spin out of control. The blades bit into the air, the engine whined to an intolerable pitch as the machine climbed.

The pilot stopped at five hundred feet altitude and a quarter mile away from the Ministry house by the time he regained control. His hands shook and, his pulse raced as he realized how close to death he came. He looked back at the gunner clutching the side of the door and retaining strap. His face was the color of bleached flour and streaks of blood ran down his features and onto his neck.

"Fuck this," the pilot said, "they don't pay us enough for this shit."

The helicopter turned toward Staten Island and accelerated through the grizzled sky.

CHAPTER 56

Joe stepped on the gas, sending the station wagon to the end of the street, and stopped. The engine idle through the worn mufflers sounded like the steady growl of a feral beast. Plumes of black smoke poured out the back and the brakes screeched as the car came to a halt.

The morning closed in on nine AM, and the narrow streets were almost empty. Two old men sat wordless on a stoop of chipped and crumbling bricks. Discarded wrappers, empty boxes, newspapers and rags littered the streets and the sidewalks where grass popped up through numerous cracks in the concrete. Slimy liquid rivulets disappeared in the sewer outlets at the edge of the curbs and the blacktop of the street held an oily sheen. Joe looked around for a long minute then swiveled his body in the driver's seat so he faced Charly in the front seat and Wu and Mai-Lin in the rear.

"We have to go back," Joe said, "the Reverend saved our lives and we just ran like dogs at the first sign of trouble."

"That was hardly a first sign of trouble," Charly replied, "Those people were clearly after us, not Jedediah or his mission."

"I'm tired of running, tired of people dropping like flies around me and there's nothing I can do. You can't keep running forever. You have to face whatever is chasing you or it will end up eating you whole."

Charly looked at him silently as Wu answered.

"The way to stop a train is not to jump in front of it with your arms out. It will flatten you in a blink. But if you step aside and jump on the locomotive as it passes, you can pull the brakes and stop the longest train."

Wu paused and Joe noticed the lines in the scientist's face deepened still more. Weariness etched every pore and he seemed to have aged another decade in the few days he had known him.

"We must," continued Wu, "stop a train. As powerful a train as you can imagine. It's already hurtling down the tracks toward a huge crash and its going to take humanity to destruction. We must stop this train and we cannot do that by jumping in its path."

"I don't understand what you're saying," Joe replied, "You haven't been straight with us. You told us nothing but little cryptic bits that nobody understands. Its time for you to talk to us, to tell us all you know or we're all so much dead meat. We'll keep running until something, human or inhuman, catches up with us and finally kills us."

Joe felt a wave of anger, pent up fear and the frustration of the last few days welled up in a torrent of rage. He slammed his hand on the dashboard, the slapping noise like a gunshot in the musty air of the car's interior.

He leaned forward toward Wu and spat out each word like a bitter pit.

"Talk to us. Tell us everything. Now."

The old Chinese ran both hands over his face as if he could wipe out the weariness like cleaning a chalkboard. Joe thought that beneath the tired eyes lay a steel backing that would somehow pull him through. His voice sounded soft, low and gravelly as if the vocal cords had exhausted all moisture.

"You already know I was head of the project that discovered the existence of the Sylvans at Brookhaven National Lab a year ago," Wu started. He paused for a moment and looked out the side window at the desolate street and the jumble of flotsam littering the sidewalks. He shook his head gently like he had just awakened to this section of the world and continued, "It actually started two and a half years ago. Two and a half years. I still can't believe that much time has passed. I was assigned director of what they called the Artifact Project. Back then it was run out of Los Alamos, New Mexico. A few months before, an archeological dig in Israel located the entrance to a cave. It had been deliberately blocked and filled with rocks and boulders. The event occurred in approximately 600 AD which placed it at about the time and place where ancient records indicate the Devil's Calix was last seen."

"What's the Devil's Calix?" Charly asked.

"Until the discovery of the Artifact in that cave, it was always believed that stories of the Devil's Calix were myths, convenient fables invented by people who had no explanations to the horrendous outbreaks of violence occurring in Roman and Biblical times. The Devil's Calix is supposed to be the cup that Lucifer drank human blood from on his only visit to Earth. Some say the Vampire legends really start there, thousands of years before Vlad The Impaler ever graced the woods of Transylvania. Whenever these epic massacres and prolonged episodes happened, the Devil's Calix is mentioned. It is always alluded to with vague descriptions and wild legends of its origins. We find references in ancient Egyptian hieroglyphics and Roman carvings. It is mentioned by the scribes of the Gaul warrior king Vercingetorix before his defeat by the Romans at Silecius. He blames the Devil's Calix for the massacres of entire villages along the Seine River by his own tribesmen. There are even hints at something resembling the Devil's Calix in the Dead Sea Scrolls."

"So this Artifact thing they dug up, you believe is that Devil's Calix. What's all this got to do with leaving behind someone who saved all our lives just last night?"

"We believe ancient people called it the Devil's Calix

because they simply didn't have any other frame of reference. We do know that someone went to a great deal of trouble to bury that thing under tons of rocks. They also died in the process. Two skeletons were found in that ancient cave. The dryness of the desert subterranean floor preserved the remains sufficiently so we identified a Roman soldier. He held a rolled copper tablet inscribed with the warnings. He evidently knew he would die in the process of burying what he believed caused supernatural madness and violence."

"If that's what you think happened, why didn't madness and violence break out again when it was first dug up?"

A questioning look, like a college professor challenging his students spread across Wu's tired face, surprising Joe at the sudden animation and vigor from the old scientist. Mai-Lin's dark eyes fixed on Joe, then back out the window again. Joe looked at her eyes and wondered why he had never noticed the size of her pupils. The shiny black orbs seemed to fill most of the space of her eyes, the white more like a margin, a punctuation to the deep indigo of the oversize pupils. Even when she looked away, the girl's spirit, her very being lightly touched the edges of his mind. It was like a gentle summer tide, warm and soothing on a bather's feet. The sound of Wu's voice brought him back to the moment as he realized he had drifted, just a little bit, under the spell of the young girl's psychic presence.

"Think my friend, think," Wu said, "what happened about that time, about three and a half years ago? What happened in that region of the Middle East, in Israel that brought the world to the edge of global war when the nations believed the new peace was working and settled at last with the Palestinians, Israel and the rest of the Muslim world?"

This time Charly answered.

"The Second Intifada, the Final Jihad of the Palestinians in 2008."

"Correct," Wu said, "and what marked this one from all the others, was its intensity and short life. No one, not even the participants, especially the participants, have ever offered any sensible explanation. It seemed as if they all suddenly went mad. Over eight hundred people died in a forty-day period ruled by unparallel savagery. Remember the Alhambra settlement massacre? The first modern Palestinian settlement built after the peace of 2007. Forty-five Palestinian police and members of the former Hamas group entered the settlement, proclaiming to be the Mujadeens of the New Millennium. They sought informers in the camp, instead, they killed. They killed, and killed, over three hundred men women and children. All the children of the settlement died, butchered in two hours of frenzied madness. So it wasn't simply Palestinians and other Arabs versus Israelis. It was madness, pure and simple. Most the issues had been settled, the region quiet for about two years. For the first time in the modern history of the Middle East, it seemed as if lasting peace had arrived. The beginning of the Second Intifada coincides to the day with the unearthing of the Artifact."

Wu paused as sirens sounded nearby. One block away on the Avenue intersecting the street where they had stopped, a six wheeled armored vehicle carrying National Guard soldiers followed two NYPD squad cars heading toward the Feed My Sheep Ministries building. Beneath the rumbling noises of the armored carrier and the screeching wail of the police sirens, something growled and tugged at his consciousness. The Maarzuk still roamed beneath them, dogging their footsteps through the fabric of the Earth, waiting, stalking. Overlaying all like a psychic gossamer blanket, woven of dreams and ethereal moonbeams, Joe felt the presence of Mai-Lin. It seemed as if the girl's powers bloomed in the last twenty-four hours, filled with newly discovered radiant strength.

"What about the expedition that discovered the Artifact?" Joe asked, returning his attention to Wu, "Weren't they affected more than anyone else?"

"You might say that," replied Wu, "Out of the original thirty two members, nine died in the first eight hours, the results of senseless and violent altercations. Mind you, this was a team that functioned smoothly during the previous eighteen months of the dig. It took most of a week for Israeli scientists to find the radiation the Artifact emitted, link it to all that happened, and shield it. Once they did that, the violence stopped. Of course by then they figured out three things: The Artifact was dangerous as hell, its origins were not from Earth, and they did not have the resources to study this thing properly. That's when it was turned over to the CIA who in turn passed it to the NSA who sent it to Los Alamos for study and development."

"Development for what?"

"Probably what they always have in mind. Military applications, national security, possible alien contacts to foster the previous two. They didn't spell it out when Assistant Director Duncan Wesley showed up and asked me to head the project. When it was moved to Brookhaven National Lab for the Nuclear Alignment procedures and the Ion Collider experiments, we had discovered the Sylvans. They were connected to it in a manner we still don't quite understand. Best theory is that Sylvans are of alien origin and the Artifact is a kind of communications device that was brought with them thousands of years ago. It somehow links with their telepathic powers. It works with them but it's highly dangerous to human life. From the animal experiments we conducted, we know that exposure to the radiation causes a veritable flood of increased brain chemicals. Serotonin, Dopamine, Adrenalin and dozens of other substances are manufactured by the body in a sort of overdrive condition. Exposure reaches several hundred miles with scattered results."

"You still haven't answered my questions," Joe said, "What does this have to do with leaving Jedediah to face those goons by himself?"

Wu looked away, rubbed his eyes and looked at Joe as he spoke.

"Last night, after everyone was asleep, I went upstairs to Jed's office and used his computer. I went on the Internet into the Brookhaven Lab Website. I know my way in there and I have the password to the computers of several of the physicists. I know how to get by their firewall and security systems. Hell, I designed most of them myself. I saw the progress and timetable of the Nuclear Alignment procedures on the Artifact. I saw the setup for the Ion Collider and sub-atomic particles bombardment and its own schedule. They are going to do it sometime tonight."

"And what happens if they do it?"

Wu's voice was soft and filled with conviction as he answered. He was like a man discussing something outlandish, something impossible that somehow was coming true.

"It's unthinkable. It would mean the end of civilization, as we know it. You see, the power of the Artifact will increase a thousand fold. Half the human population will die within twenty-four hours, perhaps more. I explained this to Jedediah last night. He understood and believed it. He is extremely intelligent, an amazing man. Under different circumstances, he could be leading entire nations. He bought us time so we could stop Wesley and this Sylvan from carrying out the procedure at Brookhaven Lab."

A thousand thoughts raced through Joe's mind in a jumbled kaleidoscope. Even if he believed all that the Chinese told him, how could they possibly stop Duncan Wesley in his own home territory?

Joe turned and closed his eyes, letting his head drop slowly until it touched the cracked plastic of the steering wheel. *Think,* he told himself, *it's your home territory also.* The reservation abuts to the land surrounding the Laboratory. It had been his home many years before Wesley ever set foot on it, and how about Wu? He wasn't exactly a stranger to the Lab. Just a few months ago he *ran* the place for heaven's sake! As far as Jedediah was concerned, he had believed it and bought them time. To attempt some kind of rescue of the minister would surely mean detention by the authorities or worse.

Joe now understood what he must do: get to the lab,

confront Wesley, and somehow stop the experiment.

He put the shift lever in gear and stepped on the gas. The big wagon accelerated down the street with loud growling of its semi-defunct muffler and puffs of blue-black smoke from the rotted tailpipe.

CHAPTER 57

Feed My Sheep Ministries House, Beford-Stuyvesant, Brooklyn, New York, 11:15AM

Special Agent Donohue lit a new cigarette with the old one and flicked the butt out of the blown out hallway window. The sharp black eyes above a slashing beak of a nose gave him the vague appearance of a wingless bird of prey. For the moment, no amount of nicotine could help his frustration. He constantly sorted out new information and none of it made any sense. It was as if the Gods were feeding him pieces of puzzles one at a time, but the pieces were from all different puzzles. Nothing fit, there were no answers in sight and every moment raised a labyrinth of new questions.

First there were troubling doubts about the NSA report on this terrorist cult. Ever since the horrendous attack of 2001 on the World Trade Center, intelligence activity on terrorism increased many folds. There were no groups that intelligence agencies were not at least, aware of. Suddenly this NSA report comes in from a single source naming a Chinese scientist, a naturalized American citizen who had been living and working in the US for decades. Not just working, but as FBI records indicated, working with a Top Secret clearance on sensitive projects.

The case gnawed at Donohue's sense of investigative logic that someone like that would suddenly take up with a cult to commit terrorist acts. Then there was the issue of TR Jackson's brother. Perhaps when TR recovered enough to be interviewed, there would be some answers. Donohue trusted the NYPD captain. He had worked closely with him on numerous cases over the years, and TR was one of the few people that Donohue knew would always do what they said they would do with clear solid judgment.

He found it unlikely that TR would make such an error about his own brother and equally unlikely that his brother would ambush TR as he tried to take him to the safe house the FBI had set up for Donohue's operations. There was no reason, it didn't make sense, no more sense than this strange operation at the Bedford-Stuyvesant self-help ministry.

Donohue sat with his notes at a downstairs table, gouged and scratched with graffiti. The odor of spilt greasy food, unwashed bodies, blood, offal and the caustic remains of gunpowder formed a gritty paste in his nostrils that he could almost taste.

Dozens of residents sat around listlessly on scattered furniture, awaiting questioning by one of Donohue's detectives.

Patches of plaster lay scattered around the floor and furniture in expanding ovals where bullets had struck the walls and ceiling. A dozen agents and crime scene specialists swarmed around the downstairs room and the upstairs hallway, offices and roof. Bullet holes were circled in red and recorded, carts of evidence bagged in clear plastic stood in three locations throughout the rooms while uniformed officers carried more evidence bags to vans outside.

A heavy police presence filled the street, backed by three squads of National Guardsmen packing M-16's with fixed bayonets. Donohue thought there had never been so much security in the streets of Bedford-Stuyvesant since the riots of the sixties.

For the first time in his career, he felt lost in a case. It felt as if he stood on shifting ground while monstrous storms came out of nowhere and raged all around.

One thing he was convinced off: the attacks were not terrorist acts. Scores of unsettling aspects popped up, things that the higher ups at the Bureau shrugged away. His reports had been filled with questions and few answers. The known facts were too nebulous, but in spite of that, they directed him to find the terrorist connections at all costs and follow the NSA leads. He couldn't fathom for one moment the terrorist-induced hallucinogenic theory he was forced to investigate.

Donohue crumpled the info-sheet and threw it on the floor. He didn't believe the people on the list from the NSA had caused these events. He did believe that they held the answers to the events of the last two days.

He sent a team of agents to track down the origin of the helicopter and assigned two more agents on the background of the two wounded men who carried out the raid. The third man had been caught a few blocks away trying to flee on foot. Although he claimed he headed a mission sanctioned by the NSA, clearly there was something not quite Kosher going on there.

Donohue assigned his best team of interrogators to shake out the information. Now he settled down to study the dossier from what he believed to be his number one lead, if not suspect: Joseph Gray, full original name, Joseph Gray-Wolf of the Shinnecock Nation.

Long Island Expressway, near the Queens-Nassau Counties border, 12:15PM

It was one of those endless projects that dotted the Long Island Expressway on any given year, snarling traffic and raising commuter's frustrations to new levels. This one was destined to be a new off ramp leading into the suburban town of Lake Success. The entire access area had been lined with orange cones, and Joe simply drove the station wagon between gaps in the cones. The site was deserted, public works having been temporarily stopped because of the recent troubles in Manhattan. A long mountain of piled up dirt lined the site with blocks of concrete pillars stacked and ready to be put in place. Two cranes sat on the left side of a construction office trailer, their long arms overhanging like watchful steel claws. Several dump trucks and other heavy construction equipment dotted the five acres of gouged out earth.

Joe parked the wagon behind the trailer, and he sat with Charly and Wu in one corner of a large hangar-like overhang that protected mounds of concrete and other construction materials from the elements. On the other side of the hangar, Mai-Lin sat on a pile of steel girders and looked out as the rising winds carried the occasional fat raindrops and slapped them into the steel, concrete and dirt of the site.

Wet earth and vegetation smells clung to the air, strange among the maze of roadways, bridges and malls surrounding the area. It hadn't really started raining yet, but it felt like the sky pulled in tons of moisture, marshalling its forces for a deluge on the earthbound creatures below. Joe caught the weather forecast on the radio as they drove eastward. The weather and news channel being about the only thing the radio could pick up from the wire coat hanger replacing a long-ago busted power antenna.

A hurricane was on the way, scheduled to hit Cape Hatteras momentarily, or maybe it would veer away and follow the coast, maybe it would hit New Jersey or maybe it would land on Long Island. *Typical weather forecasting*, thought Joe, covers all the bases just in case.

Luck brought them to this fairly safe resting place. There were several portable construction bathrooms, and the back of the station wagon contained two cardboard boxes filled with donated peanut butter, canned meat, white bread and bottled water that Jedediah had not had time to unload.

Not exactly lunch at the Waldorf, but for the moment it suited them just fine. Joe took a swig from a half-gallon generic plastic jug of water and turned to Wu.

"Okay," Joe said, "If we accept this premise of an experiment wiping out half the human population or worse—that leaves a few major league questions, like, why? Even a murdering bastard like Duncan Wesley would surely hesitate before committing the worst mass killings in human history. Does he even know what the results could be? And how about the people working with him? Surely they must know the potential."

Wu exhaled with a rattling noise in his throat and looked off to where a small band of crows picked apart some garbage spilled from a steel drum.

"Oh he knows all right," Wu answered, "He is like a very few men I knew a long time ago in my native land, men who had power in Beijing. Human life did not exist for them except as a means to continuing or expanding that power. Mass killings are just a way to reach a goal for men like that. The numbers and scope of death and suffering carries no meaning for them. As for the scientists on the project, I was the only one who knew and compiled the results from the animal experiments. When I realized what he planned, how he had set up this unholy alliance with one of the Sylvans, I threatened to stop the entire project. He tried to kill me but I escaped into a network of people I knew in Chinatown. I am the only one with full knowledge and I am his main threat. This is why he sent you to track me down. Once you found me, all he had to do was kill us all with that Sylvan helping him. That's what the last few days have been about."

"Why Joe? How was he chosen?"

Wu shrugged as he answered, "He was probably the first one with latent psychic powers to come into the Sylvan's reach. It couldn't just be anyone, it had to be somebody who would be sensitive to various forms of telepathy. I would wager there is a history of paranormal activity in your family, Joe. It's inherited you know, like the color of your eyes or hair. It's in the genes."

"Okay," Joe said, "Now let's get to the practical side of it. How can we have any chance of stopping this? We don't have time to convince any authorities. Right now we're on a wanted list. We have practically no resources and I'm sure this project is guarded up to the eyeballs."

The old Chinese shifted on the hard wood bench. His back straightened as if someone had inserted a steel rod in his spine. Something strong and hard shone in his eyes and his voice carried the timbre of cast iron as he answered.

"It was over thirty years ago, in Beijing, when I lost everything I truly loved. I should have acted with strength and the resolve to die if need be. Not one day passes that I don't regret the terrible weakness that allowed the killing of the two people dearest to me. I made the mistake of a lifetime. My youth has long since fled, and this old man will have lived for nothing if I fail to stop the evil that will soon overtake my adopted land and the rest of the world. I have some resources. I know the Laboratory and its machines and control systems, and I am ready to die. Surely that has power, would you not agree with me Joseph Gray-Wolf?"

Joe held his eyes while his mind raced. He grew up on the Poospatuq reservation, among the wild pine forest and the Bays next to the Lab. He saw a way, a dim chance maybe, but still, the only chance they had.

"I can get us on the Lab grounds, but then what?"

Wu shrugged, "We succeed or we die among the millions."

"What about her?" Charly said with a slight wave toward Mai-Lin, "We know she's not your daughter. There's something different about her, something strange. Who or what is she?"

Wu paused, his eyes on the girl who seemed absorbed in watching the crows screech and fight over the scraps of food. He turned back to Joe as he spoke.

"She is a Sylvan."

CHAPTER 58

Willis Avenue, Mineola, Nassau County, half a mile from the Long Island Expressway, 4:25PM

The emergency strobes on the two Nassau County Police cruisers punctured the gray afternoon light with explosions of red and white. Both cruisers were stopped behind the big station wagon parked at the curb. Puddles of green antifreeze mixed with water and sooty oil gleamed in viscous clumps beneath the car. Some of the black electrical tape that spelled out "Feed My Sheep Ministries" had begun to peel and flap in the moisture-laden breeze. Clearly something happened to the big old engine, stranding the car like a dying whale on a cold beach.

That section of Willis Avenue is dotted with million dollar homes and the usual parked vehicle normally cost a couple of years worth of an average working man's salary. The neighborhood is very quiet with the occasional domestic dispute or motor vehicle accident the only serious event. Consequently, police patrols are not very frequent, just enough to show the flag once in a while so the residents feel they are getting their money's worth from the exorbitant property taxes.

By this time, about a half dozen uniformed officers milled around the car along with several plainclothes detectives. There had been a rush to the scene soon as the first patrol unit called in the plate number of the car. The number turned out to be the one described in the FBI bulletin relating to the possible connection with the killings in the city. The lead detective had just started the examination and search of the car as a captain arrived, and began issuing instruction for searches to the uniformed officers on the scene. The detective tried to find out how long the car had been parked there. The police lab could determine that from the current ambient temperature of the engine block, but it still couldn't provide a definitive answer. What if they had left it idling a while?

Actually the car had been parked there about two hours and it had not been left idling. Barely ten minutes passed since Joe and the others had gotten back in the wagon and left the construction site, before the "check engine" light started flashing red on the dashboard.

Joe didn't pay it any attention. Nothing he could do about it anyway. Besides, he was more concerned about a police car spotting the wagon. Surely somebody must have reported it.

Streams of white steam and dirty smoke had started to snake out of the gaps between the hood and fenders, blown back by the wind soon as they emerged. A burning paint and scorched metal smell filtered into the interior.

"Joe," Charly said, "what's happening with this car?"

Joe didn't answer right away as a bright red light with the word Temperature printed on the lens started blinking.

"In case you didn't notice," Joe finally replied, "this is not the latest word in automobile circles. This thing is older than my grandma's smoking pipe."

Noises like empty Coke bottles knocking together in a sack came from under the hood and the white puffs of steam erupting from under the sheet metal soon turned into clouds.

"We should get off the road with this car," Wu said from the rear seat, "If we are stuck on the Expressway, the first police car will take us in, and we have to get to the lab."

Okay, thought Joe, *this is like the old joke about the guy who drove faster so he wouldn't run out of gas.* Up ahead, about fifty yards, Joe saw the green road sign on the overhang:

Willis Avenue--Mineola.

Clanking, banging and smoking, the old wagon made it to the off ramp and onto the four lanes of Willis Avenue where less than five minutes later, it stopped with a noise like an explosion in a drum and drifted to a stop at the curb.

Joe knew they only had one choice. They had limited cash, not enough to hire a car to take them where they had to go, in Eastern Long Island. They split up, each walking on the opposite side of the avenue, Joe with Mai-Lin and Charly with Wu.

Willis Avenue is a four-lane street filled with stores, shops and restaurants, and flanked with broad sidewalks filled with people going in all directions. Nothing as crowded as a Manhattan sidewalk, but still enough people so they blended in without attracting attention. *Another plus,* thought Joe, is that there were seldom any police around, except for the occasional patrol unit looking for cars parked at expired meters.

He walked with Mai-Lin at his side. Every once in a while, she would look up and their eyes met. He would say something soft and inane and of course she wouldn't reply, but somehow, she acknowledged him. He felt her presence, her communications, like someone entering a room and smelling a whiff of perfume, a hint of pipe smoke or a soft voice, something announcing the presence of the person before they come into sight.

Joe had a sudden flash, as if he straddled two worlds. He walked down the broad sidewalk, the familiar visible world of people all around him. He felt this other world, felt it with senses not developed sufficiently to be a full part of it. He realized that in this other world, he was like a newborn puppy with eyes still closed. He felt different dimensions and sensory experiences at the fringes of unseen elements where auras and dancing tendrils of psychic energy existed as the mainstays of communications and touch.

They had reached the Mineola Long Island Railroad station and purchased their tickets. They boarded the train, an express on the Montauk line with stops at Manorville and the Shirley station on the edge of the Poospatuq reservation. By the time the first police car came up behind the abandoned station wagon on Willis Avenue, they were all on the train that pulled out of the Mineola station at four PM sharp.

Rain pelted the windows of the car as it hurtled on the track in continuing metallic roars and screeching wheels. As it passed the Nassau County border and left behind the first town of Huntington, Joe began to feel the coming proximity of the Pine Barren forests of Eastern Long Island. He recalled the first night he spent in the Pine Barrens after he was "Mapped" and tried to escape by just running out. The jarring memory of the horrendous physical pain caused his hand to tremble slightly. It was an involuntary twitching, a tiny residue of the pain experience that lingered in his nerve cells.

The Mapping, Joe thought, *I was mapped and I ran, and now I'm coming back into their clutches.*

But there was a difference now, there was Mai-Lin, or as Wu had called her: the Maiglin. He thought he had misunderstood, as if some quirk of sound changed what the Chinese scientist had said: Mai-Lin was a Sylvan.

The explanation, whatever passed for an explanation anyway, left him with more doubts and questions than before. Joe remembered the calm, matter of fact way that Wu had spoken. Perhaps it was the very calmness of his voice that lent it credibility.

"When the Artifact was brought to Brookhaven Lab, is when the first contact occurred," Wu had said, "But the contact was not through the creatures that we later came to know as Sylvans, it was through her. In many ways, dealing with her was stranger and more difficult. She would appear in sealed chambers and locked rooms and disappear. She was pure ghost and left no traces in the memories of those assigned to catch her and guard her. The contacts with the other Sylvans came shortly after."

"But how can she be a Sylvan when she appears so human?" Joe had asked.

"I think that by now, you should be aware that things are never quite as they appear. We believe the Maiglin, or Mai-Lin as I named her, has somehow acquired a mixture of Human and Sylvan Genes. It was probably done deliberately by the aliens who originated Sylvans, maybe their attempts to populate the planet. We can only speculate. But we do know that a Maiglin comes about once a Century and their full abilities remain a mystery."

CHAPTER 59

Temporary FBI field office, Feed My Sheep Ministries, Bedford-Stuyvesant, Brooklyn, New York. 4:40PM

Special Agent William Donohue was furious. His assistant wisely backed away while his boss yelled into the phone. At times like this, the thin face and hawkish nose reddened with anger and the ever-present cigarette jumped up and down on his lips like a witch's familiar. Donohue looked more like some of the violent criminals he normally hunted than one of the Bureau's top investigators.

"Thirty minutes," he screamed, "You've had this information for thirty goddamned minutes and you idiots are just getting around to faxing it now?"

Donohue didn't have to wait for the fax. The automobile abandoned at Willis Avenue in nearby Mineola at the Nassau County border had been identified as the station wagon belonging to the Feed My Sheep Ministries. County and town police searched the area for the last half hour or so with no results. Wherever and whoever the occupants were, they had disappeared from site.

As Donohue and his investigators started to unravel the events that had occurred this morning at the ministry house, he became more certain, with each bit of information they extracted, that the three suspects they sought did not cause the mayhem that recently plagued New York City. He was equally certain they held answers that would lead him to the guilty parties.

As the interrogations of the wounded raiders and their leader progressed, evidence began piling up that members of federal agencies were involved. He just couldn't quite put it together at this early stage. Another thing bothering Donohue was the girl that accompanied this Doctor Wu and his two companions, Joseph Gray and Charlene Wright. This girl Mai-Lin was connected to them and to the events, but no records of her existed anywhere. *Christ,* thought Donohue, *she didn't just pop up out of thin air.*

Donohue spread the tactical map of New York City and Long Island on the table in front of him. *East,* he thought, *that's where they are headed.* Two of them were connected to Eastern Long Island according to their files. Joseph Gray, born and raised in the Poospatuq Reservation, lived in the town of Ridge about fifteen miles away. Wu had worked at Brookhaven National Laboratory at Upton, also a few miles away.

What he didn't find in the files, was what TR Jackson had told him, the story of his brother's involvement in a fantastic tale of a hidden race, capable of mind control, with origins leading to Brookhaven Lab.

One of the leading factors in Donohue's success as an investigator, was a totally open mind. He rejected nothing until the weight of contrary evidence was strong enough to rule it out, until that time, nothing remained out of the question. So far in this case, nothing had come in to dispute TR Jackson's story.

Donohue looked at the map and placed an X at Willis Avenue, near the thick red line denoting the Long Island Expressway. With his index finger, he traced Willis Avenue to where it intersected with the black line of the Long Island Railroad. He followed the black line eastward until he reached the station in the town of Shirley. The Poospatuq reservation was right there, less than a half a mile away. Brookhaven National Lab was about six miles North.

Donohue turned to the laptop powered up on the table. He activated the Internet connection and brought up the Long Island Railroad website and schedules for the South Branch. The Montauk Express left the Mineola Station at 4:35PM, made one stop in Huntington and one stop in Shirley at 5:10PM.

"Shit," he growled, "they're on that goddamned train. That's why the local cops can't find them. They just walked to the station and got on the train."

Donohue stood from the table in one violent motion. The chair fell over backward as he yelled orders at his two assistants.

"Get a hold of the local cops down there. I want that train stopped at Shirley. Have them rouse the Sheriff's Department if they need more manpower. I want everybody on that train positively ID'd. I don't want anything bigger than a gnat's ass to get off without me knowing. Tell the chopper pilot to get his ass moving, we're going out there, now."

On the 4:35 Long Island Railroad train from Mineola.

A dusky, damp evening started to settle as the train flashed by the Ronkonkoma Station. The medley of loud noises accompanying a fast moving train was changed in subtle ways by the rain. A muffled quality accompanied the moisture laden atmosphere, altering the texture of the sound. Joe felt the dampness in his pores, and the changing pressure that foretold the arriving storm.

Mai-Lin, he still thought of her as a young girl named Mai-Lin, in spite of what he now knew of her origin, leaned her head against his shoulder. Her eyes were closed, hiding the oversize dark pupils. Joe thought she looked like any young girl emerging into her adolescence.

Outside he saw another deserted platform flying by, the name Manorville barely readable as the green lettered sign passed in bare wet seconds. Shirley would be next and it was a scheduled stop, they were almost there.

Joe felt the train slow and lurch a few times as if a giant pulled it back with invisible cables. The interior lights blinked off and on, and the train slowed to walking speed. The raised track outside was lined by dark, wet forests, and the rain made noises against the windows like flailing cat-o-nine tails. Mai-Lin sat up, her eyes wide, dark pupils scanning the hidden ground ahead like radar.

The train passed through a shallow curve, still at crawling speed. Joe could now see ahead in the gloom. Multiple flashes of red and white blasted the growing dark of the evening and reflected throughout the surrounding woods and against the walls, platforms, and rails of the approaching station.

Joe stood and in a sudden movement, opened the top window and stuck his head out. The train was about a hundred or so yards from the station. Dozens of police cars lined the railhead and it seemed as if the entire local police force had gathered and surrounded the platforms and adjacent structures.

He turned to Charlie and Wu in the next seats. His voice low and urgent, but not low enough that several passengers looked around in alarm.

"There're about a hundred cops out there. We've got to get off this train before it hits the station."

Charly got up and grabbed Joe's arm as she answered.

"How? Everything's locked until the train stops."

Joe pushed down on the window. It came down another couple inches and stopped, opening for only about two feet. He looked at the door and tried to pry it open with his hands but it wouldn't budge. Several passengers sitting on the nearby seats moved away from him. He reached up and with a violent downward movement, yanked the red emergency cord.

At normal operating speed, if he wanted to, the engineer would have sufficient time to override the automatic emergency stopping system. However the train moved at the barest speed as it approached the station. The system halted the train immediately and the doors opened automatically.

Joe held Mai-Lin's hand and they jumped down on the dark graveled bed of the track. He turned and caught Charly as she came down from the car. Wu reached the edge and squatted down as he lowered himself, legs dangling from the opening.

The door closed and Joe dimly heard passengers inside screaming as the automatic doors caught Wu. Joe hopped back on, leaning outside as the automatic sensors kicked in and the doors opened again. The old scientist winced in pain and groaned as he slid out of reach of Joe's grasp and fell to the ground with a dull thumping noise. As the doors closed and opened again, Joe leaped down and squatted next to Wu lying on the ground.

Thunder rumbled in the distance and heavy raindrops pelted them in a wind driven barrage. It seemed almost as noisy outside as it had been on the train. Closing in from the station, a dozen or so uniformed cops in shining yellow rain slickers ran on the sides of the track toward them. They were still too far off to be sure, but Joe thought he saw the gleaming black of gunmetal in their hands. Yelling came from inside the train, mixed with shouted orders from the approaching police officers. Joe felt the sharp slippery edges of the graveled track bed as he tried to help Wu to his feet. The old man gasped, his eyes dull with pain and fatigue, his breath labored and ragged. Joe realized there was no way they could escape with him. Charly came on Wu's left side and placed his arm over her shoulder and propped him up.

Joe still held Mai-Lin's hand. He felt a wave of energy passing from the girl into his very being. It was as if she charged him like a faltering battery. He led Charly and Wu down the track and to the edge of the woods. It was painfully slow as he saw the officers closing in, the weapons in their hands, now all too clear. Charly slipped and fell hard on the border of the sloping track. She gave out a sharp cry as her ankle twisted. Wu fell again, collapsing like a sack of grain and sliding down the last few feet. Joe turned toward their sprawled shapes, just twelve feet away at the edge of the track. The light from the windows of the stopped train augmented the gloom in a surreal environment of rain-glistening muted colors.

The first two officers reached them just as Charly tried to stand and fell back on her twisted ankle and groaned in pain. The first two cops stood over Wu and Charly, their guns trained on the woman and old man in tight two-handed grips and barking short, clear orders.

"Let me see your hands, place your hands in the air. Don't move. Slowly place both your hands in the air."

Two more officers came behind, one holding a gun in a straight arm combat stance, the tip of the barrel shaking imperceptibly in the nervous young cop's grip.

"Get down on the ground. Down on the ground with your hands behind you," He shouted to Joe and Mai-Lin.

The air thickened and the moment stood still for Joe like a fast running movie suddenly frozen in one frame. He felt Mai-Lin slide in front of him, felt the girl's grip on his hand and arm. He felt a tingling where she touched him, and for a moment he thought he saw thin wisps of vaporous smoke rising and dissipating from her gripping fingers. Fat drops of rain rolled down her forehead as the large dark pupils locked on the young cops eyes. She held his gaze for a moment, and turned to his partner who came up behind him with his weapon held out straight. The second cop lowered his weapon, placed his hand on the first cop's shoulder and spoke softly.

"Christ Jimmy, you're spooking me," the officer said, "You're chasing shadows man. There's nobody there. We got the two who got off the train."

The young officer lowered his weapon and slowly turned away. He could have sworn…

More officers arrived. They gently helped Charly to her feet and placed handcuffs on her. One of the officers took off his raincoat and covered her. Another one did the same with Wu's form on the ground. They would have to wait for a stretcher for him.

Wu raised his head and looked at Joe and Mai-Lin,

standing barely a dozen feet away. He gently waived his handcuffed wrists and mouthed a few words toward them.

"It's up to you now."

His arm in a mutual grip with Mai-Lin's hands, Joe stumbled back into the darkening forest surrounding the track.

CHAPTER 60

As Joe walked farther from the stopped train, the lights penetrating the dark of the surrounding woods, diminished, as if the woods soaked up the glow from the train, kept it for its own and let nothing escape. The air felt damp with the raw wet chill of the approaching storm. Joe's newly awakened senses felt waves of invisible energy riding the molecules of the atmosphere. He was back in the domain of the Pine Barrens Sylvans, and their psychic senses had already found him.

Tendrils of psychic power pulsed and rose like waves from a demonic ocean as Joe felt the first tingling approach like an electric current aimed for the pain centers of his brain.

He moaned as the memories of that first night of excruciating agony returned, an evil deja-vu. He broke into a sweat as nauseous waves of pain started pounding into his very core. He stumbled and fell in the darkness and small sharp branches tore across his face. He got up again and screamed and ran in a blind headlong rush. He had entered a nightmare of dark pain, and black shapes that chased him with pokers of glowing hurt.

He didn't know how long he ran, it could have been hours, it could have been minutes. The air thickened and time itself seemed frozen as he slowly became aware of the presence.

It glowed and shifted in his mind, familiar, yet bearing a quality tinged with strangeness, whispering of alien worlds and undiscovered dimensions of the mind.

It was Mai-Lin, the Maiglin.

He could no longer think of her as Mai-Lin. He knew instinctively what his intellect had accepted earlier from Wu. She was a blend of human and Sylvan, a mind of earthly qualities, yet endowed with remote outlandish power.

He felt her invisible strength meshing with his spirit like entwined beams of light. He saw his shield extending around them as it had done the previous day at the base of the Brooklyn Bridge.

This time, he felt her power as the Maiglin blended her incandescent aura like sheets of steel in his warriors' shield.

The pain vanished, having never really taken hold as it had done that first night. He tried to focus on his surroundings instead he saw a second world, superimposed on the first. A dim purplish glow filled his vision and dark shadows danced at the edge of his consciousness.

One of the shadows detached itself and flitted across his vision like a patchy cloud flung across a gale-blown sky. The shadow stopped in front of him and turned into a tall figure wearing the vest, feathers and bones of the Shinnecock tribal Shaman.

Joe recognized his grandfather.

The old man's eyes locked with his and Joe felt his spirit reach out to him across the chasm. His grandfather raised his hand, holding a staff with feathers and bones dangling from the carved ends. He pointed with the staff then turned and vanished.

It felt as if a switch had turned off. The glowing light and energy of that other world disappeared all at once and Joe felt the lashing of the raw wind and dark woods at the edge of the road. The far-flung air carried the sweet, crisp pine scents layered with the sharp tang of oak from the Pine Barrens.

He stood on the edge of a hard packed dirt trail with no conscious recollection how he got there. A few yards to his left a car passed on an intersecting road, the headlights throwing moving shadows that danced on the trees and shrubs.

A familiar sense came to Joe. He hadn't walked that far while his mind had been wherever it had been. He stood on the side road that entered the Poospatuq reservation, a scant half-mile from the Shirley train station.

He walked the few yards to where the dirt path ended on the blacktop of the main road circling the reservation in a twisted U.

Joe stopped and turned and looked at the Maiglin close behind him. Her psychic voice resonated in his mind, pleasing, feminine and smooth.

"You are home."

It took Joe a few moments to realize what had just happened. At first, he thought she had actually spoken, even though Wu had said that she was not capable of speech. *Her lips had not moved,* thought Joe, as he realized that she projected her thoughts into his mind, into a part of his brain that could only interpret her communications as language, and changed those psychic waves to a form of speech created by the receiver's own mind. Joe imagined that if she *could* talk, that would be how her voice would sound.

He felt no sense of invasion at her thoughts projected in his brain. It was a different and more effective means of communications. A part of his mind fell back, the left brain-analytical part considering the experience too fantastic to really exist. But the other side of his mind, the side that dreams, wonders, and creates, the artistic intuitive side of him grasped it and answered.

"Yes, I am home."

His eyes were on the Maiglin's wide alien pupils in the beautiful adolescent human face. *"Home,"* he continued, *"the home that dwelled inside me when I left. I felt the call of my people for so many years. And now I am back, but to do what? And how?"*

"To do what you must do," she replied.

"You haven't answered. How? I believe I can get into the grounds of the Lab, but then what? I don't know where to go, what to do to stop this coming horror. Even now we may be too late."

He felt the power of her mind, the steel beneath the feminine resonance as her answer floated in the confines of his brain.

"I can sense where it is being done. I will light your way. You carry the memories and power of your ancestors inside your soul. When the time comes, they will help you to know what must be done."

They walked on the shoulders of the road as the gates of Joe's memory opened and the old world of his childhood flooded back. Much of the reservation remained unchanged. They went past the war memorial ground with the statue of the soldier with the noble Indian face, past the pow-wow ground and the sacred Totem that his grandfather had revered.

He saw the signs of economic resurgence all about him. They passed the playground where mobs of children played on new structures of multi-colored bright plastic beneath powerful sodium lights. A two-story youth center rose next to a baseball field flanked by bleachers. Farther down, he saw the outlines of goalposts on either sides of a newly seeded football field.

He remembered all of this as a large expanse of scrub oak and wild grass littered with trash. The playground of his childhood consisted of half dozen old tires and several holes in the dirt. Alcoholism, unemployment and welfare had been the mainstay of the reservation back then. Now, comfortable-looking track houses sprouted throughout with their attached garages and blacktopped driveways.

They continued walking until the houses thinned and the road curved away from the woods. There, by the bright pool of a street lamppost, Joe found the secondary dirt road that he walked so often as a child.

It had been a main road then, Joe remembered. It was

like he was twelve again, coming home after one of those endless childhood summer days, home to the cabin where he lived with his grandfather.

They kept going on the dirt road until it ended in a circular clearing some forty yards down. A bare porch bulb glowed at the side of the door of a wood cabin on one corner of the semi-circle. The weak beams of light were gobbled by the surrounding woods like a giant dark sponge absorbing white liquid. On the other side of the clearing were two more cabins. They stood in the dim light as shadows, filled with dark angles where the boards covering the windows warped and stuck out. They resembled abandoned soldiers of a past era, rejected by the modern times that would inevitably bulldoze them into the ground they had sprung from, replacing them with plastic and bricks and steel. Tall weeds filled the clearing, waving in the night wind and lapping at the edges of the cabins like encroaching oceans. A rusted hand pump stood near the entrance of the outermost cabin, the handle seized shut, pointing to the sky as if beseeching divine intervention.

Joe walked to the door of the outermost cabin. He felt the presence of the Maiglin as she followed. When he reached the door he saw that it had been boarded shut and plywood covered the windows.

In the cabin there was something Joe needed. He could sense it calling to him, singing in his blood with screaming recollections.

The cabin had been boarded up when his grandfather died, and it had not been maintained. The nails rusted, the wood had rotted and bent. Joe grasped the edge of a plank and pulled. The wood gave and the corroded nails pulled out with groaning noises as if the ghosts of the cabin's past protested this intrusion.

Each board gave way with loud moans that echoed in the deserted clearing until the door stood alone, its obstacles removed.

Joe pulled the little penlight from his jacket pocket and examined the latch. His grandfather had never locked a door in his life. After he died, someone had placed a simple hook latch and secured it with a cheap little lock. Joe grasped the lock and pulled hard. On the third try, the rusted screw pulled out of the wood and the door opened.

Joe stepped inside, the beam of the little flashlight swinging back and forth. The Maiglin stood on the threshold, wide luminous eyes glowing in the pale reflected light.

The cabin remained pretty much as Joe had remembered except for the appliances. His grandfather's only concessions to modern times, a gas stove, a heater and a refrigerator, had been removed leaving gaps like pulled teeth.

Joe walked around the small rooms, the beam of light darting here and there casting shadows on the rough wood furniture and bare walls. There were only four rooms. What had been his bedroom, his grandfather's room, the larger kitchen-dining combination and a small utility-room. There had been electricity but no running water and Joe wondered if the little outhouse was still there at the edge of the woods.

As he stood, the silence soaked into his bones and the ghosts of the little cabin haunted his spirit, and he realized what he had come for. He had always known but did not want to admit it, did not want to drag it out into the light of his full consciousness. To do so would have been a total revocation of the life he had led since leaving the reservation.

He stood in the center of his grandfather's room as he played the flashlight beam around him. The thin circle of light lingered on the two photos on the wall, ancient yellowed photos, in the sepia style of its days. Dark smoldering eyes looked out at him from the other side of a bridge spanning nearly a century. Long beaded hair the color of midnight framed a high cheekbone face that set off the slight Asian fold of the eyes.

His grandmother had been full blood Shinnecock. Next to her picture hung a photo of his grandfather, young and tall wearing the "Ike" jacket and overseas cap of the US Army of 1945. The camera had caught a thin gleam of reflected light from the double rows of medals on his chest. Above the photos hung a ceremonial bow and feathered headdress. Only three pieces of furniture remained in the room. A frame bed elevated just inches off the floor on short thick oak legs, a night table and a long armoire where his grandparents had stored their clothing.

He opened the doors and drawers of the armoire.

Empty.

He looked under the bed. Nothing, yet he knew it was there, he could feel it calling him.

A gust of wind blew outside and whistled in some desolate crack of twisted wall planking. A few wind-driven raindrops splattered against the outside. Leaves and vegetation rustled and the air carried smells of burning fuel oil from the modern houses nearby.

A sharp twinge of pain brought Joe out of his reverie as he realized he had been digging into his palm with the nails of his clenched fingers. He felt a touch, gentle and light as floating silk. He followed the Maiglin as she held his arm and led him to the far corner of the dark room. She went to her knees and her hand hovered in circular motions, inches above the planks of the floor.

Joe squatted down and felt the rough wood where she placed her hand. The boards at that spot seemed a little higher than the rest. He inserted two fingers in a knothole and pulled up. Three planks nailed together rose on tiny pivoting brass hinges revealing the open top of a cedar chest secured under the floor.

He shined the thin beam into the chest and he saw it. It was lying there, nestled in one corner and cushioned under a pile of cedar shavings. He reached inside and imagined it leapt into his hand.

But of course it couldn't. It was just a stone.

The Vision Stone, the Manitou's gateway to the ancestors, the most sacred relic of his tribe, passed from each Shaman's hand to the next since anyone remembered.

He felt its magic like a distant puff of fragrant smoke carried on autumn breezes.

There were other things in the chest, things he recalled from his childhood and things he had never seen before, the aura of distant pasts and people long gone, clung to the contents and tugged at his heart.

He reached inside and pulled out his grandfather's vest, the ceremonial Shaman's vest the old man had worn on the day of Joseph Gray-Wolf's thirteenth birthday, the day he fought the Abaasy in the land of the ancestors across the dream-river.

He straightened and stood there, the Vision Stone smooth and warm in his hand and the Shaman's vest across his arm. He soaked in the feel of it, trying to let the meaning come to him.

A powerful light pinned him at that very moment like a skewered bug in a collection case. The person holding the light stood just outside the room, invisible behind the beam that lit the interior as if the sun rose in the confined dark space.

Joe blinked and squinted under the sudden brightness. He looked off the center of the beam and saw the protruding business end of a double barrel shotgun, the openings resembling close-set evil black eyes. He heard the metallic click of the hammer being cocked and the smooth confident voice that followed:

"Don't move a muscle friends. A blind man wouldn't miss at this range and I'm the best shot in this here county."

CHAPTER 61

Joe averted his eyes from the blinding light. Something seemed familiar about the voice. The beam slowly dropped to the floor and lit the room a little more evenly so now Joe could see the man holding the light and the old-fashioned double barrel shotgun.

He was old, somewhere between eighty and ninety. Only the face betrayed his age, pocked and wrinkled like leather cured without being stretched. Dark-skinned, the man's features held a mix of Asiatic and African under wide brown eyes flanked by networks of laugh lines and deep wrinkles like desert canyons. His voice filled the room with clear resonant tones.

"Well I'll be jumped up and down if it ain't little Joseph Gray-Wolf all growed up. Your Grand pappy told me you'd come back. He just didn't tell me you'd be a burglar. Inept one at that with the racket you made."

Joe heard the soft clicks of the hammers returned to their safe position and saw the twin barrels lower toward the floor. The man stepped forward and Joe recognized him instantly.

"Benjamin Two-Crows."

"The one and only," Two-Crows said as he stepped forward. He stopped a few feet from Joe and looked him over for a silent moment.

Two-Crows opened his arms and the men hugged like long-lost relatives, which indeed they were.

"Darn if you ain't the spittin image of your grandpappy," Two-Crows said, "Come on, let's get over to my cabin. You both look like you could use something warm."

Two-Crow's cabin was the one on the farthest side of the clearing with the porch light on, a throwback to the old days of the reservation with a few concessions to the amenities of the modern world. It had electricity, a refrigerator, and a Sony High Definition TV, no central heating, and no gas or electric stove. A cast iron potbelly heated the cabin and a fragrant stew bubbled atop its surface. There was no running water and Suffolk County's only operating outhouse stood just twenty feet from the back door.

Two-Crows had been Joe's grandfather's closest friend. They were raised together, fought together in the Great War, married and raised children with their families' homes practically touching. Joe remembered listening as if under a spell, his brother and cousins all around, as the two men took turns telling stories. There were tales of tribal lore, tales of magic, heroic warriors and the tragedies and tribulations that befell them. And afterwards, came the stories of the Great War. Everyone could tell those were different. The intensities of their voices and the shadows that ran across their faces signaled to all that it had been real, and truly happened. They were communication specialists, commo men in General Patton's fighting units. Their voices went out with no codes in clear tones that were immediately interpreted to the field commanders. There was no need for codes because Two-Crows and his grandfather spoke the old Shinnecock tongue. No German on earth could ever crack that language. They fought from North Africa, to Anzio, to Normandy and Remagan until they reached Berlin.

Two-Crows poured ladlefuls of stew into ancient chipped bowls decorated with tribal symbols. Wisps of steam rose from the bowls and the flavor of pungent herbs and spices filled every cavity of their mouth with glowing warmth and taste.

When Two-Crows handed a steaming bowl to the Maiglin, her wide eyes locked with his. Two-Crows' hand lingered on hers and something seemed to pass from the old man to the young alien girl. Something out of a deep level of the mind where mystical rules apply and everything is not as it seems.

"You said the Seer told you I would be back?" Joe asked.

The Seer had been what everyone called his grandfather. Bits of knowledge and wisps of information seemed to come his way. Many a tribal member had been delighted, baffled and comforted by stories and messages from relatives and friends who had passed on, stories and messages the Seer could not possibly have known by any normal means.

"What he said," Two-Crows answered, "is that you would return home to fight a battle for the people. You know how your grandfather was. Sometimes you understood what he said, other times you knew he looked at something that no one else could see, and he just left us behind without explanations."

"There is something I, we, have to do, that is, Mai-lin, she has to guide me to a place where something terrible is about to happen. There is no one to stop it but me, if I can. If I fail, the results will be horrible for all people. I guess my grandfather saw that somehow."

"What is this about and how can I help you?" Two-Crows asked.

"I can't even begin to explain what it's all about. Some day when I sort it out myself, I'll be able to tell you. What I need now is a ride to the woods behind the Lab. We have to get in there and we sure can't go through the front gate."

CHAPTER 62

———◆———

They left the cabin as Two-Crows led the way with a big lantern. The rain had stopped but the wind picked up. Two-Crows brought them to a small dirt road off the clearing. The road ended at an ancient run down barn that looked like it would collapse in any good storm. The old Indian pulled back the wide planked door on its wooden rollers, stepped inside and hung the electric lantern on a wood peg.

It stood there in the middle of the dirt floor, ancient as the dinosaurs but preserved like the classic it was, a 1941 Willis Jeep. Thousands of them carried armies of GI's through World War Two and Korea. This one sported a fresh coat of paint, original olive drab, and here and there patches of new metal had been welded or screwed in to replace rotted spots. The top was green canvas and Pepboys mirrors had been added as a necessary concession to the demands of the New York Motor Vehicle Bureau to receive the Historical license plates affixed to her bumpers.

"Ain't she a beauty though," Two-Crows said, "She'll pull four people up a forty degree incline and go through mud or sand like shit through a goose."

Two-Crows went to a corner of the barn and kicked off some dirt revealing a wide plank. He grasped one end and pulled it up leaving it standing against the wall. He reached into the opening and took out a long bundle wrapped in oilcloth. The greasy smell of gun lubricant and linseed oil filled the barn as Two-Crows unwrapped the bundle.

"Here's my other beauty. Your grand pappy and me carried one of these from 41 to 45. I shoot it at least three times a week, still can blow off the left eye of a flea at a hundred yard."

Joe looked at the rifle. Small with a long barrel, it looked vaguely familiar until he remembered that his grandfather used to have one also. Maybe it was the same one.

"M-1S Carbine, S stands for Scout, only a couple thousands of them made," continued Two-Crows as he put a short clip in the belly of the weapon. It locked in with a positive sounding click, "Best darned infantry and sniping weapon ever made. Don't care what they say about their new plastic rifles, gimme one of these babies in any situation and I'll be right as rain."

"Benjamin, you can't…"

Two-Crows cut him off as he stepped closer.

"Don't Benjamin me boy. I'm so far past eighty years old, I stopped counting long time ago. I married me a fine woman when I was a young man. She died when I wasn't a young man anymore and I married me another fine woman. When she died I knew there wouldn't be no more. I got so many kids and grandchildren and great-grandchildren, I can't keep track, done everything I cared to do and saw everything I cared to see. I only got one fear now, and it sure ain't dying. Know what that fear is boy?"

Joe shook his head no.

"It's the fear of losing it, stuck in some home with your body leaking from every which way while you sit in your wheel chair waitin, prayin, to die. So you see boy, when you come here, full of some need, fairly crying out for help with that quiet little gal over there, I can't help but think that maybe that's why I been here so long and can still move like I do. I believe that your grandpappy knew that. I believe he saw this night coming where we all got to do what we gotta do, even if we ain't so sure what that is right now."

They got in the Willis as Two-Crow clicked a toggle switch, there was no ignition lock, and stepped hard on the gas, activating the electric starter.

The old Flathead-four engine turned over twice and started with a noise like a dozen typewriters doing 200 words a minute.

"Don't pay it no mind, they always sound like that," Two-Crows said, "It still runs a damn sight better than those itty-bitty modern luminem motors."

They pulled out on the main road and left the reservation grounds into Montauk Highway, the main street that looped around the territory. They drove just two miles before Two-Crows turned into a smaller side street.

The street was straight as the arrows that Joe's ancestors had made in the same woods that flanked this blacktopped road. The houses stood scattered with dark patches of thick scrub oaks and gnarled pines between them. After a few minutes of driving, the houses and lights disappeared. The blacktop changed to a hardscrabble path, barely wide enough for the Willis. They drove a few more feet until they came to a gate constructed of two logs lashed together, and held between posts by heavy chains and a padlock.

On either side, the shoulders of the road gleamed with wet sand and pine needles. A green and white sign glowed in the headlights with the New York State Department of Conservation logo.

UPTON PINE BARRENS.
MOTOR VEHICLES FORBIDDEN. NO ENTRANCE
WITHOUT SPECIAL PERMIT. NO HUNTING. NO
TRESPASSING.

Two-Crows backed up on whining gears. He engaged the four-wheel drive lever with a clunk and turned hard right into the sand. The tires dug in, slipped and kicked as each one stuck here and there, and was pulled out by the other gripping wheels. Sand, dirt, pine needles and sticks ejected out from the spinning tires. Branches and long pine boughs scratched and rubbed on the canvas sides as if they were trying to hold the Willis back and crying out to stop the occupants.

They went around the thick post and returned to the path where the darkness behind them swallowed the log gate.

From that point, Two-Crows followed Joe's directions. A couple of miles farther, the path ended in fields of tall grass and scrubby bushes. The headlights lit parts of the field, revealing small hills overgrown with weeds.

"Okay," Joe said, "this is where we would ride our bikes to go fishing, it was part of the old Camp Upton. They shut it down in fifty-seven and took a big chunk of the land for Brookhaven Lab. Those little hills are where the soldiers on exercises would bury garbage and empty ammo casings. They weren't particularly concerned about the environment twenty years before the creation of the EPA."

Joe guided the Willis across the field between grassy weed-choked mounds and brushes like sentries for the scattered tall pines and big oaks with their crooked branches and twisted reaching limbs. The wind held steady with occasional bursting gales that bent the tree trunks and sent smaller branches flying. Any lights from the surrounding towns had been absorbed by the thick woods. The stars and moon were hidden by the mass of storm clouds and darkness filled the area around the tunnels of light created by the headlamps. Intermittent gusts blew the canvas top and sides of the Willis like storm sails. They had to shout for their voices to rise above the tumult of the wind and thousands of shaking branches and leaves. The smell of pine and rotted vegetation lay thick in the stormy air.

They reached the end of the field and the ground dipped some five feet into a slope of mud and dirty sand that ended at a twenty-foot wide stream.

It was the last tributary of the Peconic River that started at Flanders Bay and ran through the Eastern Long Island town of Riverhead. Joe knew the stream ended some miles into the absorbing sands of the Pine Barrens that composed the surrounding woods of Brookhaven National Lab.

Two-Crows turned the Jeep into the stream heading west.

The two right wheels sank in water and mud that rose halfway to their hubs while the left wheels rode on the muck of the narrow bank. Two-Crows drove the Willis like it wouldn't quit and of course it wouldn't, the old machine had been built war-tough. The cast iron Flathead Four coughed and sputtered when the wheels sent great splashes of water in the engine compartment. The little vehicle followed the stream, the occupants clinging to whatever protruded in the interior as the wheels rocked, spun and jammed only to be brought free with careening lurches that threatened to capsize it at any moment.

They continued this way, Two-Crows barely in control, until they reached a spot where the stream widened into a small pond before continuing into the woods. The banks narrowed and a half buried log blocked the way.

The part of the log that protruded was only about a foot high. Two-Crows looked at it for a moment through the leaves and mud spattered windshield. Then he engaged the clutch and gave it more gas.

Both front tires screeched, their rubber smoking from the friction as they ran on the slick sides of the log. The rear wheels jerked and jolted and the front wheels climbed over the log.

When the rear wheels hit the log, they disturbed some pockets of sand, soft mud and waterlogged piles of vegetation the log had rested on.

The rear wheels spun on the top of the rotted wood and the log gave out. The part of it that stuck out on the bank rose up as the rest of the ground collapsed. The nose of the Willis reared up like a bronco and the rear wheels slid into the water. As the log spun out, the jeep turned over on its side, unable to maintain its center of gravity and splashed sideway into the stream. Cold mud-choked water covered the Willis and poured through the gaps in the canvas and the side door that had been blown open from the impact.

CHAPTER 63

Brookhaven National Lab, Ion Collider Building, 7:30PM

Duncan Wesley paced behind the rows of a dozen computer consoles, each manned by technicians as endless figures and symbols flashed across the glowing screens.

A low squeaking noise came out of Wesley's mouth as he ground his molars to dissipate the rage he felt coursing through his system. He lit a cigarette and watched the blue smoke puff up in a cloud that floated toward the heights of the corrugated ceiling. He wished one of the nerdy little bastards at the consoles said something about the cigarette so he could have the pleasure of bashing his head in. Of course, they didn't, no one dared.

Two things frosted his pumpkin tonight. The first was that dammed Prabinwah. He was certain the little shit was deliberately stalling. They were behind by about an hour. The Artifact event should have taken place already; instead they were just positioning it now. The Artifact container resembled a half football shaped cylinder about three feet high and a foot across, composed of stainless steel lined with two inches of Boron-Silicate Lead compounds. The container was composed of three hermetically sealed sections that would come apart under the direction of the computers. That would happen one hour from now and fifteen seconds before a pulsed array stream of Ion-Plasma would be hurled through the Artifact at the speed of light.

That moment would mark the beginning of his reign, his stewardship of mankind with his Sylvan partner.

CHAPTER 64

———◆———

Two-Crows pushed open the driver's door and stuck his head above the water. Joe kicked out the side canvas and stood on the overturned vehicle, holding the Maiglin and pulling her out. They were at a point where the stream started to die out until it turned to a trickle that finally disappeared in the woods. Hardly any current remained at that spot, and it was barely deep enough to cover the little Willis.

They dragged themselves up on the riverbank, wet, shivering and muddy. Two-Crows managed to pull out the old M-1S carbine and Joe heard the clanking of the spare magazines in the old man's pockets. He pulled the little pencil light from his soaked jacket as he remembered that model had been waterproof. He clicked the little light and looked over the old man and the girl.

"Shut the dadburn light off," Two-Crows said, "You're ruining my night vision. We got some passel of shit now don't we boy?"

Two-Crows shook water out of the old M-1S and wiped mud away with a soaked handkerchief.

"Might as well leave that alone," Joe said, "we're finished now."

"Sheeit," replied Two-Crows, "maybe you're finished,

but we ain't, this old rifle and me. I carried her through Bastogne with old Blood-and-Guts Patton, in blizzards, mud and cold a sight worse than this. If this was one of them fancy plastic guns they use now, I'd say okay. But there ain't no stopping these two old warriors."

No stopping what? Joe thought. He felt lost, a kind of alien in a landscape of desperation. He barely knew where he was, had no idea how to get where he had to go, and no idea what to do if somehow he got there. He was drenched and cold, trailing one young, or old—how could you really tell?—strange outlander girl and one old armed coot, both equally drenched and cold.

Joe waved the little penlight beam between the Maiglin and Two-Crows. The girl's black hair hung plastered to her forehead and her water logged clothing dripped dark muddy stream water. She was still and her pupil-filled eyes seemed to reach through on a separate plane of yet unformed communications. She was totally unaffected by the cold wind blowing around her soaked body.

Two-Crows was another story. The old man shivered as if someone had hooked him up to a wall outlet. His face looked like bloated dough and he clung to the carbine with hands that trembled like gnarled branches in a gale. Hypothermia was beginning to set in, and Joe felt himself shaking also. He wondered how long it would take before their core temperature dropped to a point where it would affect their logic and thinking. Probably a lot less time than it would take to find help.

CHAPTER 65

———◆———

6th Precinct, Suffolk County Police, Yaphank, Long Island, New York, 7:50PM

Donohue had not gotten to be one of the Bureau's top investigators by following the well-trodden path. It wasn't that he chose not to follow accepted investigative methods; he did. He accepted nothing as fact until it had proven itself. That kind of thinking often drew him into areas where he produced results that others had missed.

When he received the information from NSA through the usual FBI channels, Donohue had used it like any other clue. He followed up, but didn't believe it until it had proven itself to be true.

So far it had not.

Everything he encountered pointed to a group of people running from some unknown enemies. He found no evidence to back the NSA information of a terrorist cult led by Dr Wu and his associates.

The Chinese doctor and the woman they arrested at the train station underwent separate interrogations for over an hour. Outrageous as their stories were, elves endowed with mental powers, ancient creatures that moved through the earth and rogue NSA agents, fantastic as they were, they corroborated each other. While the scenario they described was hard to swallow, nothing in the evidence actually contradicted it.

Donohue opened a fresh pack of Camels, his third of this long day, and lit the new cigarette with the old butt. Wu's assertion of impending doom this very night disturbed him more than he cared to admit. The old Chinese carried a certain dignity, a presence and command of facts that could not be shaken by interrogations. The girl Charly had no scientific background but her story fit and they hadn't tripped her up.

It was time to visit the lab.

CHAPTER 66

Near Brookhaven National Lab

Joe couldn't feel his hands. They had turned into large lumps, attached to his body but feeling like they belonged to someone else. The dunk into the near ice of the stream, followed by exposure to the cold blowing wind, rapidly sapped his strength. He had stopped shivering and weariness was taking hold through the depths of his body. They walked a few yards from the spot where the Jeep Willis sunk, and stopped. Two-Crows half-sat half-lay in the dark of the muddy banks, the old M-1S wrapped inside his arms as if it would provide life saving heat.

He dimly sensed the Maiglin's presence. He thought he could see the young girl's eyes in the wind-swept darkness like the glowing orbs of a giant cat. Now he felt her touch through the icy sleeve of his soaked jacket and the numbness of his body as it entered the early stages of hypothermia.

I will light your way.

Where she touched, smoky warmth penetrated to his skin and he felt the heat diffuse throughout his body in glowing whorls. It penetrated each organ and the marrow of his bones, it flashed throughout his nerves and rode each molecule of pulsing blood. The weariness lifted as he felt the icy grip of hypothermia tear its shroud from the recess of his brain.

Restoring beams of energy blinked and whirled like summer fireflies on all the surfaces of his body and by their glimmering flashes, he saw the Maiglin's other hand resting on Two-Crow's head. The old man revived with the same life-giving warmth Joe was experiencing.

Something else also went on. Joe's perspective altered in a way he could not fully understand. He felt as if he looked out from a place different than where he stood. The air filled with a glow, a kind of crepuscular light emanating from the trees, bushes and soil. It stretched in the distance and revealed the tiny ripples and waves of the stream. At that moment, Joe saw himself, leaning against a great oak, and he realized the source of the light.

He was seeing through the Maiglin's eyes.

I will light your way.

Off in the distance, maybe a mile or so, a shimmering wave of light rose above the glowing treetops. Undulating and shifting shapes of dim energy rose and dissipated until they disappeared hundreds of yards into the night sky.

He heard the Maiglin softly echo in his mind:

That is the signal from what your people call the Artifact. They have covered it with metal and dimmed its call but they cannot hide it completely from the eyes of Sylvans. That is where you must go.

They walked on the bank of the stream, every footstep clutched by the sucking mud. The wind continued howling among the shaking trees, drowning out Two-Crows mutterings. The old man had recovered and clutched the M-1S as he followed behind them.

The stream narrowed when they came to a cleared path two yards wide running at a ninety-degree angle to the stream. The path contained a twelve foot fence topped with razor wire, and circled the entire perimeter of Brookhaven National Lab. Climbing the fence would be impossible for any one not trained in such things. To make matters even more difficult, sensors wired together every ten feet would bring security running if the fence was climbed or rattled.

The stream remained the weak spot that Joe remembered from decades ago when he sometimes breached the security of the Lab on dares from the other reservation children. In those days, no sensor or razor wires adorned the fence. It had been a pre-terrorism game back then.

The tidal based ebb and flow of the stream left a foot and a half gap at the bottom of the fence where the soil had been eroded away, and Joe got on his knees, then flat on the ground. He crawled, face in the dirt, the top of his body less than an inch from the bottom of the fence. When he reached the other side, he turned back to Two-Crow.

"Hope you don't expect an old man like me to do that," Two-Crows said.

"Just lay down flat and hold out your arms under the fence. I'll pull you through," Joe replied.

"Okay, okay. Here, take my rifle and be careful with it."

"I don't think you're going to need it. Why don't we just leave it here and…"

"Blast it Joseph Gray-Wolf," Two-Crows said, "the longer you been away, the stupider you got. I know we're going to need it. I can feel it in my bones."

Joe took the M-1S, pulled it under the fence and rested it against a tree. He grasped Two-Crows' forearms, pulled him to the other side of the fence and helped him up. He turned to help the Maiglin, but the girl had already passed under.

They walked through the forest by the glow reflected all around them. It seemed as if the entire woods were made of some glow-in-the-dark stuff. The luminescence surrounded them and wrapped itself all around like ghostly lights. They followed the glistening beacon of the Artifact, rising in the sky like pastel smoke.

As they approached the edge of the woods, the bright lights from the building chased out the glow of the woods. Joe felt a twinge in his mind like a solitary, nocturnal whisper, and the night vision the Maiglin provided, disappeared.

They stood just a dozen or so yards from where the woods changed into a manicured lawn. The lawn continued for a hundred feet and stopped at a curbed blacktop road. Inside the semi oval formed by the road, the physics building was lit by dozens of in-ground spotlights, and Joe saw four pairs of guards and a Chevy blazer slowly patrolling the grounds around the clustered buildings. Another guard stood at the door and farther down a Hummvee blocked the road from the rest of the grounds.

Joe looked at the Maiglin and addressed his thoughts to her.

"It's inside this building that I'm supposed to stop whatever is going to happen tonight?"

He felt her reply like whispers of silk.

"It is inside and it waits. I have done all I am able to. I will help shield you from the Sylvan, the one who would stop you. I cannot shield you from all the humans, nor can I protect you from the Maarzuk whom I can feel growing near."

"Now what son?" Two-Crows whispered, "Is it that building you've got to get into?"

"Yeah, but look at those guards. I'll never get past them much less figure out what to do when I get inside."

"All right," Two-Crows said, "better let this old soldier do some strategic thinking for you. See that small building on the edge of the woods, across the road from the entrance to the big building?"

"Yes, it looks like some kind of storage. No lights, no windows."

"That's the one," Two-Crows said, "Follow the wood line, stay well back so they don't see you. Don't worry about making noise, ain't nobody going to hear nothing with this wind going on. Get directly behind the building and get ready. I'm going to cause a ruckus with these good folks, believe you me. When they're all taking care of business with me, you run across the road and into the building. You got that boy?"

"What kind of ruckus? These guys look serious. You're going to wind up getting hurt."

"Sheeit," Two-Crows said, "you forget who I am boy. The best hunter and wood scout the Shinnecock nation ever produced. If old Blood and Guts was alive, he'd testify to that, yes sir. I scouted for old Patton from Normandy to Berlin itself. This is going to be easier than falling off a log. You just do what you got to do and don't worry about old Two-Crows."

Joe looked around for the Maiglin but the alien girl had disappeared. He sensed her, somewhere inside the blackness of the woods. He nodded to Two-Crows and walked inside the woods to the back of the building that the old Indian pointed out.

Two-Crows lay down in the shrubs and weed choked scrub oaks. Barely enough light penetrated from the building across the road so he could set up his hiding place. He dragged branches and weeds and prepared the spot until he was satisfied, then he lay down again and positioned the old M-1S.

Two-Crows was unafraid but not as confident as he had told Joe. Ever since he surprised Joe and that strange girl in the boarded up house, Two-Crows felt the shifting tides of fate. Maybe it was the Airwalker that brought the news on the wings of one of its animal tribes, or maybe his ancestors sang to him in the blood that flowed in his old veins. Whatever brought these events to Two-Crows, he knew this day would end like none other.

Enough time passed for Joe to reach his objective, so Two-Crows positioned the M-1S. He sank down even farther, feeling every twig, pine needle and pebble under his body. He splayed his legs in the classic sniper position with feet pointing out. He rested the barrel on a branch, locked his elbows, sighted and squeezed the trigger with the slow pull of the expert marksman.

CHAPTER 67

Outside the front gates of Brookhaven National Laboratory, 8:12PM

Donohue didn't like traveling this way. He preferred the quiet unobtrusive approach, not letting anyone know you were coming until you showed up. He sat in the passenger side of a borrowed unmarked Suffolk County Police car while his assistant, drove. The rear passenger compartment had been designed to carry prisoners with a hardened glass partition separating front from back and rear doors. It only opened from the outside. Dr. Wu and Charly sat in back.

They followed a Suffolk Police cruiser with two uniformed officers and flashing lights and howling sirens. The 6th Precinct was only a few minutes from the gates of the Lab and when they arrived, a Laboratory security car waited to take them to the physics building.

They stopped at the roadblock, a Hummer parked sideways across the semi circle of road flanking the physics building, and adjoining Ion Collider housing.

Gales of wind blew heavy damp air across Donohue's face and threatened to rip the cigarette from his lips. He closed the buttons on his coat as he walked to the Hummvee where the Lab security men spoke to the two guards manning the roadblock.

"Look pal," one of the guards told the Lab security man, "nobody gets through here. These buildings are under direct NSA control and considered Federal property, plus, whatever is going on in there tonight has been classified under National Security."

Both guards stood over six feet with no possibility of fat on their body. Brush cuts and a hard look pegged them as military, as much as the familiar and professional manner they wielded the wicked looking machine pistols dangling on shoulder straps. Waist high, hand resting lightly on the wire stock, Donohue got the impression that these guys would have the guns leveled and firing accurately in a blink of an eye. The contrast between the two guards and the private rent-a-cop security of the Lab was startling. They were clearly outclassed and certainly outgunned.

Donohue walked slowly to the group and stopped just two feet from the nearest guard. He slowly reached inside his coat pocket and pulled out a small leather case. He held it up to the guard's eye.

"Ever see one of these before Buckaroo?"

The guard glanced at it. His fingers traced the outline of the machine pistol stock before he returned his gaze to Donohue.

"I don't care if you're the Pope himself, nobody gets through tonight."

Donahue appeared more annoyed at his cigarette going out than the guard's refusal. He held the ID steady in front of the guard as he spoke again.

"Maybe you better take another look Buckaroo. The top part is standard FBI Special Agent ID. The bottom part is National Security Emergency Task Force. It identifies me as the agent in charge of this little cluster-fuck. Since this is a domestic matter, I outrank your boss. If you look closer, you'll see some green eagle shit there. That's called a Presidential Seal. You have reached a career-defining moment. So I tell you what, Buckaroo, you let me in and tell your boss I'm coming, escort me if you want, I really don't give a shit, or I will make two phone calls, long distance, Washington DC. Within an hour there will be so many agents swarming over these grounds, you won't ever know which way is up. One thing for certain though, your next job will be handing out flyers at Wal-Mart. Comprendo buckaroo?"

The guard looked at the ID again and licked his lips. He turned to the other guard who answered his look with a shrug.

"Call Wesley," the guard said, "tell him he's got some visitors he's got to see."

Two-Crows' first bullet hit the left rear quarter of the Blazer right at the gas tank filler. The interior of the truck instantly filled with the odor of spilled gasoline. Both men inside jumped out cursing. Two more rounds hit so quickly it sounded like someone doing a rap-tap with a hammer on the sheet metal. The two men dropped to the ground as one keyed a small shoulder mike.

"This is mobile patrol, we're taking sniper fire, we're…"

The man's next words were cut short by the thumping woosh of the exploding fuel tank as Two-Crows' next bullet sparked off the gasoline. Both men ran from the burning vehicle and rolled behind a tree. There wasn't any way to tell where the sniper fire came from as the wind howled and the shaking trees and branches set off a din that drowned out the noise. The edge of the woods and the building flickered red in the flames of the burning truck. Black greasy smoke swept immediately sideways by the wind into the faces of the patrolling guards. The smell of burning gasoline, melting plastic and rubber permeated the grounds.

Two-Crows traversed the M-1S and sighted just above the heads of two guards crouching next to a parked station wagon. He blew out front and rear door windows. Thousands of tiny pieces of shattered safety glass rained down on the guards who now lay flat on the ground trying to become part of the earth.

Bathed in the light from the buildings the guards could not see into the dark woods where the shots came from.

The howling wind tore away the crack of the carbine and flung it to be lost among the cacophony of the windy forest.

Two-Crows fired another half dozen shots. Caged light bulbs blew out in showers of sparks, tires exploded and another fuel tank burst into flames, so now two vehicles were on either side of the buildings like giant torches.

Three guards ran to the front of the structure and climbed a zigzag metal staircase to a platform where a spotlight was mounted on swivels. Two of the guards took up stations on either side of the spotlight, M-16's resting on the rails. The third guard turned on the powerful light and started playing it across the surrounding woods.

The genes of Two-Crows' tribal ancestors carried a quality paramount to the battle success of the warriors of the Eastern forest tribes like the Shinnecocks.

The quality was stillness.

Two-Crows pushed handful of leaves over the M-1 and quickly set up some surrounding pine branches over his prone body. With the dark brown and gold cammos he wore and the pine branches over him, he blended in the surroundings like an acorn.

Two-Crows put his face against the dirt and pine needles of the forest floor and became still. He became part of the environment, still as the stones in the dirt and the thick fallen branches about him.

The spotlight slowly passed over Two-Crow's body. The shooters on either side of the light sighted down the barrels, ready to loose streams of 7.62mm steel jacketed slugs into anything that moved.

The trees moved, the branches moved, the scrub oaks moved and shifted under the storm wind.

Two-Crows and the ground were indistinguishable. Neither moved a hair.

A glowing noonday circle from the spotlight passed over Two-Crows. The moment the light left his area he opened his eyes, raised the carbine and put four rapid-fire, tightly grouped rounds into the spotlight.

The halogen beam exploded out, showering the guards

below with slivers of thin glass. The three men on the now darkened spotlight platform hugged the perforated steel floor of the stand. One of them let out a three round burst that whizzed aimlessly into the dark woods.

The guards all ready called for the security helicopter and re-enforcements. The weather made it dicey for the chopper to even fly in the rising storm and re-enforcements were at least some fifteen minutes away.

Covered by the commotion Two-Crows caused, Joe dashed across the road behind a pair of crouching security guards, pushed open the door and entered the building.

Two-Crows had himself a grand old time. Six decades dropped from his life like the late autumn leaves on the storm-tossed oaks. He was the young Shinnecock warrior again, the one who scouted for Patton as they approached the noose of Bastogne that held the 82nd airborne. He felt like screaming out the war cry of his people as he had done at Remagen when they took the bridge, and later on the outskirts of Berlin as scores of German soldiers fell to the deadly fire of his M-1S carbine.

Two-Crows heard the war cry of his ancestors calling him in the gusts of wind that ran through the forest. He raised the carbine and sighted again on the scene of disrupted confusion fifty yards ahead of him.

CHAPTER 68

It didn't know anger for it had no glands to produce adrenaline and the other chemicals that incited emotions in the race of men. But something was bred into its very being, something operating on molecular, atomic, and sub-atomic levels, incomprehensible and as alien to humans as the moon would be to a praying mantis. For in that molecular and sub-atomic environment, thrived the force that drove the Maarzuk to fierce bouts of deadly rage and purpose.

It sensed the humans it was charged to kill. It had stalked them but always the dreaded light was there until they cocooned themselves in hollow steel tubes that flew above the surface on shiny rails.

The Maarzuk had the ability to move fast. Its atoms formed and reformed, shifted and surged through the composition of matter, of soil, rocks, dirt and water.

But it could not keep up with a train.

The Maarzuk sent out feelers the width of just one or two atoms that danced and stretched and weaved through the surrounding matter. It felt the location of each of its prey in the light filled world it could not reach, above the ground.

The Maarzuk was aware of its foes splitting into two groups. It sensed the one called Joe who had taken the

Maiglin with him. The memories bound in its electrons remembered the Maiglins. They had been the implacable enemies of his kind, half-Humans half-Sylvans, they led the war that raged across the planet, the war resulting in the destruction of his kind, leaving him the only survivor.

There was no regret, sadness or fear in the creature's makeup, only the imperative to hunt and kill the designated humans and the Maiglin. Since the group split up, the Maarzuk had to make a choice which to hunt first.

It chose Joe and the Maiglin.

For long moments the Maarzuk tracked them, sensing them in the dark forest, a perfect environment for his task, away from the deadly Photon rays of the light It had not been able to reach them until now, when the Maiglin and the one called Joe were back in the protective light.

Yet there was another, one who had chosen to accompany them. Even though this human had not been on the destruction imperative, still he was now part of the group simply by joining them. If no other purpose, the destruction of the new human would help assuage the ravenous psychic hunger for death that coursed in the atoms of its being.

And now, that one was out there, in the forest, in the dark, alone.

Two-Crows fired again, blowing out a side mirror on a car next to a crouching guard. The guards moved up, infantry squad fire and movement style. Only the fire came from Two-Crows in the black recesses of the woods.

Two-Crows lined up the sights of the carbine for a shot at one of the surviving spotlights, when he caught a whiff of sulfur and almonds.

The smell overwhelmed him, acrid with sulfur and stomach-turning sickly sweet almonds. He felt a choking dread envelop him as the night blackened with a shifting cloudy presence holding the call of death.

He dropped the M-1S and raised his torso from the ground. The woods were black as the inside of a tar pit.

Inside the darkness, indigo clouds of shadow enveloped him and he felt the wind of flashing silvery swords and metal claws.

The Maarzuk came out of the ground as if forced through a sieve, and the shifting ebony cloud enveloped Two-Crows. A tongue of black smoke solidified into a whirling razor sword that flashed down and cut his body in half. Two-Crows felt no pain, and died in less than a second as whirling blades cut his body into bloody pieces no larger than shopping bags.

On the light-bathed perimeter of the physics building, several guards saw the flashing and whirling blades appear and disappear like sparks in the night. They fired long bursts of automatic weapons fire that hit the pieces of what had been Two-Crows, making them hop and jump like bloody stumps in a *Dance Macabre.*

The bullets passed harmlessly through the Maarzuk as its smoky form retreated into the ground.

CHAPTER 69

Inside the building, Duncan Wesley's first reaction had been anger when the guard informed him about the FBI visitor at the roadblock. He left the physics building by the rear door so he could meet those people himself. He walked the hundred or so yards to the barricade where they waited. As he approached, he recognized Wu sitting in the rear of the unmarked police sedan.

Wesley stepped up to Donohue, exchanged a few words, verified his ID and told him to follow him to his office. He intended to stall them until the event.

As he led the way, Duncan glanced at his watch. Less than six minutes to go before they unshielded the Artifact, but this time it wouldn't be a tickler like the last two days. This time, within one minute from unshielding, the Artifact would receive the full dose of a Pulsed Array Ion stream from the Collider.

From that point on, the world belonged to Duncan Wesley and the Sylvan. It was all ready too late for any of it to be stopped.

Donohue, Wu, Charly and a uniformed Suffolk County Officer had crossed over half the manicured lawn. It was a large field more than it was a lawn. A particularly strong gust of wind rocked them a little, and they leaned away from the gale sweeping across the bare grass. It was at that moment that Two-Crow's first bullets found the gas tank of the blazer. They saw the guards roll out of the vehicle as it went up in garish orange flames.

"Hold it. What the hell's going on?" Wesley said, the words torn out of his mouth by the storm winds.

Now they saw guards running on either side of the building, diving for cover as bullets blew out car windows, lights and ricocheted on the concrete walls. Someone punched an alarm and the wail of a siren added its noise to the screaming wind, the shouting and running and the muffled pop of the second gas tank going off.

"Come on," yelled Wesley to Donohue and the others, "let's get the hell in the building. Whatever's going on, we'll have it under control real quick."

As they approached the building at a run, they saw several guards aiming a spotlight into the woods. The spotlight went out in a shower of glass debris and sparks. They reached the back door, and Wesley ushered them in. Donohue's face was red and coarse from the unexpected exertion. A couple of packs of Camels a day didn't do much to improve his performance.

Just as the last person went through the door and Wesley prepared to slam it shut, he saw the lone figure running from the darkness of the adjacent building, across the road and into the side door.

"Sonafabitch," Wesley muttered to himself through clenched teeth, "Joseph Gray-Wolf. I'm glad you're in. No more chasing your illusive ass anymore. You just walked into the lion's den you dumb bastard."

They stood inside the hallway as Wesley pulled a tiny radio from his pocket and clicked the mike.

"Exterior security, draw close to the building. Seal the entrances and shoot anything that approaches."

"Yes sir, we're on it."

"Interior security, we have an intruder, came in the North side door. I want him found and I want this place tighter than a duck's ass in water."

Wu held Donohue's coat and spoke to the FBI agent, his tones fevered with urgency.

"You've got to act," the Chinese scientist said, "You know something's not right. You checked my record and Joseph's. We're both clean as a whistle. You've been fed disinformation and it's up to you to see through it. If you don't stop what 's going to happen here tonight, this procedure I told you about, there will be no tomorrow for any of us."

Wesley turned his attention to the conversation between Donohue and Wu.

"He's not feeding you that crap he gave me before he disappeared, is he Special Agent? That bullshit about fairies and space aliens, that's what he uses to cover his terrorist activities, him and that cult."

"I have a few loose ends to tie together," Donohue shrugged, "I want to see what's going on in this building."

"What's going on is a national security classified matter. But suit yourself, I'll show you around since you pulled rank with domestic priority," Wesley replied as he led them toward the interior of the building.

CHAPTER 70

Joe burst through the side door like a linebacker charging a quarterback. The guard assigned to the door crouched outside behind a metal waste can, automatic weapon pointing to the interior of the dark forest. He didn't see Joe dash inside.

Joe had no idea where to go or what to do to stop whatever Wu told him would happen. He had a vague idea of some sort of alien shaped thing, of course it would be glowing in some fashion and maybe if he just broke it somehow…

But first he had to find it.

He ran down the short corridor from the entrance and turned into a wider hallway, crashing into a desk blocking the way, and two guards standing next to it. Joe had a flash of their surprised faces eyes open wide, mouths just starting to form words.

It was just animal reaction, a move of pure instinct dredged up from the non-thinking part of Joe's brain. The part that reacts, that fights or runs with adrenaline filled energy. He launched a running, windmill roundhouse punch that landed square on the side of the first guard's head. The punch knocked the man out cold and sent him sprawling into his partner as both men fell in a tangle of flaying arms and legs.

The second man struggled to push the inert body of the first guard when Joe ran past and landed a kick that caught the rising man in the chest.

The second guard fell back, the wind knocked from his lungs. He was young, strong and well trained. He recovered fairly quickly and rose on shaky legs, holding the desk for support. He drew the automatic pistol from his holster and fired three rounds at Joe's fleeing figure.

The guard's actions came too late, and the bullets hit the far wall where Joe all ready turned the corner, and disappeared in the adjoining hallway. The guard took a small device from his belt and keyed the solitary red button in a small pad.

A shrill alarm klaxon sounded in blasts spaced two seconds apart. The sharp piercing noise filled the interior of the building. Red lights mounted in a corner flashed out revolving red streams of light.

Joe ran the length of the hallway and pushed open a wide double door with red radiation warning symbols. His heart pounded and he smelled ozone permeating the atmosphere inside the building. He sensed tingling undercurrents of invisible forces around him as he turned yet another corner.

He had a split second impression of giant curls of wire in a gymnasium size room when a tremendous weight hit him between the shoulder blades. He fell heavily. His outstretched arms could not prevent his head banging into the painted concrete floor. He tasted blood in his mouth and bright sparks went off in his eyes followed by a still darkness.

Duncan Wesley preceded Donohue and his party into the Artifact chamber, and waived them inside. Banks of computers lined a double leaded-glass enclosure with re-enforced steel doors. Behind each computer console sat technicians, their faces highlighted by the dull green glow of the screens as they made continuous adjustments to the electronic controls of the giant Collider and Phased Array Pulse Radiation Generator wrapped around the room like giant electronic pythons.

Dr. Prabinwah paced on a small raised platform, going from one console to the next, speaking rapidly to technicians and regulating the minute corrections like a conductor in an invisible and silent electronic orchestra.

Inside the shielded room, a three-foot high case shaped like half a football, made of titanium composite denser than lead, sat on a stainless steel table. Knobby extrusions extended from fastenings and controlled the three doors that would release and fall away from the case, exposing the Artifact. The doors were so finely machined that only a hairline revealed their existence to a close scrutiny. The computers controlled the precise opening of the doors, and the exposure of the Artifact to the Ion stream and pulsed radiation.

Dr. Prabinwah turned from a console and saw the group that Duncan Wesley just ushered in. His face lit with surprise as he recognized his old boss, Dr. Wu, and their eyes met across the expanse of the vast room.

Donohue looked around at the imposing array of electronic controls and strange machinery, operating in total silence, and he knew that here he was out of his element. Something vaguely disturbing about this operation flitted around his mind, something hovering just out of his reach. Still, he could find no justification, no base of evidence outside of Wu's say-so to halt the procedure.

He also doubted that he could stop it even if he decided he had to. Pulling rank and intimidating a guard to gain access was one thing. Stopping Duncan Wesley and the arrayed manpower around him would be something else. In spite of his earlier bluster, he didn't have the authority to do so and a misstep of this magnitude would surely end his career.

From the corner of his eye, Donohue noticed the quick hand signal interplay between the Indian scientist on the platform and Dr. Wu. He saw Wesley had not noticed as he stood facing Donohue.

"Well Special Agent," Wesley said to Donohue, "do you see any sinister plots going on here. Please point it out if you do. All you will find here is science."

Wesley now caught the interplay of hand signs between Prabinwah and Wu. He was about to throw his visitors out of the room and deal with Prabinwah when the far doors burst open and two guards came in half dragging a stumbling man.

The man seemed like a dwarf between the mountainous guards who would have been at home playing linebackers for the NFL. He had one side of his face black and blue with the eye puffed up and closed, and his mouth bloody and swollen. Partially dried blood spotted his chin, neck and down the front of his torn shirt.

Charly recognized him and screamed, "Joe," she pulled hard against the guard who grabbed her handcuffed arms, "let go of me you bastard."

Her scream echoed shrill throughout the empty spaces of the steel walled room. Donohue winced as she turned her high-pitched screams toward him.

"Look at him. They beat the shit out of him, do something, you're the FBI, can't you see there's something wrong going on."

CHAPTER 71

Inside the shielded room control knobs whirred and clicked under the computer-controlled tiny servomechanisms and relays.

Three composite titanium sides suddenly fell away exposing the Artifact. It looked like a thick stemmed mushroom tapering at the top. A dull gray surface was striated with veins of muted gold and orange, pulsing and throbbing as shadowed sparks ran across the surface.

Everyone in the room felt it like a door opened to a blast of stormy air. Pulses of invisible radiant energy passed through the shielded glass as if it didn't exist. It spread out at the speed of light in concentric circles as it had done two days previous. When the radiation passed through each human brain, unfelt as radio waves, it instantly began to alter brain chemistry starting the process leading to chaotic and violent madness for at least one third of those it touched.

Three people in the room were not affected. Wesley felt the covering shield of his Sylvan ally reach out from the depths of the Pine Barren forest. The radiation passed through Wesley but the psychic energy of the Sylvan prevented any changes in his brain chemistry.

Rippling gossamer waves of psychic power undulated around Wu and hovered over Joe's prone body. The power came from the Maiglin and prevented the malignant energy from reaching them like pebbles skipping over a lake.

Wu backed up to a green computer console marked in block letters "PMC23." This was what Prabinwah had signaled him. Primary Master Control, Console #23.

When he reached a spot just three feet from the keyboard, Wu suddenly lunged and hit a number of keys in rapid successions. The master console was usually set on certain permanent functions and would only be used as an override in case of emergency. In this case there were only two men in the room who could operate its complex override codes. Wesley wanted it that way.

And Wu had designed it. He knew every line of code and every electronic space of its construction. But fast as he was at the console, he couldn't operate it quickly enough. Before he hit the final key, shutting off the power and starting the procedure sealing the Artifact, a whirring, humming noise came from the giant coils wrapping the tubes that led into the chamber.

Trapped in powerful waves of electromagnetic energy, the thin plasma field hurled through a round accelerator chambers until it reached the pulsed-array generator. The primary pulse hurled the plasma to near light speed and sent it into the exposed Artifact.

The procedure started.

No obvious outwardly manifestation revealed the tremendous forces hurled at the Artifact. It blinked, glowed and darkened again, but something powerful and invisible radiated from the still and alien surface.

A pulse of enhanced energy erupted from the Artifact, a form of microwave stronger than anything human science had yet experienced. Spreading from the epicenter at the speed of light, it rose and bounced against the ionosphere, and reflected back downward to earth only to bounce up again. Wherever it passed living matter, it left a subatomic imprint of energy. In most living things it would not matter. In the higher order animals like apes and humans, it spelled disaster.

Every person in that room felt the surge like a powerful drug suddenly kicking into the central nervous system.

But that was only the beginning. Inexorably, its protocol now unstoppable, the Collider and phased array generator prepared the second surge. Even more powerful, this one would start the reaction setting the Artifact in the non-stop pulsed radiation mode that would savage humanity.

The Collider hummed again and the second pulse of Ion plasma began the seconds-long journey that would send it into the Artifact.

At that moment, in the few seconds before the event, Wu tapped out the final codes. He finished just as Duncan shoved him violently away from the console and all the lights went out. Total darkness filled the room like thick smoke, but it was too late to stop the second Ion pulse.

When they dragged Joe into the collider room, he just started to come around. He felt a painful tattoo pounding in his head. His mouth filled with the metallic taste of blood and he smelled ashes in his gore-crusted nostrils. He couldn't feel his wobbly legs and his arms barely responded, as his body leaned against the guard holding him up.

He sensed the conscious presence of the Maiglin as the girl's mind reached into the recesses of his brain and her psychic energy washed into the sensory mass of his cerebellum. The results were like holding smelling salts under the nose of a person who had fainted. Joe opened his good eye and took in the scene.

I will light your way.

He heard Wesley and Donohue arguing and saw Wu slowly backing to the console and start working the keyboard. He felt the first pulse of energy from the Artifact and he understood as he felt the Vision Stone through the material of his jacket. The relic pulsed warm, and strong with the power of destiny that placed him in this spot at that moment. He felt its reviving energy spread throughout his body like a powerful tonic.

I will light your way.

Joe exploded into action with newfound power, shoving the guard holding him and sending him flying onto a console. He ran across the floor in a mad dash that would have made Jesse Owens proud.

The blood of the Shinnecock warrior raged in his veins, and he barely reached the door to the Artifact room when the lights went out and he was plunged into absolute darkness.

The impression of the room burned in his retina and his brain. He hit the door running and it opened. It had no lock, they only designed it to hold radiation in, not keep out intruders.

After it killed Two-Crows and returned to the dark below the surface of the earth, the Maarzuk stretched beneath the building. Its atoms formed and pulsed, reshaping like a fantastic dark and malevolent amoeba. It sensed the humans, the ones whose life force it had been charged with extinguishing.

At that moment a new directive launched itself inside the Maarzuk. Built into the network of sub-atomic receptors that provided its consciousness, ancient as time and endowed with the power of its alien creators, the directive took control of the creature.

Screaming into every electron composing the Maarzuk, pushing it with a relentless savage rive. The newly awakened directive called it to blend its atoms into the object above, what the humans called the Artifact and absorb it whole. The directive drove everything else from its consciousness.

But the deadly light held it at bay like a huge murderous beast in a cage. It could not break through into the deadly radiance that filled every inch of the building holding its objective.

Suddenly the light disappeared and the darkness beckoned the Maarzuk.

Like the creature of pure, reactive consciousness that it

was, the Maarzuk immediately sent every atom of its body into a massive shifting cloud, penetrating through the very matter of the concrete floor, and erupting into the Artifact chamber.

In the silent total darkness, Joe sensed the Maarzuk enveloping him. He felt its atoms entering his body and the beginning of a dismemberment that would reach down to the molecular level of his cells.

He dove the last few feet and his arms enveloped the exposed Artifact. His head smashed into the alien surface at the same time that the Maarzuk closed in and the pulsed-array driven Ion stream hit the Artifact.

The nuclear structure of the trillions of atoms comprising the Maarzuk set off a trigger within the Artifact, a trigger the alien builders wove millions of years ago into the elements of its operating sub-atomic engine.

The Artifact sucked in every atom of the Maarzuk and everything that it touched including the case, the table it stood on and Joe's body. It used the nuclear energy of the pulsed array Ion stream as additional fuel.

The Artifact instantly transformed itself into what its cosmic designers intended when triggered by the Maarzuk: A powerful inter-galactic signal.

A column of incandescent beams of compressed light suddenly appeared, bursting upward through the cloudy atmosphere and into the reaches of space, the strongest, most compressed laser beam, powered by unimaginable forces that man would not begin to fathom for centuries.

Two potent and simultaneous blasts echoed throughout Eastern Long Island from the Lab. The first was the air vaporized by the energy of the beam. The second blast followed so quickly it sounded like one giant thunderbolt. A hole appeared in the roof as the beam vaporized everything it touched.

Parts of the wall blew out from the air pressure and sharp odors of melting steel, ozone and smoke permeated the room.

As quickly as it appeared, the white-hot beam of light and alien energies disappeared. By the time the dazed witnesses regained their visions and the interior lights came back on, the beam flashed past the orbit of Jupiter on its way to the deepest reaches of space.

Joseph Gray-Wolf stood on the bank of the vast, copper colored river. The waters moved with a slippery swiftness and under the rushing waves multi colored shapes flashed and danced. The air washed smooth and warm on his skin as a slight tang of wood smoke filled his nostrils.

He recognized where he stood, the same river he crossed many years ago in the Vision Stone ceremony. The place of dreams and nightmares, the spirit world of his ancestors where he had once fought the Abaasy, only now the dream-feeling vanished, leaving only a sense of smooth reality, of true belonging.

A path of stones appeared, rising out of the flowing water and leading to the other bank. He saw the shape of his grandfather and others, waiting on the opposite bank.

He stepped on the first stone. The water swirled, warm and fragrant and it felt good around his feet. He took another step with the rich scent of vegetation from the far bank filling his nostrils. Clean pure white light flowed throughout, and his vision extended endlessly. He felt every sense coming alive, every feeling that was good and clear abounded in his spirit.

With strong sure steps, no longer chained by physical limitations, Joseph Gray-Wolf, warrior and Shaman of the Shinnecock tribe, crossed the flowing river on the stone path to his ancestors.

EPILOGUE

The media called it the October Madness. Like Pearl Harbor and the Twin Towers, it would be remembered around the world for its sharp brutality and deadly casualties.

Random acts of insane violence occurred around the globe almost simultaneously. Many were individual acts while others came from groups inflamed with bloodlust. Madness and deranged violence danced in the atmosphere like summer fireflies.

In Beijing a Tianamen square celebration painted the concrete grounds in blood as rioting erupted and police fired on anyone within reach.

In Sao-Paolo a rampaging mob invaded a Catholic orphanage killing scores of nuns, priests and children.

The effect was especially terrible in the teeming slums of the third world. All ready enmeshed in poverty and desperation, the inhabitants turned on each other with murderous ferocity. Fires swept through shantytowns built of plywood and cardboard. With no fire fighting or rescue available, hundreds of thousands died in cities like Bombay, Calcutta, Karachi, Rio De Janeiro, Mexico City and countless others.

High places seemed to have a particularly murderous

effect on human brains absorbing the altering radiation from the Artifact. In places like the Chrysler building and the Empire State building, the Sears tower, the Eiffel tower and countless other skyscrapers, strangers attacked strangers and bodies hurled to crashing deaths thousands of feet below. One hundred and twelve crushed bodies were recovered from the base of the Las Vegas Space Needle.

By far the largest number of casualties came from individual attacks, neighbor on neighbor, family members on family members and strangers on strangers. Accurate accounting of the deaths was impossible but estimates ranged upward of a million world-wide.

Thankfully, these events came to a halt within hours of their start. It seemed as if some switch had been briefly turned on then shut off. Speculations ran the gamut from solar flares to environmental toxins to psychic activities.

The only common thread was found from research at the University of Southern California. Studies of the autopsies and analysis of brain matters from victims and perpetrators alike revealed very high contents of certain brain chemicals.

No one knew what to make of that.

The handful of people at Brookhaven National Lab and in the higher reaches of government who understood what had happened were not yet ready to talk.

Everything had been squashed at the top level and massive studies continued under the highest security ever.

They placed Special Agent Donohue in charge of the team working with the CIA and NSA to ferret out the truth of the events at the Lab and New York City. Duncan Wesley faced a military tribunal and was condemned to life without parole in a federal prison. Although eligible for the death penalty, the government accepted plea-bargaining to maintain the cloud of secrecy currently surrounding the Sylvan project and the events at Brookhaven National Laboratory.

Dr. Wu had been re-instated in charge of the Artifact project. Of course with the Artifact gone, vaporized to condensed light and on its way to God knows where, it turned into the Sylvan project.

A new building was constructed in record time for the project. Wu hired Charly who had a sort of affinity with the alien girl, the Maiglin.

Once a week the Maiglin appeared at the building, one moment she wasn't there, the next she walked into the building from the surrounding forest. The focus remained on communications with Sylvans and progress was being made.

Wu anticipated public announcements in the next few years as Mankind and Sylvans edged closer to recognition of the mutual needs of each race and how one could compliment the other.

Perhaps then, it could be explained why the building bore the name of The Joseph Gray-Wolf Memorial Research Center.

Feed My Sheep Ministries, Bedford-Stuyvesant, Brooklyn, New York

The zig-zag scar danced on the face of the Right Reverend Jedediah Mosely-Wilson as he maneuvered his wheelchair closer to the desk in his refurbished office. On the surface, squatting like evil gargoyles, were piles of paperwork that needed his attention before his scheduled physical therapy session in about two hours. He tried to pass some of it on to his assistant director, Manuel, with absolutely no luck. The Mexican was a veritable wizard at organizing the affairs of the ministry but soon as you put some papers in front of him, he reverted to Spanish and claimed difficulties reading "That *Pendajo* language, English."

Manuel had recovered nicely from the leg wound.

Jedediah's wounds had been more complicated. The doctors told him that one of the rounds nicked his spinal cord and walking would be iffy at best. Jedediah knew they were wrong. He felt his strength growing and he was certain he would walk again someday.

Jedediah didn't know which had been the greatest shock. His wounds or what happened to the Feed My Sheep Ministries a few days after the attack.

Dr. Wu had accessed Wesley's computer codes. It hadn't been very difficult since he was an expert in those things and the rogue agent used some of the codes Wu had written.

Illegal operations of the sort that Duncan Wesley ran, took lots of money. He had gotten vast sums from working clandestine connections with Chinese tongs in Macao and Hong Kong. He facilitated the operations of the "Snakeheads" bringing in illegal Chinese immigrants for large sums of money paid by the servitude of the new immigrants, servitude very much resembling old-fashioned slavery. And of course there was the ever-present drug running facilitated by Wesley's NSA position. All that resulted in generous payoffs in multiple accounts overseas.

The whole thing hadn't been terribly difficult for Wu. Coded instructions went out over safe and encrypted lines, seven figure sums transferred from banks in Switzerland, Bonn and Prague. The transfers were routed through Cayman Island trusts and Bermuda Corporations and channeled into the main branch of the Chase Manhattan bank in New York.

From there, the total charitable contributions from overseas benefactors to the Feed My Sheep Ministries totaled a bit over seven million dollars.

Not bad for an account that usually had difficulties maintaining three figures.

With Manuel's help, Jedediah Mosely-Wilson stepped to the occasion. The ministry purchased adjoining buildings and hired staff. Now a large kitchen filled with everything from cooks to dieticians provided thousands of free meals daily. Full time drug and alcohol counselors worked on the premises along with psychologists and career counselors.

Jedediah appeared on CNBC, Dateline, 60 minutes and Larry King. "The miracle of Brooklyn" continued to expand as donations poured in from all points of the country.

Sunlight, warm and glowing like polished gold poured down on a meadow in the Pine Barrens of Eastern Long Island. It was late spring and the remains of the old encampment blended into the land, covered with weeds, bushes and scrub oaks.

They had all left, the occupants of the camp that Joseph Gray-Wolf knew for a short while. But they took something with them, a healing of the mind, a golden touch of the spirit provided by the Maiglin.

The old occupants of the camp returned to society. No longer scarred, their diseases of the body and mind had vanished. The word soon spread in the communities of the ultra-poor, the homeless and disenfranchised, the throwaway communities cast away from society.

The word was healing, a mystic spot of hope that burnt out ailments and despair like a torch on thin plastic. They came to this spot. They came and came, and they left healed and full of hope.

But none knew why. None ever saw anything. They just felt the healing powers of an alien presence in the surrounding forest.

And they left whole.

In the center of the meadow, a beautiful young girl sat on soft cushions of wild grass. Her face was a timeless beauty more than just physical. There was a graceful spirituality born of alien worlds permeating her features, shining out of voluminous pupil-filled eyes.

Out of all those who have come to the meadow to be healed, only a precious few have ever seen her. She showed herself rarely, and only to those whose spirit and body were so broken that the view became a necessary step toward healing. Someday they will know, someday all humankind will know.

But until the work at the Lab was completed, the Maiglin would continue to be "The Madonna of the Meadow."

Turn the page for an

excerpt from

THE
DEVIL'S
CALDERA

The Apocalypse Series
Book Four

Patrick Astre

Captain Bernard LaChasse never expected his patrol to be caught in this storm. After all, it wasn't one of those trial and error fishing expeditions. There was supposed to be solid intelligence. The terrorists crossing into France were to be met just outside Passe-Du-Diable by their French counterparts. Bernard had orders to intercept, capture or kill, and not necessarily in that order. Superbly trained and handpicked from the ranks of Special Operations Commandos, his men were veterans skilled in mountain warfare.

Howling gales drove horizontal sheets of snow and ice droplets that hissed ferociously as they pinned the chemically heated suit against every fold of Bernard's body, sandblasting the H&K-P19 light machine pistol slung around his shoulders. It felt as if he struggled in a field of gray fog, the barrel of his weapon deflected slightly down, ready to traverse upward to killing fields. NVG's (Night Vision Goggles) were useless in this storm, and the infrared heat sensor marginally better. Red and purple blobs danced in the UV window of his goggles, representing Corporal Ladron and Private Benoit on either side of him. They advanced in V formation spread one hundred meters wide at the opening of the V and moving forward like a deadly maw to ensnare the terrorist killers that intelligence declared would be there. A French Air Force surveillance plane packed with electronic gear monitored the operation. Each soldier wore a locator transmitting a constant signal to the aircraft circling unseen above.

"Moulon one," the voice in his earplug said, clear and low, riding the bone structure of his skull so no sound wave leaked, "you're about a hundred and fifty meters from the Joffre Precipice. You're starting to get strung out. Wheel to your left twenty two degree West to the ambush site,"

"Copy that, Eagleye. Ladron, did you hear that? Twenty Two degrees west, one hundred and ten meters."

"That's close enough for me Lieutenant. Make sure I don't fall off that cliff, can't see shit here."

"Don't worry *mon vieux*, I'll keep you as safe as walking the *vignes* back home," replied Bernard.

Ladron hailed from a village near Bernard's hometown of Libourne in the heart of the Bordeaux wine region.

"Hey Lieutenant," came the voice of Private Benois to his immediate left, "if he does fall off the cliff, that means I become point and I get the *beefsteak-frites* dinner you offered, right?"

Before Bernard could reply, another voice came on the net.

"*Attention*. There's something out there. Directly to my twelve o'clock." Sergeant Berthon, point guide on the opposite side of the V, cut in.

Immediately the seven men squad hit the ground, weapons deployed. No command had been given as training took over like primitive war instincts. Each man became an invisible mound, white on white in the howling subzero gale. They held a deadly array of force, the most effective infantry weapons devised in that year of 2016.

"There…there, it's in front of me now…what the hell is it…Lieutenant…" The radio voice of the soldier directly below Sergeant Berthon immediately cut off by a deep sustained rumble, the tearing growl of an automatic weapon firing a storm of inch-long explosive flechettes.

"What the fuck is that?" Sergeant Berthon's voice

exploded in Bernard's earphone, "It can't move that fast…it's changing, look…look…"

Muffled, thumping explosions sounded to Bernard's right, followed by more to his left as the men detonated the "Perimeter Sweepers," modernized versions of the old American Claymore mines. More automatic weapons growled, this time on either sides and forward of Bernard as the men on both flanks of the V opened fire.

Warnings, screams and curses poured into the headset followed by howls of pain, every note tinged with bloody primitive fear. Still Bernard saw nothing. He stood, weapon at ready, advancing into whatever attacked his men.

"Eagleye, Eagleye, Moulon One, we're under attack, I have nothing visible and no heat signatures…"

Bernard's voice was cut off by another scream, choked by the gurgling noise of death.

"No…No…" it was Benoit to his left now, screaming as two more explosions came, fast and heavy, intermingled with hundreds of rounds of automatic weapon fire. The violence of the storm absorbed the noise as the concussion waves of the explosives rode the terrible wind. The sound of his men dying around him drove Bernard out as he ran toward Benoit, the closest to his left.

"Moulon one," came the voice from the surveillance aircraft four thousand feet overhead, "there's nothing, repeat nothing. We're picking up some movement from the sensors but no heat signatures and no laser sightings, nothing but your weapons firing. Repeat; We see nothing there. What do *you* have?"

Bernard didn't reply as he ran toward Benoit's dying scream. A shape loomed in front of him, shifting, imprecise and vacuous as blowing smoke clouds. Suddenly a crumpled mass came into view on the ground in front of him: Benoit, facemask and goggles torn away along with the bottom half of his face. Eyes open wide in unspeakable terror, intestines red and gray spilled in the driving snow, already partly covered in white like a morgue sheet, satiny red spreading, wisps of steam from the claw mark that had torn him from gullet to groin, swept away in the artic gale.

The voice from the aircraft continued, "Nothing, we pick up nothing…what's going on down there…" the voice droned on as Bernard ran to his left, toward Ladron. He fired at shapes that shifted and swirled like phantoms but never came close as he heard Ladron scream.

"Lieutenant, the Garridon, oh God, no, the Garridon…" The voice ended in a high pitched scream, unspeakable pain and terror rising until it seemed beyond any human vocal chords.

Bernard continued to run toward Ladron to his left, unheeding the voice from the aircraft droning in his ear set.

"Moulon One. Stop. You're the only one moving now. Stop, you're near the Jouffre precipice. What's happening down there…we have nothing, repeat, nothing…"

He ran farther, screaming to his men as if the throat mike and radio didn't exist, as if he could save them all by sheer volume. He tasted bile and ashes as he inhaled the chemical coated smell of the suit fabric, adrenaline and fear pouring out through his sweat. The calm droning voice of the operator in the aircraft continued like a counterpoint to the death screams of his squad.

"Shut up, *shut the fuck up*," he screamed at the unseen operator. He scanned the few feet of terrain in front of him before it vanished in swirling frozen white clouds. Left to right, center, right to left. Nothing. He thumbed a lever on the machine pistol and a three round magazine popped into the small grenade launcher barrel beneath the weapon. He slowed to a fast walk, scanning over the gun-barrel.

Something darker then the driving snow turned and moved, formed and reshaped. He fired, the small popping noise, torn away by the wind. A second later came the red flash of the exploding grenade as white-hot shards expanded in a lethal thirty-yard circle. He fired bursts of flechettes from the machine pistol as shapes danced around him and nothing showed in the heat sensors. Whatever was out there was so ethereal it emitted no heat signature.

Yet it disemboweled men—well-trained, armed and

deadly men.

Bernard sensed movement from the corner of his eye. He whirled, running backward as he fired. The grenade exploded, barely out of reach. He ran back when the figure came into full view.

He felt his bowels heave as mindless terror overcame him. He was no longer the fearless warrior, the macho commando squad leader. He suddenly became the little boy sitting on his grandmother's knee beside the flowing Gironde River as night fell and she spun the folk tales of the Garridon, tales born from primeval terrors of ancient times when magic, death and sorcery ruled the world.

His finger tightened on the trigger and the weapon sent a long burst of deadly flechettes into the screaming wind. It was more a reflex then a defense as he stumbled back against the figure approaching at impossible speed.

The ground gave way under his feet and the world turned into a quilt of swirling white as the ledge he stood on broke away, and fell into the Jouffre Precipice.

Four months later
Somewhere off Highway 4
Everglades, Florida, USA.

The fourth man had to die. It was simple as that. The first and second didn't have to, although they did, but the fourth man, he had to die.

It'd been a day hot as the breath of Hades, under a sky blue like English porcelain, the sun an incandescent cinder near the horizon, trying to singe the dark vegetation outlined on the horizon, just at the edge of the Gulf of Mexico. The air smelled late-summer rank, bringing the particular stink of drying mud flats and effluvial streams, and the carcass of a deer rotting at the edge of the road.

An eighteen-wheeler geared down as it approached the solitary curve just a mile before Alligator Alley, the road that ran straight as a longitude line, bisecting the state of Florida all the way to Interstate 95 on the East Coast. The truck passed the curve, picked up again and vanished, trailed by a few cars that had missed their chance at passing, except for one car, a vintage seventies Dodge Charger, blue, the paint dotted with oxidized spots, the kind of stuff that didn't happen anymore on modern, sterile and bug-like autos dotting today's highways. An air scoop stuck out of the hood, hooked up to a big Hemi engine from the era of sixty-five cents a gallon gas. The Charger looked like a throwback, something that'd lost its way from another time, oversize, ravenous and worn. It gave you that impression…at first glance.

But first impressions aren't always correct. A closer look revealed a well-tuned engine refitted to NASCAR standards and a chassis where corrosion appeared as infrequently as larceny in a Jesuit. Equally deceiving, the interior held some quirks of its own, front seat upholstered to exact standards, digital state of the art gauges and controls, but the rear passenger area told a special tale, one that reflected on the sometimes violent occupation of its owner, a vocation that he and his partner performed with consummate skills.

The Charger coasted into an area that had once been a parking lot. The place wasn't visible from the road, wedged like a toothache in the encroaching vegetation. A sign that looked homemade hung at a nearly ninety degree angle, one of its posts having been torn out of the ground when a drunk slammed into it a few years back. Weather beaten to a bleached white, you had to get close to read the faded letters: Gator's Place.

The parking lot itself was an odd mixture of crushed oyster shells, dirt, gravel, broken beer bottles, cans, and paper debris, all covered with a patina of dried mud and salt when the vast waters of the Everglades had overrun the area during the last hurricane. The building itself wasn't much more than some extended shack, as if it'd been cobbled out of leftover construction materials from a looted site, thrown together best as possible and opened for business too quickly. It'd been the kind of place where patrons fought outside with knives and broken bottles, a refuge of men and the occasional women steeped in alcohol, sprinkled with drugs easily found in South Florida, a place for those who'd missed a rung on the ladder, not quite making the twelve-steps and rarely staying on the wagon. In most cases, such establishments didn't last too long and Gator's Place was no exception. Boarded up, penetrated uncountable times by squatters, set on fire once and defecated on often, its remains stood like a rotted tooth that didn't quite hurt enough to yank out.

Long shadows darkened the area as the sun passed below the horizon. Thick mangrove lined the edges, belying the presence of nearby water linked to the great swamp. It was nearly dark, but the driver of the Charger didn't turn on the lights as he rounded the building. The kind of business he needed to conduct was best done in darkness.

The Charger glided around the building, its engine muffled to a nearly inaudible growl, the tires susurrating against the ground with only the occasional pop from a crushed oyster shell. It didn't have far to go as the driver pulled behind a silver Mercedes Benz.

The driver stopped the Charger and got out of the car smooth as quicksilver. Standing a shade over six feet tall, he wore a dark tee shirt hanging a few inches past the waist, over jeans that held particular items at the belt. The body was lean with muscles hard as steel cables, the kind of built not developed for shows, but the result of a lifetime devotion to martial arts. His blonde hair, and fair, pleasant features, clean-shaven except for a geometrically trimmed soul patch, indicated some sort of Viking ancestry - Another case of wrong impressions, for he was actually Jewish and from Brooklyn. His name was Israel Iskewitz, but only his partner and girlfriend knew that, to everyone he was just Ike.

As he got out of the car, he saw four men. Two stood on either side of him, the one on the right wearing a tank top, arms heavy with muscles and gang tattoos like red strings burned into brown skin. A long scar ran across his face, past a nose that had once been broken and never properly reset. His face was pockmarked and the eyes brutish and feral. The other man was whip-thin, with slicked back oily hair, short and wiry. His eyes burned, the light in them fierce and electric. Two small teardrop tattoos ran from the corner of one eye, the mark of EME, a Mexican Mafia symbol of jailhouse murders. An aura of violence hung about those two like dirty ground fog. The third man stood well behind the first two. He wore a sharkskin suit, jewelry flashed under an open silk shirt. He looked at the driver who'd just got out of the Charger, his eyes hooded and dark in the murky light, and when he spoke his voice carried inflections of the distant Urals and the mountains of Chenchnya.

"You are Ike, da?" He said to the man from the Charger, the tone neutral, bored.

Ike said nothing. The big guy to his right grinned at him, and pulled heavy brass knuckles from his pocket and slipped them over his right hand.

"You still got a chance to get out of this," the man in the sharkskin suit said. "It's because of your partner Francois I give you this chance."

"Not without him," Ike said, nodding toward the fourth man.

The man in the sharkskin suit shrugged, nodded at the thin man to Ike's left. The man pulled a gravity knife, flicked it down and it opened with a muted click. He moved on Ike, his stride easy, center of gravity low, knife held to the side, the mark of an experienced knife fighter, one who played for keeps. To Ike's right the big man with the brass knuckles also moved in.

Although instincts may tend to belie it, geometry is paramount in personal combat against multiple opponents. Ike whirled to the knife man's right who crouched, blade ready. But with that one simple maneuver, the battle scene had changed. Whereas Ike had been between the two men, vulnerable, he now stood directly to the knife wielder's right with mister Brass Knuckles aligned directly behind him. For maybe an entire second or two it was one on one, and that's all Ike needed.

In a movement so fast it rendered the knife man to slow motion status, Ike whipped the blackjack from its quick release place on his belt. Eight inches of rubber hose, thin for flexibility, stuffed full of steel ball bearings for bone crunching hardness, Ike brought it smashing into the forearm that held the knife, shattering the bone as the knife flew away. One blazing sweep kick sent him horizontal to crash down into a fetal position as blood pumped around jagged splinters of bone protruding through the shattered forearm.

Brass knuckles stumbled over his fallen partner's leg, recovered and started a swing at Ike's head.

Ike dodged, whirled and caught the man with a snapping sidekick that could have shattered a brick wall. Both of the big man's feet came off the ground as his body flew back a couple of feet to land, collapsed like dead meat.

That was the only diversion the man in the sharkskin suit needed. If he'd expected a different outcome he didn't show it. He pulled a black automatic from his pocket and fired three shots into the fourth man who was tied to a skinny Royal Palm tree with bailing wire.

The fourth man had to die.

Now sharkskin suit whirled and fired two more shots at Ike.

Ike dove to the side, pulled out his own Glock Nine. By that time the man had jumped in the Mercedes and slammed the door shut. The engine had been left running. He jammed the gearshift in drive and floored the accelerator.

Ike stood and fired four shots at the car. Hollow point bullets ricochet off the windshield, kicking off sparks, pinging and whining, but not even leaving a single star in the glass. Bulletproof, obviously a special kind of vehicle.

Ike rolled off to the side as the Mercedes leaped at him, then corrected. Two soggy plunks sounded over the whine of the engine as the big German sedan ran over the bodies of the men Ike had taken down. So much for the hired help, Ike thought, a unique retirement plan, one that he'd seen before.

Ike looked at the fourth man, not recognizing him. Three steel-jacketed large caliber rounds directly in the face from less than three feet away will do that to you.

Now Ike muttered a curse, leaped into his car and went after the Mercedes. Wide tires bit into the hardscrabble, throwing a spray of sand and debris over the three corpses, whipped around the defunct building on two wheels and hit Highway 4.

But Ike had a problem: Gator's Place sat on the apex of a curve on Highway 4 and Ike hadn't been able to follow closely enough to determine if the Mercedes headed north, toward Fort Meyers and Naples, or toward the more desolate south, more roads running through empty swamps and sparsely populated Everglades City. He didn't pause, slammed the wheel to the right, south. No time to debate, one choice was as good as another.

Dodge Charger, 450 turbo charged horsepower against Mercedes Benz's finest, no doubt also tricked out. Ike knew he'd take it, but it would be close and he couldn't narrow the gap fast enough. By the time he reached the intersection of Highway One he hadn't even caught a wink of taillight. Right, left, straight ahead, the odds rocketed down. He chose right.

Twenty-two miles later he gave up. The dices hadn't rolled his way. The fourth man had died and he didn't even get to find out why.

THE DEVIL'S CALDERA
available in print and ebook

THE
APOCALYPSE SERIES

◆

The Boomer Protocols
Cold Fusion
Sylvans
The Devil's Caldera

Also by Patrick Astre
<u>Remnants of War Series</u>
The Last Operation
The Doppelganger Protocol
The Devil's Eye
Twilight of Demons

Award-winning author Patrick Astre served in the US Army Infantry, stationed in Germany during the height of the Cold War. Rising to the rank of Sergeant E-5, Astre finished his last year of service as a Drill Instructor at Fort Benning, Georgia.

Now, Patrick Astre, CFP, EA, RFC is a recognized tax and financial expert specializing on the economic issues of longevity. Patrick is independent and has been advising individuals and corporations since 1969.

Patrick's second financial book was released in mid-August 2007 by Entrepreneur Media Publishing. It is Entrepreneur's "cornerstone" retirement book. *This is Not Your Parents' Retirement* is one of the top sellers in its field, addressing the convergence of the longevity revolution and the aging baby-boomers, woefully unprepared for retirement.

In addition to his financial books, Patrick is the author of numerous articles as well as fiction thrillers. His novel *The Artifact* won the Salvo Press Mystery Thriller of the year Award in 2005.

Patrick is a professional public speaker and member of the National Speakers Association. His seminars, speeches and keynotes are a lively, enthusiastic mix of entertainment, motivation, humor and unique insights.

Some of his clients include Celebrity Cruises, John Hancock, Princess Cruises, LIBOR (Long Island Board of Realtors) Passaic Board of Realtors, and many others.

Patrick lives in Long Island, New York with his wife Lynn. The couple has two children and two grandchildren and enjoy traveling throughout the country in their motor home.

www.ingramcontent.com/pod-product-compliance
Lightning Source LLC
Chambersburg PA
CBHW030919050726
47498CB00003BA/821